THE CONFESSIONS OF A CATNIP JUNKIE

ALLAN GOLDSTEIN

For Jordan.

THE CONFESSIONS OF A CATNIP JUNKIE

A Novel

by

ALLAN GOLDSTEIN

OVERTURE

When it comes to me, it comes to me in flashes....
I see hands, Kathy's chapped hands, reaching down for me on the forest floor, lifting me three feet high and three thousand miles away. Doug's great big mitts, an athlete's hands, stroking his troubles away on my magic pelt. Edgar's rough, workingman's hands, murderous hands, angry as hell, tossing me into a burlap sack.

I remember sounds, the silence torn apart by a roaring twister that trapped me in the scablands. Lightning so close it ate up all the sound in the world and spat it in my ears. The godawful noise of old Charlie's rickety airplane, and the fear, which was louder.

Places parade past, so real—a cat *never* forgets a place—I feel I own them, even now, even in dreams. I see a baseball diamond on the high Colorado plains in summer. That was my home once, for a season. I dream of sunning myself again, on the wing of a tiny airplane parked in the grit of a dusty airport in Nevada, in the thin, winter sunshine. Dreams of terrifying places—stranded and starving on a frozen lake, chased by a charging metal beast in the subways of New York—nightmares. I have those, too....

When it comes to me, it comes as a stranger. Because none of this happened to me, it happened to him. *Keep that in mind or this won't make any sense. I am two cats.*

I remember people, the crazed, meth-fueled trucker I "hitched" a ride with. Doug the minor league pitcher, who almost stole me away forever. Charlie and Clarence, pilots, old war buddies, who saved me, twice. Half-drunk Edgar and cheating Donna, thinking I was the ticket out of their boring jobs and miserable lives. Fiona, the lesbian goth girl who set me free. And so many others....

You must try to understand. I used *to be him. We share the same genes, the same mother, the same history, the same name. But I'm not him anymore.*

I have dreams of that used-to-be-me cat being trapped all the time. He was always plotting an escape, making an escape, escaping. I wonder, how could a cat could get himself stuck so often? Fourteen years later that is still a marvel to me, even more than his whiskersbreadth escapes. He still brags about those, the cat-who-used-to-be-me thought he was pretty slick. He was, but he was also an idiot. I can see that now, but he couldn't.

I remember our buddy Rass. I don't have to be dreaming to remember *him*. It's been fourteen years and I still miss him, every day. Stupidest cat I ever met, and the best too. I wonder whatever happened to him....

I am two cats. The Doo Doo who was born of this story and the Doo Doo who lived it, fourteen years ago.

That cat-who-used-to-be-me and the cat I am now don't see eye to eye about what happened to us, and why. I suppose that's only to be expected, I'm sixteen, worn-out and content, he was two, fresh and full of lust, mostly wanderlust. But there is one thing we agree on ... make that two. Doc and Fern.

Doc and Fern—my people, *our* people—the precise point where our lives intersect, young Doo Doo's and mine. He had them then, I have them now. But in between, fourteen years ago, there was a discontinuity. A ragged gap, six thousand miles long and fifteen months wide, separates his life and mine. It's a bloody gash in our life, he is on that side, I am on this side. It's a divide I can never cross. But he did. He *did*.

He brought me back. The idiot who destroyed my life gave it back to me again. He gave me the chance to grow old, to be loved, cherished, pampered and catered to by the only people I ever wanted to feel that way about me, the only people I ever wanted to feel that way about. Back to Doc, back to Fern, back to *home.*

When it comes to me, it comes to me in flashes. But he remembers everything.

Sometimes I want to ask him, why? Why did you do that to us, why did you risk so much, why did you take us through hell and back?

I know it was because he was young, half-feral and totally foolish.

But if you ask him?

He blames catnip.

CHAPTER 1

You'd figure, if I was going to fly the coop, I'd do it on the way to the hated vet, and not afterwards, on the way home. But if you did, you'd be wrong on two counts. First of all, that assumes I was *thinking*, and second of all—mindless impulse that it was—the temptation never presented itself until it did, and when it did I went for it.

Let me set the scene. Spring day, late afternoon, returning from a routine visit to the vet for vaccines, weighing, and, just because I'm so cute, that thermometer thing stuck up my ass. So I'm not in the best of moods on the way home, and I'm letting Doc know the only way I can, by yowling my head off.

All of which is routine, except for two little details. Fern usually took me to the vet in her buttoned-up Chevy sedan, but this time I was with Doc in *his* car, a boxy, noisy Jeep, with—and this is the central point—a soft top with plastic windows zipped down for ventilation. And why did that drafty Jeep need more air than it usually leaked anyway? Because I got so damned mad I took a dump in my box and the stink drove Doc to it.

I want to be gentle here for those of you with delicate sensibilities, but, the feces in question were, how should I say … rather more pungent than otherwise. Get it?

Doc sure did, because his nose and compassion compelled him to make a horrible mistake—for both of us.

He opened the box and took me out of that mess to hold me in his lap for the remaining couple of miles home—which mollified me not at all. I was an ingrate in my youth, and not inclined to thoughtfulness, which shows how things have changed. Back then I was always looking for trouble, and I found some, right there.

We were cresting a hill, just short of Twin Peaks, at a five-way intersection where the road gets wide and traffic-y. Bordering it on our left was a gorge, filled with brush and eucalyptus so dense as to be virtually impenetrable—unless you're one foot tall. As we slowed for the light it *hit* me. That smell….

Catnip. Sweet, fresh, growing catnip, like the kind Fern would plant for me in the backyard and I'd destroy in an hour, pouring through that open window above the hot rubber and diesel stink of an afternoon rush hour, coming from those woods. Catnip. The grassy scent I'd gotten hooked on by the very same hands that held me now. Catnip. The *only* thing that could make me stupid enough to run away from the only home I ever had and the only two people I ever loved. Catnip.

I can't expect you to understand what I did next, because I don't understand it myself. All I remember is being mad and soiled, disoriented from riding in the noisy car, loosely held in Doc's lap, with a zipped-down window three inches from my nose, which was catching drifts of the heavenly herb wafting my way from, for all I knew, nirvana. It was all too much for my addled little brain (if you believe that you're a bigger sucker than *I* was), and I bolted.

How can I re-create the giddy rush of freedom I felt back then, so long ago? The Doo Doo who is telling you this story knows what happened to him in the harsh year that followed. He knows what price he paid for the joys and jolts of the free life, the time spent wild, lonely and lost, his initial thoughtlessness turning slowly into nostalgia, longing, and finally to remorse and the long, long road home.

But at that moment? Oh, I remember; it's with me yet. If I close my tired eyes, flare my nostrils, and catch the scent of that faded catnip chew toy I knocked under the chair last week, the one Fern brought home with the mushy "senior chow" I'm reduced to gumming for supper in my old age, I'm back there again.

It felt like life. It felt like being born again, full-grown this time, with all my strength and wiles, let loose on an unsuspecting world. I followed that scent where it took me, and brother, it took me places I could never have imagined. It took me so far I didn't know which way was back. It shames me now to admit it, but for a long time I never gave a thought to what, and whom, I'd left behind. For a time I forgot all about "home." I damn near forgot myself....

CHAPTER 2

I wasn't always Doo Doo. People gave me that name. I was born wild, in a litter of four, my mother's first, and, for all I know, her last. My two brothers, sister and I came into the world in an urban jungle, near the ocean in a place called San Francisco. It must have been early spring, because my first memories are of cool rains and sprouting grass.

We were city cats, living on a steep strip of unclaimed land between the backyards of the houses below and the balconies of the apartments above. It was idyllic, for the big city, a mini-forest one curving block long and fifty feet wide. Later I found out just how tiny and precious that place was, how strange and beautiful and tilted. I thought everyplace was a hill, steep angles and precarious perches seemed natural to me. I had no concept of flat, of prairie and plain, of mesa and meadow, but I'd see them all and more, because I did something very foolish.

Momma was beautiful. If I'm handsome, and I am, I got it from her. All I can do is ask you to believe me—I know I'm prejudiced—but in the sixteen years and thousands of miles I've lived so far, I've never seen a more beautiful cat. She was tiny, delicate as a doll, creamy white all over, tipped by just enough black on the point of her tail and the peaks of her ears to set off her color to best effect.

Momma was just a kitten herself. Her looks were her fortune, and ours. She was too small and skittish to be much of a hunter, but she never lacked for food and neither did we. I was there; I *saw* the effects her passing vision had on people—the oh-my-god gasps, indrawn breaths, the unrequited come-hither calls that trailed in her wake whenever she was seen— and the fruits of that angelic attraction fed me for the first sweet months of my life. Momma couldn't cross a backyard without some human cooing like an oversized pigeon, and shoving out a dish of Friskies for the pretty little thing that never let you touch her. Half the houses on our block sprouted bowls of food and Momma took that food when she got the nerve, when all the lights went out. That rich bounty fed her, and she fed us, sweet milk and mother love that never seemed to end. Until it did.

She left us too soon, her skittishness got the better of our little family, and we became orphans before our time. One of my brothers, White Spot, was playing with a grasshopper one summer day, and he wandered off, far enough to be out of Momma's sight, but I saw the whole thing. A couple of kids from the apartment complex nearby spotted him as he pronged straight up chasing the bug, popping above the weeds like a toy, and the inevitable happened. He was in their hands and around the corner in no time, destroying our little Eden forever.

Momma missed him within minutes, but it was too late. She paced and meowed and moaned and howled and sniffed for hours, crying for him until dusk.

And then she'd had enough. Whether out of fright or pique, or just because it was her time, she turned her back on the three of us and ran away. She turned tail—her black-tipped, white tail flashing in the sunset—leaping in that curious fore-and-aft gait of hers, bounded over the fence at the end of the block, across the street and into the infinity beyond. I'd see the infinity beyond, in my long life. But I never saw her again.

Food got scarce when Momma left, and those first nights were nights of fear. Noises that were invitations to play when she was at my back now brought shivering terror. My pretend forest turned into a house of horrors. I felt exposed, vulnerable and *so* hungry. One by one my siblings disappeared. I never knew if they got lost or picked up or run over or taken in by a nice family. They were just gone, and gone forever.

But I've always been a lucky cat. With Momma gone the toms went away and I had the little strip of land mostly to myself. Those same nooks I had explored as a half-blind infant now became places of refuge, and as I grew my terrors faded. And did I ever grow! I found Momma's old feeding stations and made them mine. I was careful to eat only at night, when I couldn't be seen. Not knowing they were no longer feeding the pretty white cat, but her lanky orange son, the neighborhood Samaritans kept the food coming, and I sampled it all. My little world was alive with rodents and birds and even small snakes, and I was fast, stealthy and strong. Before long I had tasted prey, or perhaps I should say play, because I hunted more out of joy than hunger. That winter I had my first fight, a one-sided affair with a big, nasty black tom who was getting a little ragged around the edges. He was more ragged when I was done with him.

My world was small, but I had a feeling of belonging, of *reigning* over all the space I ever thought I needed. I grew into twelve rangy pounds of power and beauty, green eyes, orange tabby markings—pale beneath and darker above—softened by long hair. But none of that overbred, pug-faced, gaping-nostril, longhaired body type for me. I hate those genetic freaks, bred to look like they'd jumped head-first for a bird without knowing the window was closed and now they have to spend their entire lives with a "damn, this litter box stinks" look on their mugs. No, I was sleek and silky and perfect. I loved my body—how it felt, how it worked—and I loved my life. But there was something missing.

* * *

It started with curiosity. We're famous for that. I wasn't looking for anything in particular, or, if I was, I didn't know it, yet.

I'd always avoided people. The last thing I wanted was White Spot's fate. But there was one house on my block that made my explorer nerve twitch, one house that drew me to it. It wasn't much of a house, just a bungalow really, with a steep, weedy backyard and a large patio door facing up the hill. But a couple of things made it different from the other homes in my neighborhood.

For one thing, the food offerings were better. Sporadic, but better, with the fresh, recognizable tastes I later came to know meant the good stuff, the expensive stuff. A big clean bowl filled with chicken or tuna or other goodies would appear in that yard about twice a week, a real treat I looked forward to. The people inside never bothered me; I rarely even saw them at first. They just put out the food and left. The situation was so comfortable I barely noticed when the bowl slowly crept down the hill, each time a little lower, a little closer to the patio door.

The other odd thing was that someone in that house was as nocturnal as I was. I'd see lights and hear little noises, smell food and tobacco smoke coming from that place, all through the night. In the soggy pre-dawn hours, as I stalked my domain, marking a tree here, licking some dew off the grass there, it was like we were the only ones alive, that all-night human and me. I got to counting on the regularity of that unseen presence. It made me feel lonely and less alone ... all at the same time.

That night owl turned out to be a he, like myself, but he wasn't the person in that house I got to know first. No, the first one I met, the first one I let approach me, touch me, love me, *capture* me, was a woman. It happened one afternoon, just past my first year, on a rare, drowsy, fogless summer day.

I was napping right outside their fence when that enticing, familiar aroma woke me up. I crawled through the gap in the bottom of their fence heedlessly, not a care in the world, following my nose through the tall grass and unkempt bushes down the hill. I hopped through the weeds towards the concrete deck, where they'd been putting the bounty lately, my paws rustling the pine-needled earth on the way down. She must have heard me coming, because she was waiting for me right where I emerged.

A pretty woman, staring straight at me, with a look of delighted surprise on her face, like she'd just unwrapped a birthday present and I was it. But *I* was the one who was surprised, and I almost ran. But I didn't. That's the main thing, the telling thing, *I didn't.*

She stepped back a little from the food and watched quietly. She had tact, that one. She gave me my space, just enough space to trap me in a web of love I never got out of. A web so strong it stretched three thousand miles without breaking.

As I approached the bowl, the woman whispered to me in a voice as warm and soft as felt.

"Oh my, you are a handsome devil, aren't you, kitty? Are you hungry? It's okay, it's for you. Yes … yes…." seducing me from six feet away. "Come on kitty," she beckoned, "that's a-way … that's a-way," singing her human, caressing words, drawing me ever closer to my prize. I began to eat, warily at first, but then with contented, purring gusto. "You have a good appetite, don't you Orange Boy?" she said as I wolfed down the shrimp. Orange boy … I liked that.

She never touched me as I emptied that bowl. When I was done I was just about to traipse right back up the hill and out, but I was so full, the sun was so warm, and this woman was so close and sparkling….

She called to me … and I came. I rubbed my face against her outstretched fingers and caught her soft scent. She sat down on the patio and lured me into her lap. I climbed on like a silly, homesick fool. Curled up like a big orange cashew, I fell asleep with the woman's soft hand gently stroking my body from that sensitive spot between my ears to the taper of my long feathery tail. I saw Momma as I drifted off, and everything was perfect—my first perfect moment since Momma abandoned me.

And that was it—I was trapped. Simple as that. All it took was one bowl of food on one delightful summer day with one human female determined to play earth mother and I was caught. The most independent cat on the block—my universe, don't forget—was halfway to becoming the lap cat I'd always, in my innocence, despised.

After that it was just a matter of time, and not much time. I began coming around looking for her. The woman, whose name, I found out later, was Fern, would call for me when she got home from work. That's how I got the name Doo Doɔ. Fern didn't know me well enough yet to pin a name on me—she was like that, considerate—so she'd just make a silly sound, *doo* doo … *doo* doo, first syllable pitched high, second lower, over and over until I heard it, and I knew it was food time, lap time, love time, once again, and came down the hill.

And beyond. Soon enough I was entering the dark house to eat and explore. I marked every corner of that place over the next few weeks, made it mine. I met her man then, about whom more later, and I began to spend more and more time indoors, reveling in comfort and luxury.

In all that early time neither Fern, or her man who had two names, Jeff and Doc, ever made a bad move. There was food and water and newspapers on top of furniture to sleep on. Someone who had lived there before must have had a pet, because there was an old cat door leading right into the kitchen, which they rehabilitated for me, so I could come and go as I pleased and I never felt trapped. I *was*, of course, but not by walls or glass.

By that fall, as the days grew short and the nights took on a chill, I was spending more time in the house than outside. Don't get me wrong, I still took care of my territory—I did a spraying tour often enough to keep the fear alive in any rivals—but *home* took on a more contracted meaning. It was where the two humans were, *my* two humans.

That autumn was a season of bonding. I believe I was the first pet that childless couple ever had, and they lavished love on me like I was triplets. And I took to it lavishly. Fern made sure I got the coddling I needed, the food I wanted—I was and remain famously fussy—and all the lap love a once-feral cat could handle. Life was play, pet, nap and frolic. Doc and Fern were cat people to the core, it was like they could read my mind. They even knew when to leave me alone. They'd worry when my wild side grabbed me and I'd go walkabout into the urban jungle for a couple days of mayhem—but when I'd come back, they'd welcome me with open arms and yet more catnip. Thus passed that happy, stoned season, we three becoming a family, two thirds of which spent most of its time genially loaded.

I haven't told you about Jeff yet, the one his friends called Doc. Fern loved me best, but Doc was my buddy. Hell, he was half cat himself. He was up all night. He knew about play and pleasure. He spent his nights reading, stretched out on his tattered couch, blanket up to his chin, pumping out heat like a boiler, with me draped across his legs so deep in REM sleep he'd have to pet me just to stop my snoring, or so he claimed.

He was real lazy, for a two-legger—like I said, half cat, maybe three quarters—and when he was awake I'd purposely ignore the cat door and claw the patio screen frantically, like I was being chased by wolverines, just to make him get off his ass and let me in. Doc was a good sort, real simpatico with cats, if a little bit rough when he played—but, then again, so was I. Sometimes I messed with him, just for kicks. I'd get him to chase me around the house, let him catch me, then I'd gnaw on his hand until he let me go. But turnabout is fair play, as you humans say, and other times he'd grab me by the front paws, pull me up so only my back toes touched the ground, and waltz me across the kitchen floor. The guy was no end of fun and no, I'm not being ironic. We hung out together playing and napping, all night, every night.

But if Doc was my buddy, Fern was The One. An absolute eat-off-her-plate, sleep-on-her-head, indulge-my-every-fuss-and-whim Goddess. And bless and damn her to hell—she's the one who turned me on to the nip.

CHAPTER 3

Picture a gray felt cube with a couple of tiny red triangles on the corners and a scraggly length of twine hanging off one end. Now imagine the triangles are "ears" and the twine is a "tail" and imagine you were stupid enough to consider the contraption a "mouse."

Neither was I. But the above cat toy had its advantages, or, rather, its advantage—it was *soaked* in the essence of a substance I came later to know as catnip, *Nepeta cataria*, high dose, concentrated, distilled domestic nip, and I went nuts for it right away.

I tore at the toy like it was a sworn enemy, which, I guess, in a sense, it was. But all I knew at the time was that it made me crazy high, happy and frantic. I'd gnaw the thing and bat it all around the house, striking and pouncing on it over and over again, until—soon enough—I'd kick the sodden mess under a couch or some other place too small for me to get to, and then I'd go sleep it off.

That was my first taste of the nip. My first *several* tastes, because Fern got such a kick out of my kicks she started bringing one home weekly.

You might as well give a 13-year-old human child, whose parents are about to allow him his first sip of wine with dinner, a big hit of crack instead. Those "mice" were *strong*. Only later did I come to know how unusually concentrated the dope was on that toy, but by then it was too late. I was spoiled ... *and* hooked.

You'd never figure Fern for a catnip pusher. She was very strict with Doc, who got his nickname because he tended to like the medicine. Sometimes he'd get pretty deep in the people nip himself, and when she caught him she'd throw a fit. She'd meow real loud and her face would get all puffy and her eyes would make water and doors would slam and they wouldn't talk to each other.

But with me she was just the opposite. She was the Catnip Queen. Catnip mice, catnip ball, little burlap sacks stuffed with catnip, catnip loose on the rug, catnip growing (briefly!) in the yard. And she loved it! I'd get all high and slobbery and she'd giggle with delight at my stoned antics. It was heaven.

I started out in the parlor, like the rest of them. I wound up tearing the fur off my back wriggling through a cracked window sneaking into a greenhouse in the dead of night. It's cost me a lot, this habit. It almost cost me everything.

So, was it worth it? If I had it to do all over again would I do it all over again? The answer doesn't come easy. I'm a much older, warier, and presumably wiser cat now, and I still can't say for sure. Lots of cats, and people too, disdain their young lives with their vices, as if to hate what they were helps to reconcile them to what they are now—old and tired.

Well, I *am* old and tired, but it's not that way with me. With me it was sheer ecstasy. Sometimes it still is. Listen. I'll try to explain it to you. If you're a two-legger you lack the necessities to understand this, but you're here; let me try.

Have you ever seen us? I mean *really seen* us? Watch us curl into sleeping position, walking a small circle as we spiral down onto that perfect, mystical spot. Notice how weightless we are, how gravity seems to cuddle us as we purr ourselves to sleep, our bodies molding like putty to fit the space where we've come to rest. See us tuck a paw under our bellies, our head sinking slowly into our own soft fur, the seamless symmetry of our repose.

Now think. Have you ever, once in your stiff-backed, tottering lives, felt that comfortable, even for a single moment? Have you known the satisfaction, the *joy*, of being inside a body so responsive, so competent, it's a form of genius? Have you ever felt Just Right?

Well, we do. We spend most of our lives that way. And a catnip high is like ten minutes of concentrated cat bliss in every second.

So ask me again. I think I'd say, yes, the price has been far too steep, it's dragged me down to a very low state. But I've been places you can never dream of....

* * *

I blame catnip, but it didn't start with catnip. The seeds were planted much earlier, in my first weeks with Doc and Fern. Because, one fine day, when my people finally decided I was theirs for keeps, they made their big move. They took me to the vet.

I will not bore you with the indignities I suffered there, the prodding and poking and man-handling by a total stranger. For me, that wasn't the worst of it. Nor was the cage—what you people call the "cat carrier" and we call "hell with a handle"—bad as that was. For me, the part I hated like death, was the car. I made an infernal racket every time I was dragged into the Rattle, Roll, Jolt and Puke.

Cats *hate* cars. Oh, I know, you want to tell me about the old lady you heard about whose pussy likes to climb in the Buick and watch the world disappear out the back window, but that woman also knits sweaters for Pookie that he wears without shame, so he doesn't count. I've known cats so far gone they ride in the car on their human's *shoulders* without clawing the idiot to ribbons, but they're the exception that proves the fool.

I feel very strongly about this, and here's why. You see, a cat *is* awareness. The greatest shame a cat can have, even greater than the loss of dignity you humans go on and on about, is to be taken by surprise. It goes against our very nature.

Those nine lives you people say we have, what do you think that's about? Of course we have, like you, only one. But we are *ready.* We preserve that life—from the way we fall to the way we escape trouble—with hyper-vigilant awareness, and it comes at a price. We are jumpy. Our deepest sleep is a fragile thing. One noise, one scent, a change in the light or the acoustics of a room and we're wide awake in an instant, ready to fight, ready to fly. You already know that, that's why you call them cat naps.

But a car cuts us off from all sense of place. With the windows up and the heat on we can't hear, see or smell a thing. The motion gives us an intense case of vertigo. Every sway and bump and pothole triggers a fight or flight reflex so strong it makes us cower, or go crazy or barf. I've done all three inside that horrible machine.

Roll down the windows and the rush of noise just kills our ears. To us, whose hearing is so sensitive we can recognize your footsteps half a block away when you come home from work, it would be like you sticking your head inside a jet engine.

And on top of that, we know what a car ride usually means. A shot. And in the presence of a dozen other cats, or, worse yet, dogs, *way* too close for comfort and not a damned thing we can do about it. Cats *hate* cars.

There is a reason I'm going on so about this car business. Because, when I was young and reckless, it was a car that provided the opportunity, the motivation, and most of all, the *excuse* for me to bolt from my happy, contented life, and go out and "have adventures."

I swear, if I knew then what I know now, and I still had my strength, I'd lick the hood of Doc's Jeep, just to show it I'd learned my lesson and that I'd never jump out of a car again. But I was an idiot in my youth. And I was about to learn my lesson the hard way.

CHAPTER 4

G *o.* Twenty claws shot into Doc's legs, I made my body into an arrow, pointed for freedom, and sproinged out that window in one lithe, powerful leap. The poor guy never had a chance, I was too fast. I flew out that window like I was shot from a cannon, and that was damned near the end of me and this little adventure you're reading right there.

Because we were *not quite* stopped when I made my move, and neither was the traffic in the adjoining lanes. I hit the pavement skidding, my claws getting no purchase on the concrete, and slid right under a truck, between the front and rear wheels, clunking my head so hard on a hot exhaust pipe that I was stunned senseless.

That saved my life, for the moment, because it halted my forward progress, and the truck's back wheel rolled to a stop not more than two whiskers in front of my snout.

I didn't have time to be scared. That awareness we were talking about kicked in and I acted—NOW.

I shook my whole body, my head cleared like magic. I scooted out from beneath the truck and hopped up on the grassy median, hearing Doc's cries behind me and feeling the forest and that tantalizing smell in front of me, three lanes of opposing traffic away.

Now I was moving, and on my game. I saw an opening, darted into the traffic, still rolling on that side of the street, and began to jump and juke my way across the road like I'd been doing it all my life. I heard horns honk and tires squeal, smelled burning rubber and my own joyous fear as I made for those woods and freedom, my senses so sharp it felt like everything was in slow motion—everything but me. I was inches from disaster a couple of times, but I made it clean and easy. It was poetry. Up the sidewalk, over the hedges, into the tall weeds and the green cool shade of the concealing forest. Inside of ten seconds I was well and truly gone.

* * *

But gone where? I didn't know, I just ran and ran hard. I wanted to put as much distance between me and that scary road as possible. Up over a last crest and down a crease in the land, paws flying on a damp, dark path where the water drains when it comes off the hill, down and down into that steep gorge, the city sounds fading behind me, the catnip smell growing in front.

But there were other scents, and as I caught them— dog crap, snake trails, mouse holes, bird droppings, even the musky smell of unwashed human—I slowed, easing towards the grassy verge of the path. I could smell the good stuff, just around the next bend, but— my senses told me—I wasn't alone. I skulked into the grass and fallen eucalyptus leaves, getting invisible, placing one paw gingerly on the ground ahead, testing it for firmness before shifting my weight, making sure I made not a sound, then repeating the move over and over, creeping forward six inches at a time. A cat, even a recently escaped, adrenaline-drunk, catnip-craving cat, is a patient thing.

But his patience can be tried. And when I turned that last corner mine was tried, stretched and wrapped around my neck so tight it gagged me like a spoonful of KittyLube (Hairballs gone overnight or your next tube free!). What I saw made me snot up so bad I got a nose whistle that scared *me* half out of my wits and alerted every hearing creature within a four-mile radius that Stealth Cat was In The House.

In that situation patience was no longer a virtue— haste was—so I made some. Two kitty heartbeats later I was at a tiny rivulet of oily water, standing paws deep in the mucky bank, seeing God.

Who knew nip could grow like this! The stuff was so tall it had bark! Or anyway, that's how it felt as I staggered from plant to plant, rubbing against the stalks, face, flank and tail, back arched like the Halloween cat, purring a motorboat bass that shook the plants from the roots up, sending a cloud of pure catnip resin drifting slowly, slowly, all the way from heaven, down to the ground with me on it. Temporarily.

Soon I was up there floating with it, higher than I'd ever been before. High enough to lose caution, to notice, but not care, that there was some stank homeless guy passed out on the other side of the tiny creek. All those warning smells that had given me pause were forgotten now as I reveled in the thicket of full-grown nip, eating the lower leaves, rolling in the pollen-y mulch till my fur was full of the stuff, blissing out.

For a while it was as good as it gets, but then it started to turn on me. I don't know if it was overdose, or coming down off the rush of escaping from Doc and my safe life, or what. Most likely it was all of the above, on top of the shots I got at the vet's, that made me violently ill, and so dizzy my legs decided they were on strike for the duration. I puked, rolled over in it, curled into a fetal ball and passed out in my own sick. It was totally gross, but I wasn't awake to enjoy it. And when I did wake up there was too much going on for me even to notice.

It was dark. The smell of smoke filled the air. And it wasn't just a homeless guy over there, ten feet away on the other bank, it was a homeless *encampment*. There must have been a dozen of them around a campfire. All sizes, shapes, smells, colors and sexes. And, just as my nose had told me that afternoon, they had dogs.

I forgot my hangover, my matted fur and deplorable condition and sat up slowly—only the patch of catnip hiding me from that human menagerie—and strained my still-dulled senses to figure out what I'd stumbled into. And what to do about it.

* * *

What I should have done is get the hell out of there. I should have taken advantage of the cover their raucous laughter and smoky campfire gave me and backed my sorry ass out of the vicinity as soon as

I was fit to stand. But I didn't. You know what they say about cats and curiosity? I think I got a double dose. So I sat quietly, peering through a gap in the bushy nip, watched and listened.

Of the dozen or so of them only a few were talking. They were closest to the fire, and I could see their faces as they leaned in to light a cigarette, or pass around a bottle. The rest of them were inert, either snoring, or motionless but awake, their eyes occasionally catching a glassy glint from the guttering flame.

One big, shaggy, bear-like man was carrying the conversation, talking to a clean-shaven small guy with a face so rat-like I wanted to bite him. A largish woman with a knotted corona of hair was leaning against the big guy, looking up at him admiringly as he spoke, his voice raspy and commanding.

"...got the idea he could unload the stuff on kids, young kids, like junior high, because they wouldn't know the difference and couldn't make too much trouble even if they did. And he figures, 'what the hell, even if I get caught it's only catnip, what can they do to me?'

"This Griff was a clean-looking dude, just like you, Mouse, (Mouse!) not the kind to attract any notice hanging around a schoolyard, right? So he does it, takes the catnip we planted right over there, bags it up and sells the stuff for twenty, twenty-five bucks a Z, moving all around town like the smart guy he thinks he is, and for a few weeks it's all good.

"But then, sure as shit, he gets pinched. Cop grabs him by the neck and damn near chokes him throwing him into the cruiser, he's so outraged, this bum dealing dope to school kids. Takes him to 850 Bryant and the whole time Griff's yelling, 'it's catnip, it's catnip!' but the cop tells him to shut up or I'll shut you up."

The big guy pauses there to wait for the laugh, which comes like he just told the funniest joke in the world. And that was yet another chance for yours truly to get a move on. Needless to say, however....

"Still, Griff's not worried, he figures it'll come out in the wash and when they find out, he'll walk.

"What he doesn't count on is this cop getting his picture in the paper the next day, shaking hands with the principal of the school, which ... and get this ... turns out the be the same school the cop went to like 15 years ago, same principal and everything. Where he's now the big hero, saving the kiddies from this sicko dope fiend, probably make nark of the year or something.

"Now Griff's just a homeless loser, no family, no dough, and they give him a lousy public defender who doesn't want to hear it. So, damned if a pound of primo bud doesn't walk into his evidence locker right before the arraignment, and about ten vials of rock too, just in case.

"Dumb ass. He has one idea in his worthless life and look where it gets him. Like a cop is going to lose a bust like that to a bum like him on a technicality. Far as that cop is concerned, he has it coming. He's either a drug pusher who sells to kids, or a con man running his stunt in middle schools, for chrissakes. His trial is in a few weeks. Too bad you never met him, Mouse, you woulda got a kick out of the idiot. Hey, Kathy, grab me a smoke out of my coat there, willya? You want one, Mouse?"

I'm coming to slowly and taking all this in. I know I'm in the presence of an unsavory character and maybe worse, but I still don't leave. I hang around. Because, somehow this scene doesn't seem so threatening anymore—the dog is sleeping and, upon closer inspection, he doesn't look like much to begin with—and also, I suddenly realize, I am absolutely starving.

My stomach is groaning like it hasn't been fed in a week, which it has every right to do, if you figure how much I upchucked before. I have a rotten taste in my mouth from trying to clean myself up that only makes it worse. I'm so damn hungry I forget that my nose is shoved up against a grove of catnip; I smell right through it. And what I smell is food, somewhere among that motley crew over there.

I know I should wait. The big guy and his woman are kind of leaning on each other and the conversation is tapering off, soon they'll be asleep and I can go check it out in relative safety. But I convince myself there is no harm in stalking a little closer, so I get up and carefully slink down to the bank of the creek, until I find a place where I can cross unseen.

I time my leap on a big yawn the rat-faced Mouse guy makes, and hit the other bank with an imperceptible-to-human-ears squish. I work my way around the sleeping bodies, and the funk coming off them, until I come to a mound of what looks like dog food sitting on a square of aluminum foil.

Now normally I wouldn't give that crap a second look. It must have been sitting out a while, because it looks kind of crusty around the edges, but as Fern always says (and that was the first time I'd thought of her since I took the big leap, but not the last, alas) "hunger is the best spice."

So I take a chance. I reach out a paw and hook a dollop of the slop with my claws, careful not to crinkle the foil, and bring it to my mouth. Edible. Tastes like food. I do it again.

The guy sleeping close to me grunts, turns over. I freeze for a moment … nothing happens … and I go back to eating, less cautious now, craning my neck over the foil, eating hearty and enjoying every gamy bite.

Then I make a mistake. I start to purr. I can't really blame myself, I always purr when I eat, if I'm hungry enough, and it's not like anyone with two feet two feet away could even hear it. But I can, and that sound rumbles in my ears just enough to mask other soft noises, noises on the outside, where trouble might lurk. Or an overweight woman's meaty hand.

"Look Marv," she gushes as I'm lifted three feet off the ground, gagging on half a mouthful of dog slop, "A kitty!"

CHAPTER 5

Why, you ask, did I not simply turn her arm into string cheese and depart the premises forever? Why take a chance with an off-smelling, slightly tipsy, not altogether healthy, overly fleshy human female of no great strength?

It's not like that, you see. I'm a *cat* if you haven't already noticed, and I tend to react to the moment. It took many hard knocks before I learned to think ahead a little, to think of *consequences.*

At that moment, I was more startled than afraid. The vibe around this woman was silly, not dangerous. And I was still hungry and hung over. So I just let it happen.

Not that she got off scot-free. I did stab a claw or three into the puckered pores of her arm trying to keep my balance, but I don't think she even noticed. She was too happy. Her lumpy face folded upwards into joyous curves of delight. In the kind, fading light of the campfire, she was almost radiant. Her body bloomed with a benevolent reek, and I was just curious enough to stay still in her hands as she carried me over to her man.

"Marv!" she squeaked, "Isn't he beautiful? And feel this fur!"

"Marv" chucked me under the chin. I would have bitten him but I didn't want his grimy finger in my mouth. He scratched me between the ears; I flattened them against my head and glared at him. He had a bad smell—not just the odor of filth, I could tolerate that, but a sour smell of anger that leaked out of him like he was full of it.

I recoiled in Kathy's hand and hissed, showing Marv my teeth.

"He doesn't like you!" she said triumphantly, like I had confirmed something *important*—that she was a better person than he was.

Marv barked out a sound I think he intended to be a laugh. "You and your goddamn strays. What next? You gonna start a zoo? I swear, Kath, he gets in my way I'll snap his scrawny neck, you hear?"

"Blah, blah, blah," she said. "All talk. You couldn't hurt a fly, you big galoot. And if I didn't like strays, you'd still be sleeping under 280. Alone."

"Yeah, whatever. Screw it, I'm going to sleep."

"Me too," said Kathy, lying down on a tatty wool blanket, facing away from him, cuddling me against her soft, warm belly.

Me three.

* * *

I woke well before they did, in the murky predawn hour. The weather had turned thick overnight, with fog so dense it felt more like drizzle. I stretched and flexed extravagantly, like the athlete I was in those days, stepped silently through the array of sleeping, snoring bodies, shook off the morning mist and groggies, and sauntered over to the creek for a drink, feeling like a million bucks.

A strip of tender young grass bordered the creek, the kind that's real refreshing when it's speckled with dew; I grazed on it before coming onto some sprigs of catnip that had sprouted here on the near bank. I wasn't that interested, for some reason nip never appealed to me much first thing in the morning, but here they were and what the hell—I took a few bites.

That put a glow on everything the sun had missed this gray morning. I decided to explore, heading slowly into the drifting wisps of fog. The route I took went up the other side of the gulch, away from the camp and the hill I had walked down the day before. I paused to rub against a bush or two on the way up, and clawed and sprayed a thick tree where I caught an aging scent of another tom, though this was clearly no cat's territory right now. But there was an increasing smell, or complex of smells, coming from dead ahead, that was enticing, drawing me on. I literally followed my nose, up the hill, through a grove of eucalyptus, down another defile, and over a scrubby ridge, where the grass was patchy and trees didn't grow at all.

Finally I came to a road, wide and windy. The fog was so dense that I heard the traffic before I could see it, not that there was much of it at this hour. But there was some, and if I misjudged the sounds, it would be flat-cat time. I should have said the hell with it and turned around, but ... you know ... curiosity. And that smell was so tantalizingly close now, coming in booming waves I could actually hear.

So I posed, stretched my neck up as far as it could go, turned my ears this way and that, and listened. First a hissing whisper, then a car zoomed by like a wraith, now two cars, then quiet, quiet … still quiet. okay, now!

I was across in three seconds. My paws landed on cold sand, loose and scrabbly. I climbed a steep dune, bare but for some wiry patches of long grass at the crest, then down, down, skidding, almost tumbling as I slid, my claws curved the wrong way to grasp the shifting sand. Halfway down I emerged from the fog which was streaming over my head like it was in a big hurry. Beneath it the air was clear, the light dull white; I was in a different world.

Now I understood the booming, rushing sound I heard on quiet nights when the wind was still, here was the source of those salty, fishy smells I'd been tasting all my life, and chasing all morning. The sea.

Actually I didn't know "the sea" from "the moon" back then. All I knew was that here was a BIG water that moved and smelled and made a bucketful of noise. I found out about the ocean later, from cats who lived alongside one on another coast, far away. I found out about *most* things later, in the course of my travels. I wasn't stupid that day, my first away from home, just a baby. Cats may not learn like, or as much as, humans, but we *do* learn.

We also play. Most cats hate the beach, it's noisy and wet, dog territory. But I was still buzzed, and I was also provoked.

Something moved beneath my front right paw. The sand was squirming under there like it was alive. First it tickled … then it didn't.

I let out a screech that would have been appropriate if I was about to go into mortal combat with a moose. That "living" sand clamped down on my toes and I shot straight up in the air, screaming like I was in the jaws of death.

Well, not quite. My pain-startled eyes found my assailant—a sand crab—dangling from my foot. Couldn't have been more than three inches across. Hurt like three yards.

Get off, get off! I shook my paw hard, the way I do when I step in something unpleasant. Which I guess this qualified as. My foot vibrated like a tuning fork, and that only made it hurt worse. But finally the crab flew off and hit the sand upside down, struggling to turn over and slink away.

Oh no ... not before I get some payback. I darted over to him (no, of course I don't know if it was a him; I'm *assuming*), stuck a paw—the *other* one—under his hard back, very quickly, very carefully, and gave it a powerful flick. Up went the crab on a cushion of sand, then back down again, on his front. He tried to burrow, I circled around him and gave him a quick swipe on the shell. Off he flew again. This was fun.

Fun yes, but clearly not food. After a minute of this foolishness, I let him go. Suddenly, I had the munchies. Somewhere on this big beach there must be something to eat; I began to prowl.

I learned a few things that morning. Seagulls are big and fast and impossible to catch. The ocean will sneak up on you and get you wet and very cold if you don't pay close attention. And the bugs they've got there are tasty, but hardly worth the trouble and the mouthful of grit that comes along with the mini-meal. I settled for some sea oats with that all-important roughage we mammals need. Which, presently, allowed me to leave my mark in the world's biggest litter box, thereby claiming it as my own.

By now I'd been up and moving for a good part of the morning without so much as a nap, and even a healthy young tom needs a good, solid 18 a day. I found a sheltered spot under the people steps to the beach, curled down until I'd made a nice bowl in the sand, and drifted off.

When I woke up I was out of sorts and chilled to the bone. The fog had turned to drizzle for real now, darkness was coming, and the big beach made me feel naked and exposed. I felt a powerful urge to get back—but back to what?

As I climbed the dunes towards the dangerous street I'd challenged that morning, I was confronted with a crossroads, literally. What to do, where to go. "Home" never entered my mind that day, that urge would come much later. My decision, as I saw it back then, was between going back to my yummy catnip grove and its weird inhabitants, or just moving on into the whatever. I decided not to decide, but my legs kept me going in one direction, pretty much.

They say that all animals are repelled by fire—though the moths will give you an argument on that score—but fire was in my mind more than anything as dusk darkened to night that soggy evening. I kept picturing myself curled up next to that campfire, belly full of food—the kind that comes in a can that you don't have to hunt—warm, flickering light drying my wet fur, and, perhaps, the soft buzz of the catnip I had for dessert lulling me off to dreamland. For a feral I'm a total slut for luxury. But, then again, so are we all. In the end the choice was no choice, I just went with what felt good.

Another thing I found out that day, I'm a born tracker. I had no difficulty retracing my steps and scent until I was close enough to hear the first crackles and cackles of my newly adopted—God help me—family.

* * *

She must have been looking for me. The whole fragrant crew was awake this time, and Kathy was by no means the closest to me when I came down that hill into the fire's light. But she saw me first.

"Hey Marv!" she bellowed, "Look! Rusty's back. I told you!"

Rusty? Oh man. This woman was no Fern, as if that issue was ever in doubt. But as she wove her way to me, slapping her fat thighs and keening "Rusteee, Rusteee," in her alcoholic version of a momma's baby talk, she said the magic word.

"Poor baby, where did you go? You must be starving. Does wittle Wusty want some *food?*"

Oh *hell* yeah, that's exactwy what Wusty wants.

CHAPTER 6

So I stayed a while. I won't bore you with the details, the days were pretty much alike. I'd go roaming, exploring and hunting to my heart's content, then I'd come back for huge doses of my own personal catnip jungle and whatever slop Kathy was dishing up that day.

The homeless folks were good to me, mostly. It didn't take me long to figure out who was okay, and whom to avoid. The latter were mostly "dog people."

Speaking of the dogs, I had no trouble with them, except for one especially stupid mutt—half shepherd, half something big and ugly—they called Ranger. I think he wanted to be friends; it's hard to say for sure, because he was so annoyingly inept at it. His version of play consisted of such amusing pastimes as chasing *my* tail, or running around my face growling, like I was a sheep and he was trying to herd me. He got in my face mostly at mealtimes, so you know he wasn't my favorite.

He never laid a paw on me in anger, though, and, with one exception, neither did I. I don't want to come off like a snob, because I'm not, at least where cats are concerned, which will become abundantly clear later in my story. But dogs, in my humble opinion, are servile idiots. They lack the brain power to think for themselves—which is why they're so good at following orders. And Ranger was rather less evolved than most.

One warm, lazy afternoon—I was being especially indulgent of myself, which is saying something—I was nodding off a major catnip buzz, deep in a stoned dream where I was hunting some kind of snake-frog monster my blitzed brain had conjured up. In my dream I had lost sight of the creature, who had submerged into a reed-banked pond where I'd been stalking him. I had my head down, trying to pick up the scent, being very careful because this monster of my fevered imagination was about six feet long and toothy. All my muscles were tense and ready to fire.

Suddenly, without warning, it sprang! A cold crocodile snout jabbed at my backside, cold and slimy! Snake-frog was about to devour me in one huge bite! I spun on the monster, defending my hindquarters with twenty slashing claws.

Poor Ranger. He had chosen that moment to play with the sleeping kitty, shoving his wet, disgusting nose right up my rear. It never occurred to him it might be dangerous to disturb a cat sky high on nip and deep in fantasy land. Hell, he had no idea the grove was catnip at all! Dogs don't get off on the stuff. One gets high with one's brains and dogs lack the raw materials.

I suppose I should be grateful he didn't come back at me with jaws agape and mouth a-foam, considering how his nose looked after I ripped it, but—not to brag—he'd had all he could take by then. He ran away howling like he'd stepped on a land mine. The homeless people, easily amused, roared with laughter. Ranger more or less avoided me after that.

My only real problem was Marv. He could be a cruel son of a bitch—not to me, he was okay on those rare occasions when he deigned to take notice of me at all—but to Kathy. They fought constantly, and it worked my nerves something fierce. Cats are very sensitive to the threat of violence, we have a sixth sense for it. Sometimes when Fern and Doc would fight, I'd get right in the middle of it and squall until they shut up. But they were class people, and they'd calm down because they "didn't want to upset Doo Doo."

But Kathy and Marv's lives were all struggle and no class. Which is why they were here in the woods, living on scraps. I just knew that sooner or later something bad was going to happen. And once again, dammit, I was right.

It all started over people dope. One evening Marv came back to the camp all pissed off, looking to take it out on somebody.

"Lazy bastards," he said to no one in particular, making his usual, stomping, top-dog entrance. He waved a fistful of money in the air. "Fifty-six big ones, right here. Took three stinking hours of panhandling to get it, I wasn't done till four. But ask me, could I find one lousy dealer with a couple balloons of tar? Nope. Not one of them was out there, the lazy bastards. Not a Mexican with some Chiva he hadn't unloaded that afternoon, not a single homey, nobody. There ain't no drought, I saw lots of guys I know junked up to their eyeballs. But not a one of 'em would part with so much as a taste. Useless bastards, I got the shakes and all I can do about it is drink this crap," he said, lifting a wrinkled paper sack. "Where the hell is Kathy? Anyone seen my goddamn woman?" He wiped his big mouth with the back of his hand, waiting for an answer.

Only Mouse spoke. "She's around here somewhere, dude. I saw her and Jessie over to the creek not long ago."

Marv's eyes narrowed. From my perch on a warm boulder, still radiating heat from the day's sun, I could see that he was not only hurting, he was already half drunk.

"Oh yeah?" Marv snorted, "Jessie huh? HEY KATHY!" he shouted, "Where the hell are you? KATHYYYY!" Then, under his breath, too softly for human ears to hear, but not mine, he hissed "bitch."

A little rustling from the other side of the creek, beyond the catnip patch.

"Right here, baby," came Kathy's voice, not sounding at all mad or offended. Soft and sweet and slurry, actually.

"Get your fat ass over here, woman," Marv growled. "What the hell were you doing out there with Jessie? And where is the SOB?"

"I dunno. What are you saying?" Kathy crossed the creek, walking slowly, half drawn to her man, half wary of his explosive mood.

"I'm saying I couldn't find a goddamn thing out there, is what I'm saying. And while I'm out there pounding the pavement to get us straight, you're screwing around with that loser?" Marv took a deep swig from the gallon of wine he'd brought, then spit some out towards Kathy's muddy feet.

But then his rage seemed to leave him then, and while his words stayed harsh, his tone changed.

"Ah what the hell," he said. "Sit your ass down, try some of this shit. Maybe it'll take the edge off. I mean, look at me." And he managed a tight smile as he patted the ground next to him.

Kathy thought she was home free, I guess. She should have known better. I did.

She sat down next to Marv on some newspapers he'd spread out, her hands on her knees, looking down, her tangled red hair hiding her face. Marv handed her the big jug of wine, she took it without looking up, but she had to lean back to drink, and when she did, Marv glared at her.

She handed him the wine, and he put a hand under her chin and turned her face towards his.

He stared at her for a long moment, his face slowly twisting into a sneer.

"Oh no. No no no. You are *not* messed up. I'm not *trying* to believe you got a load on while I was out there bustin my ass for nothing! You're eyes are pinned! You holding out on me, *bitch*?"

Kathy cowered away from his hand.. "No, Marvin, it's not like that! I wouldn't do that to you baby! How long you know me? It's Jessie, he had some…"

"*Jessie!*" Marv's face grew even redder than usual. "You got high with Jessie? While I'm gone?" He stood up, towering over Kathy, who was hugging her knees, shivering scared.

Marv's voice softened ominously. "You doing Jessie now, Kathy? Is that why he's hiding in the woods, cause you two are getting it on out there? Huh? Tell me baby," his voice raising in pitch but not in volume, "you do *anyone* who's holding now? Come on, tell me. You a full on dope-whore now, Kath?"

I'll give her this, Kathy would try to defend herself. Weak as she was, she didn't like getting stepped on, and, in her wimpy way, she'd let you know it.

"Stop it," she was sobbing. "No! Jessie just had … he's a friend. Can't I have friends? Nothing happened."

"Nothing happened?" Now Marv was roaring. "Looks to *me* like something happened! I'm jonesing my ass and my woman's fried to the gills! I tell you what, you don't level with me, something's *gonna* happen, real soon."

Kathy scooted back on her butt; Marv stood spread-legged over her menacingly.

"Go away!" she said. "It's all lies. You have no right…."

"No *right*?! I'll show you who has rights, you slut!" and he reached down and backhanded the top of her head, hard.

Kathy yelped softly, whimpered, and curled into a ball.

"Get away … away," she gasped between sobs. "You're a bastard! I hate you!"

Marv lost it. He swore incoherently, swiped at her again, and when she ducked, making him miss, he kicked out at her with a booted foot. She caught it square in the ribs. I heard a sound like a broken twig.

I didn't know what to do. My body was cranking out fight-or-flight juices like a fountain. I was a good fifteen feet away, but I could smell the anger and fear coming off both of them, I could hear the gasps and ineffective entreaties of the others to knock it off, I tasted my own steely readiness for … for whatever. I didn't know *what* to do, but I sure didn't want to attract attention to myself. I got as flat on that rock as I could, kept my eyes wide open on the craziness happening in front of me and got poised to move fast if I had to.

It got worse, much worse, but the action moved away from me. Marv reached back to kick Kathy again, but this time she grabbed his boot, holding on to protect herself. Marv, none too steady to begin with, toppled like a rotten tree, face first.

He reared up making animal sounds, blood streaming from his nose. Kathy knew she'd done it now. She scrambled to her feet before he could, hightailed it over the creek towards the woods. Marv twenty feet behind, stumbling, roaring, out for blood.

The rest was hidden from my view, mercifully. I heard enough though, to know that he'd found her, and she was catching it hard. It didn't last long, but long enough.

Marv came back alone, wobbly and blown, blood and drool around his mouth. He collapsed near the fire, breathing hard. I thought he was staring straight at me; I felt my back hair bristle, my whiskers bent back, claws straining silently for purchase on the rock. But I doubt he even saw me. His mind, what was left of it, was elsewhere. Inside of ten minutes he was snoring like he was choking to death. If only.

Don't ask me to explain why I did what I did next. I'd only been around this woman for maybe a week or two, and she wasn't my idea of a perfect human companion, any more than she would be yours. With my sharp hearing I could tell where she was, about 100 feet over the other side of the creek, breathing raggedly, whimpering. And however long it had been, she'd fed and petted and loved me the best she knew how. I felt the need to go check.

She was awake, crying softly, her breath catching from the pain of what turned out to be a broken rib. It was very dark over there in the trees. I think she felt my breath on her nose before she saw me. But she was beyond being startled, I guess. All she did was sigh, "Oh Rusty ... sweetie. You came...." And she petted me until I purred.

* * *

The next day, I was having a morning nip in my beloved patch after stealing some of Ranger's cruddy food for breakfast. Last night's fight had me a little antsy, but cats face danger all the time, and if we dwelled on it we'd be too scared to go on being cats. It happens to some of us, though. You must have known a cat or two like that, afraid of every noise, perpetually nervous and jumpy. Ferals need a little of that instinct, but a little goes a long way. So I was just doing my thing, nice, mild buzz on, when stuff started happening, too fast.

Kathy woke up with a plan, and I was part of it. Like I said, she could stand up for herself when she absolutely had to, and today was the day. She came limping into camp and had it out with Marv, who was much diminished and oddly contrite this morning.

She wasn't going to take it anymore. She was going away, away from here, away from him. She didn't need this crap, she had family.

Marv actually started to cry. Amazing. If I walked on two legs, like you, you could have knocked me over with a feather. "Don't go. I love you. I'm sorry."

Kathy was having none of it. She walked away from him, wincing, each stab of pain from her busted chest visible on her face. Slowly, gingerly, she gathered up her stuff, saying goodbye to her friends in the camp, a few of whom were standing between her and Marv, anticipating trouble that never came.

The last thing she gathered up was me. And here I thought she was only coming over for a farewell pet. Next thing I know I'm in a cardboard box with a couple of holes poked in the side letting in almost enough air, bouncing up the hill and away from that camp, and my grove, my beloved catnip grove, forever.

CHAPTER 7

I didn't like the airplane any better than the car. Worse even. First of all, they give you a shot. You might think a nip head like me wouldn't mind a nice buzz to take the edge off, but you'd be wrong. I want it to be *my* choice when I get messed up, and the stuff they shoot you full of before they shove you in that metal beast feels awful.

Nip heightens me; that crap made me feel like I was made of lead. It put me to sleep, but not a normal sleep. It was a disorienting, dizzy swoon that came and went in sickening waves. Each time I "woke up" I was terrified—trapped in a plastic cage inside a buzzing drum, the noise a huge, roaring drone, the air thin and stagnant, the smells strange and vaguely poisonous, the weird motions nauseating. I didn't know where the hell I was, but it *was* hell, that much I knew for sure.

The worst part was that my brain, in those fleeting moments of semi-lucidity, kept screaming "RUN!" at the top of its lungs. But my normally responsive body, my one unfailing asset, was dead from the eyes down. I weighed a thousand pounds, it was all I could do to twitch my tail. I had to lie there in paralyzed horror until the next wave of the drug put me back under for a little while. Then I'd wake up, un-remembering, and do it all again. Even now my throat gets tight and my ruff hairs bristle when I recall those endless five hours.

I say five hours; at the time I couldn't tell you if it was five minutes or five days. But, as I found out later, that's how long it takes to fly from coast to coast inside one of those hollow trees you humans build to take you into the sky. As for me, I'd rather walk. Which—as you'll see when my story unfolds—is pretty much what I *tried* to do, on the way back.

But forgive me, I have the advantage of you. A cat's thoughts aren't as linear as a human's; sometimes I forget where I left off. As I remember, we were just leaving that homeless camp, Kathy in a tizzy, me in a box....

Once she snatched me from the woods Kathy got busy, right away. It turned out that she had a sister living on the East Coast, in a place called New Jersey, within smelling distance of another place you may have heard of, New York City.

This relation was the recipient of Kathy's sad story, sobbed over a pay phone that very afternoon. And, though the bonds of family had been strained through the years by Kathy's repetitive sad stories, said sister offered Kathy a helping hand in the form of a one-way airline ticket east, and a severely temporary place to stay when she got there.

I was the joker in the deck. Where old Kath got the money for my fare I'll never know, because her sister—whose name was Brenda and looked just like Kathy would have looked if she hadn't gotten her three squares a day from a bottle for fifteen years—certainly wasn't expecting me or anyone like me.

Which was the cause of their first argument.

"He can't stay here. Timmy's allergic. Gives him asthma."

"How is my little nephew? Don't worry, he's an outdoor cat, he can sleep in the box."

Like hell I could. But I was hung over bad, trying not to puke myself in that box as the jalopy careened towards "home," so I kept my peace.

"I'm serious Kathy. It was all I could do to talk Tony into letting *you* stay. Why you always gotta make things difficult?"

"He's just a kitten, Brenda. He won't be no trouble. You shoulda seen the way he come to me after Marvin got done whaling my ass, woulda broke your heart. I couldn't leave him there with those degenerates. Leave him stay in the backyard, okay? It'll only be for a little while."

"You got that right," Brenda said.

* * *

I slept off the groggies and woke up, still in the cage, in the weedy backyard of a disheveled house, so lost it made me dizzy. Actually "lost" doesn't quite say it; *everything* was strange here, nothing was familiar, nothing fit. Even the air was odd—heavy, sticky, smelly, close. The sun fuzzed hot out of a white sky, warping the plastic cat carrier, baking its iron bars like an oven shelf. Someone had thoughtfully placed a dish of some kind of fish parts in my cage, ripening faster than I could eat it, and I was plenty hungry. To wash it down I had boiling water in a metal bowl. A four inch tattered square of carpet—which I suppose was there to "comfort" me—completed the furniture.

What they'd forgotten was kitty litter. I peed on the rug. Thankfully, the airline dope still had me constipated. This was not a good situation.

Kathy came out to see me when the sun went down. I heard her coming, limping heavily, smelled whiskey on her breath as she whuffed down painfully in front of the cage. She called me "poor thing." I thought the same of her. It never got dark here, the white sky just turned livid gray at night, and I could see the contours of her lumped-up face as she leaned over, blowing me kisses through swollen lips.

Very carefully, she opened the cage, just a crack, groping for me. She must have thought I would bolt if I had half a chance, and I thought the same thing. We were both wrong. I let her drag me out of that damned box, and I let her hold me, too. Oh, I squirmed around some, made a halfhearted squawk or two, I even got out of her arms long enough to relieve myself. I could easily have made a move. But I stayed.

Kathy had a napkin on her lap, filled with overcooked hamburger, which she unwrapped and offered to me like it was kitty caviar. It was dry and hard to swallow, but it tasted great. She even trusted me enough to put the napkin on the ground so I could more or less eat in peace. But she never stopped petting me.

When I was done I circled around her, rubbing up against her hips and back, purring like a lap cat. Kathy lit a cigarette and looked at the sky, sighing with every puff.

This isn't so bad, I thought, stretching my legs luxuriantly, delighted to be out of the box and free. I can live with this.

And then the bitch snuffed out her smoke, snatched me up, and shoved me back in that stinking jail. I had a few choice words for her too, as she wobbled back inside, but if she understood me, she didn't let on.

* * *

I couldn't have taken much more of that, and I didn't have to, thanks to Timmy. How long it would have taken me to get oriented, feel brave, and head out on my own in this new, confusing place is a matter of debate—my pride says soon, my memory calls my pride a liar. But Timmy, bless his black heart, saved me the trouble.

I wish this was a picture book so I could show you what that brat looked like. The best I can do with words is "Red." Red in color, red in mood, red in fear and anger (I know that cats don't see color like people, but, contrary to popular belief we're not completely colorblind, and "red" is how Timmy looked to me). He was one itchy, twitchy kid, allergic to everything, apparently. I think what he was most allergic to was himself.

A few days after we got there, he waddled out to take his first close look at me. By this time Kathy was leaving the cage door open and I was doing some limited exploring, though sticking close to "home."

Timmy must have been told to leave me alone, because he tried ineffectively to hide that morning, cowering behind a rusty barbecue on the porch, waiting until his aunt had come to feed me and gone back inside. Then he kind of spazzed over to me while I ate.

Stealth wasn't in the kid's arsenal; he wheezed, snorted and stomped—I forgot to tell you he was fat as a beach ball—as he came up behind me. The vibe coming off him was so bad it made me back away from my food, which really pissed me off because it was leftover roast chicken, my idea of gourmet cuisine even though Brenda cooked it in a kiln.

"What's so special about you, stupid cat," Timmy began our beautiful friendship. "You look like a regular stupid cat to me, stupid."

Clearly this was a child of great promise, if only he could get over his prejudiced ignorance. I took it upon myself to enlighten him.

"Hisssss, hiss, hiss, growl, spit!"

"Mommeeeee!"

But mommeeee wasn't there, luckily. Kathy was babysitting while Mom and Dad went out to hunt and gather at the local Wal-Mart. She came running.

"What's the matter, sweetie?" Kathy fawned like she thought she was being videotaped.

"Your stupid cat scratched me!" Acting was another of Timmy's skills; the kid could make tears over a broken shoelace—assuming he could reach his shoelace while still attached to his foot, a doubtful proposition.

What I didn't count on was his being able to raise welts on demand, because, as The Lion Goddess is my witness, I never touched the brat. But that didn't stop the boy from swelling up like a balloon animal.

"Oh sh … oh no!" Kathy gasped when she took Timmy's proffered arm, red and glowing like Brenda just took it out of the oven. "Where did he get you?"

She shot me a glare, "Bad boy! What did you do, Rusty?"

Rusty. I almost forgot. Who's rusty now, I thought, watching Red blubber and wheeze like I'd gutted him.

"I don't see, Timmy, show me…. There? He scratched you there?" Kathy, to her credit, looked closely at the "wound" which looked no worse, or better, than any other part of his flabby wing.

"You're not bleeding, sweetie," Kathy smiled, making light, trying to soothe the monster.

"He scratched me! He made a chhhh sound and then he scratched me! I hate him! Make him go away!"

I swear, if cats could laugh or cry I wouldn't have known whether to laugh or cry. When he imitated my hiss it sounded like he had someone's thumbs on his windpipe—a happy image. But I could feel the worry starting to pour off Kathy, and that frightened me. I made a quick, judicious slink into the rangy shrubs that passed for a hedge in this dump and waited for the crisis to pass.

CHAPTER 8

It never did. When Brenda and Tony (picture little Timmy all grown up, with his baby fat replaced by man fat) got home the litter really hit the fan.

That family could make some serious noise, when they put their minds to it. You humans are, as a rule, rather too loud for feline comfort at the best of times, and these were far from that. I was prepared to see Kathy stagger out of the house a bloody mess, because if cats had been fighting at that volume anything less than torn flesh would be considered bad form by the Feline Street.

I couldn't make out much of it, only an occasional snatch like, "What did we tell you?" or "...back in the gutter where you belong..." or "He goes or *you both* go. That's it!" But what I heard was enough to frighten me half to death.

Back in my kitten days, in my private jungle behind Fern and Doc's place, I'd heard talk from adopted cats about what happens when you "go." I knew all about the place of no return—or, rather, the place from whence you return either croaked or cut—and I had no desire to be either. I hadn't put it together yet, but I was facing two bad options—the pound or the street. And it pains me to admit that my tiny brain might not have processed the danger in time for my superhero's body to get me out of there with soul and sack intact.

But my luck held. Have I told you that I'm a lucky cat? Well, I'm telling you again, because for all her disheveled incompetence, when I met Kathy, I met gold. I was lucky.

"Rusteeee! Here boy, c'mon, Rusteee! Kittykittykitty.... Let's go boy, we're getting out of here."

I poked a pink nose out of the shrub. Back in her arms, back in the box, back on the road.

* * *

I'd never seen her let go before, not even when Marv had been pounding the crap out of her, but now she was dripping tears like a baby. She held it together long enough to talk the bus driver into letting her buy one ticket if she held the box in her lap, sat down in a corner of the rear bench, and commenced to bawling.

I felt bad, and not only for her. Between the diesel fumes, the constant stop and go, and Kathy's belly shaking my cage with every sob it was all I could do not to barf. She tried to cry quietly, but the more she suppressed her gasps the more that box jerked and rolled. After a while she subsided and her choking breath turned into whispers of self hatred.

"Why I'm such a loser ... all I had to do was ... oh Rusty, you poor thing...." Deep sigh.... "She always hated me ... can't hardly blame her ... what we gonna do now?" Kathy stuck a finger through the bars of my cage, I rubbed my cheeks up against it. "You're all I got now, kitty. Just you and me. I'm *so* sorry!" Another sigh, "Oh Jesus … why I have to be me?"

Hell, I was just glad to be out of that crazy house. Not for the first time I ached to be able to speak people. "Come on, Kathy," I would have said, "don't be so hard on yourself. We're going to do just fine. And by the way, the name is Doo Doo."

* * *

For a self-loathing alky, Kathy was a survivor, and she knew how to work the system. It wasn't easy getting the welfare bureaucracy to do something for a stranger with an alley cat in a box. But she succeeded by sheer persistence and tenacious loyalty. "They" wanted her to take me to animal rescue, if only for a few nights, until she got set up. She wouldn't hear of it.

"He's the only thing that makes me feel good," Kathy told the frazzled case worker. "Plus he helps keep me straight." (Did I mention she could lie like a cat doctor with a scalpel and an agenda?)

The welfare woman mumbled some discouraging words, like she was reading from a form. Kathy was undeterred.

"I'm not going anywhere without Rusty. I'll sleep in a doorway if I got to, he stays with me. Don't you understand? I rescued *him*. He makes *me* feel useful, he *needs* me." The welfare woman wavered. Then Kathy tried a magic word, and it worked.

"How am I supposed to get it together if I fail all the time? We're good for each other, the cat and me. He helps my *esteem*."

Bingo. They sent her on her way with a hot meal, a few dollars, and an address. If she wanted more she'd have to come back later and jump through the hoops again. Kathy was effusively thankful to the welfare woman, like she'd just talked her way out of a ticket, all smiles and promises.

And there was something in it for me. Dinner. I got a paper plate full of some foodstuff that was supposed to resemble turkey, I think. She snagged it from the cafeteria where we got supper with the meal ticket they gave her. The place said "no pets," but as long as I stayed in the box nobody seemed to mind. I ate under the table, surrounded by a forest of feet, which, if only by contrast, helped neutralize the funk coming off the food.

So I was fed, and we were out of that madhouse in New Jersey: so far so good. But I was sick and tired of living in a plastic box and pissing in a pie plate. If this new city—which made my home town seem like a farm—wasn't scaring the bejesus out of me, I'd have been laying plans for a break.

But not yet. The noise, the smells, the crowds, the invisible sky; it was all too much. I'd have to lay low for a while, figure it out. And I hadn't had any nip for days. I could sure use a taste right about now, but would I ever find any again?

* * *

We spent the next few nights moving around. A church for a couple of days, with a few other down-and-outs who got a kick out of the lady with the cat.

Then one night in a shelter, where Kathy smuggled me past the guard by leaving the box in an alley and shoving me under her dress (never again!). But we got tossed after I "made a mistake." I saw some kids tagging the shelter halls with spray paint and got inspired. When Kath wasn't looking I darted out of our room and "tagged" the place with some of my own highly-ripe spray, and we were busted. Back in the box, back on the street.

Our luck changed for the better when Social Services found us a place that took pets. It was an old tenement—converted to a welfare hotel.

That building was a dump if there ever was one, but our fifth floor walk-up, dingy, dark and acrid, meant freedom to me, and once I got out of the box for good, the place felt like the Ritz.

I spent a lot of time alone in that apartment. Kathy would leave in the morning, come back and feed me once or twice during the day, then go back out again. I don't know what she was getting into out there but she always came back before my food ran out. The longer we lived there the more often she'd come home late, smelling of booze, but she never got as ripped as I'd seen her back in San Francisco.

When she was home I got lots of affection. The food she brought was pretty good, too. She tidied up the place, got me a regulation litter box, and generally tried to make a home for us. When she slept I'd crawl on the narrow bed and curl up between her legs, tucked into the crook of her knees.

My days were pretty boring. The only exercise I got was chasing cockroaches around the floor and up on the sink. That was fun for a while until I made my big mistake. I ate one.

Talk about sick—I puked so much I thought my tail would come out of my mouth. That bug was so full of poison it could have been a weapon. And the worst part was that I'd just had a meal of my current favorite stuff, beef hearts. When Kathy came home and saw the mess she figured it was the food. She worried over me for hours. And I never got those beef hearts again.

The one saving grace of that place was the window. It faced the street, with a nice windowsill for me to sit on and watch the world below. On warm days she'd leave the window cracked a bit, and gradually I got used to the noise and smells of the neighborhood. There were cats out there, I could see that even from five flights up, and dogs too. There were lots of cars moving real slow and honking real fast. There was a symphony of smells, all mixed together: food of every imaginable kind, smoke, sewer gas, people sweat, dusty rain, even the smell of sparks coming off the power lines.

The one scent I never found was catnip. And believe me, I was trying. The closest I got to that stoned feeling was at dusk sometimes, when I got the crazies— bouncing off the walls, clawing furniture that was so tattered it was an improvement, and jumping on top of the bathroom door playing king of the mountain. It was good fun, but it wasn't the same. High on life isn't exactly high, not even for a cat.

I got restless by degrees, so slowly I barely noticed it. Comfort—and that snug apartment became comfortable once I'd scoped it out and found my places—goes a long way with a cat. But the world outside my window began calling to me, my fear at its noise and chaos fading with each day.

It happened suddenly, just like that time back in Doc's Jeep. And it was an impulse, the decision of a moment. I had no idea, when Kathy scratched my ears on the way out that day (and it was an especially happy day for her) that I'd never feel her touch again, never smell her boozy breath, never see her sweet, collapsed face.

It all started the night before, a warm, humid night in early summer. I was nodding on a cool corner of the bed when the sound of her footsteps on the stoop outside woke me up. Yes, I know, it was five stories down, and you humans with your weak, immobile ears couldn't have heard, much less identified, that sound, but we can, and I did. I could always tell when she was coming, it meant food and play, and I looked forward to both.

But this time was different. This time, as I woke up and bounded to the door, I heard another set of footsteps with her. For the first time ever she was bringing someone up to our place. And when the door swung open—me doing my "Kathy's Home" dance, tail up, purring like a bimbo—there he was. Barrel-chested, bald, thick, ham-fisted and big footed. He carried a paper sack, Kathy a plastic grocery bag and both of them were grinning like teenagers. Kathy had a fella!

Introductions were made, though if it cost me the rest of my ninth and last life, I couldn't remember his name now. I do remember he was a nice enough guy, nice to me, nice to Kathy for the few hours I knew him, and he gave off a nice, easy vibe.

The two of them had a fine night of it; they weren't drunk, much, and Kathy whipped up some dinner, a rare event that filled the apartment with yummy smells. Barrel-chest even fed me some scraps off his plate, to Kathy's insincere "no!" and obvious pleasure. Then they went to bed and thrashed around so spastically that I got bounced onto the floor. I'm amazed there are so many humans in the world, your reproductive techniques are so ... *protracted* ... and so clumsy. Those two spent half the night writhing in that little bed, making woofing noises as the screeching springs played their tune. Ridiculous, but they obviously enjoyed themselves and I didn't mind, except for the noise and the overcrowded bed. It was dawn by the time they fell asleep and I could take my place behind Kathy's knees again, and I had to curl into a tiny ball to fit.

That night was warm and tolerable, the next day was stifling and not. The heat woke them up early, but, despite their whining, they seemed as happy as the night before. Kathy got up, splashed some water on her face, threw on some clothes and said she was going out to buy some eggs for breakfast. Barrel-chest asked if it was okay if he stayed here and showered. Kathy kissed him, said sure honey, the towel's on the rack, use mine, then skipped over to me, and said, I'll feed you when I get back, Rusty.

Then she scratched me between my ears.

CHAPTER 9

Barrel-chest wasn't too bright. Or maybe he'd never had a pet in his life and didn't give me a second thought, because he made his mistake before Kathy had been gone five minutes. He hauled his sweaty body out of bed, padded right up to the window, cracked open just enough to slide in his fat fists, tugged and said out loud, "What's this thing, stuck? 't'sn oven in here!" And then he gave a mighty heave.

Next thing you know he's clutching his back, howling like he'd been kicked in the kidneys. The window flew up so hard it banged off the stops and bounced halfway back down. Barrel-chest was bent over like a hairpin.

His injuries only *sounded* mortal, however, because he straightened up, groaning, and arched his back—which made a scary series of clicking sounds—said "ahgghh," and goose-stepped off to the bathroom. There have been occasions when I envied you two-leggers your posture and height for the ease of far-seeing standing up gives you. But you pay a big price for it, don't you? Every one of you has back trouble, sooner or later, and you're always on the verge of falling. Give me four solid legs, every time.

And I was going to need all four this morning, because, just beneath that open window, through which poured the noise and humidity of a summer city morning, was a fire escape.

I could see right through it, that was the scary part. Five stories of flaking paint and rusty metal, ladders and slats, rickety bolts and crumbling brick between me and the rest of the world. There it was, fifty feet down a catwalk of skeleton steel. Freedom.

But was I ready? I leaned forward, perched on the edge of the sill, to take closer look. Bad move. When I got my nerve back I tried easing one paw down to the metal landing, but it was too far to reach. It was jump or nothing. I looked through the jungle gym down to the street. Go or stay?

I heard water running in the bathroom, I felt the dark room behind me, the dazzle ahead, I got that herky-jerky rush of fear that comes right before I "do" something. Poised, feet close together, rocking back and forth, getting my timing right, head bobbing, little sub-vocal noises in my throat, I picked a spot. And then I jumped.

* * *

Of course I made it, haven't you been listening? That was one thing I could count on, in those wild, youthful days—my body wouldn't fail me. I willed something to happen, and my body made it happen, just like that. Years would pass before the question changed from could I, to could I *still*? Back in that New York apartment I was just entering the long, broad prime of my life. Back then when I jumped, I *stuck* it.

What never occurred to me, as I scrabbled down that fire escape, floor to floor, down the shaky steps, hitting each landing with my front pads and claws, making the metal ring, was how poor Kathy would take it.

I did think of it later. Kathy had been good to me, in her way, and while she would never replace Fern in my affections—no one could—I felt bad for her. Not bad enough to stay, mind you, but bad enough to remember her from time to time and to hope against reason that she was doing well. I would sure hate to be Barrel-chest when she got home from the store and found her cross-country companion gone, after all she'd gone through to keep us together. The old gal had a temper, and he seemed like a nice enough guy.

But right then the world beckoned; I was looking ahead, not back. And I wasn't free yet. The trickiest part of my getaway was the last bit. The fire escape ended one story above the sidewalk, at a pull-down ladder my twelve-pound body couldn't budge. There was nothing for it but to go over the side, down about ten feet. Either that or hop into the open window at the second-floor landing, belching loud music and the screech of a squalling baby through its filthy curtains, an even less inviting prospect.

One last jump. I hesitated for a moment, picked a spot and made my leap, and while it stung when I hit the concrete, it was mostly the unfamiliar heat on my paws. I was a little soft, for a few weeks I hadn't stepped on anything rougher than wood. My paws would toughen considerably, as would my body and soul, in the months ahead.

* * *

There was a haze coming off the streets of the city that day, a dusty smell I can remember even now. Everything seemed to glow with heat and energy, every sound was heightened. The scuff of strangers' feet on the sidewalk, the bubbling thump of tires on the hot asphalt, my own breath, lingering on my face in the damp, still air.

I wandered, driven by a relentless need to take it all in, that survival instinct you people call curiosity. But I was cautious too, and for the same reason. This was all unfamiliar territory. I hugged the walls to stay away from the from the street and found out that brick *hurts*, it pulls out fur like crazy when you rub against it. I peeked around corners, sniffing the air before turning into the next dangerous block.

And they *were* dangerous. I hadn't been gone twenty minutes before I got my tail tromped on by some oblivious idiot jawing on his cell phone as he weaved down the sidewalk. He never heard my yowl. I watched him as he crossed the street, fervently praying for him to get run over in traffic, but my prayers weren't answered. At times like that I believed that God must be a human, but pain makes cynics of us all.

I soon learned to avoid the feet and tires, the human dangers of the streets, but others lurked. Dogs were everywhere, most downright unfriendly. Luckily the worst of them—to judge by the racket they made when I passed by—were tied up on leashes, and merely rattled my nerves. My first real trouble came not from them, but from a member of my own species.

It was late afternoon that first day, still hot as hell. I'd found some food in a dumpster—food was everywhere in that city—and plenty of water too, oily tasting gutter water, but it did the job and my digestion was rock solid in those days. I was getting sleepy and wanted to find a quiet, shady place to nod off. I wandered into an industrial area and found a narrow alley in the middle of the block that looked promising. I rounded the corner and the smell hit me like a wall.

Female cat. In heat. Very, very close. This wasn't the first time I'd encountered that smell, just the first time I'd been in a position to do anything about it.

She was beautiful. Not that it mattered; a healthy tom's reaction to a female in heat is pretty much automatic, but she was beautiful nonetheless. Silver coat, long-limbed, thin, black-ringed tail pointed straight up, quivering in her need. She was rubbing against some cardboard boxes, almost stumbling as she painted each surface with her scent. Only the confining space and still air of that narrow alley kept her chemical message from attracting every tom within a ten-block radius. But it was only me there, me and her. Just lucky, I guess. Or so I thought.

They say you never forget your first, and while that may be true, you can't judge by me, because I have a souvenir that makes remembering easy. All I have to do to recall that long-ago day is clean my left ear, lick a paw and run it over the bump I've had there for so long. The bump that was once a hole, right through the middle, like it had been pierced for an earring (don't laugh, I once saw a punk girl whose black cat had so much metal in his ears he looked like an antenna).

It wasn't my (temporary) beloved that inflicted that scar on me. No, she was a total sweetie. It was her first time too, and we circled each other coyly and nibbled gently before coupling in that honeymoon alley.

But once wasn't enough for Stud Boy, and the second time around she played hard to get. I had to chase her around the boxes and garbage cans, nipping at her tail, before she finally stood still and let me get on her back. Confident now, a worldly tom of legendary prowess, I showed my ardor by biting her on the neck—maybe a little too hard.

Because, whether out of ecstasy or pain, my silver honey screeched out a howl that could raise the dead. And yes—I'll admit it—I was proud. When I was done (shortly, stamina not being an asset in feline sexual performance) she bolted away, whistling a claw past my nose in goodbye.

I let her go. All of a sudden I was so tired I could barely see straight. It had been an eventful day, full of excitements. I'd found everything I could have hoped for when I made my impulsive leap to freedom that morning—food, water, adventure, even sex—and only one thing was needed to make it perfect. Sleep. Right now.

No such luck. Little Silver Fox didn't go far. Before I could snuggle down in a crushed cardboard box at the far end of the closed alley, there she was again, silhouetted against the light of the street, as haughty as if she hadn't bestowed her favors on a total stranger twice in the last ten minutes.

I wasn't interested anymore, or so I *thought*. But that scream had brought company, and when *he* showed up instinct kicked in. Not with *my* girl you don't!

It's amazing what we do to protect our genetic survival. We might not know about Darwin, but we sure know what it means to let another tom mount our females. It means we don't know *whose* kittens they are. You humans might think, as briefly as cat families stay together, it doesn't matter much to us who the daddy is, or even the mommy.

True, for most of us, love is fleeting. But it is nonetheless intense. And sometimes it lingers. Haven't you been paying attention? Don't I dream of my long-gone mother to this day? Call it love or lust or reflex, I had no choice.

I *launched* off that box—blew right past my fatigue, let it settle on the cardboard and told it to wait for me—and streaked down the alley, blood in my eyes.

He was an alley cat, black and mangy. He looked like he'd been through the wars and I was going to give him another. He outweighed me a good three pounds and was so tore up ugly it didn't matter anymore. I humped my back, skittered sideways big as I could get and growled a deep baritone that echoed menacingly off the alley walls.

He laughed at me—or the feline equivalent, a wet gurgling hiss—and then jumped on me hard, attacking with four mangled paws and breath like a crap-eating dog.

Now out west, where I'm from, it's customary to pose tough awhile before any actual fighting ensues.

First of all it gives you a chance to "work up to it," and secondly it allows a face-saving retreat if you're out-muscled or decide that the issue at hand just means more to the other guy. But New York rules were different, as I learned to my cost.

The first rule of fighting, cat or human, is whoever strikes first usually wins. Stanky McFunkbreath struck first, but he didn't win. He got in the first bite—ripping a jagged hole clear through my left ear that infected before he got his rotten mouth off me—but he didn't win. In fact, he's lucky he lived. If he did. I was so pissed off I lost it for a good half minute. And back in my prime I could do a hell of a lot of damage in thirty seconds.

I can't give you a blow-by-blow because I don't remember. I kind of blacked out, or maybe redded out is a better way to put it. I do know that when he staggered away, dripping blood, I'd gotten my pound of flesh out of him, most of it stuck to my back claws. I stood there in full, panting glory for a triumphant minute, every sense hyper alert, so full of nervous energy it felt like I could fly. Then the adrenaline wore off and the pain rushed in.

All of a sudden my legs were jelly, I was so spent I could barely hold up my head. My left ear swelled up like a marble, blood clotting fast and itchy down my cheek; it hurt so bad my eyes watered. I squinted through that veil of tears and pain to make sure all was clear.

My enemy was gone, Silver Fox was too, I had the alley all to myself. I wobbled back to the corner, *behind* the box this time, and curled my aching body into a ball.

"Well Doo Doo boy," I thought, "you're not a virgin anymore. And you almost got yourself killed in the process. Maybe those 'fixed' cats have the right idea."

With that morbid thought running around my head, I fell into a deep, dreamless sleep.

CHAPTER 10

I woke up sick as a dog. I don't know where that cliché came from—most dogs I've seen were pretty healthy—but that's how I felt. Unlike us cats, if a dog gets sick enough, he dies. We get nine lives, which means eight near-death experiences, and this was one of them.

It was full dark out now. The soft drumming noises of the city hurt my head like the worst nip hangover I've ever had. My body ached and shivered with chill, ached and boiled with fever, back and forth; only the ache was constant. The swelling in my left ear was so bad it twisted my scalp into a painful knot, and that ear was deaf to the world; all I could hear with it was the horrible rushing of my infected blood. My mouth was so dry I could feel every prickle on my tongue standing up, scraping the roof.

I could barely move. It was all I could do to pick up my head and focus my crusty eyes. Fortunately, the alley was still deserted, but there were strange scents nearby. This was very bad. This was life or death. I needed to gather my strength and get out of there, get somewhere sheltered and safe, someplace where I could heal in peace, if I was going to heal at all.

I needed to make a supreme effort, I had to drag my hurting carcass out of that alley *now*, under the cover of darkness, and find a place to hide. I gave it my best shot, sat up on my haunches, waited for the dizziness to pass, and passed out instead.

This time it wasn't even sleep, it was more like unconsciousness. I have no idea how much time passed before I finally came to. From the hazy light I thought it might be late afternoon. But the heat wasn't unbearable, and I was feeling better.

Not all better, not by a long shot, but a little better. The pain was still intense but my head felt clearer. When I asked it to move something, something moved. And did I ever need to move. If I was thirsty before, I was dry as dust now. I didn't have the slightest appetite, but I knew I'd have to get some food in me pretty soon. And that blind alley was a trap. Somehow I'd survived there for the past … who knows … hours? days? But I wasn't going to push my luck. It was time to go.

I willed myself up, through the haze of pain and dizziness. And this time I made it.

Out of that never-to-be-forgotten alley and onto the busy sidewalks of New York. Here the heat was worse, the sparkly concrete hurt my eyes, loud sounds attacked my ears. Big trucks smoked past, workmen hollered to each other with annoyed good humor from loading docks, forklifts and pushcarts, stomping around, booted feet everywhere. It was too much too soon.

I got a hard jolt of energy and it turned to panic. I started running. This was the kind of thing that *never* happened to me; I never lost my cool, my sense of where I was and what I was doing. But now I was out of my mind. I flew down the block, darted blindly into the street, driven by pain, fear and a desperate need to get away. Away to what? I couldn't have told you. I wasn't thinking straight, I wasn't thinking at all. This is how little kitties get killed, we lose control for a fatal moment in the land of giants ... and *squish*. It's all over.

Somehow I missed the cars, or the cars missed me. I told you I was a lucky cat, right? Back on the sidewalk, running wild, paws scraped up, adrenaline wearing off, overheated and out of gas, I hopped over a passed-out drunk ... and landed on a cushion of air.

It came straight up out of the sidewalk, a cooling blast of wind that riffled my fur and filled my tortured lungs. If I hadn't heard metal ringing under my claws, I would have thought I was standing on nothing.

It was a grate, a steel grate of square mesh set flush on the pavement. Cool air was rushing up from a hole beneath it. When that wind subsided I settled on the grate. What mystery was this? I leaned forward and turned to get the sun at my back so I could see down.

There was some kind of dim light coming from the hole; I stepped gingerly on the mesh to get a better look. And the whole grate wobbled. The corner opposite where I stood tipped up a few inches, I guess the thing was warped a little. It felt like an invitation.

Maybe, I thought. Just maybe. I stepped off the grate and waited to see if the lifted end fell back down. It didn't. I walked around on the sidewalk and put my nose under the warped corner for a closer look. There was a ladder running down into the hole, and a landing beneath that dim bulb, maybe a dozen feet down.

Here was shelter, refuge, cool and dark. It might cost me a little fur, but it was worth a try. I got as flat as I could, splayed out, and began working my head under the sharp flanges of the metal. There was one very bad moment—when I scraped my swollen ear on that jagged steel. But the pain was worth it, I felt my blister ooze, lanced, and the pressure in my scalp eased. I kept pressing and twisting until I got my head through, and where I could get my head, my body could follow. I clawed halfway down that vertical ladder, then jumped the rest. Light as a feather. A broken feather, perhaps, but pretty damned smooth, if I do say so myself.

And there in the dim light, just a few feet away, was a puddle of oily water, dripping from the rocky sides of the tunnel. I never tasted better.

Cooled, safe, and sick with toxins dripping down my face and into my veins, I curled into a corner and let the pain wash over me, knocking me out. My sleep was broken intermittently by a loud, threatening roar, accompanied by a rush of wind like I'd felt on top, but it wasn't so close that I had to flee. After a while I got used to it and slept right through.

What finally got me moving was raging hunger. When I woke up the fever had broken, replaced by a gnawing emptiness. It didn't feel like I was going to die anymore, and the pain in my ear had backed off enough that I didn't want to. But the hollow in my belly took possession of my mind and told me to find food *now*, somehow, somewhere.

There was no going back up that round-runged ladder, and I didn't want to face that grate again anyway. Instead I wandered deeper into the tunnel, or, rather, maze of tunnels, my eyes so dark-adapted now even the feeble light of the occasional bulb was enough to guide my steps. But food proved elusive. I was reduced to trying another bug or two, and while they didn't make me sick they couldn't begin to fill the hole.

So I pressed on, down blind tunnels, through narrow conduits, ever downward in a series of small jumps to the next level, until, finally, I caught the scent of prey.

Mice, hopefully, or maybe rats. Just around the bend. I tracked until I heard their skittering, got them in my sights, and pounced. I was so focused on the hunt I didn't notice how much louder and closer that rushing noise was getting; there was only room in my consciousness for one thing—food.

Human sensibilities keep me from detailing what I did to that coven of mice. You guys get your meat all nice and dead and wrapped for you by professionals. For that matter, so did I, when I lived with you. But down here it was murder or die, and despite my soft life recently, I was still a predator par excellence. I picked 'em off one by one, must have snagged five of the little things before I was done, and the last one made a good chase out of it before I caught him, too.

But it almost cost me big time. I never came so close to death before or since without losing a drop of blood or a hair on my body. That last mouse ran right past me and hopped on a narrow landing.

I missed my first swipe, then jumped for him, got him in my mouth—and tumbled down about four feet to a flat-bottomed tunnel with a gravelly floor that rattled beneath my paws.

I should have known trouble was coming, but I was too busy devouring that last mouse to pay any attention, until....

I saw my shadow. That was the first hint, my shadow stretching out in front of me, and a horizontal light glistening off metal rails. Then the now-familiar roar began, and grew, much faster and louder than ever before. I turned and was transfixed by a spotlight, blinding as the sun, rushing towards me at an impossible speed. For a moment, almost a moment too long, I froze, my hair standing straight up at the roots, making my shadow huge when I spun around and tried frantically to flee from the apparition. It was no use, the thing was gaining on me fast, a rush of air blew me forward as it powered through the tunnel, but not nearly enough to help.

I smelled sparks, oil, hot metal, my own electric fear. Death came on like fate and I couldn't outrun it. Every muscle, every sense strained, desperately searching for a chance, a way out.

Then I saw it. At the very last moment, almost invisible, a dimple, a darker spot in that black hole of death. It was just an indentation on the right side of the tunnel, a small nook down low that I could get to, right now, if I didn't miss. It might be deep enough and it might not. I dove in head first, flattened myself against the rough back wall, and suffered fifteen seconds of the most stark-staring, brain-burning terror it was ever my lot to endure.

The subway train—for that's what it was, as I'm sure you figured out already, but which was entirely new and foreign to me at the time—screamed past not two feet from my face. I tore my claws trying to keep a grip on the stone walls, so hard did the suction of the passing train pull at me. The sound was raw pain, so unbelievably loud I felt I'd gone mad, and that fifteen seconds felt like an eternity—like an earthquake does.

And then it was gone, the roar fell away until the only thing I could hear was my heart jack-hammering in my chest, and my breath coming so fast I whistled like a tea kettle.

When my shredded sanity came back, urgency struck—get the hell out of here before another one of those beasts comes along. That's what keeps cats alive—or at least this cat—you don't have to tell me twice. A part of me was so scared I wanted to stay in that nook forever, but the smart part got me moving, down onto the tracks, looking for an escape. I ran in the same direction the train was going, thinking it would put more time between me and the next one. I didn't know it yet, but I had about ten minutes. As it turned out, I only needed five.

The first thing I did was hop back on the narrow ledge that paralleled the tracks, about four feet up. That was better, but precarious. I didn't want to risk being there when the next train went through. So I pressed on, not full-out running, just sort of galloping along, avoiding the debris and wires on the greasy ledge, pausing from time to time to sniff for a change in the air that might signal a way out, and listening for anything that might be close, especially another screaming metal beast. Mostly I was careful not to fall into that pit of death again; I couldn't count on my fairy godkitty to make me a lifesaving nook twice.

The tunnel began to turn slowly left, limiting my vision forward and back. This was not good. But there was the hint of a glow on the walls ahead, not a moving, jumpy light like the train's, but a yellower, steady illumination whose source, though not terribly close, obviously wasn't moving. I also thought I might have heard some murmuring, as of human voices, just at the very edge of audibility. I stopped dead still to listen.

I was straining to hear forward, my ears, even the wounded one, pointed straight ahead. The last thing I expected was a sound directly across the tracks from me. When I heard it, I jerked my head around so fast I almost lost my footing on the slippery landing.

"Pssst," it said. "Pssst. Over here...."

I tracked that sound to a pair of bluish-red dots, glowing softly in the feeble light. Two glowing dots only a couple of inches apart. Eyes. Cat's eyes, and a cat's voice, all the way down here in hell.

"Pssst! You. Over here."

CHAPTER 11

You were about to ask me a question: Can cats talk to each other? So let me give you the answer: It depends. If by talk you mean speak English, then of course not, don't be an idiot. But if you mean do we have ways of making ourselves understood to one another, through meows, coos, purrs, screeches, postures and other signals too subtle for human senses to detect, the answer is yes.

Some cats are more "evolved" than others, and there are regional differences too. What you read here are my translations. I'm an especially well-traveled feline; I've been with the hicks and the city slickers and, in the current case, the troglodytes. To show you the local accents, to explain every squeal and whisker-twitch would be tedious in the extreme. You're just going to have to take my word for it; this is what they said. And if you find the above explanations unsatisfactory, find another damn cat who writes books and complain to him.

Meanwhile, back in the subway tunnel of death, I had just been thrown a lifeline…. Or had I?

"You talking to me?"

"Yeah, you," the cat said. "Come over here."

"What's there?"

"My place. Big and safe. No trains."

"Uh, I don't know...."

"You better!" the wraith across the tracks said. "There'll be another train soon. But if you're a-scared...." And with that he turned away.

When I lost sight of his eyes I lost sight of him. But it was like he *knew* me. That challenge was all it took.

I bounded across the tracks and up the other side in three long leaps. My momentum drove me into my new friend's tail before I could claw to a stop. He turned on me like he was ready to fight. Cats in the wild aren't nearly as unsociable as we're made out to be, in fact, the absence of human contact makes us hang out together much more than otherwise. Still, there are protocols, and saying hello by ramming your nose up another cat's ass is an invitation to conflict.

But the moment passed as quickly as it came; he gave me the oddest little chirrup, then turned away: "Follow me."

We walked about ten paces along the ledge until we came to a hole in the tunnel wall, about two feet up, the size and shape of a manhole cover cut in half.

"Up here," he said. "It lands flat, but then it gets steep. Try not to fall on me." And he hopped into the archway. I could see his cobby body for the first time as he flew through the dim light of the tunnel. He was coarse-haired, dusty black and runty, with a short, scrawny tail and stubby legs. But he moved with precision, making almost no sound when he landed above me.

I followed, almost as gracefully, considering that I could barely see where I was going and didn't know the terrain. Inside the archway it was very dark, the floor was flat, like he said, and manmade, some kind of rough, pebbly concrete.

"Wait a second after I go," he said.

"Go where?" But by then my new friend had disappeared, his heat and scent gone in an instant, replaced by an avalanche of sand, gravel, and cat.

It sounded like he'd thrown himself into a bottomless pit—he seemed to fall forever, and half the dirt in the world went with him. Committing to that death ride was going to take a lot more trust than subway cat had earned in the ninety seconds of our acquaintance. But then he called me—reasonable evidence that he'd survived. His voice was hollow, a long way down, yet megaphoned by the hole.

"Yo!" he said, "Anytime now big guy."

Another challenge. Well, anything that scrawny mutt could do, so could I. As long as I didn't land on my ear.

I put out my left paw, groping the emptiness beneath, until, finally, I hit sand, at a very steep angle. No way I was going to be able to control this drop by running down. The best I could hope for was a controlled fall. I leaned over the ledge with both front paws, tucked my rear ones flat against the ground, under my belly, and, claws out, gave a little tug.

Whoosh!

Dirt flew up in my face, my front legs skittered over the sand, plowing up furrows, as I struggled to slow down without having them dig in and launch me into a butt-over-head summersault. I kept my weight back as far as I could, trying to steer with my tail, but basically I just slid down that dirt chute on my ass.

Undignified yes, and unhygienic too, but effective. Finally, I crash-landed into a mound of sand that the hole had collected from its previous victims. And before I could get up and out of the way, a couple of fresh quarts fell on me.

I stood up, shook off as much dirt as I could out of my long hair, and saw my friend just a foot or so away, looking highly amused.

"Laugh and die," I said.

He didn't. And on his turf yet. A very good sign.

"Just a little further," he said.

We walked another few steps and emerged into a vast, high-ceilinged cave, lit softly by a green phosphorescent ooze dripping from the walls.

"What is this place?" I asked.

"My home. Do you like it?"

"It's, uh, sure. I've never seen anything like it. It's huge!" It stank too, but I didn't say that.

"Sometimes there's other cats, but mostly it's mine. You can stay if you want."

"Like I have a choice. I don't think I can make it back up that chute right now, I'm a little sick. Hey, what's your name, anyway?" I asked.

"Rass. And I seen worse coming down that pipe the first time, believe me. What's yours?"

"Doo Doo," I said, and the sound was sweet to my ears, even my throbbing one.

"Doo Doo…" Rass drawled like he was trying it on for size. "Is that a human name?"

Maybe it was all the crap I'd been through the past few days, but I was touchier than usual. "Yeah, matter of fact, it is. You got a problem with that?"

"Nuh uh…. Doo Doo, huh? That's a nice name. You musta had good humans."

Had…. That got the images of my first and only real home flashing through my head. There was Doc and Fern, there was my green backyard. *Had….* I felt a surge of emotion, truly missing that place and those people for the first time. It was a bittersweet, nostalgic memory. Soon enough it would turn to longing.

"Yeah, Rass. They were real good humans."

"Where are they now?"

"I wish I knew…."

"I never had people," Rass said, sounding like he knew he was missing *something*, but having no real idea what. "I've seen some, even let a few of them touch me up at the station. I kinda like being around them— that's why I was up top, where I found you. But I've never had people of my own."

"You call that 'up top?' Where the trains are? Haven't you ever been outside?"

"Outside?"

"Yeah, you know, like in the sun and all."

"The sun? What's the sun?"

The poor guy. "Never mind, I'll tell you later. I don't feel too good, I think I'm gonna sleep now."

"Okay," Rass said brightly. "You'll be safe here. See you when you get up!"

* * *

"Hey Rass, you awake?"

No response. I gently tapped a paw on his sleeping head.

"Rass, you awake?"

"I am now."

"Not much of a watch cat, are you?"

Rass got up on his short paws and stretched. He puffed out his chest fur and made a big show of looking around.

"Nobody bothers me, I'm the boss down here."

I had to suppress a laugh. "Well, boss, where's the food? I'm starving."

"You in good enough shape for a little walk?"

"How little?"

"Okay, not so little."

"And what do we find when we get there?"

"Food. That's what you want, right?"

"I meant what kind…." But it was no use. Subtleties were lost on this dwarf. "Sure, let's go." And as I followed, I must admit, it crossed my mind—I wonder how the "boss" would taste.

The good news is that we didn't have to climb that chute again. Instead, Rass led us around the side of the cave, passing innumerable branching tunnels and warrens that pierced the walls at about ground level, until we got to one that looked just like all the rest.

"In here," said the cat of few words.

I smelled it right away, food, *old* food, *rotting* food— garbage.

Down a curving tunnel through a corrugated metal pipe into a huge, reeking sewer. Drip, drip, stink.

"Oh man, is this the best you got?"

Rass stared at me; he actually looked hurt. Then he bounded up onto a huge pile of compost and trash.

"It falls from up there," he said, pointing with his face. "This stuff on top is good, mostly."

"Good for what?" I asked, stepping around the heap, trying to look up without slipping into the slime.

"Really, that's the old stuff down there. See?" he said, bending down and coming up with a fish head in his mouth. "Fresh!" he gurgled around it.

"I'm not hungry anymore," I said. And, truth to tell, I wasn't, even before I smelled this pile of crap. I didn't know if it was my still-raging infection or something I ate, like maybe those mice were full of rat poison, but my hunger had turned to nausea. My legs were wobbly from that little ten-minute walk. By the time Rass came traipsing off the pile, I was flat on my belly, dizzy as hell.

"You okay, Doo Doo?" he asked in a frightened voice. "Here," he nudged the fish head with his nose towards mine. "See? I told you. Fresh."

Damned if the boy wasn't right. But it wasn't fresh once I got done puking all over it.

Of all the godforsaken places to pass out and be delirious, this had to be the worst. On the other hand, it beat being conscious in this dump. When I woke up just long enough to wharf out another hairball-and-bile cocktail, it barely affected the overall stench. But lordy, was I sick! Those little illness membranes that I can never remember the name of filmed my eyes, I couldn't tell what was real and what was delirium, sometimes I knew where I was—which was revolting enough—other times I thought I'd died and gone to kitty hell. And, occasionally during this out-of-body experience, a pure, sweet, bliss would wash over me.

That bliss was home. It was all jumbled up and crazy, even my visions were blurry, but the *sense* of it was wonderful. I remember flying around the living room of our house, Doc chasing me as I floated just out of reach. It felt like I could swim on air—even in my hallucination I knew that was impossible—but the feeling was pure delight.

"I can *fly*," I thought, and promptly crashed to the ground in a sewer pipe.

Well, all good things must end. Bad things too, unless you die, and I guess it wasn't my time yet. Whatever I got out of my system, which, to gauge by the mess I saw when I came to was everything, it must have helped. Because my sick swoon turned to sick sleep. It was an improvement. Waking up was another matter entirely.

CHAPTER 12

They say when it itches like hell you're starting to get better. So my ear must have been doing just fine, because if I could have scratched the thing off, I would have. And what stopped me wasn't common sense or a lack of agility. Nope, it was my head. It hurt so bad I couldn't bear to touch anything connected to it, rancid ear included. Every heartbeat was like a big bass drum inside my forehead, trying to beat its way out. My skull felt full and hollow at the same time; it was awful.

But I was so strong, back in my youth, that I could take it. And with great effort I managed to get my wobbly pins under my body and weave drunkenly to a puddle of almost clear water Rass led me to. It didn't taste too good, but then again, neither did my mouth. Let's call it a draw.

In fact, let's call the next couple of days a draw and pass them by. I ate a little, drank a little, moved a little more, slept and healed a lot. Rass followed me around like he had a crush on me or something. Sometimes he'd tag along quietly, which was okay, other times he would jabber on about nothing, which wasn't. Not when my head hurt so bad that the faint rumbles of the trains far above could make me see stars, not when

I was still too sick to be curious about what the caver was saying.

But, I must admit, I found his presence kind of comforting, which is why, when we pick up our story a few days later, and I'm finally feeling myself again, more or less, I notice that he's been gone for a while when he comes walking up.

"Where you been?" I ask.

"Hey, Doo Doo. You look better!"

"I'll live. Weren't you gone a while there, or was I delirious?"

"Both! You were out of it and kept telling me to get lost. Once I was pretty sure you weren't going to croak, I did."

"I don't remember," I said truthfully, "but sometimes you talk too much," I continued, equally truthfully. But I didn't really want to hurt his feelings, and I was curious, so I asked again. "So, where you been?"

"Up top." He said.

"Yeah? What's there?"

"Well, you know … people and all."

"You went all the way up that pipe just to get a look at some strangers?" I asked.

"No, silly! You don't go *up* the pipe. There's another way around, the long way!"

"There's *another way*? You made me take that sand enema and there's another way?!" I got up and stretched to my full height, which was a good four inches taller than Rass. For the first time in days I felt steady on my legs, weak, but steady. "Why?" I practically shouted down on the runt.

Rass backed away a step or two.

"It's a *long* way," he apologized, "and there were trains coming!"

"Yeah, well, still...." But I had to admit, he had a point.

"And anyway," Rass continued, the spunk coming back into his voice, "the chute's kinda *fun*, don't you think?"

I chuckled a little despite myself. I had to admit, he had a point there, too.

"So, did you see any?"

"Any what?" Rass asked.

"People, you dunce, did you see any people up top?"

Rass never took offense, that's what I remember most about him to this day. That and his odd, inexplicable devotion to *me*, which, odder yet, made me feel the same about *him.*

"Nah ... well, yeah, sorta, but nah."

Sometimes the best way to communicate with the runt was to shut up and wait.

"I mean," he went on after a bit, "I saw people up there, but I never got too close."

"I don't get it," I said. "Why'd you bother?"

"Cause of you..." Rass said and winced, like he knew there was an argument coming. He was right.

"Me? What the hell did *I* do? I've been unconscious for days!"

"You ... talked. In your sleep, like."

"What? I tell you to scram and you *do*? I was delirious, I'm sorry," I said sarcastically.

"No, not that. You talked about your home, your *people*, over and over. It made me—I don't know—want to *see* some, but I chickened out in the end."

I won't deny it, the wise ass in me wanted to make a wise ass remark, but I didn't. Who could, hearing something like that?

"It's okay," I said instead. "Lots of cats don't have people, I didn't when I was a kitten. Hell, I don't now...." The sting of that admission brought me up short for a second. "And you got this," I looked around the dank cave and hoped my voice didn't show what I really was thinking. "You have a *home*. Hell, you *are* home. Which is more than I can say. What's the big deal?" I ended bitterly.

"I'm not, I mean, it's not ... you know..."

"Yeah, I *do* know," I was the one motormouthing now. "I know you can't miss what you never had. You want people so bad, go back up there and grab you some. Go on. It's not like you need anyone special, it's not like you're so far from home you don't know where to turn. Dammit!"

"You don't know everything, Doo Doo." While you couldn't offend Rass, you could hurt him.

"What don't I know?"

"It wasn't always like this. I can remember a little. I wasn't born here. It's hard, but I can remember a little. And I'll know it when I find it, again."

This discussion was taking its toll on me. I walked over to the half-eaten frog that Rass had dragged here from somewhere and had a few nibbles. It stayed down, thank God. When I looked up from my snack, I saw Rass watching me, eyes full of ... something ... eagerness maybe, hope.

"Tell me," I said.

"Not here. You were talking about the sun, too. I think I know now what you mean, maybe. Want to take a little walk?"

"How little?"

"Well, maybe not so little," and the little cave cat jounced away inviting me to follow.

Once I hit my stride it felt great to work my legs, to get my body moving again. With each step around the base of the cave, up into a branching tunnel, around some narrow conduits where I had to scrunch down to follow, I could feel the power coming back into my muscles. A couple of decent meals and I'd be ready for anything. But I didn't know what "anything" meant yet, which was probably a good thing.

Finally, after a long trek that led us ever upward, we emerged into a round concrete shaft that looked like a smaller, deeper version of the one that brought me down here in the first place.

Diffuse light poured down from the opening high above.

"Here," Rass said.

"Here what?"

"Just wait," he said brightly.

That was okay by me. Our "little walk" was more exercise than I'd had in a week. A nap would do me good.

It was not to be. Rass, who had been silent the whole trip, chose this time, this place, to tell me his story.

"I've been up there," he began, nose pointing up the shaft to the brightening hole above.

"I was just a kitten, and it's all fuzzy, but I remember. That 'sun' thing you talk about is bright, so bright it hurts your eyes when you look at it, right?"

"Yeah...." I nodded, trying to pay attention. But that hole in the sky was getting brighter by the minute, points of light began to glint off its metal grate.

"There were four of us," Rass said, "in a cardboard box. She took us down to the station and left us there."

"Who did what?" I asked.

"I don't know who she was. Some person. I remember living under this house, I remember my mommy, and I remember a bright light, maybe the sun. I remember getting shoved into a box with my brothers and sisters one day when mommy was gone, and being carried away. When we stopped, we were here."

"She just dumped you here? The bitch! What happened to the rest of your litter?"

"They were bigger. People took them—not me. For a little while I was stuck, but then I tipped the box on its side and ran away."

"Ran away to where? How did you live?"

"To the station. Not the one near here, another one, far away. That's where I got dumped. I just hung out, kept out of trouble and away from the trains. There was always a lot of food around, people would leave it, sometimes even, I'd beg. There's people who live down here too, and they'd feed me, but I never trusted anyone enough to stay with them."

A semicircle of blindingly bright light burst through the opening above, lighting one wall of the shaft, crawling down towards us, slowly.

"But, uh, you still want people... Huh?" It had been so long since I'd seen the sun; I was distracted. A little more than a week down here had made me half cave cat myself.

"I want ... something. I want *that*," Rass said, staring upwards.

"Yes, me too." The cone of light got closer and closer, but it never reached all the way down to us. I ached for that warmth so bad I would have climbed those sheer walls if I could.

"See? I told you!" Rass glowed.

Well, he would have glowed had he not been mud colored. This was the first time I'd seen him in a good, strong light, and he looked pretty homely, in a cute, runtish way. That fur, sticking out of his stubby body like wire, his big, pale, almost yellow eyes, that dingy pelt, not black or gray, really, more sludge than anything else. His spiky tail held high and proud as if he was best in show. How could you not you love a guy like that?

I poked my nose straight up, trying to smell the sunshine I couldn't quite reach. "Yeah, you sure did.... Rass, I gotta get out of here."

"You're going to *leave*?" Rass said with a touch of panic in his voice. "Take me with you!"

"Take you *with* me? Why haven't you done it yourself, all this time? Do you know how?"

"Maybe. There's the station, I've seen the light from there, but there's a lot of stairs and people. But maybe there's another way...."

"Like this?" I asked, thinking of that ladder I came down and how hard it would be to climb back up, *if* I could find it.

"No, different," Rass said. "I've passed it a couple of times, even peeked out. It's like a hole."

"It takes you outside?"

"I think so."

"You never checked? You never went? Why?"

"Cause I'm scared," he said, ashamed. "But I'd try it with you!"

Cats travel light. I didn't know where I was going, but I knew my best shot of getting there was alone. All I wanted was out of here; I wasn't counting on carrying any burdens with me.

But I *owed* the guy. And he did know the way out, or so he claimed.

"So where is this magic hole?" I asked.

Rass practically lit up—as if the sun, receding up the other wall of the shaft now, had reached him after all, and he was still glowing from its touch.

"It's not far," he said. "Do you think you're up to a little walk?"

"How little."

"Well," Rass said in the cat equivalent of a giggle, "maybe not so little."

CHAPTER 13

"Are we there yet?"

"I'm *looking*, Doo Doo." Rass complained.

"You've been saying that all day. My paws are tired."

"It's around here somewhere. I can smell it. Can't you smell it?"

The only thing I could smell was the ass whupping I was gonna give Subway Boy if he didn't find us a way out, real soon. I'd say screw it and let's try another day, if not for a new element adding to my impatience—nip crave.

It had been forever since I had a good catnip buzz, and down here in the underground it had been almost as long since I'd even thought about it. But the hunger was on me now, and it was all Rass's fault.

"Tell me more," he had asked me for the dozenth time as we trudged endlessly up, down and all around that godforsaken pit looking for his magic hole. "Tell me what's up there. What's so good? Do they got lots of cats? Are the people better? Tell me more, Doo Doo."

"You'll find out soon enough if you can get us out of here," I answered, my patience wearing thin as the skin of my pads. But his constant questions got me thinking, and what I thought about was what I missed about being in the real world, and that, inevitably, brought my mind to dreams of nip.

Yes, I know, there are more important things. The sun, good food, grass to nibble, trees to climb, moonlit hunts with the wind in your fur, people to pet you, *my* people, out there somewhere. But youth wants it *now*, and we cats are creatures of the present. Once Rass's nagging put that picture in my head, of being high, happy, outside and nipped, it grew and grew until it blocked out those more important things. One of which was patience.

"Come *on*, dude. Find that hole. You get us out of here and I'll show you a good time like you never imagined."

"I'm sorry, Doo Doo. I thought I remembered. Maybe I don't..." Rass sighed as we mounted yet another ledge to nowhere. Down below us, through a lattice of beams, I saw a hint of a gleam. Rass saw it too.

"See that?" he offered hesitantly, "I think those are some rails down there, near a station. Want to try the tracks?"

There's no denying I was tempted. It wouldn't be the first time I made a bad move on impulse—the whiff of nip that started this long exile, for instance— and it surely wouldn't be the last. But it *could* be the last if we made a wrong turn on those rails, and the only thing that could trump my crave was fear. Luckily, it did. And, even luckier, a puff of sweet, fresh air hit us both, at just that moment.

This was too easy. No climb, no metal grate, no mineshaft of dirt. Just a two-foot hop up to a three-yard-long tunnel that led outside. A narrow, two-cat diameter pipe made of rusting metal, some forgotten airshaft perhaps, or a place where wires used to run.

"This it?" I asked Rass.

"Uh … yeah…"

"Finally." I hopped into the pipe alongside Rass, who was shaking like he had frostbite.

"Something wrong?" I asked.

"N, n, no…"

"Cool." I stepped off the last few paces and stood poised at the far end—alone.

"You coming?"

Rass hadn't budged. He was welded to the entrance of the pipe, big-eyed and trembling. It wasn't ten feet, but he looked so far away it was like he was at the wrong end of a telescope.

"Well?"

"I … I can't, Doo Doo."

"Why not?"

"I … I just can't.…"

It was pathetic, the poor guy was so scared he was almost crying. Deep wellsprings of compassion surged inside me.

"Suit yourself," I said, and hopped out into the big bad world, all by my lonesome.

* * *

I emerged into a night so dark I could barely tell I was out of the hole. The pipe was set into a crumbling brick wall about a foot above the ground. I hopped down and took a step sideways.…

"WAIT!"

Rass came blowing out the pipe like a cannonball. If I hadn't moved out of the way he'd have knocked me clear to Canarsie.

"Change your mind?"

Rass opened his mouth and nothing came out.

"I see," I said.

He tried again; this time brought forth an asthmatic wheeze.

"You all right?"

He managed a step or two, his lungs whistling like this fresh air was poison. It was a good thing we'd come out into a quiet park at night. The way the boy sounded he couldn't outrun an earthworm.

"Just stay close and do what.... Hey Rass! You want to watch where you're peeing? That's my tail."

"Oh...."

"He speaks!"

"Sorry…"

"Damn, dude…." I shook my tail, trying to fling off the funk.

I really should have left him right there and then. Clearly I hadn't done him any favors by luring him out here in the first place. But I couldn't just slink away. I had to tell him why. I turned around and saw him shaking on his stubby legs, hair all ruffed up, mouth open like an out-of-breath dog.

"Rass," I said as gently as I could, "I think you should go home."

"Nuh uh."

"No, really, this isn't the place for you. You wouldn't last a day."

"Don't wanna."

"I can't look after you. Cats travel solo up here."
I was almost begging now.

"No."

"Rass, I have to do this alone. You need to go back where you belong...."

"I helped you when *you* were hurt."

Oh man, I was afraid of that. I stared at Rass, staring at me. As my eyes grew accustomed to the darkness his seemed to grow until they were as big as saucers. I could already feel his weight on my back. Damn it all.

"If you cost me a minute, I swear...."

"Yay!"

* * *

We passed the night in some nearby bushes. That was strike one against Rass; I was so ready for a buzz I would have walked the city all night until I found some nip, but Cave Boy was worn out from the excitement and I didn't dare leave him alone. I even let him sleep touching me, his back curled up against mine, his subway smell funking up that sweet air I was enjoying—though I guess I stank just as bad. And, tired as I was once the nip crave left me, it was all I could do to nap. Every time I dozed off I heard something that woke me up. I think I'd been underground too long, because being out in the open made me nervous, and, what's worse, having this sniffling, wheezing presence glued to my flanks made me feel—even remembering this feels strange—kind of *responsible.*

That was strike two. I was thinking of excuses for what I wanted to do come strike three—and it wasn't pretty—when a fortunate nod overtook me.

* * *

"Hey, Doo Doo! What do we do now?"

Right out of a deep sleep to a baby morning, the sun was up maybe five minutes.

"Don't you know that cats are supposed to be nocturnal, Rass?" I yawned. "This is my bedtime."

"Nocturnal?" Rass was radiating eager.

"Yeah ... you *wouldn't* know the difference, would you?" I said, rousing myself. "Okay, let's go."

Luck smiled on us that morning. As soon as I woke up I realized that I was starving to death, but finding food was easy. We were in a big park, at dawn, before the trash men were out, and food was everywhere. Actually it was kind of disgusting, it was summer and this garbage had been ripening since yesterday, but I managed to find some edible stuff. Rass thought he'd died and gone to heaven.

"I like it here!" he said, mouth full of day-old wiener.

"So I notice." I also noticed that the foot-long was almost as big as he was. In daylight he looked even smaller than he did down below. He was no more than two-thirds my size, I doubt he weighed eight pounds. The real world didn't suit him at all. If I wasn't around to watch his tail, he'd be dog food on the hoof.

"Rass, you really should think about going home."

"No way! I like it here. And what about that catnip stuff you've been talking about? When do we get some of that?"

"Will you go back down after we've found some?"

"You mean you're not?"

"No, Rass. I'm up here for good."

"Then me too!"

Oh, no. What did I ever do to deserve *this*? Well, screw it. Deal with him later. Right now it's time to get high.

"Try not to get lost," I said. "I don't want to go looking for you."

"I'm right here."

"Tell me about it."

In the end, it was Rass's silliness that paid off for us. We hadn't been nip hunting for more than an hour when boredom hit and he got goofy.

I was on the trail of a likely scent, my head under a bush, rooting in the roots, finding what turned out to be the nub of a damned marijuana joint (they smell similar, as you probably know), when Rass jumped my tail.

"Yang!" he said, which is the sound of a cat playfully gnawing the current object of his attention. In this case it meant, roughly translated, "You're it!"

I spun around, leaf litter on my nose, and got a mouthful of Rass's ruff, letting him know I wasn't in the mood. But I was, of course, we always are.

Off to the races.

Soft grass, bright sky and muscles that craved action after being cold, cramped and sick for days, this was gonna be fun. A surge of joy flashed through me as I stretched it out, running full speed, cutting, juking, chasing Rass until I caught him, then letting him chase me. That sweet air was like sunshine in my lungs, and Rass must have felt the same way. He was going like a three-month-old kitten, tumbling, twisting, paying not the slightest attention to where he was headed. His eyes were wide open, showing white all around, like a marble in an egg. It was a kick seeing how much he got off on this romp, one of the simple joys of catdom that he'd missed out on all his life, till now. We went at it forever, flying through the park, through the flower beds, the asphalt paths, little groves of evergreens that the city had planted, skittering up to the edge of a pond where Rass almost fell in, then ducking under some bushes lining the shore.

I was so high on the game we were playing, I almost didn't notice. Almost.

"Hold up…"

"Wha?" Rass hopped over to me.

"Something," I said, nose to the wind. "This way."

We snaked through the underbrush, thick with thorns, down into a little hollow so heavy with weeds you couldn't see it.

But you could smell it, or I could, anyway.

Nip. Wild. Right there, growing. Maybe half a dozen plants, three feet high. And this silly oaf had led us right to it.

"That it?" Rass said breathlessly.

"Oh yeah."

"How do you…."

"Watch me."

I don't know how it is for people, but I had big fun watching a friend get high for the first time. I got off on him getting off, while I was loading up like a Dumpster. It had been a while, and this stuff, so sweet and unexpected, was pretty good. I was surprised some local hadn't beaten us to it, but I chalked that up to my usual good luck. And then I reached that place where reasons don't matter anymore.

As for my new best friend Rass, he could barely stand up.

"Wow," he said (actually the sound he made was more like "rowwrrr," but I said I wouldn't trouble you with translations).

"You like?" I purred, full of stoned affection.

"I, uh, I like it … all!"

"Sure beats the subway, don't it," I said and immediately regretted.

"I ain't *never* going down there again," Rass said emphatically, reinforcing my regret.

I had to let him know this couldn't last forever. I wasn't sure where I was going, but I knew it had to be alone. The time to tell him was now, before he got used to the idea of me always being around. But how could I? The sight of his stubby little body rolling around in the nip shards warmed my lonely heart.

"Wait a minute," my head said to my head, "did you just say 'lonely'?"

Rass picked that precise moment to ask the question I was avoiding asking myself.

"Hey, Doo Doo," he slurred, "Tell me again. What's it like being with people? I mean your *own* people, like you used to have and all. Don't you miss them?"

Why'd he have to ask me that then? Did he know that there was a hole in the pit of my buzz just waiting to be filled with melancholy and loss? Could he understand that having loving humans was like the late-morning sun on your back, a belly full of food, and a head floating in the bright clouds of nipland, only better?

No, he couldn't possibly.

So I told him.

* * *

Rass had no idea what I was talking about, I might as well have said "good, good, good," for fifteen minutes. But he knew he liked it.

"So, you mean you just showed up and they took you in?" he said.

"More or less," I said, replaying those first days with Doc and Fern in my mind. "It kind of happened little by little."

"How'd you know? Why'd you pick them? You lived where there were lots of people, right?"

Why *did* I pick them? Looking back on it, it seemed predestined, like it was meant to be. "I'm not sure, Rass," I said, wearying of the subject, which was bringing me down. "It took me a while. But I knew from the first that they liked me."

"Do you think they'd like *me*?"

"Oh … sure," I said to the cobby, coarse-haired, runt, unlovable by any standards. And I felt quite proud of myself for saying it.. Kindness costs you nothing, I thought, wrongly, of course.

"Really? That's good…. Yeah…." Rass sighed. "You sure?"

"Sure I'm sure," I said, munching some more nip in a vain attempt to get back to nirvana. "Why do you ask?"

"Because I'm going with you."

"Going where?"

"Back with you to your people. You are going back there, aren't you? Wasn't that the plan all along?"

"I don't *have* a plan, Rass."

"Yes you do! You're going back home!"

"No."

"Yes you are! And you're taking me with you!"

What was I supposed to say? Rass was talking nonsense—stoned nonsense. So why was he getting to me like this? What the hell was I doing in this strange city, with this strange cat, blitzed and confused, feeling lost and stuck at the same time? And what Rass wanted was impossible, wasn't it?

Impossible for him, my dark side whispered. But not for you.

"It's too far. I wouldn't know where to begin."

"I'll help," Rass said brightly. "We can do it together, Doo Doo."

"You've been above ground for twelve hours and now you're gonna get me home?" I laughed, despite myself. His innocence was ridiculous.

"You just don't want me along!" Rass mewed, hurt.

"It's not that. I wasn't even thinking about finding them before you started jabbering about it. Let a cat enjoy his buzz in peace, will ya?"

"Not until you tell me I can come with you," Rass insisted.

So the big decisions are made. We think we think, but really, stuff just happens and we find ourselves ... elsewhere.

"Okay," I said.

Just like that.

CHAPTER 14

The sun was the hint. I remembered they lived where the sun sank into the ocean. I knew that if I just followed the afternoon sun, sooner or later I'd be, well … I'd be closer.

But I had no idea how far, how long, where on that "other" coast I was going. I just had a direction—west— though I didn't know the name for it then. There was a softly glowing spot on the horizon pulling me towards the far waters, but that's all I felt, all I knew. Hell, I didn't even know that I was on an island, but I found out, soon enough.

Rass slowed me down, just like I thought he would. He had never crossed a street in his life; now we had to cross dozens of them. Alone I would have skipped across between cars, no problem. With him I had to wait until there was a big gap in traffic—in Manhattan. By the time I found water again, it was dark.

You have to promise not to laugh, but … I thought I was There.

Quit it! You promised! I was crazy drugged when I was on that plane, I had no idea of time or distance. Not to mention the fact that I'm a cat, remember? All I knew was that I had to go west until I hit water, and by nightfall, I hit water! Then I saw the lights across the river. Ouch.

"See over there, Rass?"

"You mean way over there?"

"Yeah."

"What about it?"

"That's where we have to go."

"Your people are there? Right there?"

"Uh, no, not exactly *right* there. But they're not here, that's for sure."

"So, how do we get across?"

"Can you swim?"

Rass's eyes got so wide in the streetlamp's glare I thought they'd drop out of his head.

"Just kidding," I said.

* * *

But how *to* get across, I had no idea. We found the entrance to a tunnel, but I didn't know where it went and even if I did I wouldn't have chanced it. Too many cars and trucks, too much noise—there was no way. Plus Rass would have been in his element, and I couldn't have taken his lording it over me.

So we turned left, or south, hoping something would turn up. Finally we got so tired and footsore we had to stop. There was a jumble of large, broken rocks lining the banks of the river. It looked like a safe place to catch some shuteye. Plus, if my weary eyes didn't deceive me, the place was infested with mice.

"You ready to rest?" I asked Rass.

"Meow."

"Me too."

We were so tired we couldn't have eaten if the mice threw themselves in our mouths. By the time we found a nice hole in the rip rap, sleep was more than beckoning—it was screaming. For the next few hours, the mice were safe.

It was still full dark, or as dark as it ever gets in the city, when a gray muzzle poked into the opening of our little nook. My sleep was broken by the cat's mere proximity, the way his body changed the acoustics, muffled the water sounds, stilled the air.

"Hiss!" the stranger said. "Get outta here. This is my place!"

Rass was deep asleep, hidden behind me, until he heard that noise. Then he woke with a start and the stranger could see for the first time that there were two of us. I hoped it would make a difference.

I took up a defensive posture, head drawn back, claws out, seeking to deter, not to fight.

"We're just passing through, needed a safe place to sleep," I said.

"What makes you think this is safe?" He said, still in threat mode. "This is my hunt, can't you smell it? Go find your own."

"All I can smell here is that crappy river. And we weren't hunting."

But screw it, this wasn't worth the hassle. He wanted us out, we'd go. I puffed up big, hissed right back at him, and said, "Out of the way."

The stranger growled, then stepped back a few feet. I climbed out onto the rocks, Rass right behind me. I don't know if that mollified him, or if maybe it was my size and presence, but he mellowed out some, and even asked a question.

"I don't know you guys. You're not from around here, right?"

"Hell, we're not even here now."

"What's that supposed to mean?"

"We're trying to get over there," I said, pointing my nose at the Jersey shore.

The stranger laughed.

"What's so funny?" I said.

"Oh nothing, except that they'll never let you. What's your name. I'm Keener, and who's that runt with you?"

"I'm Doo Doo," I said. The runt was struck speechless, so I answered for him.

"His name is Rass and he's a caver who'll eat you soon as look at you."

Rass rose to the occasion by grunting satisfactorily.

"Yeah, well, he's pretty small. You don't look like much to me, Rass," Keener sniffed. But then he let it drop.

"Who won't let us," I asked.

"Huh?"

"I said we wanted to cross the river and you said they'd never let us. Who'll never let us, and how they gonna stop us?"

"There's only one way over there, less you want to risk the bridge, and trust me, you don't. The ferry. But the ferry cats got that sewed up. You'll never get on."

"The ferry?"

"Yeah, like that one," Keener pointed to a well-lit boat heading south, mid-river. "Only not that one exactly, that one goes to Staten Island. You want the one goes to Port Liberte, or maybe Highland, New Jersey. That'll get you past all the water. But you'll never get on. The ferry cats won't let you."

"A boat, huh?" I said. "I never been on a boat before."

Keener laughed again. "So what were you gonna do, swim?"

"That's what *he* said," Rass piped up helpfully.

A couple of nearby rats took that moment to make a break for it, scurrying over the rocks just below. Keener and I snapped to attention.

"You guys hungry?" he purred at us.

"Yeah, kinda," Rass answered, sniffing the air.

"Go for it," Keener said. "And leave me some."

* * *

I never worked so hard for a meal in my life. Between Rass and me we must have missed on fifteen strikes, before he finally chased an old one right into my grasp. And the damned rat tasted like rope, though Rass and Keener didn't seem to mind.

"What'd you do, kill off all the slow ones?" I said to Keener as he groomed himself afterwards.

"Never were any slow ones. I didn't think you could do it. Nice job."

"Thanks for nothing," I said. "Next time you want someone to fetch you dinner, get some people." But I was secretly proud of myself, and little Rass, who showed well on the rocks.

"I'm not partial to people," Keener said. "We get some mean ones down here. Some of them put out poison."

"We're going to find Doo Doo's people," Rass said brightly. "That's why we need to get across the water."

Keener ignored him. "You good with people?" he asked me.

"Mostly."

"Well then, I think maybe I can help you get on the boat. Whether you can get *off* or not will be up to you."

"It always is," I smirked.

Keener led us around the riverbank, through a wispy fog that reminded me of home. But everything was reminding me of home today. The wet grass, the smell of water, the first light of dawn that we cats can sense an hour before humans, all happening in a strange city among strangers, yet all strangely familiar.

"You see that one," Keener said, "the boat on the far side of that pier?"

"Yeah."

"I think that's the one you want."

We were about three hundred yards away. The big ferry had a few lights on, some people moving around it on the pier; the decks looked deserted.

"I can smell the toms," I said warily. "This whole area is marked."

"There's a ton of them," Keener said. "You can't imagine the amount of food that gets tossed around here, this place is a jackpot. If the big toms think you're trying to poach down there you'll be lucky to get away with both eyes. And your friend will be a wet spot with fur."

"Hey!" Rass spat.

"It's good to know you're paying attention," I said to him. "Now shut up and listen."

"I'm not going to stick around and watch," Keener said, "but here's your best chance. In about two hours that wharf will be full of people, most of them getting on the boat. You gotta sneak on with them."

"That's it? That's your big plan? No wonder you live on the rocks...."

"I *know* where I live. You don't even know where the hell you're *going*. Now, one last time ... the wharf cats won't stand for you guys hanging around. But they're used to seeing all kinds of animals going on the boat with their people. If you can get lost in the crowd, get on the boat fast and disappear, I think you can make it."

"Okay," I said, "that doesn't sound too hard."

"Maybe it is and maybe it isn't; that depends on you and the runt. But that's not your only problem. This girl cat I knew got pregnant and thought the boat would be a nice safe place to have her kittens. She was afraid of the local toms, so she snuck on the boat, down low in a dark place where she thought nobody would notice her."

"So what happened?" I asked.

"She got *adopted*. By the crew. Had her litter there and everything. But after they took her kittens away, and she wanted to leave, it took her months to escape."

"Yeah, well, I've done that before," I said.

"And then they found her again. Or at least I think so. Last time I spoke to her, she told me they were looking for her, and I haven't seen her since."

"We'll take our chances," I bluffed. Actually the idea of even being on that monstrosity was giving me the chills.

"Whatever," Keener said, losing interest. "I'm going home. If you get stuck in a cage out there, don't forget to meow at me when you sail by."

"Nuh uh!" Rass sneered at Keener's tail as he walked away.

Attaboy.

CHAPTER 15

As usual, the hard parts were easy and the easy parts were hard. I wasn't worried about the local toms—anyone I couldn't outrun I could outfight—but I had to get *both* of us on that boat, and one of us was Rass. It wasn't far, just a few hundred yards to the pier, but the scent markings were as thick as soup. My job was to plow us through nine hundred feet of enemy turf so fast and strong that the runt would be towed in my wake. That would be the hard part—once we made the pier the rest should be easy as a ball of yarn, or so I thought.

Rass was sniffing around like a bulldog with the snots, which might have been useful if he had half a clue what he was looking for. That would be giving him fifty percent more credit than he had coming, but what he lacked in effectiveness he made up in entertainment.

"Notice anything there Champ?"

"Uh … wait," Rass said. He got up on his tippy toes, shoved his snout as high as it could go, snorted wetly, then dove his nose straight into the ground and sniffed some more, took two steps to his right and repeated the performance, then four to his left where he did the dance all over again.

"You tracking or praying, Rass?"

Irony wasn't his strong suit. He turned to me with worry in his eyes—or maybe he was just dizzy from hyperventilating.

"It's cats everywhere, Doo Doo!"

"Uh huh, that's the word on the street all right. Now tell me, how fresh?"

"How what?"

"Fresh. How old are those scents?"

"Old…? How am *I* supposed to know?"

"Exactly. Watch and learn."

Now, I already knew that these marks weren't new. Otherwise there wouldn't be time for this little lesson.

"You see here?" I led him a few feet upwind to the base of a boulder. "This is the strong spot, here's where he left the mark. And over here…" I trotted to the stump of a tree, "this is another one. Different cat. The scent's weaker and it's spread further. That means older. Get it?"

Rass made a show of understanding, mimicking my moves as well as he could in that ungainly body.

"I, uh … *snort* … think so."

"That's okay, you'll figure it out. You see anyone around?"

Another awkward sweep of his senses, this time with his eyes.

"I don't think so…"

"Good boy. Neither do I." I poised silently for a few seconds, then whispered to Rass.

"You ready to try?"

"You mean now?"

"Yeah, right now. Stay behind me. If we get split up, run like hell, then meet me on that pier."

"Nothin's gonna split us up, Doo Doo," Rass said, trying to sound fearless. "Lead the way."

I nodded, then set off at a nice easy canter, acting like I was the only cat for miles around. I felt eyes on me so close I *had* to turn and look, but I didn't, and neither did Rass. Bit by bit I picked up the pace; it felt like a tunnel was closing around us. We did the last hundred feet at a dead run and damned if we didn't make it onto the pier unmolested. Sometimes you just have to go for it.

"That wasn't so bad," Rass said, panting.

"Shhh, not yet." I whispered. "Follow me."

There wasn't much activity on the wharf, at first. But the more I thought about it, the less I liked the idea of trying to mingle with the people who started to gather there. There were too many uncertainties, you never know with people; I had to find another way to get us on that boat. In the meantime I tucked us behind some tall wood pilings at the edge of the pier, unseen and safe, for the moment.

That other way presented itself to us shortly. Rass and I were still hiding silently—I have to hand it to the little guy, he was rock solid even when he was scared. Maybe I was nervous enough for both of us, but his faith in me was touching. As long as I was close he was calm and content.

I saw the opportunity, but it wasn't going to be easy. Just to our front, on the other side of the pilings from where we were hiding, some workmen began stacking boxes. Actually they were more like crates, great big things with wooden frames. Some were sealed with plastic, some cardboard. But one, all by itself and over six feet tall, was wide open at the top. I could tell because there were two rolled-up things that turned out to be rugs poking above it. I was sure I could leap into that crate in one bound, and probably not be noticed doing it, if I was quick and timed it right. And I thought Rass had a fair to medium chance of doing the same.

And, truth to tell, I realized that if he didn't make it, he would still be on his home turf with a decent shot at finding his way home. And I would be relieved of my burden—not so much him, I was getting to like the little caver, but of responsibility, which never comes easy to a cat and was weighing on me.

Then came the clincher: Some burly workmen started to haul those boxes down a ramp into a big door that had opened in the side of the boat. So the crates were going on, and on meant across.

"You think you can make it to the top of that box?" I asked Rass. "The one with those two rolls sticking out?"

"Oh man, it's kinda high."

"Yeah, but the sides are cardboard, you can claw your way if you come up short. Anyway, that's our best shot. We get inside there without being seen and we're golden."

"If you can, I can."

"Don't jump right after me, wait half a minute or so, make sure no one is looking at you, and *do* it. And don't you miss, dammit!"

Rass purred and nodded. Like he was telling me he *knew* where my sudden vehemence came from.... And the runt was right.

When the workmen took away a big crate two stacks from my target, I knew it was time to go. I squatted down, coiled … and then had to wait for them to turn their backs on me. That pause messed me up bad. I got so psyched I damn near jumped over the box. My tensed-up back legs sprang hard, and I flew!

I don't know how nobody saw me. I jumped far higher than I had to, soaring above the crate, way too much hang time, then plunged down, down, four paws splayed, about to crash to the bottom of that box and make a ton of noise, when I snagged one of the rugs with two outstretched claws. My momentum snapped me around to the underside of the roll; I grabbed it for all I was worth, and wound up hanging there upside down, completely exposed, feeling like an idiot and waiting for trouble.

None came. I stayed on the back side of the rug, somehow managed to get turned around, and slowly scootched down the roll, trying to get out of sight. My claws stuck to the rug like Velcro; every time I moved a paw it sounded like I ripped out another inch of fabric. But I got to the bottom okay, and found—surprise!—a soft pile of shredded newspaper. I nestled in, turned to look up at the steely dawn and waited for Rass to drop in. Minutes passed.

Come *on*, dude, I thought, watching the sky for falling cats. Now or never, I urged silently, not sure which I would prefer.

I was beginning to think about how free and easy it would be to travel alone from here on out, when the crate exploded.

Or that's what it sounded like. Where I jumped long, Rass went short. He slammed into the side of that crate about six inches low. The damned box boomed like somebody fired a cantaloupe at a bass drum.

"Nice job lame-o," I growled deep in my throat, "now you've got us both busted." I saw his claws ripping through the cardboard as he flailed to the top, his round body teetering on the edge for a long second—like a "Cats Here" sign—then watched in horror as he tumbled helplessly to the bottom, totally out of control. If the box hadn't been lined with paper he would have busted his chin wide open.

"Whoops!" That was what Rass giggled when he emerged from the confetti. *Whoops!* The little puke was *enjoying* himself.

"Get your ass under that rug and hide, idiot!"

That shut him up; I think I hurt his feelings. He turned silently towards the corner where the rug met the wall. But he was trying to walk in two feet of shredded newsprint, and he waddled like a drunk. Strips of paper clung to his body and draped over his nose. The higher he lifted his legs the deeper he went, the more ridiculous he looked. By the time he reached the corner he was buried; all you could see of poor Rass was his tail. I was trying like hell not to laugh out loud.

Maybe if you act like a drunk you get drunkard's luck. Because no suspicious human heads poked over the top, looking for clumsy feline stowaways. Not even when we heard a bunch of men draw close, jabbering orders to one another, their bodies separated from ours by a quarter inch of cardboard. And then the box started to tilt, sway, lift and finally, move. Thirty seconds later it stopped, the daylight gone, replaced by still, oily air and darkness. We were in.

* * *

"You okay?"

"Yeah. I, uh, kinda fell."

"I noticed."

The boat was vibrating and began to lurch a little as we got under way. From what I could smell and hear, I thought we were probably alone for the moment. We had a decision to make.

"I think we should get out of here, Rass."

"Why?"

"Because if they take these rugs away we'll be stuck. We can't jump off this stuff," I said, pawing the newsprint.

"Nuh uh."

"What?"

"I don't wanna go. This feels safe to me. We can hide here. Who knows what's out there."

"You've been gone two days and you already found yourself a new cave?" I sneered.

"So?" Rass sounded angry.

"So I thought you were following *me.*"

"You ... you're not always right."

"And you don't know anything!"

"Look, Doo Doo. They put this box on the boat. They'll take this box off the boat."

I'd had enough. Without another word I hopped on the rug, ran to the top, looked around ... and froze.

Two big guys in overalls were cadging a smoke in the corner of the hold. Only dumb luck had them looking the other way. The noise and diesel stink had fooled me; I backed down the way I'd come.

"Fine," I said to Rass, who was staring up at me like a baby bird at his momma with a worm in her mouth. "We'll do it your way."

* * *

Rass was right. They did take the box off the boat—with us still in it. So now we get out and we're safely on the other side of the river, no problem, and I should thank him, right?

Wrong. We never got the chance. They hauled our crate off the boat and loaded it, rugs, newsprint, cats and all, right onto a truck. A possibility that never even occurred to me—or Rass, damn him. They shoved the box into the guts of a semi, and then they closed the door. Clang, click. And then we rolled.

* * *

Cats can be a little slow on the uptake sometimes, even such a cat as yours truly. But I knew this was not good, and I knew it right away. It was noisy and hot inside that trailer, it bounced up and down and rattled and dulled the senses something awful.

I got the fear. For a few minutes I cowered in the crate, quivering, disoriented, freaked. Then I *blew* out of that box, up the rug and over the side in a reflex of rage that verged on panic.

I landed in a ghost world. The truck was old, I guess, because its rivets leaked a little light and air, and the back door shimmied in its frame and did the same. That let in just enough daylight for me to see that there was no obvious way out—but the main thing was, I *could* see. *You* couldn't, but I could—there was just enough light for a sharp-eyed cat. And that cooled my nerves considerably.

Because now I had a job to do. I had to survey every inch of the place, and it was big and full of stuff. We might be stuck in this box a long time. I didn't smell any food, but maybe the place had mice, or roaches, or maybe an old puddle of water somewhere. Maybe there was a hidden hole that we could squeeze through to the outside. And maybe there was nothing and we'd die in this grinding, pounding, steaming tin box.

"Hey Rass! Get your ass out here! We got another cave for you to explore."

* * *

I went high and Rass went low. There were couches and dressers and boxes galore, there were mirrors and pictures wrapped up against the wall, there were kids' bikes, pole lamps, fake plants and plastic drop cloths by the yard, but no food, no water. And, it was getting very hot.

As long as we kept rolling it was almost bearable. The old truck leaked a trickle of outside air—a poor trade for all the pounding and noise, but one that kept us from roasting alive. But, when we stopped, and it must have been several hours later, that box really started to bake.

Precious seconds ticked away before my ears stopped ringing, before I roused myself. My legs were shaky, I was parched and spent. This was not good.

"Hey Rass."

"Yeah?" he wheezed.

"I think we better make some noise."

"You think?"

"Ain't you feeling hot? You're looking a mite peaked."

"You don't look too good yourself."

"We gotta get out of here. Whatever. It can't be worse than this."

Rass tried to yowl, bless his heart, but he wasn't very loud. I took up the slack big time, making as much noise as I knew how. My dry throat burned as I screamed and I clawed the sides of the trailer for good measure, sending horribly unpleasant vibrations down my paws and up my spine. We must have kept up the racket for a solid minute, but it didn't work. The truck's motor started and we began to rumble away. We were as trapped as ever and twice as exhausted. Damn.

"Next time we better hit it quicker," I said to Rass.

"If there is a next time," he panted.

"Don't be a quitter," I said to both of us. "Come here, sit by the door, there's almost a breeze."

Rass sat beside me, I saw his spirits rise as the temperature dropped. As did mine. I still couldn't see a way out of this mess, but it felt good having him right there. Somehow we'll get through this, I thought. Together.

CHAPTER 16

It was a long, grim afternoon. That driver just kept driving. He must have had a big supply of sandwiches and an even bigger bladder, because by the time he stopped Rass and I were getting desperate.

We'd spent the day sleeping and dehydrating. The lack of food was no big deal, yet, but the heat had baked us dry. We started out using the shredded newspaper in the crate as our litter box, but then the jump up and down became too tiring, and we did our business on a stack of rags by the back doors. By the time the light leaking into the truck turned red we were peed out and sleeping most of the time. The scorching day had taken a heavy toll on us. Rass was a curled-up lump, breathing shallowly, his back hairs standing up porcupine-like. I was worried about him. In those moments when I came awake I was worried about me too.

It was full dark when I felt the truck finally trundle to a halt. The air brakes squealed and puffed, the motor ceased its popping drone. My head rang from the all-day noise, I was achy all over. It took me a few moments to get moving. I nudged Rass with a paw.

"Get up, dude. Make some noise."

Rass picked up his head, looking weary and confused.

"Huh?"

"Time to get out of here, Rass," I said. "Give it all you got."

It wasn't much. He tried, but his voice was a dry croak. I knew we couldn't take another day trapped in this moving tomb. It was all up to me.

At first, I didn't do much better. I let loose some strangled cries at the back door, so weak they couldn't have penetrated tissue paper. But the effort woke me up. The very act of making noise gave me a rush of mad energy; I howled and pawed the doors again and again, getting wilder and crazier, almost hysterical in my desperation. Throwing myself bodily against the steel, I succeeded only in knocking myself silly. I fell back, breathless and defeated—but then I heard something.

A metallic clunk, followed by a wet, gurgling rush. The sound came from the front of the box, on the right, or passenger's side. I found out later that's where the fuel tank was—the driver was gassing up.

"Follow me!" I told Rass. We staggered through the furniture and boxes, got to the corner nearest the sound. "Now, do what I do."

I reached up and clawed the corrugated metal sides of that box like I was trying to shred it. It hurt like hell, and that gave my screams some real punch. Rass did the same thing, with much less energy; he was pretty far gone. But the wall there was a lot thinner than those heavy back doors and it rang like a tin drum with each agonizingly painful scrape. We kept at it for what seemed like forever. *What the hell is* wrong *with that driver? Is he* deaf? *Surely he has to hear* this, *he* has *to!*

And then the rushing sound stopped. I heard footsteps crunching along the right side of the truck, towards the back. Then a wrenching grind of metal on metal as the doors opened, the bright lights of the fuel island flooding in, silhouetting a big, burly man. *A miracle? Maybe.*

"Who's there?" boomed an angry, frightened voice.

"Rarrrk!"

The driver clicked on a huge flashlight, bright as the sun, pinning Rass in its blue-white beam.

"Rarrk!" he insisted. "Rarrk!"

Now the idiot speaks up.

I ran. Stealth wasn't going to work, Rass had seen to that, so I ran. Or, rather, I told my legs to move real fast, but somehow they didn't get the message. I *should* have made it out of there. The driver had the light on Rass, he wasn't expecting two cats—hell, he wasn't expecting one cat—so I had the element of surprise working for me. But not speed. I urged maximum effort out of my crampy muscles, weaving through the boxes towards the open door ... but it wasn't good enough. A big, meaty hand got me by the neck.

"Whoa, little buddy," the driver laughed, pinching my scruff so tight I couldn't claw him. "Take it easy."

I hissed at him. My throat was so dry it came out like a cough. I was trapped.

But Rass was free. If he made a move right now he could get out of there, and maybe distract the driver enough that I could scramble away too. Rass wasn't big on initiative though. The driver hoisted me off the floor and the damned caver never moved.

"Where did *you* guys come from?" the driver said, holding me up by my front paws. "Nice looking cat," he added, examining me like I was a piece of meat. He turned the flashlight back on Rass, still sitting in the truck like he was glued there, the idiot.

"You're an odd looking thing," he said to him. "If this isn't the strangest.... How'd you all get here?"

Rass's big eyes reflected the light like blue mirrors. He stared at us, transfixed.

"Rarrk," he demanded. "*Rarrk!*"

* * *

They sell everything in truck stops nowadays. After our driver tossed us in the cab of his rig he disappeared for an hour—an hour I spent in high dudgeon with an oblivious Rass—and came back with cat food, two small hubcaps, and some bottled water. He filled one hubcap with each, put them on the floor by the passenger seat, lit up a smoke, and waited for us to eat.

That took a while, for me, anyway. Rass the Prideless went for the food while our benefactor was still opening the cans. I hid under the seat. The driver, I never did get his name, coaxed me in his deep baritone.

"Come on there, little fella, have some food."

Screw you, I'm not hungry. And I wasn't. It was the water that got to me. Nice cool water in a chrome hubcap, already dripping with dew from the humid air. I shouldered Rass out of the way, made sure to keep my hindquarters pointed at the driver, and drank about a pint. Then I had a few nibbles. Rass scarfed so hard that he puked as soon as we got rolling again, and serves him right.

You know how I hate cars? Well, riding in that truck made being in a car feel like riding on air, but I made the best of a bad situation. There was a sleeper compartment behind the seats; I got in there and claimed it. And I didn't wake up until we stopped again, this time so briefly the driver left the motor running. After a few minutes he came back with a plastic litter tray and a couple of boring cat toys for us to play with (boring because no catnip, just yarn and bells, but that didn't stop Rass). I used the litter box, ignored the toys, and fell asleep again.

It was still dark when we finally pulled over. Our driver left, being careful to open and shut the door quickly so we couldn't escape. I couldn't have, I was still in the sleeper, but Rass might have been able to. He was on the driver's *lap* when we stopped.

"Done barfing yet?" I asked sarcastically.

"That was hours ago," Rass said.

"Plan on getting out of here anytime soon?"

"Get out? Why should I get out?"

"You're kidding me, right?"

"Uh, no. I like him."

"You … *like* … him," I drawled. "Wanna be his pet?"

"Hey, we're moving, okay? Why not see how far we can go? Unless you want to walk."

"Man, you'll trust anybody. Me—I'm gonna stick here until tomorrow, then take my chances outside."

"The food's good too," Rass said.

"Slut."

When the driver slipped back into the cabin Rass perked up like a puppy and got scratched between the ears for his trouble. I was disgusted, and a little jealous. Here I'm the one who is supposed to be civilized, used to people, and Rass is getting all the love. Well, so be it. I'm not that easy.

The driver, who was a big guy to start with, stretched alarmingly, and began to peel off his shirt.

"I need a little shuteye, Tuffy," he said, leaning into the sleeper.

He reached for me, scooped me up in his meaty hands, and put me at the foot of the bed. I stayed there for about a second, then sulked out and went back under the passenger seat. The driver chuckled.

He patted the bed, "Come here, Fluffy," he said twice. And I'll be damned if Rass didn't hop right in.

Fluffy? I thought. For *that* hairbrush? Tuffy isn't bad though. I've been called worse. I consoled myself with a few bites of food and then did what cats do best. Slept. Yet again.

* * *

I don't know why I ever bother to make plans. They never work out the way they're supposed to. First of all, I'm lazy, a characteristic I share with all cats and almost as many humans. But not, apparently, our driver.

We started our second day on the road early, as the sun shot long shadows in front of us. My curiosity got the better of my attitude, and I was tired of hiding under the seat while the world went by. After yesterday's rough ride, today it felt like we were floating. After a while I lost all sense of motion, only the drone of the engine and the whistle of the wind to mark the passing miles. I just had to look out and see.

And there was only one perfect spot to do so, one place high enough for a little cat to look out and see the world. The top of the passenger seat back. That morning, after breakfast, instead of crawling back underneath, I jumped on top of the seat and perched.

The view was mesmerizing. Flat as a table top, straight and deep. The still-low sun behind us made everything at a distance sharp, while our hurtling gait blurred everything close. After a while, staring at the fields flashing by the side windows and the road unreeling through the front, I became strangely detached. It felt like we were standing still, and the scenery was a movie projected on the windshield, always changing, yet always the same, in an endless loop.

And endless is the operative word. I had flown over this place, tranquilized and stuffed in the belly of a plane. Now I was *seeing* it, and the impression was vast. Vast and overwhelming.

Yet, as I drifted happily between barely awake and barely asleep for the next several hours, one feeling was constant. I knew, just *knew*, that we were heading in the "right" direction. I don't know how I was so sure, "west" doesn't mean the same thing to a cat that it does to a person, we don't navigate that way. But our sense of direction is famous—and earned. Maybe the angle of the sun had something to do with it; I knew that home was where it set, close by the ocean. But not all days are sunny, and nights never confused me. Home was like a hot spot out in the far distance—how far I had no idea—and I could always turn around and point my nose towards that glow, night or day, and almost feel its distant warmth.

This was too pleasant. I put my escape plans on hold and let the day fly by, rising from my torpor only when we stopped, as we did sparingly during that long day, or to eat when the driver refreshed the bowl, or to use the litter box he carefully groomed at each stop.

I think he was on drugs—the driver, that is. He drained bottle after bottle of water, and, if my nose didn't fool me, the occasional beer too. I could hear his teeth clash in his closed mouth, see his jaw muscles work. He threw a disk in the player and for an excruciating hour bellowed along with the mournful country music blaring from speakers mounted in every corner of that cab.

Then he decided he was going to have a conversation with Rass—mostly one sided, though the little guy did manage to squeeze a squawk or two in the infrequent gaps. I'd seen Doc like that, when he was on speed. The sweet memory of my first, best, human buddy mellowed my annoyance with the noise spewing from the driver's mouth. I'd grown used to the boring sameness of the long day, watching the glaring scene of intolerable heat in quiet comfort from my air-conditioned cocoon. Now that twilight had come, as the headlights clicked on and puffy clouds piled up gray and ominous in the western sky, our driver couldn't shut up. I'm sure he was on drugs.

Rass wasn't on his lap anymore. The driver was too fidgety for that. Now the cobby caver lay balled up on the doghouse, a fake leather cushion that covered the compartment between the two front seats. But the look on Rass's face was still adoring as he listened to, and occasionally interrupted, the driver's monologue.

"Lorraine's gonna get a kick out of you two, I can tell you that. She used to sleep right back there, Fluffy," he said, tossing a thumb over his shoulder "where we were last night. After a while, she says, too much of a grind for me. But hell, I told her that when I bought the rig!"

"Mroowr?" Rass interjected.

"Yeah, she stays home now. Stays home and gets lonely. I hope! Ha ha. She loves the animals, though. Damn place is a zoo already, two more won't hurt. Hope the dogs won't mind. And she'll have your ass if you mess with her rabbit. Ha ha."

"Chirrup!" Rass laughed right along with him.

This nonsense went on half the night. Normally that much racket gets on my nerves, and I guess it did now too, a little bit. But I had decided to wait it out until morning. Tomorrow, some time, I'd look for my chance and get out of here. In the meantime I could relax, eat, sleep, and try not to feel too bad about what was happening to Rass. One thing I was sure of, it wasn't going to happen to me. Not with this guy, anyway.

He was good to us, I'll give him that. But he wasn't cat people. We can tell right away. Your cats can tell too, but you already know that from the way they act when friends come over, don't you?

But Rass didn't know *any* people, and he *couldn't* tell. With his inexperience, it was just the luck of the draw. I couldn't make out everything the driver said, but the vibe told me this: Dog Person. Rass had hitched his star to a dog person. Poor needy fool.

CHAPTER 17

Escape day dawned gray and cool. We hit the road early and made miles and miles on the plains—the floor-flat road gradually rising, sloping, finally rolling, but never turning. The driver cracked a window, wedged a cigarette between his knuckles, draped a wrist over the steering wheel, and went through a whole pack of smokes before he ever hit the brakes. But when he did—finally—I was ready. Feigning sleep, curled up on the passenger seat, I watched his every move through slitted eyes as he left the cab for a late lunch.

What I saw was sloppy. The driver was getting careless. Where before he had angled the door just enough to slide out his bulk, now he swung it wide open and stretched for a moment before turning around and closing it. The whole process took maybe two seconds, but that was one more than I'd need. I knew how to get out of here.

Getting out would be the easy part, getting away *clean* would take some planning. I jumped on the dash and looked around. We were off the freeway, in a cluster of gas stations and fast food joints. The driver had parked his truck at the far end of the parking lot; a dense hedge fenced the pavement from the flat, plowed fields beyond.

Tricky. I could hide under those bushes easy enough, but I'd be open and exposed for a few hundred yards once I went beyond them. My best shot seemed to be to stay low, get to the hedge line, snake my way into the roots and wait. If the driver kept searching for me, I'd have to work my way down the line without shaking a leaf, wait for him to look the wrong way, and make a mad dash through the fields to freedom.

Freedom. The thought ran through my mind and my body bristled with anticipation. I felt my ruff hairs rise, my tail grew big. I'd been cooped up *way* too long.

"This is the place," I said to Rass. "Time to get out of here. You coming?"

"How you gonna do it?"

"Right out the door. He's not so worried about us bolting anymore; I've got it all figured out." I jumped off the dash and down to the floor.

"There's enough room here for both of us," I said, tucking myself between the driver's seat and the door. "He's got to open it when he comes back, soon as he does, we go."

Rass nosed around, checking out the tight space. He looked and smelled nervous. "I dunno," he said.

"What? You want to stay with this loser? Move in with his old lady and a bunch of dogs?"

"I'm scared, Doo Doo."

"When ain't you?"

Rass stared at me, then looked away. I felt bad.

"Okay, buddy," I said softly, "I understand. I don't know what the hell is going to happen out there, and this ain't your quest. I'm looking for something and you're looking for anything. That's cool. I hope it works out for you. But it's time for me to go."

"Aw hell, Doo Doo," Rass sighed, "I was just saying...."

And the door swung open.

* * *

I only made one mistake and, when it didn't cost me, I was kinda happy about it. I exploded out the door—that "second" I needed wasn't half gone before I was. But on the way out, flying through the air, I caught the driver good with my back claws, using his thigh like a starting block. He howled in pain—which scared me at first—I didn't want to make him angry.

And it probably did make him angry, but mostly it helped me get away. Once again in the heat of battle I abandoned my plans. I went straight under the hedge and blew across the freshly plowed field beyond. I was out in the open for a solid half minute. The driver never came after me. I'm not sure why. But maybe if he hadn't been distracted by the blood running down his leg, he might have come screaming for mine.

Or maybe I flatter myself. Maybe he was glad to be rid of the antisocial cat who shunned him like a leper. Maybe it was a case of good riddance to bad rubbish and hello to the *nice* cat. He still had Rass to bring home to his lonely Lorraine.

But, whatever the reason, I was *free*, and I didn't look back. I cut loose and *ran*, bounding over the dirt furrows of the naked field, feeling the humid air jetting into my lungs, ears back, eyes narrowed, snapping my paws together beneath my bent belly, flinging them out as far as I could reach, flying two feet off the ground, barely touching with each leap. I felt light as light, uncatchable, alone and on my way.

Cats are built for speed, not for distance. I landed in a clump of trees that marked the line between two fields, blown and happy. I had been running for nearly a minute—a long time for a cat. Looking back over the field, catching my breath, I could see how far I'd come. The hedge I'd escaped through was just a line in the haze, I could barely hear the noise of the parking lot, and the driver wasn't following me. My escape was made.

So now what? A little catnap, of course, in the cool grass. There was something different about the air here, humid under piling clouds, but also thin. I found out later I was in a place called Colorado, almost a mile up on the plains. That thin air made me sleepy after my mad dash, a fine excuse for some shut-eye. But then again, I never needed much excuse.

I walked deeper into the wooded patch to be sure I was out of sight, trod a circle in the grass until I'd made a little nest, sank down and slept the sleep of the free.

I woke up with my hair standing on end. This was something new. It felt—how to describe it—*ominous*, like danger was just around the corner, the oddest feeling. Very strange and tingly. I got up and looked around warily, but there was nothing to see. I couldn't figure it out, there was just this weird sense of trouble, an odd tinge to the air, the little sounds from the trees too close, magnified.

Then the world exploded and I went blind.

*   *   *

Okay, you can stop laughing. I'd never seen lightning before. Just my luck that I damn near get hit on the first encounter. My vision came back slowly, I was still seeing spots fifteen minutes later. Which was an inconvenience, because, once again, I was running like hell.

I *had* seen rain before, or so I thought. But I'd never seen the sky turn to solid water. I'd never felt drops so heavy they stung, clear through my fur. And I'd never fought against a driving wind so furious it blew me sideways as I tried, desperately, to get away.

But away to where? The only shelter I could see, and I couldn't see much in this cataract, was that stand of trees. I couldn't go back there—that place was haunted—so I ran away from it, squinting through soaked eyes, fighting to keep a straight line. The warm air had turned now, I was drenched and cold, my fur pasted to my body, carrying away the heat of my panic as fast as I produced it.

Soon my paws got so clogged with mud it felt like I had boots on. Heavy boots. Maybe that was a blessing because it slowed me down, and my panicked dash turned into a slog. The rain might even have eased up a little, I'm not sure. I was already half drowned, a few drops more or less in that gusher wouldn't make much difference.

The whole ordeal kept piling on and on. On and on *me*. I got so disgusted it almost became funny. The fields had turned to swamps, sheeted rain merged with muddy earth at a horizon that was very close, but never got any closer. For all I knew I was standing still—or running in circles. And my mind was doing the same thing. I sagged for a moment and let the rain pour down on me, almost laughing at the ridiculousness of it all. What's a cat to do?

Move, that's what. I tucked in my head, let the rain stream past my face and ears, down my chin, and booked. I bowed my neck into the wind and picked up a steady rhythm, not too fast, not too slow, trot ... trot ... trot, like a machine. If I had to—and I might—I could go all day at this pace.

Trot, trot, trot.

Trot, trot, trot....

Splang!

Head first into a chain link fence. That's what I get for not looking. My body accordioned, water flew off my pelt like a prizefighter when he takes a hook to the head. Luckily the fence had some give and I bounced. Three feet away was a concrete wall, and *that* would have hurt. When I stopped rolling I got up, looked around and saw an open gate.

Good deal. The fence was only a few feet high, but I was so waterlogged and leg weary I doubt I could have jumped it. Instead I walked right through, onto solid green grass. Flooded grass with two inches of standing water, but not a bit of mud. After slogging through those gluey fields, this felt like ice skating. The grass was short, even, manicured, wonderful. Now if it would only stop raining!

Shelter would be the next best thing. At this point I'd take what I could find. But as I walked around the field, flat as a table top, the tallest thing I could see was me. Not that I could see much. And then it got worse. What had been a slight letup in the storm—so slight I hadn't noticed it—ended abruptly in another flash and boom, followed by a blast of wind that drove the rain sideways into my flanks. That I did notice.

This sucked. Looking back on it now, I can see I was never in any real danger, but at the time I was desperate—leaning into the wind like a drunk, skidding like I had a sail on my back, fighting to stay upright. It hurt like hell to open my eyes in that gale, but I kept trying. I had to find a way out.

Just when it seemed like nothing more could go wrong, I stumbled off the edge of the grass and plunged neck-deep into a muddy moat. That was the breaking point. I swam through most of that mud hole and swallowed the rest, cursing the world. Choking and crying inconsolably, yowling like a baby who's lost his momma, harsh, trilling meows, and pointless ones, too—it embarrasses me to this day. Momma was long gone, and the storm so wild she couldn't have heard me if she was ten feet away. Nobody could.

But somebody did. Maybe it was wishful thinking, a sound mirage in a drowning world, but I could swear I heard *something*. I stood still and shut up. And then I heard it again, off to my left, barely audible above the storm, but *there*.

"Hello?" I said.

"Rarrk!" the voice answered. I stumbled towards that sound and it came again, louder, clearer.

"RARRK!"

You *got* to be kidding me.

* * *

I'm going to let my pride take the hit and come right out and say it: Rass was my guardian angel. Nine times out of ten the little caver was a hopeless, indecisive dolt—a burden I couldn't, or wouldn't, shake. But there were times—the tenth time, like in the subway—when he was a lifesaver. And this was one of those times. In the midst of this biblical torrent, Rass had found the one spot that was high and dry. And his voice led me right to it.

I found him perched on a wooden bench inside a long, open-sided lean-to. Its overhanging roof was deep enough to keep the rain off the bench, but the floor was flooded and gusts howled through the structure like a wind tunnel. Rass had barely a drop on him, but he was scared witless. His eyes were swimming in his head like marbles in oil and I couldn't get a straight story out of him.

"Dude! How'd you get here before me?" I hopped on the bench with him, shook off about a quart of water, and surrendered to the useless instinct that makes cats try to dry off with a tongue.

"I was following you…." Rass began.

"What, from the truck? I thought you were gonna take your chances with the driver. And no way! I would have heard you…"

"No, not then. After. By those trees."

"By what trees?"

"Where you ran. I came after. I was following *you*. I didn't like that guy, once you left...."

Boom! Thunder shook the field, rattled the lean-to. Rass twitched like he'd been hit with a cattle prod. "Doo Doo," he moaned, "I'm *scared*. I thought you was dead for sure back there! And me next!"

"Settle down, squirt. We're not dead yet." My voice seemed to calm him. I moved a little closer and my presence seemed to calm him more. But my curiosity bone was still throbbing. I waited quietly for a lull in the storm, then tried again.

"I still don't get it, Rass. Where were you? How'd you get here ahead of me?"

"... Rass?..."

"Wrssssp..." he snored.

I'll be damned—the little punk had fallen asleep.

I was annoyed, for a moment. But upon mature reflection, I saw the force of his argument, and joined him.

CHAPTER 18

I got the whole story when we woke up. The stormy day had turned into a drizzly night, placid and cool. Crickets and frogs and locusts made a foreground for distant dog barks and the odd coyote howl carrying across the plains. The effect was big, open, feral—not scary, exactly, but lonesome and wild. I was a city cat, remember, and this was all new to me. Same with Rass, but he seemed oblivious. He jabbered away like he was making up for lost time.

"He turned mean once you got him, Doo Doo. He was cussing *me*, like *I* clawed his leg. He didn't hit me or anything, but I got a bad feeling. When he was in the sleeper, fixing his cuts, he left the door open, like he wanted me to go. So I did."

I dropped off the bench and gulped down a grasshopper that caught my eye on the lean-to's floor. It tasted pretty good. I must have been hungry.

"So you followed me?" I asked.

"No, I tracked you. It was easy, you left a trail in the dirt, and I found you sleeping under that tree."

"Really? You just watched me? How long?"

"Until … you know…" Rass sounded embarrassed, "until you got zapped."

"Why didn't you let me know you were there?"

"Cuz I thought you might be mad at me."

"I don't get it. Why would I be mad?"

"On account I didn't come with you in the first place, like you told me."

"Wow. I'm that much of a son of a bitch, huh?"

"No, I didn't mean that...."

"Forget it. So, did you get hit by that lightning too?"

"Nope. I felt it, but it missed me. You shoulda seen yourself, Doo Doo," Rass enthused. "You lit up like a sign!"

"I wouldn't know. I was blind at the time."

Rass chuckled. "You must have been. Otherwise you would have seen this place, like I did. Once it started raining, I ran right over. That's how I beat you here."

"Let me get this straight, I'm half drowned and blind, totally lost, and you just watch me?"

"No, I couldn't see nothing in that mess. I sure *heard* you though! Mroowr! Meowww!!!"

"Hey Rass, you want to die young?"

"No! Why?"

"Tell somebody about that and find out."

* * *

I tried hunting on that drenched field during the night, but, aside from a few bugs and some tasty grass, all I caught was the sniffles. Rass was asleep on the bench when I came back; I curled up right next to him. The drizzle had stopped, finally, giving way to a chill fog. Tomorrow would be sunny and dry, I hoped. And that's what I dreamed—sort of.

It was a simple dream, but one that kept me going for months, when I remembered it, when I needed it. I was back in San Francisco, in Doc and Fern's place, lazing on a window seat, the sun streaming in, warming my back. A catnip mouse was wedged between my front paws, but I wasn't buzzed, I couldn't even smell the nip. That wasn't unusual—I never dreamed "high," it was always the next thing I was going to do. But it wasn't frustrating, either, it was comforting and homey. In this dream I had a belly full of food. Fern's scents surrounded me, the smells of my people, of home. Doc came over and rolled me on my back, an indignity I always resented until he seduced me by scratching my stomach, which he did now with long, spidery fingers. As he petted me, he said my name over and over in the deep, rumbly voice he knew I loved. Sing-songy, "Doo Doooooo, Doo Doo boyyyy, who's my Doo Doo boy...."

I could dream that forever. And I had variations of it, often. Waking up each time was a disappointment— yet it left an afterglow that stayed with me, warmed me, and motivated me. I was going to get back there, no matter what. But, as I found out time after time, "what" had its own ideas.

* * *

Life is a matter of minutes; timing is everything. Timing and chance. This particular adventure wouldn't have happened if I hadn't been so exhausted by the previous day's storms and trials. That made me sleep late, which is where the timing came in. Normally I'd be up and gone by this hour. The chance was where we wound up spending that night. I called it a lean-to, though in that torrent I never gave it much thought, it was just shelter.

But it wasn't a lean-to. It was a dugout. As in baseball dugout.

All I knew about baseball was that Doc was crazy for it. He watched it all the time on TV, but cats have a hard time seeing television; two-dimensional pictures don't compute properly in our brains. But I understood it was a people game, that it had players, and, because Doc liked it, so did I—whatever *it* was. And I was about to meet some of those players.

* * *

"Hey Friz, check it out! There's two of them."

"Tchee, Dougie, one of 'em is black. I doan like no black cat."

"Nah, he ain't black. More ashy, kinda."

"Where they come fron?"

"Hell, I don't know. Hey, little guys! Where you come from?"

I popped open one eye to look at the humans making all this noise.

Big. That was my first impression, they were big. Both of them, the tall white one and the stocky brown one. The pale guy, the one called Dougie, had cat person written all over him. He approached me slowly, smiling, almost cooing.

"Who are you, Orange? Where'd you come from? Who's your buddy?" He reached out with his left hand, about the biggest paw I'd ever seen on a person, and touched my fur. I let him.

"Are you craze, Doug? What if he bite you on your pitch hand or sonethin, what you gonna do then?"

"He ain't gonna bite me. You aren't gonna bite me, are you Big Orange?" he said chucking me under my chin.

No, I don't believe I will, I thought. But I'm not so sure about your friend.

Rass wasn't having any of it. He'd scuttled under the bench and hid while I got all the attention. That was a complete turnaround from the way he'd acted with the truck driver. Maybe something really had happened to him after I ran away, maybe more than he told me. He sure was acting afraid of strangers now.

"You think they're hungry, Friz? You guys hungry? Hey Friz, be a pal and snag some of that sausage from the clubhouse, okay? I think they'll like that."

"What you thin, I'm your servand? Tchee, Dougie, is jus' a couple of stray gatos."

"No, Friz, I don't think you're my servant. I think you're my catcher. Now be my *pal* and grab me those sausages. Otherwise I just might miss a sign and put a hole in your chest today."

"You thin we gonna play? Look kinda wet to me."

"I hope so. I'm feeling lucky. This orange guy—you are a guy, aren't you?" he said, lifting my tail.

Don't make me take a chunk out of your arm, I thought, but I submitted to the inspection with a small meow of protest.

"...I think he's lucky for me. And lucky for me is lucky for us."

"You loco Dougie, and you a leftie too. Nothing worse than a loco leftie...."

"Friz. The food?"

"Okay! Hesus! I'll get the puto sausages. They ain' fit for people anyway."

That's how it began. Doug knew cats well enough to toss us the food and leave us alone. Rass came out of hiding, grabbed a big, greasy, white link between his teeth and dragged it to the far corner of the dugout. I took a few bites right in front of them, then followed Rass. The guys started tossing a ball back and forth on the still-wet field. After a while they seemed to forget about us. After a while longer there were *dozens* of them around. Then hundreds of people in the stands behind us.

I liked it here. But clearly, it was time to hide. We found a perfect spot, cool, shady and hidden, under the wooden bleachers at the far end of the field. As we scooted out there before the game started it felt like a spotlight was on us. I could hear people calling out from the crowd—"Look! Down the line. Cats!" Like they'd never seen any before. But people will do that when they see familiar animals in unfamiliar places.

They did play a game that day. The noise of it was driving Rass mad, but I was fascinated. I peeked between the fans' legs to the field beyond, where the action was. It was hard to make sense of it all. Mostly players standing around doing not much for a while, then frantic bursts of activity on the field accompanied by loud stomping from the fans above. I had to look sharp, then—a rain of beer from kicked-over cups would follow within seconds. But also the occasional French fry, or better yet, hot dog stub.

The best part was that nobody could see us. That's the only thing that kept Rass from going stark-staring nuts that first day. He told me later it felt like he was back in the subway, hearing a train coming, and no way to get off the tracks. He said it freaked him out, big time.

But that didn't stop him from falling asleep before things got interesting.

I'd been looking for my guy the whole time. I couldn't see in the dugout, and I found out later he spent most of his time in the bullpen down the right field line, where I couldn't see either. But I could hear everything, and when I heard "Now pitching for the Miners, number 49, Douglas Twitchell!" boom through the speakers, two things happened.

First, there was a groan from the crowd. A fat guy sitting right above me bellowed, "Damn! Not Twitchy again!" and someone answered, "How many you think he's gonna walk before Gus pulls him?"

Second, I saw my benefactor, the one who fed me that morning, loping slowly towards a dirt circle in the middle of the field. And the booing rose to a crescendo. I didn't know what it all meant, but it couldn't be good for Doug or Dougie or Twitchy or whatever his name was.

It pissed me off. The brown-socked loudmouth above me was whining like he'd lost some money. It took all my willpower to not bite his flabby ankle and give him something to cry about.

I learned something else that day: Baseball fans are fickle. My pitcher friend hadn't been out there two minutes before the booing stopped. The brown-socked dork above me spoke for the crowd.

"Damn," he said. "Twitchy's throwing strikes!"

"Another K! Give it to 'em, Dougie!"

"C'mon, Blue! That was right there!"

"One more … one more… Yeah! Miners win! Let's go get some brewskis. Man, that dude can *pitch*, when he's on the plate."

The bleachers drummed as the fans clambered down, happy and loud. Rass picked that moment to wake up and start wailing.

"Shhh! Quiet," I said. "You want to blow our cover?"

Rass shut up and cowered behind a post, which couldn't hide him, his fur being all perpendicular. He was puffed up like a blowfish.

"How'd you like it if half those idiots up there came down here, looking for us?" I hissed in his ear. "Keep it down. They'll be gone in a minute."

"This place is too crazy, Doo Doo."

"Maybe so," I said. "But we've been eating pretty good since we got here, haven't we? I want to stick around a while. You want to go, go."

Rass whimpered and stayed put. I don't know what it was about the guy that made me be so hard on him, but I always felt bad afterwards. I gave him a few licks on his neck, soothing down his fright-wig fur.

"See?" I purred. "They're going now. Want to get out of here and look around?"

"Well, uh, maybe. But not yet, okay? There's still too many people...."

"All right, Rass," I said, indulgently. "We'll hang here for a bit." And I didn't mind, really. There were cars starting and players barking and a grounds crew working the field. And all the excitement had made me tired.

When in doubt, take a nap. That's the Cat Manifesto. I needed to sort some things out. Like where I was going to go from here. And when. The kind of decisions a cat makes best at night.

Darkness comes late to Colorado in summer. It was only dusk when we ventured out from under the stands. A soft haze had settled on the grass, the air was still and humid. I couldn't be sure in the confusion of smells left over from the game, but from what I could see and hear, we were all alone in this big empty field. Yet the whole place felt ... how to describe this in terms a human can understand.... Safe. We were outdoors, but I felt like I was in someone's living room, or, better yet, big backyard. And not just someone— but *my* someone. Some kind of feline instinct made that place feel like *my* place, like I'd owned it so long I could take it for granted. I felt like I belonged here, like I was *wanted*.

Again, all this was only instinct. But my instincts were about to be confirmed.

CHAPTER 19

Food. Somebody had left us food—and I had a pretty good idea who "somebody" was. I found it while Rass was digging a crater on the dirt hill in the middle of the field, preparing to leave his calling card. Not wanting to invade his space while he went about his business, I wandered over towards the dugout where we had spent last night.

"Hey Rass. Take a look at this!"

The caver came trotting over, tail held high.

"Wow."

"Yeah. Did I tell you?"

"Mmfff!"

He was already nose-deep in the stuff. A huge pile of crumbled hamburger and scraps of fried fish, filling a big ceramic bowl almost to overflowing. It was enough food to feed ten hungry cats for a week. I dove in on the other side of the bowl, relishing the best tasting meal I'd had in months.

And there was something else—a scent—just sensible through the powerful food aromas, all over the outside of the bowl.

Doug. I could smell him, sure as anything. I was right. *He'd* brought us this feast. I purred like a diesel as I stuffed my happy face.

You'd think that getting so full would call for another nap, and you wouldn't be wrong, usually. But that big, empty stadium was like a playground, and we'd been cooped up all day. It was time for the crazies.

Rass and I hadn't had a romp like this since the park in New York, where we found the nip. And catnip was the only thing missing to make tonight perfect. Warm air, full moon, giant playground with convenient sandboxes and more food than we could eat. Hell yes.

I ran Rass ragged, all over that place. First he was "it," then I was "it," streaking the infield and outfield, up the grandstand and over the fences, climbing the mesh of the backstop and pouncing on each other, hiding behind the foul poles, the outfield signs, in and out of the dugouts. I forgot all about my quest, my home—I was having way too much fun, right here and now.

When we finally ran down Rass crawled back under the bleachers for a nap. I was still too keyed up, so I explored until I had a good mental picture of the place, inside and out. I found a ventilation duct that led into the musty clubhouse, nosed around, reached the trainer's room and took a drink out of a big metal tub that turned out to be a whirlpool. It tasted heavily of chlorine, but it was either that or the rusty toilets, and I have *some* standards.

I was still inside when the sleepies overtook me. It's never a good idea for a cat to corner himself—I should have gone back outside to sleep. But I was feeling carefree, and like I said, this place felt like mine, somehow. I nodded off on a padded bench in the weight room. I thought I could smell Doug here, and maybe I could, or maybe I just wanted to see him again. What I didn't know was that he had his own reasons for feeling the same way.

* * *

Have you ever heard a human wharf up a hairball? Neither had I, until that morning. Turns out every clubhouse has a "boy." This clubhouse boy happened to be, oh, about 70, but I didn't know that yet. I heard someone come rattling into the place, pushing what sounded like a laundry cart and smelling of aftershave, a particularly rancid variety. Before he hove into sight he paused, lit a cigarette ... and gagged up enough phlegm to drown a moose. He retched so hard I thought he was bringing up a beach ball. Scared the hell out of me. I fully expected to see an ogre, eight feet tall, with horns and a taste for cat blood, coming straight at me. I dived under the bench and prepared to meet my gargling doom.

What I found was a cherub. An old cherub, true, but the happiest-looking, weather-beaten, round old guy you can imagine. He was too busy to notice me— bustling around, stacking weights, folding towels, humming to himself in a voice like wet sandpaper. It made me feel silly—being so terrified by this happy grandpa. I was tempted to go rub up against his leg, just to get a contact high on his joy. But then I heard the door screech on its hinges again, and a voice I recognized barked out.

"Hey, Murf! Whatchya know?"

"That you, Twitch? Damn, you're up early!"

"I could barely sleep. I was so stoked, the way I threw yesterday. Hey, you haven't seen any cats around this morning, have you? Especially a good-looking orange one?"

Murf snorted like a foghorn on a drowning ship. "Friz told me about that. Nope, can't say I have. But I just got here."

"Well, lemme know, willya? Now, mind cranking up the tub for me? I have a hunch Gus might call my number again tonight."

"What, you stiff, you old goat? What'd you throw, like ten pitches yesterday?" Murf said, turning dials on the whirlpool, which rumbled noisily to life.

"Yup. Ten exactly. Ten strikes, too, though the ump missed one."

Doug rolled a stool to the tub's edge, stripped off his tee shirt, and dipped his knotty arm in the water.

"Yah!" He said. "This thing's freezing! Serves me right for getting here so early."

"Give it a minute." Murf regarded the pitcher through cheek-pinched, smiling eyes. "You still want it bad, don't you Doug? Must eat you up seeing the kids run through here, guys who can't carry your rosin bag, while you keep hacking away." Murf grabbed a broom and started raking the floor—one stroke got so close it almost swatted me. "Well," he continued, "from one old fart to another, I hope you make it. You keep throwing like you did yesterday and you'll be sending me postcards from the show. Now scoot that chair back, I gotta get under the tub."

Doug rolled the stool around the side of the whirlpool, never taking his arm from the water. He was only about six feet from me now.

"Let me know if you see that cat, Murf," he said as the clubhouse boy swept a pile of dust through the door. Murf answered "Glug," near as I could tell.

Now we were alone. I don't know why I hesitated; I really wanted to go to him. Yet I felt shy as a kitten. And there was something else, that pull of a faraway place I needed to go. I watched him as the water swirled over his arm, his head drooping forward, eyes closed. After a while his breathing steadied, like he was falling asleep. I could leave now, be on my way, and he'd never know I'd been here.

I stepped out from under the bench, walked over to Doug's stool. His face was turned, I was behind his right shoulder. I watched him peacefully soaking, then started to sidle away. As I passed him, I paused and took a last look good-bye. I was so close I had to crane my neck straight up. And then, to my complete surprise, a tight meow forced its way past my throat.

Doug's eyes opened and he scanned the room without seeing me.

"Lucky?" he said. "Is that you, Lucky?"

He looked so funny, blinking awake and looking everywhere but down. Right here, I was about to say, I'm right here. But instead, I leapt into his lap, landing so softly that he never even twitched, despite his name.

"Lucky!" he said. "How you doing, boy?" His big paw ran across my back, starting my motor. I tiptoed in his lap, rubbed my side against his belly, staggering with glee. "You found *me*." He said with wonder. "You found me...."

I propped up with my feet in his lap and my paws on his chest. My claws combed his fur tenderly as I kneaded him like my momma's belly.

* * *

They did call Doug's number that night, and he pitched a perfect inning again. That clinched it. I was now officially a mascot, the source of one Douglas Twitchell's newfound control and the Miners' first two-game winning streak in a month. But before that happened I had a dizzying day in the clubhouse and on the field. Never had I attracted so much attention in my life.

It got to be *too* much, what with all the large humans galumphing around and either making too big a fuss over me or totally ignoring me, depending on whether or not they were cat people. I stuck close to my pitcher friend most of the afternoon. Later on, after yet another ample meal—steak this time—I realized I hadn't seen Rass since last night. I wondered if he'd wandered off, or gotten himself into some kind of trouble. I got a case of the guilts, imagining him trapped by dogs or lunch for a coyote. So off I went, on a Rass hunt.

I must have spent an hour at it. The first place I thought to look was under the bleachers where I'd left him. No sign. I covered the field and the stands from one end to the other—even picked up his scent a couple of times, which was reassuring—but I never saw him. Still, he must be around here somewhere; worrying about it wasn't going to help. So when the sun got low and shadows spread over the field, and I heard Doug's voice calling, "Lucky. Hey Luckeee!" I trotted over to the dugout with an almost clear conscience.

"I don't want you out here during batting practice," Doug said, picking me up and tossing my front paws over his shoulder. "We're gonna go inside."

Now, I usually don't like being manhandled like that. But the move Doug made was exactly like the one Doc used when he wanted to carry me around. Like Doc, Doug is a big, solid guy. Too tall for comfort, perhaps, but rock steady. Cats like the high view; it was fun seeing the world from six feet up. Even if I did get petted by about ten ham-fisted strangers on the way to the clubhouse—my poor head dribbled like a basketball under those passing hands.

I'm going to let you in on a secret. Cats can read human intentions. We especially know what you're trying to do for us.

Did you ever wonder how your little Precious knows that throw pillow is meant for her? Or why the corner you set up for us near the heat vent seems to suit us just perfectly?

It's because we know. And as long as you do a good job and don't try to pawn off the rankest blanket in the worst room of the house (in which case we pee on your sweaters) we'll use it. Because we know it makes you happy. Like Doug was now.

Do I know cat people or do I know cat people! That's what ran through my head when I saw the spot

Doug had prepared for me. Or perhaps I should say spots: on the floor of his locker was a litter box, food and water dish—thoughtful but nothing special. The real treat was up on the shelf above his clothes.

He made me a nook, way up high. There was a bed made of some kind of delicious fluffy stuff, like soft shag over foam rubber, a ball of yarn in the corner, and, the piece de resistance, a cylindrical scratching post with a toy dangling from a spring at the top. A *catnip* toy.

Credit where credit is due—Doug hadn't pitched yet that day. He didn't know if the magic would hold. But he set me up in his locker like a king. I climbed off his shoulder into the bed, rubbing my face against his fingers for luck.

"See you in a few hours, Lucky. Don't go nowhere."

Don't worry, big guy. For once I wished he could read my meow. It said, "Go get 'em."

* * *

Doc used to say you had to have a lot of kid in you to play baseball. He would have loved what I saw that night. Players had been filtering in and out of the locker room during the game, but quietly, with concentration on their faces. Then I heard the muffled roar of the crowd outside, sounding just like it did yesterday. A minute later the team came jiving into the clubhouse, stripping for their showers, yakking it up. Someone turned on a boom box loud, and the voices rose higher as they shouted over it.

"Did you see Friz run? Man! Size fourteens kicking up clods all the way to the bag!"

"For *days*. I thought he'd never get there!"

"Yeah, Frizzie, how much you pay Contreras to boot that ball? He a homie of yours or something?"

"Doan laugh," the catcher said. "Eighth inning an my legs feel like elephan's foot. I doan make first Ritso doan score and we *still* out there."

"Dougie don't go one two three in the ninth and ditto," said a tall black player. "And I got a date tonight."

Another black guy, this one pot bellied, grizzled and gray haired, said, "Just make sure you get her in the sack by midnight, hot shot. Tomorrow's a day game and I expect to see you here ready to kick ass and take names by ten. That goes for the rest of you, too. We're still three under five hundred. So go enjoy yourselves real fast and get some sleep."

A chorus of "Okay, Skip … You got it Gus ... Yes Mommy…." trailed behind the manager as he made his way out.

I was watching all this in a happy catnip haze, my first in forever. So I wasn't exactly ready for what came next. Doug marched to the locker, tossed his glove on the shelf next to me, grabbed me in his big sweaty hands and swung me around, displaying me to the team.

"Gentlemen and hitters!" he announced. "Allow me to present Lucky O'Cat. The O stands for orange. The Lucky stands for the fact that I haven't thrown a bad ball since I found him, and we ain't lost either. You may pet him if he approves. But mess with him and you mess with me."

Doug bowed so low my paws almost hit the ground. Then he placed me back up on my throne with a flourish. The response of the team made me understand the word catcall for the first time.

I was in a good enough mood that I enjoyed the pets and pats and tobacco-breath coos I got over the next half hour. But when it was over I was ready for it to be over. Plus I had to use the litter box and I don't like an audience for that. So, I figured I'd take a stroll outside to do my thing, and also take another shot at finding Rass. Where *was* that stupid cat?

I jumped down, doing a bank shot—from the shelf to the shoulders of Doug's uniform hanging below, then down to the hard floor.

Slick. But not slick enough—the hangers banged and clanged like an alarm. Before I could scramble away a freshly showered Doug grabbed me from behind.

"No you don't, buddy. Not now. We're going home."

"But Rass!" I howled.

Doug was unmoved by my protest. Next thing I know, I'm stuffed in a gym bag, mad as hell and making sure he knows it. Doug is going "shhhh" and laughing at the same time. Worst of all, I wasn't alone in the bag. My fellow passengers included sweaty gym socks, a funked-up tee shirt, gaggy shorts, and a ripe elastic thing the players call a cup for some reason that escapes me. I'm swinging and swaying in this dank mess and not liking it at all, as my suddenly brutish hero hauls bag and baggage out to the parking lot. Big swings, too, his arms were *long*. And me with a bladder so full I like to burst.

Screw it, he has it coming. I let loose a long, fragrant stream and felt much, much better. That bag had mesh ends so the stink juice came *flying* out of both sides, making Doug feel much, much worse.

"Oh Jesus!" he said, breaking into a trot.

He wasn't laughing anymore. But I was. You should have let me go outside, you big lunk.

CHAPTER 20

Every single day for the next week, back and forth, back and forth. To the ballpark early, back home late—that was my life. And no Rass. After a couple of days even his scent was gone from the stadium. I began to forget about him—forgive me, I'm only a cat. I had other things on my mind.

Like my new "house," for example. The best thing about it was how close it was to the ballpark. Only five minutes—though in Doug's rattletrap pickup that was long enough. The worst thing about it was that it wasn't a house at all. It was a cheap, crummy apartment.

As you know by now, I've lived in cheap, crummy apartments before, worse than this one. This one was "suburban" and it had a balcony. And, though it was on the third and top floor, it wasn't so high that I couldn't jump down and split, worse come to worst.

The worst was some of the friends Doug had over. The ballplayers were okay, mostly. Even when they were boozed-up, their respect for Doug, the oldest among them, kept them within bounds.

But the hangers-on and townies they partied with could be real jerks. Some of those farm boys took an unromantic view of animals in general, and this one in particular. Even some of their womenfolk shooed me off the couch—*my* couch—when they sat down.

One total jagoff poured beer in my water dish for yucks. After getting my tail pulled and toes stepped on one too many times, I learned to make myself invisible when the joint got crowded. And it got crowded damn near every night. Once the place cleared out I'd go to sleep on Doug's pillow, unless I was real pissed off, in which case I'd hide and let him worry for half an hour—then I'd go to sleep on his pillow.

If I was lucky, I'd get a few short hours of quiet before it was time to go to the ballpark and be with a zillion people again. People, people, people—back and forth, forth and back. It made my head spin. Doug was a sweetheart and fed me great and soon learned—and indulged—my taste for catnip, but the pace was making me wacky. Is it any wonder that after about three futile days of looking, Rass began to fade from my mind?

The Miners were rocking. They were 7-1 since I showed up, and Doug hadn't pitched in the one game they lost. He was a perfect 4 for 4 in his save opportunities in that stretch, and best of all, as he never tired of telling anyone who would listen—including me—he hadn't walked anybody in all that time.

No one could accuse Doug of being a braggart. He'd been around far too long for that. From what I picked up from his conversations with Murf, he'd always had the talent, the fastball, and the head for the game. What he never had before was consistency; sometimes his control would desert him and he'd get wild when the pressure was on. Murf said the only thing holding Doug back was his nerves, and that it wasn't luck I was bringing him. It was calm.

I didn't think of it that way. What I thought I brought to our "partnership" was *cool*. You know I'm pretty cool, don't you? If I haven't gotten that across, I haven't been telling the story right. I'm cool. And yes, I *am* bragging.

And, despite the modesty kicked into him by ten years of falling just short of good enough, so was Doug. Not about himself, about *me*. He bragged about me and he bragged about the effect I was having on his game—to his teammates, to the other team, to the clubhouse boy, to the manager, to anyone who would listen. He made a big deal about our rituals—how I'd rub his fingers for luck before every game, how he'd feed me shrimp after every save (he discreetly left out my catnip rewards), how petting me helped keep his mind clear and focused. He talked so much that, finally, word got out.

* * *

"Gus wants me to do an interview, Murf," Doug said one evening after a day game. He'd stayed around after to do some leg work and soak in the tub.

"That's great," Murf said.

"No it ain't."

"Why not?" Murf asked. "Be good for you to get a little ink, wouldn't it?"

"Me, yeah. But it's not just me they're interested in. And it ain't ink. It's TV. They want to know all about Lucky here."

I perked up hearing my name. I was in the middle of a lick frenzy, grooming myself tail to toes—and I needed it, too. Just a word to the wise for you cat folks out there: never pet your pet with rosin on your hands. The taste made my tongue curl up like a soda straw.

"TV? You mean that sports idiot they got over channel 36?" Murf gargled a laugh. "He don't know enough baseball to trip you up, Doug. The guy thinks a blown save is something you do with a broad. And what's so bad about Lucky getting some attention? He's about all you talk about lately."

Then Doug did something I'd never seen him do before. He tried to keep something from me. Ineptly, true—he underestimated my hearing—but he still tried. Crooking a finger at Murf, he called him over and whispered.

"But what if he's ... you know ...somebody's? And they recognize him on the tube? Hell, I could *lose* him."

Murf stopped the line of tobacco juice he was drooling into a paper cup and whistled a brown spray. "Whew.... I never thought of that."

Doug kept whispering, "I don't know what to do, Murf. I can't say no to the boss...."

Murf looked straight at me with a corn-colored grin. "Maybe you can paint him black or something."

"Shhh!" Doug hissed. "It's like he *knows* stuff."

"Well then, don't sweat it. Maybe you'll be lucky. That is his name, ain't it?"

"Yeah well, there is one thing."

"Whazzat?"

"It's not the sports guy. It's Kimberley Jinks."

"It's who?"

"Kimberley Jinks. Don't you watch TV?"

"Wrestling sometimes."

"She's death, Murf. Total death."

"Is that good?"

"Oh yeah."

* * *

I'm no judge of human female beauty. But even I could tell this woman was something special, by the way everyone around her acted.

Now personally, I'll take a nice sexy Siamese every time, even if they never shut up. And this Kimberley woman was a lot like that. Pale, slinky, regal, and a voice that said "I love you" with every honeyed word. Doug was trying his best not to pant in her face.

"Is that him?" She asked, pointing over his shoulder towards me on my perch. The crew was setting up lights and wires in the other corner of the room. Doug nodded and Kimberley marched right past him like she owned the place.

"Oh, he's *darling*!" she gushed. "Can I pet him?"

"Sure!" Doug beamed. He would have said the same thing if she'd asked "Can I eat him?"

I shrank away as the little goddess reached for me. The top of her head barely reached my shelf. She turned back towards Doug and shrugged.

"Oh, sorry," he said like he'd stepped on her foot. "Allow me."

If I could have backed right through the wall I would have. The way Doug was acting gave me the creeps. But there was nothing I could do, other than bite his nose off, and he didn't have that coming—yet.

Sweaty hands wrapped around my trunk as my eyes burned holes in his made-up-for-TV face. He held me out to the reporter like a diamond ring.

"Go ahead," he said.

I hated everything about this moment. The crew, the lights, the girl, the way Doug was behaving. And then she touched me.

There are some things you can't fake. If cats know anything about people, we know that. Kimberley Jinks, who seemed as false as a rubber doll, ran her perfectly manicured hands over my head—and turned into a six year old girl. She *meant* it.

After a moment that went by like slow motion, she spoke to Doug, and I swear, her eyes were shiny and damp.

"There's something … He's kind of … special."

"Yeah," Doug said ruefully, like he was a little jealous. "I know."

Kimberley shook herself like she was coming out of a spell. "Well," she said, "are you ready?"

Doug was ready all right, but not for what she had in mind. He looked at her, perplexed.

"The interview?" she said. "Guys," turning towards her crew, "all set?"

* * *

I couldn't keep my eyes off her. Every word she spoke, even in her fake TV voice, called to me like a song. But those lights! It was like staring at the sun. I was in Doug's lap, his hands stroking me nervously as he answered her questions.

"...baseball players are famously superstitious, some of them eat chicken every night, some won't change their clothes as long as they're winning. Is that what's happening with you and Lucky?"

"Well, kinda," Doug answered. "But it's more than that. I mean, I'm as superstitious as the next guy, and we do have our little rituals. But something about little Lucky here," he chucked me under the chin, "helps me stay focused. It's like he keeps me calm, and keeping calm helps me get fired up. You know what I mean?"

"Not really," said Kimberley. "But yes, in a way...." Her voice was different then, not her TV voice at all. I stole a painful glance at her. She was leaning forward, staring at me. The lights had my eyes slitted so tight I saw haloes around her golden head.

"Let's try that again, Douglas," she said.

Douglas. My pitcher swallowed heavily, licked his lips, and croaked out some words.

This went on for an eternity. The heat had me mouth-open dizzy, panting in Doug's lap. I'll never understand why people love being on TV so much. To me it seemed like torture.

"So, do you have any idea where he came from?"

"No," Doug answered. "They just showed up last week, after the storm."

"They?"

"Yeah, there were two of them. The other one was a runt, and real skittish. He disappeared after a day or two. Haven't seen him since."

"That's a shame," Kimberley said. "Why don't you tell us what he looked like, in case someone is looking for him?"

Doug stiffened, that was the question he'd been dreading. He stammered through a bad description of Rass, like he was afraid we'd both be claimed if someone recognized him. But he was a lousy liar and only changed a few details, like calling Rass black instead of dark gray. I guess to him a lie wasn't so bad if you only cheated around the edges. I could feel his discomfort in his hands. But then it was over.

"Okay," Kimberley said. "I think we have enough."

The lights went out and the crew started wrapping up their equipment. It felt like I'd been trapped in an oven and somebody just opened the door. Doug put me on the ground.

"Was that good?" he asked her.

"It was fine," she said, coming over to shake his hand. I was on my way back to the locker, but I stopped to look at her as she drew close. She noticed, and for a moment we made eye contact.

"Sorry if I was a little nervous," Doug apologized.

"You were fine," she repeated. "Lots of people get jumpy first time on camera."

"I can tell you're not a sports reporter," Doug said, smiling. "I've been on lots of times. Even in the minors baseball players are news, you know."

I don't think Kimberley liked that. Up till then, she seemed interested in Doug, maybe more than as just another interview. But now she turned reporter on him.

"Well then," she said, "why *were* you nervous?"

Busted! I thought. But then the bad liar got out of his fix by telling another truth.

"I guess I'm worried," he said. "I'm going on the road after Sunday's game, and I can't take him with me."

Kimberley softened at that. "Are you afraid your luck will change if Lucky's not there?"

"Well, sure. But that's not all. I'm worried about *him.* The whole team's traveling. I guess I'll have to get a cat sitter, and I don't know if he'll like that. Maybe he'll think I've deserted him and he'll run away."

Kimberley squatted down beside me, gently scratching my back with her long nails.

"You know, Doug," she cooed, "if you can't find someone, I'd love to watch him for you."

Doug knew an "in" when he heard one.

"You would? That would be great!"

Kimberley never even looked at him. "I'd be happy to," she said to me. "You'd like that, wouldn't you Lucky?"

No, I thought. But my damned purr sold me out again.

CHAPTER 21

It wasn't so bad, really. No more crappy apartment, no more obnoxious rubes that hung around Doug's place. Kimberley lived in splendid isolation, in a rambling house that felt like a mansion to me, way on the outskirts of what the locals were vain enough to call "town."

And she pampered me like a baby, feeding me people food right out of her silky hands. This was the plush life, I never had it so soft. But for all the silky words and silky beds and silky purr-fests in her silky lap, a rough-edged restlessness began clawing at me.

It started with boredom. Kimberley was never home. She left early for work and came home late and exhausted. What energy she had when she *got* home she gave to me, but an hour after we ate our late dinner (and what she ate, *I* ate) she was passed out in her oversized bed and the house would go dead quiet. It was just the opposite of Doug's pad, this place was placid as a tomb. And her tired vibe was contagious as a yawn. The temptation to curl up on the pillow and cocoon in her golden hair was overwhelming—but she was squeamish about it. She'd pick me up gently and deposit me at her ankles with a wag of her head and a tut tut tut. No, Lucky. We don't do that.

In fact there were "rules" all over the place. Don't scratch this, don't go there, don't get fur on that. Anyone else said "no, no, no" to me that much I'd crap on their rug. But she said it in that voice, and her eyes glowed like I was her firstborn. So I put up with it—on those rare occasions when she was around—and passed a reasonably contented few days in a gilded cage.

But it couldn't last. It wasn't long before I was feeling claustrophobic and antsy. It wouldn't have been so bad if there was a cat door or some other easy way out of that air conditioned prison, but there wasn't.

So I gave myself a task, find a way outside. There never was a place I couldn't escape from, this big house should be easy. But Kimberley was a door locker, a cabinet closer, a window shutter. Her place was locked down tight; when she was gone my "run" consisted of the living room and kitchen. And I couldn't find any way outside from there.

When she was home I could go pretty much anywhere, but I still couldn't find an open door or cracked window, not even a vent I could crawl through. For a couple of days I was stymied.

Okay, where stealth doesn't work, loud annoying caterwauling might. I started giving out "hints," like clawing the front door and hopping on the windowsill. She ignored me; when I kept at it she'd pick me up and pet me like a colicky baby. When that stopped working she'd hand-feed me tuna. When I got wise to that trick, she'd carry me into the bedroom and cuddle. That worked until she was asleep. Then I'd jump down and do laps—up on the bed, breathing right into her face, touching her nose with a paw, jumping off when she shooed me, then doing the whole circuit again. After a few hours of that she'd lock me in the guest bathroom with food and the litter box. She couldn't hear me from there.

For all her softness, Kimberley had a steely will. But I don't give up. There's no telling how long our stalemate would have lasted if Doug hadn't called her from the road to see how I was doing.

Okay, maybe that wasn't the *only* reason he called. Kimberley's tired "hello" turned perky when she realized it was Doug on the line.

"Yes! How *are* you?

"I know, I asked Gary, our sports anchor, he said you had a rough outing. Are you okay?

"Oh, I'm sure you'll figure it out.

"Me too! I'm looking forward to it. When will you be back?

"Great.

"Oh, Lucky's doing fine. We're getting along famously. He's such a dear. One thing though, he really seems to want to go outside. But I'm afraid he might run away. What do you think?

"Are you sure?

"Of course I could. I'll take him out back and stay with him. I'll be careful.

"How nice! But really, Douglas, you don't have to do that.

"Well then, I'd love to. I'm putting it down right now, dinner next Sunday at eight.

"You take care of yourself, Douglas. Next time you pitch, imagine you're petting Lucky. I'll do it for you.

"I sure will, bye bye now."

Kimberley put the phone back on the nightstand and reached for me. I was curled up at the foot of the bed.

"Douglas says hi," she said to me, patting my backside. "He misses you. And he says it's all right for us to go outside! We'll do it tomorrow, okay boy?"

Gotchya!

I don't think Kimberley took many days off; she was always dressed and out early in the week or so I'd been with her. But that next morning she slept late and came out of her bedroom wearing sweat clothes and the most relaxed expression I'd ever seen on her face. I don't think she even had any makeup on; she looked like a kid.

After feeding me and making herself a giant mug of coffee, into which she stirred an ice cube so she could gulp it down faster, she gathered me into her arms and took me to a room I hadn't seen before, a spare bedroom, I think.

Thick drapes ran across one wall, the whole room was in darkness, until she pulled the cord. Light blasted into there like that day she interviewed Doug, the entire back wall was glass. She rolled open a patio door open and we were out. Fresh air at last.

"Now you be a good boy and stay close, okay?" she told me.

Absolutely, Toots. She sat on a lawn chair, legs propped up on another, and watched me, the morning paper resting unread on her lap. Those blue eyes said, "don't disappoint me, now" and I had no intention of doing so. Not "now."

You know how people always talk about Fort Knox when they mean a place that's buttoned up tight as a choke collar? Well, I only half understand what they mean, never having been there myself, but if it's as cat-proof as Kimberley's backyard I could stash a year's worth of catnip there and still sleep like a kitten.

She's a local celebrity, I guess that explained it, that and being a pretty woman all alone way out here. But I'd never seen redwood fencing ten feet tall before. No brush was allowed to grow anywhere near the base, no trees overhung the top. "Stay close"? What choice did I have?

Well, some. But it could take me a while to find it. She needed to trust me enough to leave me alone outside. If I could get her to do that, I'd figure out something, I just needed time. Meanwhile I nosed around casually, getting the lay of the land.

It was a large yard, maybe an acre or so, and whenever I wandered too far from the patio Kimberley rattled her newspaper and called me. I wouldn't give her the satisfaction of coming to her, but if I didn't at least stop where I was she'd get up and haul me back. Every time I got fifty feet away, there'd be that "no, no, no" again. Sweet voice or not, she was working my nerves.

Play it smart, Doo Doo, I told myself. I not only needed to find a way out, but a way back in again. I had no intention of running away, yet. But I'd be damned if I'd let myself be turned into a house pet, begging for master to let me out once a week. Kimberley, however, needed to think exactly that if I was going to be left out here alone. So I stopped my wandering, after spraying one of her shrubs for spite, curled up at her feet and tried to fall asleep. It was hard; I was frustrated. Must have been all of ninety seconds before I could drift off.

That first session lasted maybe an hour. Next day she worked, and I only got out for a few minutes of twilight. The third time was the charm, because by then I knew something.

It wasn't going to be easy. She'd have to leave me alone, or at the very least be seriously distracted for me to pull it off. But it was doable—if you're a world-class feline acrobat, like your humble storyteller.

Here's the shorthand of the thing—sloping roof, drain pipe, trellis, patio. That's the way I saw it—in reverse, top down. Luckily, the rosebush climbing the white-painted trellis was scraggly and half dead. If I couldn't avoid the thorns, at least I could see them. The big challenge would come at the top of the lattice. It was hooked up to a downspout that connected to the rain gutter at the edge of the roof, but it was short by a yard or more. I'd have to rear up on the X-shaped top of the trellis and somehow reach the gutter with my front claws. If I could do that, I'd be home free. Except for the little matter of being stuck on a twenty-foot roof with no idea what was on the other side or how to get down.

I was sort of surprised she took me out at all, that day. Kimberley came home early enough, mid-afternoon, I'd guess, but the weather was unsettled. When it wasn't storming, those Colorado high plains were always hot and dry the summer I was there. But today was hot and dry and gusty, a whippy kind of wind that couldn't seem to make up its mind which direction to blow, and hazy dust uglied an otherwise clear sky. Not a day for a pleasant drink on the patio. But nonetheless, once she got changed she yielded to my hints and came outside with me, just because I'd been so good.

We'd been out there ten minutes. I'd walked my circuit and peed on my bush, edging close to the rose trellis for a quick look on my way back to her feet and nap time, when the doorbell rang.

This was what I was waiting for—the Moment of Truth. But I didn't twitch a whisker. I sure *looked* asleep, but would she fall for it?

Yup. She didn't say "stay" or anything. Just waggled her narrow butt through the patio door and disappeared into the house. I counted five seconds.

I wish I had a video to show you; my next move was a gymnastic work of art. Two running steps on the concrete, up about five feet of trellis in a single bound, picking my way through the thorns to the top without getting the tiniest pinprick, then to the serrated edge, pausing for a tottering moment—my only shaky one—and finally a vertical hop so well judged I barely touched the rain gutters on the way to the roof. Sweet.

I did a quick scuttle around the roof, looking for the best way down. The walls on the back and sides of the house were sheer. The easiest jump was out front, where there was a nine-foot drop to the front door awning, then maybe another eight to the ground. I found it in time to hear Kimberley shut the door as a big brown truck crunched down the driveway. I had about fifteen seconds before she got back to the yard. For some stupid reason, I hesitated. I'm a cat; we do that.

"Lucky? Luukeeee!" Her shrill voice, burbling on the gusty air, gave me the kick in the rear that I needed.

Hop. Leap. Down. Gone.

This wasn't farmland around here. Kimberley's place was close to the foothills, in a cul-de-sac of big homes and long, gravel driveways. Her house had large picture windows that looked down on the agricultural valley below, with planting boxes where the sills should be. I put that in memory for my return trip. If I couldn't find another way back in, I'd get her attention jumping there and clawing the glass.

But for now, I just wanted to put a little distance between us. I curled around the homes towards the hills behind, in the direction of the afternoon sun. No grass grew past the fenced yards of those houses, only scrub and stunted bushes and dirt. Lots and lots of dirt.

Her voice trailed me in snatches when the wind blew my way, until I climbed a weedy rise and down into a mini-canyon that looked like a dry creek bed—and that cut me off. I was well and truly hid. Time to explore.

I had no intention of going too far, but this place was fascinating! The wash was deep enough to protect me from the worst of the wind, though I did get a snoot full of dust from time to time. But for a place that looked like a desert, it was crawling with life. Shiny bugs as big as a human thumb, with shells that looked like metal, nasty lobster-like things that I gave a wide berth, clouds of gnats dark as the blowing sand, that, fortunately, didn't bite. And lizards, about five different kinds, some as small as salamanders, some almost as big as me, if you count their skinny tails. The place was like a petting zoo for house cats, but petting wasn't on my agenda. I thought of it more as a game preserve, but I don't want to offend your ecological sensitivities. Suffice it to say that I frolicked. And that I wound up much further away than I planned when I made the Big Leap.

The farther I went up the wash, the stranger it got. Black streaks of crunchy dirt ran across the sandy bottom, a heavy, glossy stain, no thicker than a crust. The stuff clung to my paws and wouldn't shake off. When I tried licking it, I got a mouth full of foul, metallic salt. The mineral seemed to be coming from the hills above, firing my already piqued curiosity. I was already further than I wanted to be; a few more yards wouldn't hurt.

The wash took a hard jog to the right and there was my answer. Piles of the black stuff, on both sides of a cut in the banks. And through that cut, a wasteland. Torn earth, steep walls, huge gouges deep in the side of the hill, rusting machinery, toxic potholes—an abandoned mine.

I stepped up to the rim of that quarry and the wind was ferocious. Blasts of sand and the metallic stuff they'd mined there blew into my eyes, so thick I could taste it. I could either go down into that deep hole, or turn around and go home. If you can call Kimberley's igloo a home.

All my life I never could stop following my nose. It is, after all, the first thing on my face. So down the gulch I went, to see what I could see. Once I dropped past the lip, I was protected from the gales, and as I got to the bottom, strange smells came to me. Stagnant water pooled in potholes on the quarry floor, abandoned machinery dripped oil from broken axles, rubber tires steamed in the sun, plastic bubbled on the cracked seats of crippled tractors, a symphony of ruins and waste. And, as if to drive home the point, nothing moved here, it was all dead. That zoo in the wash a hundred yards away might just as well have been on the other side of the world. Nothing lived here, nothing *could* live here.

So why did I smell … Rass?

CHAPTER 22

Caves. Of *course*. Where else would he be? But how could he survive here? Was my nose fooling me? I couldn't tell in this chemical stew if his scent was fresh or old. Was he still here? Was he alive?

Only one way to find out—my trip home would have to wait. The problem was there were too many places to check, so many holes and nooks in this enormous dig, it could take all day. The easiest way would be to start screaming, but I wouldn't do that. Not after our last reunion at the baseball field when I cried like a baby. This time *I* wasn't lost.

The next couple of hours was a filthy, grinding, fruitless bore. I'll spare you the details—it was just one smelly, empty hole after the next. And while I did catch Rass's scent from time to time, pretty much confirming that he'd been here, I never saw snout nor whisker of the boy.

It was getting late; I decided to quit. I could always come back another day—if Kimberley didn't cage me after pulling this stunt. Plus, I was used to food on demand lately, and I was getting hungry for something more substantial than lizard. I turned around to go, feeling frustrated and guilty.

And then—what the hell—I let out a two-county shout.

"MEOWWWRRR!"

It came back to me three times, bouncing off the walls of the big cut. When the reverberations died, I held still and listened. All I heard was the whistling wind whipping the sand into streamers. But at least I tried. I started up the hole, back the way I came.

Halfway to the top, out of the corner of my eye, I thought I saw a shadow moving on the right side of the rim. The quarry floor was darkened now, the sun on the lip low and blinding. I stared up there and all I saw was glare.

This was not good. If that was me on top there, stalking my prey, I'd have the sun at my back too. I already knew about the coyotes hereabouts, and I was sure I could deal with one of them, maybe two. But coyotes travel in packs. The hair on my back bristled and my heart started pumping overtime. My little day trip was turning scary.

Fear got my mind working, I had a tactical decision to make. I could stay down here until nightfall, when the darkness would give me an edge, but it would cost me being passive for hours. Another option was to slide to the left, away from that shadow, up the other side of the hill, but then I'd have my back to the trouble. Or I could get low, snake my way up close, then fly straight at whatever was lurking there—if I wasn't imagining things.

You should know me well enough by now to know what my choice was. Right into the jaws, baby. And those jaws better be sharp, because once I topped that hill, I was going in with twenty razors.

Lesson One in quarry warfare: You cannot charge up a 45-degree slope in loose sand. You can *try*, but all you'll do is dig a hole. For about two seconds there I was going *backwards*, before I gave it up as a bad job, stopped my thrashing legs and walked—hell, crawled—to the crest. If there *were* coyotes up there they'd have had time to call a convention, finish their afternoon meetings and dress for dinner—tonight's special, cat on the hoof—before I showed up.

But there were no coyotes. Near as I could tell, there was nothing. I must have seen a tumbleweed—or a ghost.

I didn't stop to puzzle about it. It was time to get home. The adrenaline slowly leached out of my body as I trotted around the quarter circle of rim between me and the two big piles of mine dump that marked the exit to the wash. Fatigue and a powerful, wind-whipped, chemical-salts-induced thirst ambushed me, filling the hole where my fear was. Kimberley's air-conditioned jail was looking real good to me now. That's where my mind was as I started down the cut to the wash—back in her place, getting royally pampered, fed and brushed. So I almost didn't notice the little murmur of earth crunching behind me. Until I heard it again. I turned around to take a look.

"Doo Doo?" a voice croaked. "Is that you?"

Rass!

It was me all right, but *that* was Rass? A sorrier, more bedraggled, goggle-eyed, missing-tufted, mangy skeleton you never saw alive. Barely.

"Dude! What the hell happened to you?"

"I runned away."

"Tell me about it."

Rass took me literally. His tale of woe was pretty much what you'd expect from a subway cat alone on the high plains. He'd gotten spooked by all the people at the stadium, lost me in the confusion, wandered away, got chased by dogs, almost run over, found and lost my scent, got chased again, by coyotes this time, and finally wound up in the nearest hole he could find. This toxic dump.

"My teeth hurt, Doo Doo."

"You been drinking that water down there?"

"Yeah," Rass admitted. "Sometimes. When there was nothing else."

"What about food?"

"Bugs, mostly. I also caught one of those scaly things one time…"

"A lizard?"

"If you say so. Anyway, I got one, but there wasn't much to it, and I almost got trapped by those wild dogs…"

"Coyotes."

"Something. There was about five of them, is all I know. I had to run down my hole and hide for hours and hours. They wouldn't follow me in, but it took forever before they gave up and left. When I finally got out I didn't try to go up the hill again, until I saw you."

"What were you going to do, die down there?"

"I was *sure* I'd find something. There's caves all over the place here. But I couldn't find another way out and there was no mice or nothing. Just bugs, and they tasted terrible. Like metal."

"Why didn't you come when you saw me? I've been looking for you all day."

"I wasn't sure it was you, until I heard your voice. I'm not seeing so good lately. And anyway, look at you. You're all black!"

I checked myself out and saw that Rass was right. I was so covered with dirt I looked like a well-fed version of him.

"I hid," he continued, "until you made that noise. I thought it might be you, so I followed you to make sure."

We were walking slowly towards the wash as we talked. The cut got steeper on the way down, Rass stumbled.

"You okay?"

"Sorta," he said gamely.

"Think you can make a mile or two?"

"Oh man. I dunno. Why?"

"Follow me off this hill and I'll take you to the promised land."

"Food?" he croaked.

"All you can eat. Good clean water too. But you gotta help me get you there."

"I'll make it," Rass said, gathering his strength. "I never shoulda left you in the first place. But I got scared. I'm sorry, Doo Doo...."

"Save it. Now try to stay close. Never can tell what'll pop up out here once it gets dark."

Rass shambled alongside me, wobbly legged. When he came near, I could hear his purr. He'd make it all right. The runt was an idiot, sometimes, but you couldn't doubt his courage. Not around me you couldn't.

You'd think we had some luck coming, after all the little guy had been through. Or maybe the miracle of me finding him—when a day or two later would have been too late—was all the luck we were going to have today.

Rass was doing okay, head down and staggering, but making steady slow progress, when I felt an odd change in the wind. First it got real quiet. Quiet enough to hear something like a train whistle in the distance that came closer and got louder in a big hurry. A sudden gust slammed into the sagebrush on the wash's bank, tearing at the roots until it groaned, just an instant before the wind hit me. I had barely enough time to think "what the hell?" when I was knocked off my feet by a sucking swirl of sand. Surging blasts whipsawed violently through the wash, raising clouds of debris. I rolled along the ground, desperately trying to claw the earth, feeling like I was being vacuumed into the sky.

It couldn't have been a tornado. A tornado would have ended this story right here. It must have been a dust devil; I'd seen some before from Kimberley's window. But this one had to be the granddaddy of them all, because it damn near blew me away. And when it passed a few endless seconds later, and I opened my sandblasted eyes, I couldn't see Rass anywhere.

"Rass! (hack, cough) Hey Rass! You there, buddy?"

Silence.

Oh, no. Not after all this! I sniffed around frantically, but the earth was so churned up by the whirlwind that I couldn't smell a thing. It didn't help that my nose was as full of dirt as my eyes. And my ears were ringing something fierce, they felt like they'd been boxed by the pressure, as I strained to hear signs of life.

Nothing. All my senses came up empty. Hell.

I didn't know what to do next. My mind was running in circles and I was still dizzy from the twister. Where the hell could he be?

When logic fails, do something stupid, I always say. Maybe Rass had been blown over the bank and out of the wash? It was a silly idea—the dust devil hadn't pulled that hard—but I was out of smart ones. And I wasn't ready to give up on Rass just yet.

Sometimes being stupid is just the ticket. Especially if it makes you keep trying. I decided to take that look outside the wash and started up the bank. Right in my path was a big, toppled sagebrush. Rather than detouring around it, I jumped over the roots. When I landed, my back paws, carrying most of my weight, sank deeply into the loose sand—and hit something solid.

"Mrrwrrfff!"

I dug so fast I almost tore his tail off, but I got him uncovered in fifteen seconds. He had been blown against the bank and about a foot of earth broke off and fell on top of him—and that had almost been enough. Rass was too weak and disoriented to pull himself out. When I reached him, his paws were going feebly, but they were pointed down, digging him in deeper. I don't think he had two minutes left.

"Can you get up?" I asked him.

"Gimme … a … second."

I had to give him a lot more than that. It took him a while just to lift his face out of the sand. His breath came in hard, ragged gasps, like he was back on the subway tracks again, fleeing from a train. I could tell he was giving it all he had. The pelt twitched over his spiky backbone and his legs shimmied in quick jerks, but he was too weak to stand.

"Lay still," I said finally. I got beside him, set my paws as well as I could in the loose sand, locked my jaws around his ruff, and hauled back hard, really pouring on the muscle.

I almost threw him over my shoulders. The poor guy didn't weigh a thing. But I got him to his feet and held him there until his wobbly legs stopped shaking.

I let go of his neck and backed away, he swayed a bit but stayed upright.

"That's a way," I said encouragingly.

But when he looked at me, his eyes were filmy and discouraged.

"What now?" he wheezed.

"Think you can walk?"

"I'll … try."

One baby step. A long pause. Then another. A shorter pause, and another. Then he was walking, sort of. Like an old arthritic tom on his eighth and half life, but still, walking.

"Good boy."

It must have been midnight before we got off that hill. It was a slow, painful slog, but we made it. Yes, slog—did I mention that we got rained on? A real prairie cloudburst, too, almost as intense as the first deluge we'd encountered in this godforsaken place, weeks ago now.

Truth to tell, I didn't mind the rain all that much. It was over in fifteen minutes and I was so filthy it actually felt good.

My only worry was that the stream of water trickling down the wash threatened to turn into a torrent at any moment. I found a spot where the banks were low, hauled Rass out by the neck, and we lit off cross country. If two miles an hour qualifies as "lit."

You might wonder if I was worried about getting lost in this unfamiliar country. No. I don't *get* lost—least of all tonight. Dark and moonless though it was, I could always tell which direction led towards Kimberley's place. And well before I could see it, I could hear it—and what I heard was commotion.

"Hear that?" I asked Rass.

"Yeah, what is it?"

"That's where we're going."

"What's going on? Is it okay?"

"I think it's us. Or me, that is. I think she's looking for me."

"So what's with all the noise?" Rass asked, fear in his voice.

"I think she has help. Lots of help."

Rass turned a paw in the slick mud, groaning in pain.

"I'm scared, Doo Doo."

"Don't be. We're almost there."

"That's what I'm scared of."

"It'll be okay. Leave it to me."

"I … uh … I'll try, Doo Doo. You always know. But I'm scared anyway."

Finally we topped the last rise and there it was. Kimberley's neighborhood was crawling with people—and the light! She must have called some of her buddies from the station because there were TV lights all over the place, powered off a truck idling in her driveway. Rass meowed pitifully when he saw that tableau. I could only imagine how it must look to a cat who'd spent the last couple of weeks in a deserted quarry. It was intense enough to me.

I nudged him forward when he shied away from all the action.

"Come on, buddy," I said cheerily. "Time for us to make our entrance."

CHAPTER 23

"Over here!" a big guy with a foghorn voice bellowed.

They came at us, flashlights bobbing, like villagers about to torch the monster. Thirty seconds later we were surrounded. I got scooped up, spun around, and handed off to a very frazzled Kimberley who wasn't sure if she was angry or relieved.

"Bad boy! Where have you been! I was worried *sick*! Thank God, Douglas would have had my head...."

She was smothering me against her breasts, rocking me in her arms like a baby, babbling on and on as the whole scrum tripped down the hill towards her front door.

I was a little concerned about Rass. I'd lost sight of him when Kimberley grabbed me—I'd lost sight of *everything*, except human female bosom. Nobody was expecting *two* cats, and I was worried he might have gotten lost in the shuffle.

"Ouch! Sonovabitch bit me!" A random male voice proclaimed.

That stopped my worrying. It also got Kimberley's attention.

"Who did what?" she asked.

"Got my thumb," said the voice.

Kimberley turned to look. Rass was in the meaty grasp of some stagehand and neither party was happy with the arrangement.

"Put the light on him, Jimmy."

A flashlight played over the trembling, wild-eyed cat. Kimberley leaned forward and aimed me at Rass, holding me so tight I was considering biting *her*.

"Oh," she said. "That must be the other one! Look, Lucky, is this your friend? The one Douglas told me about?"

I don't ever want to hear any dumb blonde jokes. This girl caught on quick.

"Okay, everyone, let's bring them inside," she commanded.

Her Highness was obeyed and we all trooped into her palace. But the footmen weren't getting overtime.

"Uh Kim, can we go now?" the big-voiced guy asked her.

"Sure guys, absolutely. I guess it is kind of late. And thank you all *so* much!"

Two minutes later it was just the three of us, locked in her hall bathroom, muddy towels on the floor and crabmeat in the dish. Rass ate too fast and puked. I was still worried about him. He didn't look good. Kimberley sat on the toilet with a phone clamped to her ear.

"...yes, safe and sound. Wet and filthy, but just fine."

"Of course, tomorrow as soon as you get in. I'll be home. What did you say the other cat's name was? The black one? I think we've got him too."

"No, I will not call him *Un*-lucky," she giggled. "But he does look sick. I need to get a vet ASAP."

"I won't have to wait. I'll get someone tonight."

"How do you think, sweetie," (Sweetie!) "Don't you know?" she said in an arch voice, "I'm a *star* in this town."

She sure was. Within the hour Rass was getting the full treatment from some veterinarian Kimberley managed to drag out of bed. He was a big, rough-hewn dude, looked like he mostly dealt with sick cows. But he gave my ailing buddy about five shots and left enough pills and potions to cure a herd. Then the SOB asked Kimberley if I had *my* shots!

"I'm not sure," she said, "probably not."

"Well, just to be on the safe side, hold him down for me, Ms. Jinks."

One in the neck and two in the butt. Made me feel sick all night. I slept it off.

Doug came the next morning, bearing gifts. Flowers and a cheap looking turquoise necklace that Kimberley probably wouldn't be caught dead in outside the house, a couple of toy burlap sacks filled with catnip for me and Rass. I appreciated the gesture, and made the most of it. After a happy, roughhousing reunion I spent the rest of the morning tearing those sacks to shreds and buzzing merrily along. But Rass couldn't be bothered. All that boy did all day, and for the next several, was eat. Which would have been fine by me, except that the vet had scolded Kimberley about feeding us, especially Rass, people food. He said it wasn't "balanced," and left a bag of the rankest dry cat feed I ever refused to eat. That crap was balanced all right—midway between unappetizing and inedible. If I had hands I'd have balanced that bag on his head.

Doug confirmed that Rass was indeed the "other" cat, and that became his human name, "Othercat." Doug got down on the floor and was all over me for about fifteen minutes, rubbing me roughly, telling me how much he missed me, how glad he was to see me, how just petting me made his arm feel better (he called it his "soup bone"). But if I got fifteen minutes, Kimberley got all day.

This was fun to watch. Doug was still nervous around her. She made him a sandwich for lunch and his mouth was so dry he practically gagged on it. He washed it down with a couple of beers. That loosened him up some. They retired to the couch, sitting far away from each other to start with. She had her legs tucked under like a kid, he was sprawled against the other arm of the sofa. I was kind of hazy from the nip by then, but I watched, fascinated, as they slowly drew closer and closer together. Then there was no space between them at all.

Doug didn't go home that night. I spent most of it on the bed, after they stopped shooing me off and went to sleep. Rass curled up around his food bowl. We were one big happy family, for one night. The next morning it was time for three of us to go back to work.

I'd missed the ballpark and I'd missed the guys, especially Murf. I'd missed the green grass and having the run of the place and the hot sun and natural air.

I hadn't missed Doug's junker truck, and Kimberley's place was no five-minute drive from the park, either, more like half an hour. But it was worth it, for both of us. Doug was called in to close the game that first night back, and he pitched a perfect ninth. Everybody knew why, too. There was a party in the locker room afterwards and yours truly was the guest of honor and good luck charm. I have to admit, I enjoyed the attention and I enjoyed the chew toys and the nice fluffy pillow somebody stuck in my nook. The post-game steak that Doug cut up and put in my dish wasn't bad, either.

I was pretty proud of myself. Some cats got it and some cats don't. And that night it was just Doug and me back in his apartment, no Rass, no Kimberley, no teammates, no party. I slept on his head, like a hat.

This happy routine went on for a week. Game days at the park, some nights at Doug's, more nights at Kimberley's. Rass grew plump and frisky at an amazing rate. Kimberley lightened up enough to let us frolic in the yard, though she kept an eagle eye on me the whole time. And I could see her getting more and more attached to Rass. He was there all the time, and I think she felt proud of the progress he'd made under her care. She was still friendly enough to me, but I think she felt betrayed by my jail break—it was never quite the same between us after that. I didn't mind. I had Doug and the team and all the attention one cat could ever want. And more and more, it looked like Rass had finally found a home. So everybody was happy. I knew it couldn't last.

I'm not a big believer in coincidences. Most cats aren't. We can smell things in the wind before people can, usually. It's one of our famed survival instincts. And when you look carefully at the coincidence that follows, you'll see there really was a connection. Me and Rass.

It started after a day game on a hot, hazy, weekend afternoon. Doug never got into this one, the Miners were blown out early and things only got worse as the game wore on. Guys were coming into the locker room cursing and spitting and throwing stuff around. They'd been winning so much lately they'd forgotten how to lose. When it was finally over the players barely picked at the post-game spread, the usual boom box noise was missing. Doug sat at his locker with me on his lap.

Nobody was talking much, so when Murf, who was always in the same gruff good mood, win or lose, barked out, "Hey Dougie, Gus wants to see you in his office!" the whole team heard. And stared, for a second, before quickly looking away.

I swear, I could feel the jolt of electricity that shot through Doug's body when he heard those words. He put me back up on my shelf very gently and slowly; his strong hands trembled. If a cat didn't know any better, he'd have thought this was bad news. But I did know better, and so did everyone else in the room. Baseball is a very superstitious game; nobody said a word or looked at Doug as he left the locker room on his way to the manager's office. As soon as he was gone, though, the whispering started.

Doug's catcher, Friz, said out loud what everybody was thinking.

"Only be two theens—call upped or trade."

It was called up. As in, after ten years of frustration, finally getting his shot with the big club, the Major Leagues.

CHAPTER 24

He was *so* scared. Doug sat me on his lap as he sped up the hill to Kimberley's place, driving and talking a mile a minute.

"How am I going to *tell* her, Lucky? She's gonna freak! I mean, we just *started*, now I gotta go?"

I was whiplashed like a bobblehead as Doug took his angst out on the clutch. For about the thousandth time I wished I spoke human. "Relax," I would have said, "these things have a way of working out if they're supposed to." I sent those vibes his way—sometimes that helps. But not if the person is too far gone to listen.

"Can you believe this?" he laughed harshly, "Ten years I work and pray for this day, and when it finally happens it totally screws me up. Why I couldn't be a schoolteacher or something?" Doug crunched into fourth. "Nah, she'd never go for a schoolteacher ... Ow!"

I dug my claws into his thigh as he snapped us into a left turn.

"Easy, fella.... Not that she's a baseball Annie or anything. Just the opposite. Class all the way. Doesn't even know the game. And so beautiful! Really," he said ruefully, "I don't even know what she sees in me."

Doug wrapped his big mitt around my ruff as we banked into another turn.

"Help me out here Lucky. What am I supposed to do?"

We'd thumped into a pothole on his last word. The bounce made it come out in two syllables—it sounded like he'd called me Doo Doo.

Great. Now we *both* had something on our minds other than dinner. Unless the main course was a big steaming pile of longing, seasoned with regret. Thanks a lot, Dougie boy.

* * *

"So did I."

"What?"

"Me too. I got the call today too."

"Okay, now I'm *really* confused," Doug said.

"Come, let's sit down," Kimberley took him by the hand and pulled him to the couch. Rass was messing with my tail, pouncing on it, then taking a sideways hop, sneaking up on it, and pouncing again.

"Not now, dummy," I hissed at him. "I have to hear this."

"Sorry." Rass's contrition knew no ends since his recent, lamented misadventure. But he still had the attention span of a kitten with fleas. I figured he'd be messing with me again in about two minutes.

"The network people in Denver saw the spots I did about Lucky and Othercat, Douglas. They *loved* them. I'm supposed to go up there next week. If all goes well—and they told me the audition is just a formality—they want me full time, doing features and human interest stuff."

"Wow ... that's great!" Doug said, but his tone of voice told Kimberley it wasn't.

"What's wrong, honey?"

"Nothing ... I mean, well, that's fantastic news and all, I know how important this could be to your career, but I'm having a hard time picturing where we go from here. Me leaving, you probably leaving, what happens next?"

Kimberley leaned over and kissed him. Doug looked a little startled by it.

"You're sweet," she said.

"Huh?"

"Worrying about *us* instead of yourself, at a time like this. That's sweet."

"Us. I guess there *is* an us now." Doug smiled and seemed to relax for the first time since he got the big news. "Well baby," he said, spreading his arms wide, "how does it feel to have a major leaguer for a sweetheart?"

Kimberley grinned at him. "Hmm, I'm not sure. Why don't *you* tell *me?*"

Rass jumped my tail again. This time I jumped right back and it was off to the races.

Discipline broke down after the celebration. We had the "family bed" thing going. Doug and Kimberley under the covers, Rass and me above. She was usually too fastidious for that, but I guess we cats were the last thing on her mind this magical evening. Doug *did* have cats on his mind—he was stroking me idly as he listened to her enthuse—but he was finding it hard to get a word in edgewise. She was even more stoked about her prospects than he was.

"…not just an affiliate. The network *owns* the Denver station! I'd be working for them."

"That's great, baby."

"I just hope I'm up to it. Everyone around here thinks I'm Little Miss Confidence, but this is so—you know—huge!"

"You'll do fine. You've got too much talent for this burg—and so do I."

Kimberley got a sheepish look. "Oh, I guess I have been monopolizing the conversation," she said. "I'm sorry. I just take it for granted that you'll do well. But I *am* sure. I have faith in you."

"That means a lot, Kim. For real. But…" and here he started whispering again, "what about *them*?"

I perked up. Yeah, I thought, what *about* us?

"The cats?" she asked.

"The cats," Doug answered. "I'll be on the road, you'll be back and forth. What are we going to do about them?"

"Jeez. I hadn't thought about that."

Well you better start, Blondie. My purr cut off in mid-rumble.

Doug was packed and gone before sunrise. I followed him out to the kitchen, he fed me breakfast and nuzzled me before he left, smelling of girly shampoo and nervous energy.

"I'll see you in Denver, big guy," he said. "Wish me luck."

Good luck, Doug. What's a Denver? I jumped on the windowsill and watched the taillights of his truck disappear down the hill. I can't tell you why, but somehow I felt like that was goodbye forever. He was a good guy and he knew how to have fun. Some folks are just meant for cats, he was one of them. I missed him already.

But it was time to move. Ever since I thought he'd called me Doo Doo I'd been thinking of home again. It was far away, I knew that much, but I had no idea *how* far. Yet the idea of home was suddenly so close it was almost stifling. Maybe it was just the itch of wanderlust, to which, as you know by now, I'm pretty susceptible. Or maybe it was envy, seeing how happy Rass was with Kimberley. But that bright spot on the horizon, that place my homing instinct marked for me day or night, awake or sleeping, was pulling harder all the time. "Come on, Doo Doo," it said. "What are you waiting for?" I meowed the window, leaving a foggy spot on the glass pointing dead west.

I was pretty moody that day, though Kimberley was too busy to notice and Rass too happy to care. She left early for work but came home twice during the day, bustling around the house and talking into her cell phone. Rass followed her like a puppy as she got him food and gave him pills. The weather had turned nasty, a steady rain pelted the house under a dark, low sky. That blew my chances of getting outside, even to sit on the patio. I kept to myself, sitting on the windowsill looking at the bleak. It matched my mood perfectly.

If I'd have paid attention I would have noticed that Kimberley had brought home a couple of strange boxes with wire fronts and handles on top. Sometimes even *my* instincts fail me.

Come morning I paid the price. I was up early again, watching the sun break through a clearing sky, feeling restless as hell. Today's the day, I thought. But then came the detour.

Kimberley showed once again that she was no dummy. She knew if I saw her put Rass in one of those boxes she'd have to put on armor to snag me. And she also knew how anxious I was to get some fresh air.

"Hi Lucky boy! Does he want to go out on the patio?" she cutsied as she picked me up.

I was feeling hinky right away, but I didn't know what was up and she was too quick for me. I had just begun to squirm in her hands when she flipped the cat carrier on its end and arrowed me in, head first.

"Clang!" The gate swung shut.

Son of a *bitch*! What now?

Road trip, that's what. In the backseat of Kimberley's fancy car, soft music playing, the opening of my jail facing Rass's. The car was all comfort, smoothness and air conditioning. Even Rass wasn't scared, sitting quietly in his carrier, grooming.

Well, I could ruin the mood, if nothing else. I started screeching like we were going to the glue factory, if cats had glue. At first Kimberley was all, "shh, Lucky, it's okay." But then I got Rass excited and he joined in. Next thing you know it's a symphony of pain in there, and K is losing it, bit by bit.

"Quiet down! Both of you!"

"Screech. Wail."

"Shut up! God! We've got five hours to go!"

This was a gal who liked her comfort, but she wasn't getting any until I was tired of making her pay. That happened eventually, before we got to Denver, but not before she was scrabbling in her purse for the headache pills. When my throat got to hurting as much as her ears, I gave it a rest.

Sitting low on the back seat, I could only see a sliver of the world outside the carrier, but after a while I began to notice the tops of tall buildings through the side window. And even with the air conditioning I could smell city. I liked this. It was familiar and exciting. I had gotten free in cities before, I could do it again.

But we never stopped, we just kept on going until the buildings thinned out and the air got that country smell again. We turned off the freeway and climbed for a good fifteen minutes up a winding road. Then Kimberley stopped, got out of the car and left us inside, with the windows cracked a notch against the heat. The sounds of farm animals seeped through, and the smells too—like cow crap. What the hell was this?

"Hey Rass, you got any ideas where we might be?" I knew I was out to lunch, asking that of subway cat who spent half his life lost. But I thought maybe he'd picked up on something I'd missed during my two-day mope.

"Uh, maybe."

"You *know*? Give!"

"Well, the other night, I heard them talking. Doug said he found this place where they let cats stay, a ranch. Is this a ranch, you think?"

I could have cussed the runt until his ears bled, and I would have, too, except at that moment the car doors were thrown open by two hulking farmhands dressed in overalls. They grabbed our cages and stomped up a hill, past barns and horses grazing and pigs grunting in mud. After a couple of minutes' fast walking, we came to a long dingy shed, wood on the front, chicken wire on the back. Inside it was divided into about thirty compartments, cages really, most empty, a few with forlorn felines staring through mesh doors. They were so depressed they didn't even meow when we went swinging past.

We came to a corner cage, double wide. The guys opened our carrier doors, Rass's first, and shook him into the cell. Then it was my turn. I tried to hold on, but the carrier walls were slick and I went sliding, tail first, into my new prison.

"Welcome to Foothill Ranch," one of the farm sadists said. "Your owner brought food for you—you're lucky, Lucky," he chuckled, pleased with his dazzling witticism. "It'll be along later. Meanwhile, try some of the house chow."

The cage had come equipped with two big metal bowls. One was filled with sulfurous water, the other with some industrial dry spicules we were supposed to consider cat food. I snapped at the bullies through the wire. They laughed, but it made me feel better. A little.

What helped more was the ration I gave Rass as soon as we were alone.

"You traitorous SOB. You knew about this and you didn't tell me?"

"I didn't know what it meant!" Rass cowered, "I wasn't sure!"

"Well you got a clue now, genius? Damn, I shoulda left your ass in the mine."

"Doo Doo," he wailed pitifully, "don't."

"Ah, hell. Why do I bother. It ain't your fault. You were born in a hole, what do you know? I should have picked up the signs myself."

"This isn't forever! I'm sure Kimberley will come get us soon."

"That's just what I'm afraid of."

"What ... what do you mean?" Rass was spitting with confusion now, backed up against the wire at the end of the cage.

"I mean I'm done. I've got to get away from here. I have places to go, Rass."

"You don't wanna wait?"

"Don't you get it? When Kimberley comes back for us, I don't want to *be* here. It's time for me to get *home*, remember?"

Rass took that in for a moment, then his eyes came into focus for the first time since I started yelling at him. His words came out in a rush, like he was afraid he'd stop himself.

"You don't even know where home is and we've been all over the place and I've found my home and I don't want to follow you anymore!"

I laughed bitterly. "This from the skeleton I found two weeks ago who told me he'd follow me to the ends of the earth?"

"It's too hard. She *loves* me. And she's coming back, you'll see!"

"Ahh," I started, but then I let it go. It's his life, I thought, and anyway, I travel better light.

"Yeah, okay buddy. Congrats," I said, trying to mean it.

"You should stay too, Doo Doo! Then it'll be you and me and Doug and Kimberley, just like before! What's wrong with that?"

"Everything," I said, but seeing Rass wince I softened it. "Well, almost everything. He's great and she's okay, but they aren't my people and this—wherever the hell *this* is—isn't my home. I have to get home, Rass."

"You really mean it this time?" Rass asked like he didn't want to believe it. "You've been saying that for so long. Isn't there anything I can do? I'm gonna miss you, you know."

"Okay, me too. You happy now? But yeah, there is one thing you can do."

"What's that?" Rass asked eagerly.

"You can help me find a way out of here."

"Uh … That's not what I meant."

"I know," I said softly.

"What … how can I…." he trailed off.

"You're a caver, you're strong, and it may take both of us to spring me. Will you help?"

Rass nodded, licked his front paw, and drew it over his face.

CHAPTER 25

"*Snort!*"

"Hello?"

"*SNORT!*"

"Excuse me?" I said.

"Did I hear you speak about getting out of here? Snort."

"Okay, what's it to ya, and while we're at it, who the hell are you?"

"I am Matilda," declared 17 pounds of ancient female cat. She was lumpy, had one dead eye, patchy fur the color and texture of bark, and a voice like a busted kazoo. It was the most regal introduction that had ever put me in my place.

I stepped to the back of the cage where I could get a closer look through the chicken wire. "Hello, Matilda, I am Doo Doo and this is Rass. One of us is leaving the premises, shortly."

"What a silly name for such a handsome boy."

"Doo Doo or Rass?"

"You are *both* handsome," she said nobly.

"See?" piped Rass.

"She's blind in one eye, dummy. Sorry," I said to her. Something about this Matilda made me want to apologize, so I apologized.

"It is true," she said sadly. "I lost my right eye in this very cage, 14 years ago. That was the last time someone young and foolish tried to escape from the Ranch."

"Did he make it?" I asked.

"She. And no, I did not."

"You may not realize it from the looks of the place," Matilda preened while Rass and I sat and listened, "but this was always considered an elite facility. It still is. Foothill Ranch is the last word in 'natural animal boarding accommodation.' The very idea of the rustic pet resort got its start in Colorado, right here. You should consider yourselves lucky. This place isn't cheap. Your owners must love you very much."

"Natural? Natural dump!" I pressed a paw against a loose floorboard. A sound like warped tin wobbled out. "This place is falling apart and I bet it wasn't much to start with. Rustic my ass! The only difference between this joint and an outhouse is the outhouse smells better."

"True."

"Huh?"

"I *did* try to escape, young one. My owners like it. Not I. They think their precious is happier spending her summers here, rather than being stuck in our sumptuous, twentieth-floor, downtown Denver condominium while they cruise the globe by sea. It *is* important, don't you agree Mr. Doo Doo, for us to stay in touch with our roots in forest and fern. I find it especially rejuvenating when a wild dove perches on the cage and the mesh is just a claw's width too narrow for me to reach it. At home I have my own loft, but I would be terribly sad if Master and Mistress weren't there to feed me, or rather, to tell Consuella to feed me, the way they do so affectionately the other eleven months of the year. Consuella doesn't cruise. But she does get to bring Matilda's food to Foothill Ranch while I'm at 'The Resort.'"

"Where you learn to talk like that?" Rass gawked.

"Breeding, dear boy. Breeding. I am but one of a long line of cats who have adorned the homes of the best people on the Eastern Slope. I am groomed daily by servants. When I am ill I am attended to by the finest veterinarians, *in my home.* Our doctors make house calls, you see..."

"I had one of those," I broke in. "They're not all they're cracked up to be."

"...and I even have my own psychologist," Matilda went on, undeterred, "for those times when all that domestic bliss plunges me into fits of depression and despair."

"Mwraak," Rass amen-ed. He had no idea what she was saying.

But I did. "Been a rough life, Matilda?"

"You have no idea, pretty one. I'd end it tomorrow if I had the courage, and the strength."

"Ms. Matilda, you wouldn't perhaps be laying on the drama a bit thicker than strictly necessary, would you? You seem to be enjoying yourself, you ask me."

"Nobody *did* ask you, Doo Doo," she said, amused. "Not that you're wrong. Just impertinent." And damned if her good eye didn't wink at me.

"You're a trip," I played along. "It's a good thing this chicken wire is here. I swear, if you were ten years younger, I'd...."

"If I was ten years younger I'd eat you for lunch, dearest. You and your cobby friend." Matilda sniffed the air pensively. "No, make that 14 years. "That's when they sent me out to get 'fixed.'"

"What'd you break, Matilda?" Rass asked sympathetically. "Your eye?"

Right about then it hit me. I was really going to miss this boy.

Our confab had to pause at twilight. It was feeding time at beautiful Foothill Ranch, and two more anonymous overlarge hands did the deed, giving us food that would be complimented to be called rustic. Fortunately, dolloped on top of the gravel that clanked into our bowls like ball bearings, Rass and I got a scoop of some decent wet stuff that Kimberley must have left for us. Not as good as her home cooking, but at least *she* didn't come with it. I was really starting to resent her, in case you haven't noticed.

I saw that Matilda got some special stuff too, but it must have been senior catizen food, because it stunk like vitamins. The ranch hands called her by name.

"Food time, Matilda. C'mon old gal, here's your chow, eat up."

The old gal, bless her heart, wouldn't give them the satisfaction. She turned away from the humans, tail in the air, showing them ... well ... her disdain. She spit a word at the pair as they left the coop.

"Peasants."

Once they were gone she tiptoed up to her food like it was prey, paused, and shoved her mush in neck-deep.

I knew better than to interrupt her, but I was dying to hear the rest of her story. Especially the part where she tried to escape. I figured I could learn something, like how to get out of here without leaving an eyeball behind. But she was in no hurry. First she ate for about ten minutes straight, cleaning the bowl. Then she padded delicately to her litter box and let loose a toxic cloud that still makes my eyes sting, just thinking about it. And by the time I recovered from that, she was asleep. Very asleep. Noisily asleep. Get the picture?

If not, put down the book and go start up your lawn mower. It was a mercy our princess couldn't hear herself. It would have ruined her self-image.

"Wow!" Rass shouted above the din.

"No foolin!" I roared. "Well, it's been a long day. I guess I could use some sleep myself."

"Uh, do you think you *can?*"

"Skreee ... Skraaww!..." went our princess.

"I'm not sure!" I laughed. I was punch drunk tired now.

"Me either."

"Well, might as well try."

"Me too," Rass said above the shrieks. "Good night, Doo Doo!"

"We'll see!" I hollered back.

And yet, don't you know, it was.

* * *

Foothill Ranch might be a fake, but they sure as hell kept farm hours. The morning feed and cleanup crew burst in there at the crack of dawn, all fresh-faced and noisy. This time there were three of them, two guys and one young woman who was actually nice. I think she was the first cat person I'd seen since I got there. And she had the dirtiest job, too. Reaching in the cages with a gloved hand, pulling out the litter boxes, emptying the mess into a big plastic drum, brushing out the sticky bits, squirting some kind of disinfectant in the empty trays, and filling them all over again with dusty industrial litter that raised a brown cloud in her face.

Yet she was chipper as if she was panning for gold and finding it. I watched her closely; she liked cats. Maybe I could take advantage of that, when the time came.

One good thing about the early morning is that it woke up Matilda. Once again she dove into her grub as soon as the crew was out of sight. But this time, when she was done, she was eager to talk. More than eager, she told us her life story. I'll compress a little. She wants you to know the rest, let her write her own book.

"I'm a shell, dear boys," she started. "I know that. You should have seen me when. I was the apple of many an eye, human and feline alike. But that was so long ago.

"But, you ask," (no, we didn't) "was I happy? No, alas. I was torn from the bosom of my mother too young, far too young, and I never saw her nor my siblings again. We were exotics, you see, and very valuable, a breed so rare I doubt you could even pronounce it. All of us went to good homes, I'm told. It is small consolation. A cat needs her mother for more than a few weeks."

I was thinking she was lucky she never had to see her mother lose all love and interest in her, like mine did, in a precious few more than a few weeks. I wondered if she'd ever had kittens herself—so I asked.

"Were you ever a mom, Matilda?"

"No, Doo Doo," she said sadly. "That pleasure was denied me. I was fed something to keep me from conceiving at first, and then, after my escape attempt, they took away my abilities forever. In a life of regret, it is my biggest one. I know I would have been a wonderful mother."

I let her ramble on. Fast forward to the question that was burning a hole in my brain.

"How did you try to get out of here, Matilda? How did you lose your eye?"

"She still *has* it," Rass blurted, "it just *looks* funny...."

"Shhh, Rass. Let her speak."

"Yes, little one, let me tell you how I disfigured myself," Matilda kazooed in her tragic-diva voice. "And you too, my rash handsome boy, you may find this instructive."

I hoped the hell so, and soon, too. As much as I enjoyed this eccentric lady's chatter, I was starting to feel highly caged.

"My plan was so well thought out," she mused. "But I lost patience." Matilda stared at me and her voice turned cold.

"Let that be a horrible lesson to you, Doo Doo. Patience!" she barked.

"Yes Ma'am ... patience," I said to fill the hard silence that followed. "Please, continue."

"You haven't been here long enough to see the way they clean the floor outside the cages, have you? Well," she continued without waiting for an answer, "they use a garden hose, flush the floor with water, and then broom it away. This happens about twice a week; I believe they'll do it tomorrow."

Matilda paused, waiting for encouragement. All she got out of me was a "So?"

"So...." she went on, "where do you think all that water goes?"

"To the ocean?" I wisecracked.

"I wouldn't know," she said witheringly. "I've never seen an ocean. But I *have* seen the two vents where they brush the water outside. And either of them is big enough for an agile, young cat to pass through!" she said triumphantly.

"Yeah?" I said skeptically. "So why *didn't* you, Toots?"

"Must you be so rude? Were you born in a barn?"

"No, in San Francisco. And this little guy was raised in a subway, but I suppose you've never seen one of those either." Which produced nothing but icy silence. I could tell that mouthing off to this aging hothouse flower wasn't going to get me very far. So, with effort, I cranked on the charm.

"I'm sorry, Matilda, no offense. But you have us all pins and needles here. Please, go on."

"You can't see them from the cages, but I've been in and out of here so many times that I know them by heart. One opening is just under your corner cage, in the side wall. The other is all the way down the other end of the coop. All one needs to do to get out of this building is to get free of one's cage for a few seconds, slip under the vent and jump outside."

"*That* was your plan?" I was trying not to laugh in my bitter disappointment. "How did you propose to get out of your cage, Matilda?"

"I was going to trick them, and it would have worked, too. You see, sometimes, if you're lucky, one of the help will take you out and pet you. They sell it as a service—play time, they call it. But like so much here, it's a fraud. They take you to the big house for a brushing right before your owner picks you up so you look all shiny and smooth, but usually they just let you rot. But not always. There was one boy, a cute little thing, who used to reach in and pet me sometimes. I just knew that if I could tempt him to take me out of here I could get loose, somehow. Sneak away, run away, even claw my way out if I had to. I'm *sure* I could have done it!"

I had the hardest time picturing this old bag young enough—*cat* enough—to claw her way out of a cobweb. But I was excited that her plan was along the lines of the idea I'd had this morning—do goo-goo eyes for the humans and hope for a shot.

"What went wrong?" I asked.

"Me, Doo Doo. I went wrong. When the boy I was targeting didn't come around for a few days, I lost patience. One night I was storming around, mad as I could be. When I jumped on the wire at the back of my cage, it *gave* a little at the bottom. That was all it took—that little jiggle—for me to discard my carefully made plans. I spent the night clawing at it, nosing it aside, trying to make a gap between the wire and the wood big enough to slide through. If I'd had a lick of sense I would have noticed that I was getting all cut up trying to move that screen. But I was on fire! I could see the grass outside in the moonlight. When I thought the slit I'd made was big enough, I turned my face sideways and tried to slither through…. Foolish, foolish, girl."

"What? What happened, Matilda!" Rass's mouth was hanging open.

I already knew. I could see the scar on her right cheek and her blind left eye. They were the exactly same distance apart as two wires.

"This is what happened, little one," she said. Matilda walked to the back of her cage and pressed her nose to the chicken wire. The scars lined up just the way I thought. "I got stuck, I was stuck all night. And when I tried to back out…."

Matilda finished with an inarticulate wail that said it all.

I was sympathetic, don't get me wrong. But a part of me was working the angles the whole time. When she calmed down I asked her one more question.

"What did they do when they found you? Did they call your vet or what?"

"No, of course not!" she said, sounding surprised I could be so stupid. "They took me to the hospital immediately. Or they did as soon as they could cut me loose."

"Why'd you have to wait all night? You must have been screaming your head off."

"Nobody *heard* me, Doo Doo," she cried. "I don't want to talk about this anymore."

"I understand, Matilda. Not another word." And besides, I thought to myself, you've told me enough already. You *were* young and foolish.

Me? I'm just young.

CHAPTER 26

My luck was better than Matilda's, I saw my mark that very same day. She appeared again at twilight, one of two farmhands on the evening food run. A big doofus of a guy who gave off bad vibes and suppressed anger, and her, a pretty young girl with short black hair and sympathetic eyes.

The day had been a creeper, too hot and too long. Rass was nerve-wrackingly restless, rooting around the ten- by three-foot cage like he was drilling for oil. Seeing him weaving like that, like a horse in a paddock, made me feel more trapped than ever. I'd tell him to settle down, and he would, for all of five minutes.

But I couldn't let it get to me. Matilda was an old blowhard, but she was right about one thing. Patience. Get your plan and work it. Opportunity wouldn't come easy here; I couldn't afford to get all crazy and blow it like she did when one appeared. As it did, that evening.

First thing I needed to do was get the right mood going, which wasn't easy at the tail end of a long, caged day, but I rose to the occasion. As soon as I heard the crew tromping into the coop, I shouldered Rass aside and parked myself behind the "window" of the cage, which was just a square of wire mesh in the center of the wood door. I posed there, pouring irresistible animal magnetism out my big green eyes, ready to trap any susceptible human that came in range.

That's where the second thing I needed came in—luck. If that big, ugly guy had our cage it wouldn't work. I needed that girl. And I got her.

"Oh!" She gasped as she turned from the food tray and saw me, as if finding a cat in a cat kennel was the last thing she expected. But that's not what caused her surprise, *I* did, face up close to the screen, eyes locked on hers. If a cat has the stuff, he can make you think he's seeing all the way down to your soul. I've got the talent, and I was working it hard that night.

"Look at *you*," she said, putting a finger through the mesh and ticking my nose. But I was looking at *her*, and she couldn't look away.

I knew she'd be a pushover. What I didn't count on was me being the same. Without breaking our stare, she withdrew her finger, opened the door, and reached for me! Suddenly I was out of the cage, in her arms, my purr so loud I could hear it bouncing off the walls.

"What are you doing?"

"I, uh, don't know, Brian. Just holding this little guy."

"Put him back, Kelly."

"Aw, come on. He's adorable, and I think he's lonely. Do you miss your people..." she looked at the name tags over the cage, "Lucky?"

I had her now. I could feel it in her hands; she was blissed out, in kitty heaven. Time to escape. I scanned the floor and there it was. A big old vent, the size of a shoe box, not ten feet away.

Right then. I should have made my move right then. But I couldn't. She had me pressed against her chest, one hand under me, the other stroking my fur. I'd have to claw her up pretty good to get loose.

And I almost did, too. I freed a paw, very slowly, and looked up at her. A silver dangle hung from her neck, cheap and shiny. I unsheathed my claws.

She saw. For an instant she knew that she was holding a wild animal against her breast, stiletto claws so close to her slender neck. And then I reached up and swatted the charm on her necklace.

Tinkle tinkle. In a heartbeat, I went from being a deadly pocket tiger to a cuddly kitten playing with a piece of string. I flicked the charm again, it made the sweetest noise. So did Kelly, she giggled like a baby.

Two big mitts grabbed me from behind and tossed me back into the cage.

"Quit messing around and feed the stupid hairbags, will ya?"

"Brian! That's not nice."

"Hey look, Kelly, this is cats. Cats is the scut work around here. I don't like the little bastards and I never will. They're sneaky and I hate their phony independence." Then his voice softened. "You're new here, don't you want to do dogs, sheep, *horses* even? You don't have to clean cat crap forever, you know."

"I *like* cats. You didn't have to be so rough."

"Ah, he didn't mind. He looks pretty tough to me."

"Yes, but I did." Kelly put the bowl of food in our cage and looked at me. I was back about two feet from the door, already hating myself for blowing my chance.

"And he wonders why I won't go out with him," Kelly muttered to me under her breath.

Not far under enough. "What did you say?"

"Nothing. I'm done here. Let's go."

"That's what I thought you said," Brian spat. He grabbed the empty food tray, tossed me an evil glance, and stomped out of there like a storm trooper.

My self-loathing turned into a raging Brian-loathing. Just gimme a shot at you, dude. One time. I'll rip your eyes out.

Patience, Doo Doo, patience. She'll be back. And so will he.

* * *

"Hey Rass, you up?"

"Yeah. Why?"

"I got a plan."

"What?"

"For getting out of here, I got a plan."

"Another one?"

"Don't be a wise ass, Rass. I need your help."

"I dunno, Doo Doo, I already told you, I don't want to…."

"For me, stupid. Just for me."

"Okay, how?" Rass's voice was raspy with sleep—or something.

"It's gonna cost you breakfast."

"Huh?"

"When the food comes this morning, don't eat any. I won't either."

"Uh, don't eat? Why?"

"Cause I'm gonna be sick."

"You're sick? What's wrong?" Rass sounded scared.

"Nothing, damn. I'm fine. I'm just gonna *look* sick when that girl comes around tomorrow night. I'm gonna roll around in that food until it looks like I've been puking my guts out all day."

"Yuck. But how's that...."

"Simple. You heard Matilda. Get sick, go to the big house. Only I'm not gonna make it to the big house, I'm gonna slip away as soon as they take me out of here.

"... Uh ... Rass?"

"I'm here."

"You understand?"

"Whatever you say, Doo Doo."

"Well, that's what I say. And don't worry so much! Kimberley will be coming for you soon enough."

Rass sighed, "Doo Doo, you may be the smartest cat I ever met...."

"But?"

"But you are such a jerk."

I should have said, I'll miss you too, runt. I should have, but I didn't.

The picture in my mind was clear as air. Kelly sees me, lying in a heap, covered in slop. She reaches in and grabs me, I'm limp in her arms. Until I'm out of the coop. Then I come to life in a big hurry. She's trying to hold twelve pounds of greasy, wriggling cat in her small hands. With any luck, I'm gone and she never gets a scratch.

And I know once I'm outside, they'll never catch me. Plus I'll have lunch to go. All I have to do is lick. Yeah.

So, patience, Doo Doo. Wait for the morning food. Then wait all day until they come back at night. Then wait until she sees you. And don't blow it this time.

Rass avoided me that night. He didn't sleep much and neither did I. And yes, I know all that nonsense about cats being nocturnal. It's true, but only a little true. Mostly what we do, night *or* day, is sleep. But not that night.

Rass padded around the cage, occasionally letting out a random mewl, just to make me feel bad. I stayed perched on the shelf at the back of the cage and rehearsed my escape in my mind, over and over again. Morning took forever to come. But when it came, it came with a bang.

Loud morning voices. But no female voices! Okay, okay, no problem. She doesn't have to be here now, only tonight. Patience.

"Hey, Matilda," I said, "what's all the commotion about."

"Good morning to you too, pretty boy," she said sarcastically. "I told you. They're going to clean the coop now."

"Before they feed us or after?"

"After, silly. They also empty our trays in the morning, remember?"

She was right. Some random guy I never saw before did the honors of dumping the litter box. I don't think he even noticed us. Then he disappeared and was replaced by the ugly face of that Brian guy. He had a bowl of food in one hand and a garden hose in the other. The hose had a thing on the end that looked like a trigger. He was sneering when he opened the cage door.

I was two feet back but God, how I wanted to go for that throat! *Patience*, Doo Doo.

"Here's your slop," Brian grunted, tossing the dish just inside the cage.

Something propelled me forward, one step, two.

Brian glared at me. "So," he said, "you're the puke that Kelly likes more than me. Well, the little bitch also likes cats more than horses! What do you think *that* tells you about her," and he stuck out his tongue and waggled it obscenely.

One more step. I was almost at the food bowl now, and the bowl was no more than six inches inside the door. Brian started to swing it shut, then he paused, looked back at me.

"Hungry, are we?" he said. And then he raised the garden hose and pulled the trigger, jetting water right into my face.

Patience be damned.

"Rraaagglhaa!" I went right for his eyes, choking on water and rage. Brian ducked and dropped the hose. I snagged the top of his head, tore into his left cheek, rebounded to the right and dove for the vent.

He made an off-balance lunge for me and fell, right onto his face. That was his last shot. I blew through the slot and out of the coop. The whole thing took about three seconds.

I was as high as I'd ever been in my short life, the rush of freedom, of *success*, was overwhelming. But there was a catch. My plan had been to escape at twilight, but I emerged into a sparkling Colorado morning and the field was crawling with life—sheep grazing down the hill, horses exercising in a corral about a hundred yards to the left, a couple of guys hammering nails into the roof of the barn to my right. I took all that in searching for a clear route out of there, working the problem at hyperspeed. But there wasn't one. I'd have to improvise.

Fortunately, no one had noticed me yet. But the noise coming out of the cat coop was scary. Brian was screaming like a raptor in there, damning my soul in howling rants of pain. That was sweet music, but I couldn't hang around to enjoy it. Boots drummed hard on the wooden floor of the coop. I had about five seconds to choose—run, or hide?

I did both. I was on the downhill side of the coop, at the left corner. The door was on the uphill side in the middle. They'd be coming around to my side, where they saw me escape, and probably look for me to be running down the hill. But I wasn't going to be there. Hugging the wall, I scooted across the back of the building, curled up the right side, and peeked around that corner until I saw them clear the door heading the other way. That bought me another few seconds.

The hill crested at a dirt road, maybe a couple hundred yards upslope. If I could make it past that ridge without being seen, I was gone. But it was too far. There was another choice, risky but close. Two big, spreading live oaks, in full summer foliage, fifteen yards to my left. They were isolated, I'd have to get there and up in a big hurry without being spotted or I'd be cornered. For the moment, the building shielded me from view, but they were running hard. I wasted two frantic heartbeats making up my mind, then kangaroo-hopped through the tall grass and hit the trunk hard, spraying bark. I was fifty feet up before those dolts even turned the corner.

Very quietly, I eased myself out on a high branch until I got to a tight "V" where the limb forked above a thick splay of leaves. The virtue of that spot was also its biggest disadvantage—I didn't think they could see me there, but that meant I couldn't really see them, either. But they were so close—I could smell their anger. Were they stupid enough to miss me up here? Could I possibly stay hidden all day? And if I got discovered and had to jump, could I make it out of the tree without breaking my neck on some hidden branch halfway down?

I was out of options, stuck up a tree, waiting for dark—hours away. The situation was not good.

But did I have any choice? It seemed like I had, not long ago. The word "patience" rang in my ears like a bad song, like a machine that needs grease, over and over. But for the life of me I couldn't figure out what it meant.

CHAPTER 27

For most of the day, except for the flies, my luck held. The ranch hands were out in force, scurrying around between the cat coop and the big house by the parking lot, calling my name like I was idiot enough to answer to it. It never occurred to them that I might not have gone north or west or east or south, but *up*. And that was also lucky, because the one place I couldn't see was down.

I could hear, though, and only a couple of times that morning did anyone come close to the trees, and only then to walk right past. It would probably stay that way if I didn't do something stupid to draw attention to myself. Which is why the flies were double torture. They were eating me alive, but I couldn't move so much as a tail to chase them away. One guy kept lighting on my nose, and I kept trying to snatch him off there with a flick of my tongue, like a frog.

But I'm no frog and I was never quick enough for him. I'd have gladly given one of my nine lives to swat him to fly heaven, but not *all* of them, and that's what was at risk here.

More than once I thought about making a break for it. Sometimes it looked like the nearest human was so far away that I'd have a good shot at escaping even if I was spotted, but I could never be sure. Better to wait for dark. I might be hot, dry, fly-bit and uncomfortable, but I was safe. Plus, after the pandemonium of the morning, I finally had all my wits about me again. Nothing, I thought, would make me lose patience a second time today. I am Cosmic Cat, calm as the night air.

After a while it seemed like they'd stopped looking. The morning turned into a warm afternoon and it had been hours since anyone came near my tree. Even the flies must have gotten as drowsy with the heat, because they stopped bothering me. I was having a hard time staying awake.

That was a little scary. I wasn't afraid of falling; the way I was wedged in there it would take another of those Colorado twisters to blow me down. But what if I nodded off and they sneaked up on me? I'd wake up, sure, but I'd lose a couple of seconds and that might make all the difference. Things were quiet, I could take a chance and climb down now, but I'd promised myself I'd be patient, and I was going to stick to it. If I fell asleep, so be it.

So *was* it.

I fell into a heavy dream—it was all mixed up, but wonderful. My mother was there, so were Doc and Fern. We were all inside the old house in San Francisco, but somehow it was full of sunshine and a cool stream ran through it. In the dream I was a kitten, looking up at my mother's flanks as I stood alongside her, both of us drinking deeply from the pure, clear water as it gurgled through the living room. My thirst had made it into that dream, and my destination too. Only the mother was lost to me forever.

I woke up to an urgent shaft of red light, beaming through the leaves, lighting my whiskers from behind. I felt that sunset like a magnet, pulling me westward. It was *time.*

Food smells drifted my way. I must have slept through the evening rounds. But, hungry as I was, there was no temptation in it. There was only the need for an hour to pass, for that big red spotlight to fall behind the hill, to get moving. That was my food—I wanted to be down on the ground, legs pumping, getting away, getting *to.* I risked a stretch, arching my back until the leaves shook, then settled back down facing the setting sun. Nobody heard, nobody came. Now all I needed was one more hour of luck.

I tried to pass the time by falling asleep again, I wanted to get back to that dream if I could. But it's never like that, is it? Not for cats and not for humans. Those dream threads get all tangled when you wake up and you can never put them back together. I was all slept out, no use in even trying.

Besides, who could sleep with all this noise?

Noise?

"Doo Doo! Doo Doooo...."

Rass. Oh Jesus.

"Howl. Wail. Doo Dooo! Come back, Doo Doo."

Shut up, man! I wedged my ears back, fighting the urge to hiss. How long had he been going on like this? I must have nodded off again after all, it was gray twilight now, and I could be out of here in a moment if that idiot's infernal wailing didn't rouse the whole damned county.

"Doo Dooo.... Where are you? Doo Doo, come back. Come on, I know you're out there, come back! Doo Doo!"

I couldn't believe this. That poor, scared cave cat was blowing it for me! And what was he crying about, anyway? In a few days he'd be in his new home, the one he always wanted. He'd be fine. Kimberley loved him and Doug liked cats, even cobby runts like Rass. Anyway, she could bring home a two pound tarantula and Doug wouldn't object, he'd just smile and tell her he'd always wanted a pet spider.

And what the hell did I care? I had my own fish to fry and Rass was peeing in the pan.

"Doo Doo?? Are you there? Doo Dooo...."

I couldn't take it anymore, I had to get going before Rass brought the cavalry. Down the tree I flew, bouncing from limb to limb like a pinball, scattering acorns and leaves and one startled pair of wrens, making almost as much racket as the moron in that coop.

"Doo Doo! I hear you! Doo Doo, is that you? I'm right here! Doo Doo?"

I did the last ten feet in one hump-backed leap. The breath whuffed out of my mouth in a grinchy groan as I hit the grass. One crow hop to my left and a quick circle to check things out. Nobody around, it was time to leave this place forever.

"Doo Doo. I'm scared. I don't like this! Doo Doo? Come here, I know you're out there!"

Damn his yellow eyes.

"All right! Just shut the hell up. I'm coming." I sped through the tall grass and hopped right through the vent. Back in the maw I just got out of, at such peril.

"You *came!*" Rass was stretched up on the door, front claws poking through the mesh, his belly hair mashed against the screen.

"Yeah. I'm here. You trying to get me caught or something?"

"No. I'm sorry, Doo Doo. But I've changed my mind."

"What do you mean," I asked, afraid I knew the answer.

"I want to come with you! I don't want to be alone in here."

"You won't be. Kimberley will be coming for you soon."

"I know. But I don't want that. I want to be with *you.*"

I didn't answer right away. In that moment of silence I thought I caught the sound of footsteps, coming up the hill.

"It's too late, Rass. You're in there and I'm out here. I'm sorry, buddy...."

"Can't you wait?" Rass's voice squeaked higher, edging into panic. "I can get out just like you did! Then we can go together, just like you said!"

"No, Rass," I sighed. "Be happy. You've got that home now. You're going to have everything you ever wanted." Yes, those were footsteps.

"Doo Doo!" Rass shook the cage door with his powerful, stubby legs. I turned away.

"*No* Doo Doo!"

I tried to think of something to say. But when I opened my mouth all that came out was a meow.

Rass's cries followed me as I blew through the vent. They burned my ears as I turned up the hill, plowing through the grass, running blind. I heard them over the footfalls of the stupid farmhands who would never catch me now. I felt them like wind at my back, driving me forward over the crest, I felt them like a magnet, pulling me back until my fur stood up on end. I ran to get away from them, until I could hear them no more. But it didn't work. I hear them to this day.

CHAPTER 28

But I was free. That counts for a lot. Breathing cool evening air in deep draughts, bounding through the dry grass, pausing every few moments to get my bearings, feeling my way west as the night grew dark. I wanted to put a lot of distance between me and that farm, and I did. Onward and upward, the air getting colder and thinner with each mile.

Exhilaration will only carry you so far and I was burning energy by the bucket. By midnight I was in serious need of fuel and water; I was so dry my fur sparked when I ran.

Trouble was, it was pretty much a desert around here, all rocky outcrops and hard going. I licked a few drops of dew from the odd blade of grass and kept moving, hoping something better would turn up. There was enough moonlight for me to find my footing, but my paws had gone soft since my city days. They were hurting already.

The climb flattened to a stony plateau, sparsely covered with dying weeds and a low, spiky bush that smelled like gasoline and sprayed my belly with sticky brambles so tenacious they dug right through my fur and halfway to my liver. I was bone tired, but I couldn't stop here. The place was too flat, too exposed; it felt like a dinner plate for coyotes.

Pushing ahead, ignoring my aches and aching thirst, I settled into a kind of fugue state of perpetual motion, step-step-stepping on cracked paws, one corner of my mind alert for dangers.

Like snakes, for instance. More than once I thought I heard a rattler; I kept my eyes glued to the ground as I walked. I was so intent on looking down that I almost crashed into a wall.

I sensed it before I hit it, a big cliff looming in front of me, blocking the stars with its black bulk. When I looked up, I couldn't see the top. I couldn't see a way around it, either, so I sidled towards the south, hoping to find a gap.

There wasn't one, just this endless blank wall that refused to get out of my way. I was so tired I could scream, so angry I wanted to bash my head against that rock until it came tumbling down. Finally, even my anger left me, and with it, my last reserves of energy. But not my last bit of luck; that held, as usual.

I found a little shelter—a small hollow at the base of the cliff. If it wasn't the perfect place to rest, it would do.

Staggering down the shallow side of the bowl—it wasn't three feet deep—on rubbery legs, I settled into its gravelly bed, my back against the hulking rock-face. It still radiated warmth from the heat of the day, soothing me like a massage. That felt good, but what came next was better—I heard a plink.

Water. Not much water, just a tiny trickle leaking out of the face of the living rock, but enough to slake my thirst at the cost of a few tongue hairs. I worked at it for fifteen minutes, trying my best to suck that mountain dry. When I'd licked my fill, I treated myself to a desperately needed grooming. My longhaired pelt picks up dirt and cockleburs like a mop, and I have never felt good unless I looked good. By the time my body was clean my mouth was so loaded with crud I had to spend another ten minutes at the magic rock just to get rid of the taste so I could catch some sleep.

I got more than some. Morning was well advanced by the time I woke up, sunlight blasting off the cliff like cracked glass. My little cubbyhole was still shaded, but already I could feel the warmth of what promised to be a blistering hot day.

Soft living had done me in. I was stiff and creaky as an old tom when I got up and stretched the sleep out of my bones. I would shake that off soon enough, but my paws were going to need some time. Stepping out on the sharp, bare rock to get to the water—still trickling, thankfully—my pads burned something awful. I was going to have to take it easy today.

But I couldn't. The food situation was getting serious. Outside of the occasional high-flying bird, there wasn't much life here. I needed to get past this rock-face, get somewhere where I could *see*. Up was impossible, back out of the question, it was either left or right.

I chose left, south, because that way felt closer to home.

It was a trudge and a long one, all that morning and deep into the afternoon. I ate a couple of grasshoppers that were just big enough to make my stomach complain about how empty it was. When the sun passed behind that big stone wall it cooled off a little, but hunger and thirst dogged me all day.

But the worst part was the "stuck" feeling. That ridge line never wanted to end. I just knew I had to get past it, home was on the other side, everything I wanted was on the other side, but mile after painful mile went by without the hint of a gap. I grew to hate it.

But it was preparing a surprise for me. I hadn't realized it, but I'd been curving west all day. I should have suspected something, the ridge seemed to fall away from me whenever I looked south into the distance, but perspective is tricky from cat height. That's why we're forever trying to go up. In the wild or in your house, up is where the truth is. Nature played a trick on cats. She didn't make us tall enough.

The first hint was an almost imperceptible slant downwards on the plain that bordered the cliff. That and an odd glow that pierced the gray haze of the late afternoon. I noticed those changes, but I wasn't sure what they meant.

I needed a better angle, I needed some height. I came upon a rockfall at the base of the cliff and hopped up for a look. At first I couldn't see it, maybe I was just too weary and sunblind. But then the perspective snapped into focus and I realized, I was looking down and *west*. I'd come so far around this curved cliff that I could see the slanting rays of the setting sun lighting the hollows just beyond its bulk. I was sure that if I kept going around like this I'd find a pass, and I was right.

It was the last thing I saw clearly when the twilight faded. Far, far down and well ahead, a snaking valley cut the walls of the cliff in two. Even at this distance, and it was too far to even think about making it there tonight, I could sense a coolness, a rising fog of humidity that meant water.

It *was* too far, but I couldn't rest with that tantalizing prospect ahead of me. Even if it meant groping blindly in the dark. Nothing stops me, not even common sense.

This was dangerous business, scrabbling down the steepening slope until I was falling as much as walking, but I kept at it until my legs ached and my lungs wheezed. The smell of moisture was getting stronger all the time, and my thirst was a slave driver, keeping me going for hours. I pushed myself on and on in the dark, wondering if I'd ever get there. And then the moon rose in the east and lit the scene ahead of me, just enough for my cat's eyes to see how far I'd come.

Damn. It was like I'd been walking in place. It looked like I was no closer to that beautiful valley than I was at sunset! But vision lied. My other senses told me salvation was but a morning's walk away. Water burbled and birds twitted and the green smell of life poured out of that place. But it was a steep and jagged road down and I was flat out of gas. I had to find a place to rest.

Nothing came easy that day. The best I could come up with was a stinky little sagebrush growing on a flat ledge maybe a hundred yards below me. Straight below me. Practically crawling, scraping along on my belly, I eventually made it there in one piece. One very sore and weary piece. I was asleep by the time my tail curled across my nose.

Paradise by noon. A river as cool and pure as that one I'd seen in my dream, back in the tree. Fish and frogs and chipmunks and lizards, grass and ferns and moss and birds, birds, birds. Even deer—but I wasn't that ambitious. I just drank from that icy river until I had a brain freeze, and then did a little, well, let's just call it grazing. It was heaven.

With survival assured, all my aches and bruises came out to play. It's a matter of priorities, and now I was feeling good enough to feel bad. So I took my time, rested and walked, rested and slept, rested and ate, day after lazy day, healing all the while. Home was there in the distance, whispering softly, but the urgency was gone, I was just happy to be fed and safe. And anyway, each step upriver was taking me closer. So what if the journey takes a while, just keep your nose pointed west, Doo Doo. Time doesn't really matter.

* * *

You have to remember where I was born. San Francisco has many things to recommend it—for persons and cats alike—but one thing it lacks: seasons. So you can't blame me if I didn't see it coming. I thought I had all the time in the world.

I'm trying to keep this all straight for you, but cats don't have the best sense of time, and this happened so long ago. My best guess, looking back now, is that I spent weeks slowly meandering up that river. For one thing, the living was easy, for another, that river never could make up its mind to go straight. First it went south a little, then north a little, then back again. Only two things were constant—it always came around to the west and it always went up. And the longer I followed it, the upper it got. Eventually the valley narrowed into a gorge, the river a torrent of constant rapids. Getting a drink became treacherous, one slip on a wet rock and I'd be in that tumbling water. Food stayed plentiful, but hunting was dangerous on those mossy ledges and misted boulders. Before too long I felt the cold coming on and the living wasn't so easy anymore.

But even now, in my dotage, I envy that cat. God, was I ever strong! My paws got thick and tough, my muscles firm, my reflexes sharp. As the nights became as long as the days, then longer, my pelt thickened up beautifully. No coyote, no mountain lion, no predator at all could have a chance against me. What I couldn't escape I could kill. I felt about as capable as I ever would in life, and I was going to need every bit of it.

The air was getting thin. I was running out of valley. The trees gave way to scrub. Game wasn't plentiful anymore. Each day the river shrank, until it was a stream, then a creek, then a trickle. One morning, in a high and barren place, I found the source. Water came bubbling out of a crack in the rocks, pooled, then slid down below, back the way I'd come. Above it was dry and barren, just rocks and more rocks, and a cold, cutting wind.

Whatever. Bring it on. I was so built up I felt like I could climb a hundred miles, nothing could stop me now. Not even this white stuff that began falling from the leaden sky. Youth is an ass.

The snow was a novelty, at first. I'd never seen it before, and the first time it fell, it didn't stick. The land here was mounting and jumbled, but with no river there was no gorge, so no danger when I slipped on the slush. And when it melted it left lots of little puddles to drink from. But a few days later it snowed again, all damn day.

Ankle deep was just annoying, knee deep was an impediment, belly deep stopped me in my tracks, or perhaps I should say trough, because that's what I was plowing through the snow. There was nothing for it but to stop and try to find some shelter—which was at a premium in this high and treeless place. The best I could do was the downwind side of a boulder. It helped, a little.

The next day was sunny and almost warm. Wading through the melt was no fun, but by afternoon there were dry spots on top of the rocks and I could hop around without getting soaked. But I'd had my warning. No more dawdling. A cat could get stuck up here and they wouldn't find him till next summer. And by they, I mean the vultures.

I told you what good shape I was in, and I had a chance to prove it in the next several days. Once again, my obstacle was a ridge line to the west, this time with no breaks that I could see, and I could see a long way in the thin air. This wasn't a cliff, and I could climb it—barely—but it was very steep and craggy, too steep to go straight up. I needed to attack it technically, using cuts and switchbacks like a mountain climber, so that's what I did, learning the trade as I went. If I found food every other day I was lucky. With the effort I was putting out—hopscotching rockfields, battling boulders and scaling steep, scary gorges—I could feel the weight falling off my bones like a springtime molt.

Hope was at the top. And this time, that knife-edged ridge didn't seem to be receding a step with each step I took. Exactly the opposite, my distant goal seemed so close I could almost rub my whiskers against it. But the same weightless air that made my eyes lie like telescopes made my lungs feel like lead. It got to the point where I was panting more than moving. And when I did move, it was on shaky, imprecise legs. I missed this one ledge, tore a claw trying to hold on, fell back about six feet and bonked my head so hard it rang. But I wouldn't quit. I'd drop dead in mid-jump before I gave up now, I was so close.

I made it late one morning, the sun high at my back. Just one leap among millions, but when I looked up for the next jump, there wasn't one. This was it— the top.

Close up it wasn't a razor's edge at all, but a flattening. After days of nothing but bare rocks there was even thin soil and withered grass on the rolling table that formed the peak.

But that wasn't what I'd hoped to find on top, I expected salvation. If you go up one side, the other side goes down, right? I imagined the trip in reverse. My mind's eye had been anticipating the mirror image of what I'd just been through—steep and barren leading down to lush and gentle. Not this mossy plain on the roof of nowhere.

But my height was playing tricks on me again. If I'd been looking out of human eyes, way up there five feet above the ground, I would have noticed that the horizon was very close, and that the false ridge was a ridge after all. One that had been worn down through the years to this bluntness. And down was only a few hundred yards away.

I didn't know any of that yet, and I was *so* tired. Disappointment and fatigue overwhelmed my curiosity that late morning as a warm sun burned through the scanty air. Drunk on a lack of oxygen, not knowing how very close I was, seduced by that screaming sun, I forgot about hunger and remembered my old best friend, sleep. We renewed acquaintances on a mossy hummock, high on this peak where for once the wind was stilled. Basking in forgetfulness, I slept the day away under the healing heat of the sun. And woke up a new cat.

You humans call it a harvest moon. It rises, full and looming, just as the sun sets on the other side of the sky. Enough light pours off that big moon to make it virtual day for a cat. Here on the flat-edged rim of the world, there was nothing to block its rays, nothing to cast nighttime's deep shadows. I woke up to that brilliant moon soaring high in the sky, high and bright as my spirits. I was ready to go, ready for *anything*—except what happened.

I came to the end of the earth. Two minutes into my walk the ground began to slope downwards, gently at first, then so steeply it felt like my next step would take me over the abyss. I took it anyway, feeling my way down. For a few, groping moments I couldn't see anything beneath me, it was like I was heading into a bottomless black hole. And then I fell.

My operatic death cry was just reaching its full, falsetto magnificence, when it was cut off in mid-shriek. I landed hard after my half-second freefall, but I landed square on my feet. If Doo Doo cat is doomed to end his days in a fatal plunge, he'll have the leather side down and the fur side up when it happens. Or so I told my pounding heart as I took inventory—everything was still working, even my wounded pride. Be careful, idiot, I chastised myself as I waited for the explosion of dust I'd raised to settle. If you can't see what you're doing, don't do it!

And that's when things got *really* strange.

Because I *could* see again, and what I saw made no sense at all. I'd landed on what appeared to be a ledge, about 20 yards deep. Tapering to a point, the ledge ended in a small mound, with a single, spiny-leaved bush crowning its tip, a silhouette growing defiantly into the blackness, casting shadows *up* into the void—*backlit.*

This was sorcery, I had to find the source of that mysterious light, caution be damned. I stalked up to the burning bush, thrusting my nose through its thorny leaves, my toes hanging ten over the edge of the cliff, risking oblivion for an unobstructed view of The Truth. When I found it the world turned upside down.

There were *two* moons, one below and one above. Vertigo whooshed through my head so hard I staggered, only the bush kept me from tipping off the cliff. Up and down deserted me, lost their meaning. It felt like I was swimming in air. But then one of the moons began to ripple and wave. The earth stopped spinning, the scene slid into focus, and I *saw*. I was looking at a *lake*. A picture-perfect mountain lake, thousands of feet below me, a mirror for the full moon.

Now I had a new goal. Down there was water and life and food and shelter. Just take it easy, Doo Doo, you're going to be just fine. In the double moonlight that lake glowed like the promised land. And if I didn't notice that on its farther shores there were cliffs just as tall as the ones I'd just climbed, standing like a wall between me and everywhere I wanted to go, well, that's no different than a drowning man not thinking about his bills when he's thrown a life preserver. All I knew at that moment was that I was *saved*—if I could get down this mountain without breaking my neck.

CHAPTER 29

Two tough days, but I'm tired of telling you about tough days. The important thing is that I got there. But you know that already; I'm here to tell the tale. You know I made it home eventually, which, I'm told, is important. Humans love happy endings.

It was happy for me, too, home was *my* happy ending and I never stopped believing. But if, like some feline Moses, I was fated never to reach my ultimate goal, I'd settle for that lake in autumn, before the freeze set in. Not only was it beautiful, bountiful and safe, but my lake—Halfway Lake, I called it; I never knew its people name—came with a bonus.

Catnip. Groves of the stuff, splayed along the shoreline, just beginning to wilt from the first frosts. Once I had my belly full of fish—mostly half-dead trout thrashing in the shallows—I abandoned myself to my vice. Call it weakness, call it my reward for making it this far alive, call it whatever you like. I got high and I stayed high in my own private wonderland and never felt a pang of guilt.

The lake was a lot lower than the rim, and warmer, too. Going down that mountain was like going backwards a month in time. It hadn't snowed down here yet, and the air was thicker and moister. The only sign of the season to come was a dusting of frost on the grass that appeared on clear mornings.

In a lucid moment I'd scoped out an arc of tall pines, curving around the lake's northern shore, partway up the hill. That was my shelter, way up a pine tree, thick-trunked and tall, heavy with resinous cones. I'd eat at twilight, get stoned at night, and be asleep high off the ground before daybreak. The routine agreed with me. All the weight I'd lost on the trek up I put back on, and then some. I was getting fat in my stoned lethargy. It turned out to be a good thing.

I should have taken the hint when the fish disappeared from the muddy shoreline and I had to get mice for my breakfast. I should have, but I was much too loaded, and not just with nip, but with the free and easy life I'd found in my mountain idyll. Nor did I notice that the sun was getting closer and closer to the southern cliffs surrounding the lake, and spending less time overhead.

But when, one intensely clear, still-aired dawn, I stepped to the edge of the water for a drink and it *crunched*, I noticed. It was only a crust of ice, rimming the lake's edge like lace, but it knew it meant trouble.

Each morning the ice grew further into the lake from the shore, each afternoon less melted back again. In a week it was thick enough to stand on. One gloomy day it began to rain, a steady, stormless drenching that started warm and grew colder by the hour. Before it tapered off, two days later, the rain had turned into pellets that bounced when they hit the ground and fused into a thick slush. I hid in the ineffective shelter of my pine forest until it blew over, thinking I might have overstayed my welcome in paradise.

When I ventured out of the canopy, driven by the first pangs of hunger I'd had since I found my enchanted lake, I saw at once that my world had changed. Halfway up the cliffs, laid out so straight it could have been drawn with a ruler, was the snow line. Above it, hovering white mounds of frozen surf obscured the grain of the ground, cottoned the trees, slumped over the rocks and cuts in deep drifts. It looked like an avalanche, holding its breath.

I was snowbound. Trapped in a shrinking belt of life between half-covered hills and the half-frozen lake. That snow line would come down and the lake freeze up until there was nowhere left to go. It was going to be a struggle to survive. Only spring could spring me from this paradise turned death trap. If I was going to live that long, every move I made would have to be smart, considered and efficient.

Worst of all, that meant I was going to have to lay off the nip. Ain't that just the way with indulgences— the times you need them most are the times you can afford them least.

I set up camp on the north shore, where the afternoon sunshine kept a long, crescent-moon-shaped part of the lake from freezing—for now. My new house was in a hollow at the base of a blackened tree, a remnant of what must have been a huge fire here a long time ago. Weathered deadfall littered the ground like pickup sticks, silvery trunks and burnt-out stumps mixed with the living forest. I kicked a bunch of pine needles into my hollow log for comfort. They kept a cushion of air beneath me when I slept, raising my body off the damp ground that worked like a heat sink, trying to suck the warmth and life out of me.

As long as that arc of lake stayed unfrozen I had water only a few steps away, and with food scarce I needed to be careful about conserving energy, most of which I consumed just keeping warm. I became a skilled tracker, finding small meals from footprints in the mud and snow. But winter was coming on hard now, and what hadn't died, flown away or been eaten was hibernating. Soon I was reduced to bugs and brown grass. It wasn't enough. Some days I wouldn't even leave my stump. I was winding down.

They say a kind of acceptance overtakes a being slowly freezing to death. They say that about humans, anyway. If it's also true of cats, I was denied that comfort. In fact, when I was awake, I was mad as hell. If I didn't give into useless rage or a make a suicidal run for the hills I'd like to think it was because I was being smart, trying to buy all the time I could. The idea that I was just a passive victim waiting to turn into a popsicle was more intolerable than the prospect of dying.

And I had a secret weapon, one that worked for me but would kill a person—sleep. My three-foot round bedroom-in-a-stump was well chosen. It had a small, arched entrance like a cartoon mouse hole, it provided good protection from rain and wind, and if I curled up tight on my meticulously maintained mattress of pine needles I could almost stay warm when I slept. Almost—but each night I lost another ounce of fat, and each night the chill got deeper in my bones. With catnip off limits, dreams were my only release, and they were very seductive. Each awakening was a small victory.

Mostly I dreamed of home, but the cold kept intruding. I used to think San Francisco was chilly, back when I had no idea what cold meant. But this was something else, something life-threatening, and it seemed like every dream that started with Doc and Fern ended with ice and snow.

It's funny the way you'll incorporate your surroundings into your dreams. One time I dreamt that Fern had burned dinner and that translated into me thinking I was trapped in a forest fire. I woke up wild and thrashing. It took me ten minutes to calm down. That's the other funny thing about real stuff entering your dreams—you always get it wrong.

It's hard to say how much longer I would have lasted. I was sleeping most of the time now. The lake froze, food disappeared, I was down to skin and bones. When I was half mad with thirst, I'd lick the ice and get half mad with cold, my only "nourishment" was dead grass and bugs.

If I never have to eat an insect again, it will be too soon. So it was strange that I dreamt of one that afternoon, like it was tormenting me in my final hours, invading my last place of peace. I dreamed I was chasing the world's biggest housefly, buzzing noisily over my head, always just out of reach. I didn't want to eat it, it was just *there*, driving me crazy. Mostly I wanted to shut it up, the damned thing was so loud it felt like it was mocking me.

I woke up confused, listening for that sound like it was real. But whatever the noise was, it was gone. When I went back to sleep, so was the fly. You always get it wrong in a dream. The fly had been real. And it was going to save me.

* * *

Survival is not a mistake. Sure, luck has always followed me, I don't deny it. But you have to be smart enough and capable enough to take advantage of luck, or even to recognize it. My saviors were a mile away around the curve of the lake. A stand of trees blocked the noise from that direction, I couldn't see them and I couldn't hear them.

But I could smell, and what I smelled this bright, snow-blind morning was cooking. Bacon, if my nose didn't betray me, and it never did. The only difference between me and a bloodhound is that I don't catch criminals for a living. And I'm prettier.

But I must have looked a sight that morning, skinny body, wobbly legs, nose poked high in the air, sniffing. The smell seemed to be coming from my right, counterclockwise around the shore. The easiest way to get there would be to avoid the trees and go straight to the lake. Not the safest, however. If the natives weren't friendly I'd be exposed on a big sheet of ice. But I was beyond that calculation; I'd depend on my "luck" and hope for the best.

First thing I saw was the smoke, trailing off above the copse of trees, just where I expected it to be. So far, so good. But when I got out on the lake I had to look hard through the dazzle before I believed my squinting eyes. There was my *fly*. A big white fly sitting on the ice, looking like a miniature version of the jet that took me across the country, so long ago. From somewhere deep inside I summoned a burst of energy and trotted towards that vision.

"Hey, Clarence, lookie there!"

"Where?"

"Over by the Cessna, see?"

"I'll be damned. What's that, a cat, you think?"

"Gotta be. Kitty, kitty, kitty! Come here, li'l fella."

"He heard ya. Here he comes."

"I bet he's hungry."

"You reckon, Charlie? I don't know how the guv'mit let you retire, mind like that."

"Smart ass. Here boy, that's it." Charlie took a sausage out of his plate and waved it in the air. "You want some of this, kitty cat? Come on, don't be afraid...."

"Mrooowrr!" Hunger made me beg. I was ashamed; if I could have blushed, I would have.

"Aww, don't cry. Here you go." Charlie tossed the sausage over my shoulder, shiny and steaming against the snowy ground. I pounced on it fast and made it disappear.

"Damn thing fetches like a dog," the one called Clarence said.

"Give him some of yours."

"Okay by me, but the way you cook we ain't doing him no favors. Want some bacon, Fido?"

"Fido?" Charlie said.

"Why not? Comes like a dog, fetches like a dog."

You can call me whatever you like, mister, I thought, tearing into the overcooked bacon, just keep the food coming.

I ran out of belly before they ran out of patience. They even gave me a saucer of some kind of fake milk they used in their coffee. The edge came off my burning hunger and attached itself to my curiosity. Who were these guys?

A couple of things I could see. They were old men, and they were black men. The one called Clarence was bald under the knit cap he constantly tugged down over his round head, Charlie had a fringe of white hair bulging around the bottom of his baseball cap. One more thing was clear to me—neither guy was what you could call a cat person, but they gave off a sweet vibe, especially Charlie. I'm sensitive to these things, and to me, he read wry and confident, sad and kindly, all at the same time. I was counting on the kindly—these guys had just picked up a pet, like it or not. My job was to get them used to the idea.

"Ready to go scare some fish?" Clarence asked.

"You get the poles, I'll cut the hole. I don't trust you with machinery." Charlie answered.

"You old fool. If it wasn't for this damn arthur-itis I'd kick your tail."

"If you didn't have arthritis I'd let you use the saw," Charlie said, making geezer noises as he stood up.

"What about Fido here?"

"What about him?" Charlie asked.

"He looks cold. Think we should zip him in the tent?"

"Tent's made of nylon, dummy. Ever heard of claws?"

"What do *you* think? You knew Lucy."

Charlie chuckled "I heard that. Damn fine woman, though."

"Best second wife I ever had, rest in peace," Clarence said.

"He'll be okay," Charlie patted my head tentatively. "Fish for dinner tonight, Fido. Unless Clarence forgot the bait again."

"Oh, Jesus," Clarence blurted. "You got the keys to the plane?"

"It's unlocked. Why, forget something?"

"Never you mind, old man, but *you* get the poles." Clarence said, gimping his way across the ice while Charlie cackled at his back.

I was feeling logy as hell, the greasy breakfast dead weight in my gut, but I still had work to do. The guys were getting ready to move, and I wasn't sure I'd made my connection yet. I needed more time to pour on the charm. If I fell asleep here I might wake up alone and deserted, and I couldn't chance that. So I kept real close to Charlie as he cleaned up camp, weaving in and out of his legs, making little chirrups as I ran my flanks over his ankles. I don't think he liked it very much, he was mincing his steps, trying to avoid me. I got the hint and hung back a few inches, but when he bent over to grab a couple of fishing rods out of the tent I was right behind him. When he turned around, he zigged and I zagged.

A big boot came down on my tail. I screeched—out of surprise, mostly, it didn't hurt much because the ground was soft and snowy—but it damn near made the old man topple over.

"Jaysus!" he yelped, staggering backwards, fishing poles clattering to the ground. He windmilled his arms comically, like he was trying to take flight, but when he got his balance and stared at me the look in his eyes gave me a scare. I crouched, hissing, expecting a boot in my bloated belly any moment. All pure animal instinct and all wrong. Luckily I got *my* balance back before he reached for me. Otherwise I would have fanged his gnarly hand.

"Did I getchya bad, kitty?" He crooned, running my tail between his fingers. I came out of my crouch and arched my back to meet his strokes.

"Nah," Charlie answered himself, "you're just fine. You *do* get underfoot, Fido," he said, scratching my ears. "You oughta watch yourself. I ain't *tryin* to fall down and break a hip way out here, shape I'm in."

Charlie bent over and picked up the rods, grunting lustily as he straightened up. My first instincts about him had been spot on, there wasn't a mean bone in his body. But it was a body in pain and I felt bad about shaking him up like that. I stayed back a couple of feet as he toddled out onto the ice.

"What?" he said, eyeing me warily. "You want to watch a couple of old farts do some ice fishing? Well, come on along then. But it's gonna be chilly out there, 'specially without none of Clarence's certified applejack to warm you up."

I made it out to the airplane without causing further distress. Clarence was unfolding a couple of aluminum chairs on the ice nearby. "This spot okay?" he asked.

"Good as any," Charlie answered.

Clarence picked up some kind of machine I'd never seen before.

"Fire in the hole!" he yelled. He pulled a rope and the chain saw screamed to life, spitting smoke.

My fur jerked up so hard it felt like I was shooting hair darts. The old men were laughing so loud I could hear it over the saw. I didn't stop running until I was back on the beach.

Not my best moment, but mission accomplished. Those old dudes had just bought themselves a cat. I spent the day in camp, curled up on the ground cloth, nestled close to the cooling metal of a folded-up cookstove.

CHAPTER 30

I could have done without the hot sauce, but, for old men two-thirds drunk and three-quarters froze, they didn't cook half-bad. My body was so undernourished it sucked the breakfast out of my gut and into my muscles by noon, so I was more than ready for dinner. The oily smell of frying fish got me going so strong I didn't notice my mouth was on fire until I'd downed most of a bass. I ate some snow and burped. Charlie and Clarence thought that was real funny, but they were pretty well greased. Otherwise, I like to think, they wouldn't have served Cajun fish to a starving cat.

Actually, I was kind of envious. The party didn't wind down for hours and the jollier they got the more I wished I could sneak out for some iced nip and join the fun. But I had bigger fish to fry (sorry).

Charlie leaned back in his folding chair, took away the hand he'd been letting me rub my nose and ears against and pulled a couple of brown sticks out of his fishing vest. He looked at Clarence with raised eyebrows.

"Don't mind if I do," Clarence said, taking one and running it under his nose. "Cuban?" he asked.

"White Owl, like you could tell the difference," Charlie laughed. "Some off-brand Hondurans, actually. Picked 'em up in Salt Lake. Ought to *be* Havanas, freight they charge."

"Well, thank you kindly," Clarence said, biting off the end and thooing it into the snow.

Charlie took a twig from the sputtering campfire, touched it to the end of the cigar and hollowed his cheeks. Rich blue smoke wreathed his face; the smell reminded me of Doc, sitting on the couch smoking, me purring in his lap.

Charlie pulled the cigar out of his mouth, turned it around and blew on the glowing end.

"I shouldn't even be doing this," he said. "Shouldn't be doing a goddamned thing, according to the medics." Charlie made a face somewhere between a grimace and a grin. "Well, screw 'em," he said. He took a deep, luxurious pull, leaned his head back and blew a cloud of smoke straight up into the night air.

"So what they tellin' ya?" Clarence said, puffing along with him.

"You don't want to know."

"Hey, Chuck, this is me. Forty Sevens, Fifty Twos, that time in Berlin when you showed me the boil on your ass. Who else you gonna tell?"

"Not the FAA, that's for sure. They want my ticket."

"No!" Clarence said, but it sounded forced.

"You think I can pass my physical like this?" Charlie punched his chest. "My clogs got clogs. Need about nine bypasses."

"So get 'em, you stubborn SOB. Where we gonna go if you can't fly anymore?"

"Don't you fret. I know how to work the system. They never worried about my health when they were getting me shot at in two wars, they can forget about it now. I ain't gonna let 'em ground me before God does."

"Do they know about it?" Clarence asked.

"A little, but they don't know the half." Charlie shook his head, continued in a softer voice. "Hell, *I* don't know the half, that's the problem."

"Uh, what's that you say?"

"That's why I haven't had the surgery yet. I was over to the VA last week. They found a lump."

"Oh hell," Clarence said, grabbing his chin. "And?"

"Next week. They ran some tests. Could be something, could be nothing. But it don't look good."

"Lord have mercy."

"Amen to that." Charlie said.

They smoked in silence for a while after that, sipping cider, leaning on the back legs of their chairs. The wind had been picking up as the night went on, which was unusual around here, it tended to get calm after dark. Clouds scooted across the moon.

Charlie tugged on the brim of his cap. "Getting chilly," he said.

"Yeah, I had about enough," Clarence answered.

"I want to get up early tomorrow, beat this weather out of here."

"You check it on the radio?"

"Yeah, not so bad. Front coming down from Montana, scattered T-storms. But you never know this time of year, squall line could form ahead. If we get out of here by seven, we ought to miss the worst."

"Be bouncy, though."

"Ain't that just life," Charlie said, heaving himself to his feet.

Clarence tossed his cigar butt into the now smoldering fire and stood up. Both old men headed towards the tent, turning their backs on *me*.

Uh oh. I got up and stalked them to the tent. Clarence unzipped the flap and held it open for Charlie, and both of them trooped in. It was like I wasn't even there.

"Meow."

"Hey, Charlie, what about the cat?" Clarence said, poking his head out the flap.

"What about him," Charlie asked.

"MEOW!"

"I think he wants in."

"Ah, he'll be okay. Still some scraps in the pan, right?"

"Yeah."

"I don't want him waking us up, needing to pee or something. Let him be, he lives here. Hell, I bet he's gone in the morning."

"Suits me," Clarence said, zipping the flap closed.

"Meow??"

"Hush!" Charlie said like he meant it.

Damn.

I wasn't sleepy, for a change, and I really wanted to slip away long enough to catch a nip buzz, but I was afraid if I left this place they'd be gone when I came back.

So I parked myself right in front of the tent flap and groomed. If I get tired, I'll sleep right here. Those guys want out of the tent, they'll have to trip over me. But I was nervous, usually I make a better impression. By now I should be curled up on Charlie's legs, him not even turning in his sleep because he doesn't want to disturb me. Instead I'm lying in the snow, nervous as hell and jonesing for catnip, praying for a second chance to bond with an old man who obviously doesn't speak cat. My whole body shivered, and not just from the cold.

Daylight couldn't come too soon, and it didn't. I was up and down all night, with twisted dreams of home that always came out wrong, and sleepless hours of whippy wind knotting my fur. But I stuck to my post and tried to stay cheerful. I was going to be Mister Sparky in the morning no matter how I felt. But Lord, did the hours crawl that night.

Down in a bowl like Halfway Lake, dawn doesn't start on the horizon. You can see it coming, especially if you're a cat, when the black sky above grays a little. That event was coming later and later with each passing day, and this morning it seemed to be extra tardy. But it came, after the four-hundredth time I checked, and then things happened fast.

A buzzy alarm inside the tent, rustling and groaning followed by a few hearty coughs, a voice so thick with sleep I couldn't tell who it was.

"Morning."

"If you say so." That was Charlie, for sure.

"Want some joe?"

"If you're buying," Charlie said.

"Comin right up!" Clarence must have been a morning person.

The tent flap unzipped from bottom to top and Clarence stepped out. I was back a foot or two, standing tall and posing, ready for my close-up.

"Ho!" Clarence blurted when he saw me. "Hey Charlie," he continued, "guess who's still here?"

"Huh?"

Clarence bent down and scratched the top of my head. "Fido. I'm petting him right now."

"Well, don't feed him any of your coffee. It'd kill him and I don't want the animal rights people coming after me."

"You don't like it, *you* get up and make it," Clarence chuckled.

"I gotta save my strength. Don't forget who's flying your sorry ass out of here. Speaking of which, how's the weather?"

Clarence stood up and scanned the sky. "Looks clear, mostly, kind of windy and warmer, I think."

"Means the front's getting closer. Hop to it on that coffee, I'll get these old bones moving as quick as I can."

Clarence unfolded the camp stove. I was being ignored again. Time for some bold action. I spun around, pointed my bushy tail straight towards the brightening sky, and traipsed right into the tent, chirruping a little so I wouldn't startle the old man.

Charlie was sitting on his cot, bent over, grunting as he tried to pull on his boots. He didn't hear me, so I nuzzled up against his straining hand, offering a cheery meow.

"Clarence!" he shouted. "Why'd you let the cat in?"

"That where he is? He was just here a second ago. And whaddaya blaming me for? He ain't on no leash."

I was getting seriously nervous about my reception here. Charlie seemed annoyed, in a hurry, and definitely not happy to see me. A part of me wanted to drop my tail and slink away. Another part wanted to say the hell with it, I'll take my chances with my tree and my catnip. But the smart part was persistent.

Graceful as I could, and that's pretty damned graceful, I leapt into Charlie's lap, landing so lightly he barely moved.

"I'll be damned," he said softly. "If you aren't the very devil...."

But he was smiling. That was the important thing. And when he raised his hands to his lap, he didn't toss me off, but cradled my head and scratched my ears. That was the next most important thing.

"What are we gonna do with you?" Charlie sighed.

Yeah, that *is* the question, ain't it, I thought.

I made sure to hang close during coffee. When Charlie went to the plane to get his flight bag I followed. When he sat back down and turned on a crackly little hand-sized radio I pretended to listen. I would have jumped right in his lap again, except that he was furiously scribbling into a pad and making marks on some sort of big paper chart.

Finally he spoke up. "We go south over towards Four Corners, then back northwest to the basin we should pass through the weak part of the front. Take a while though, what with headwinds on the first leg."

"Fine with me. It ain't like I got to get back to work or anything," Clarence said.

"One good thing about being old and useless," Charlie said wryly.

"You make sure you see that doc when you get back, and you call me, you hear? You call me one way or the other—though I'm sure it's nothing. You'll outlive us all."

"Already have," Charlie said. "All but you. And you ain't worth a damn." Charlie deadpanned for a second before they both cracked up laughing.

I was enjoying this lovefest as much as the next cat, but, like, what about *me*, guys? Clarence was already up and moving stuff out of the tent. I was hanging around looking eager. But my performance was going to waste, nobody was paying me any attention.

"Mrrooorr!"

Charlie folded his maps and stared right into my eyes. His expression was so strange, full of pain and pity and something I couldn't quite make out, maybe resignation. I thought he was about to speak to me, but I was wrong.

"Hey, Clarence. You bring those ski gloves of yours this trip?"

"You mean those old, thick ones? Yeah. I hate 'em though, hard to move my fingers. You want 'em?"

"No, you do."

"Me? Why?"

"Cause I ain't gonna let Fido here loose in the Skylane to crap all over the upholstery, that's why."

"You serious?"

"Serious...." Charlie paused. "I was *gonna* say serious as a heart attack," and he cackled until he coughed.

CHAPTER 31

Charlie shouldn't have worried about me crapping all over his precious airplane. I can hold my bowels, even under extreme provocation. The problem was at my *other* end. But with the greasy slop they fed me and the way that bird bucked and rolled, what did they expect? I barfed on Clarence, heaved on the floor, spewed on the back seat, launched on the luggage, and ralphed on the rudders. I couldn't get out a decent meow without going splat somewhere.

Here's the thing about little planes: They bounce a lot. And they make noise like it was on purpose. But here's the other thing: Once you get over the stark staring terror, the wobbling, the brain-splitting racket, the cold and the drafts, they're kind of fun.

I'd only lasted about ten minutes in Clarence's grasp, through a takeoff that felt straight up and the slewing, swoopy climb that tied my guts in a knot. But after I'd bolted free and decorated the upholstery for a while, the flight smoothed out and I stopped hurling and howling—not that my saviors could hear, they both wore headsets—and before long curiosity had me peeking out the windows.

The big surprise was how slow we seemed to be moving. It looked like the whole world was laid out below me, and we were barely poking along. The only time I got a sense of speed was when we blasted through clouds—which I didn't like because they blocked my view and always came along with a sickening bump. But when we popped out and I could see the horizon again, my innards calmed down and I was almost happy.

I tell you one thing, I'd rather be free and clear-headed in a little plane than doped and boxed in a big one. The only drugs I like are the ones I give myself. And you already know how I feel about cages.

That day was all flying, with one little break. About noon we came out of the sky long enough for the guys to clean up and fuel up the plane and themselves. They offered me some food, too, but I wasn't going to make *that* mistake again. Charlie put me down under the wing of the airplane, parked on a grassy patch just off the runway, and gave me a bowl of water to slurp, which helped a lot. In the meantime, Clarence went at the seats with a roll of paper towels, cussing me under his breath the whole time.

"...more vomit here than cat, gawddammit. Shouldn't be nothing left of you but a empty bag of fur."

"Quit bitching and hand me some oil, will ya?" Charlie said as he poked around the front of the plane. "We're down a quart."

"You the one who's down a quart, fool." Clarence griped. "Bringing a damned wild animal up in the air like that." He grabbed a plastic bottle from behind the back seat, handed it to Charlie. "I thought we was going fishin, not cattin."

"Last time we went cattin you caught more than you bargained for, way I remember it," Charlie said, laughing.

"I got sicker than Fido here," Clarence said. "Stunk worse, too, till I got that shot back at base."

"I *told* you 'bout messin with those bar girls. Had almost as good a laugh on your ass then as I'm having now. You done cleaning that puke yet? Be nice to get back home by sunset."

"Yeah," Clarence reached down and tossed me in the plane. "But I was kinda hoping Barf Boy would wander off," he said, as he climbed into the passenger seat.

"I thought the same thing about you forty years ago," Charlie smirked as he buckled up, "and there you are. Still."

"You gonna jaw or fly, old man," Clarence said.

"Clear!" Charlie shouted out the open window. Two seconds later he turned the key. Two seconds after that my ears were flat against my head, trying to block the noise. I don't think I'd mind flying at all if someone would come up with a cat headset.

Believe it or not, I spent most of that second leg of our flight sleeping. The novelty was gone—I ran out of fear, got used to the noise, and my curiosity took a nap. I didn't wake up until my stomach—which had stopped bothering me since I threw it out of work— gave a sudden lurch as we banked for our landing. I dug my claws into the seat and held on tight. But Charlie put that tin bug on the ground so softly I could hardly tell when we stopped flying and started rolling.

Pretty soon we coasted to a stop and the motor shut down. Charlie picked me up by the scruff and hauled me out of the plane. I was in a whole new world.

It was chilly and there were patches of dirty snow around, but it was nowhere near as cold as the lake had been. The air was thicker too, but so dry it made my nostrils burn. Not much grew here, that I could see, and I could see plenty in the clear desert air, even as dusk dimmed the picture.

I didn't know what a real desert was, of course, but I knew the craggy landscape that surrounded this little airport was the deadest I'd ever seen. There wasn't any grass underfoot, just packed earth with metal bolts sticking up where the guys tied down the airplane. I stretched my legs and took a leak behind the only greenery I could find—some scrubby bushes planted in front of a big trailer, up on blocks, just off the runway. Charlie's office, as it turned out.

When I finished my business, they were inside that trailer, with the door open. I was starving and decided to let them know it.

"There he is," Clarence said when he heard my yawp. "I think he's hungry again. We got anything left to feed him, Chas?"

"Bait?" Charlie answered.

"Nah, I chucked it. Got a can of Spam I brought, though."

"Hell, that's cat food, near enough. Give him a little."

Clarence unzipped a big duffel bag and started rooting around in it. "Speaking of cat food, want me to go get some before I leave?"

"Ah, thanks, but I can do that on the way home, well as you," Charlie answered.

"You taking him *home* with you?"

"Tell you the truth, I hadn't thought about it, but what else?"

Clarence scooped a generous helping of mystery meat into a soup bowl and mashed it down with a spoon before offering it to me on the office floor.

"Well," he said, "I guess it is a little late for Humane to be open tonight. Or maybe they're there twenty-four seven?"

Charlie shook his head. "I don't like that idea, Clarence. Hardly seems fair, snatching him up just to do him like that. It might come to that, but for now I think I'll take him home. 'Less you want to do it?"

"Rather not, all the same to you. I don't care much for cats, never did. Though this one *is* different, I gotta admit. Why don't you leave him here at the field?"

Charlie reached down and scratched the top of my head, still bobbing in the yummy meat. "That's okay," he said. "We'll try it this way awhile."

Charlie drove a great big old car and he was fussier about it than his airplane. He newspapered the passenger seat and plopped me down.

"You mess my Caddy you'll ride in the trunk, Fido. Swear to God. If you got to get sick, do it on the paper."

Okay, whatever. All I was sick of was riding in vehicles. The big sedan rode like a dream, though. It was like riding on air, which is funny, because riding in the airplane was like riding in a truck.

I was a good boy and stayed quiet, right through a stop at a convenience store and on to Charlie's townhouse, ten minutes away. We bumped up his driveway and into a garage that was just barely big enough for the car. But the groans Charlie made squeezing out the door were about more than the tight fit. He didn't look good at all.

"Oh me…" he sighed, setting me down on the shag rug next to his easy chair. "Don't go nowhere, I'll be right back."

But I was so happy to be on solid ground, in a warm place that didn't jump, roll, or fly that I just had to pad around and check it out.

Charlie's living room wasn't small, but it was too small for all the stuff crammed in there. A big, sectional couch covered in plastic, footstools and armchairs similarly laminated, coffee tables filled the floor, pictures cluttered the walls, knick-knacks crowded every surface. It was like he once lived in a much bigger place and didn't have the heart to throw out anything when he moved.

The odd part was nothing seemed used—not that the stuff was new, just dead, like it was in a museum. The place even smelled stale. Only one corner, with Charlie's recliner, a folding tray and a TV showed any signs of life. And it was dark, too. There must have been a dozen lamps and Charlie had turned on exactly one of them, a tall ornate metal thing with a shade big as a roof—also covered in clear plastic. I wasn't sure what the deal was, but if he came back with a roll of Saran Wrap I was going to run.

Matter of fact, he did come back with a roll of plastic, but it was just a runner for the rug.

"We'll set you up right here," he said, putting down a couple of bowls and a litter box on the runner alongside his easy chair. "Now don't go making trouble. Jessie'd be real upset if she knew a damned cat was scratching up her stuff, you hear?"

I knew those words were for me, but he spoke them to a picture on his folding tray. He sat down with a heavy groan, picked the picture up by the frame, kissed his fingers and touched the glass.

"I sure wish you were here to take care of me, baby," Charlie rasped. "I'm *so* tired...." Charlie put the picture back on the tray and clicked on the TV. His big head settled on his chest facing the television, which was blaring out a laugh track.

Something must be funny as all get out, I thought. But Charlie wasn't laughing. He wasn't even watching. His eyes were closed ... and wet.

My human alarms were going off so strong my fur stood on end. Charlie sat up, rubbed his eyes with his palms and swiveled his head from side to side as if he'd just gone blind and was trying to shake it off. He started a deep breath, made a sound like half a cough that seemed to catch in his throat, grabbed the arms of his chair and held on tight. I thought he was dying.

Charlie's mouth twisted in pain, like he was struggling for air. Time stood still for a moment ... two moments ... three.... A gasp, a strangled squeak— he was fighting—and then a sudden whistling rush as all the pain and loneliness and who knows what inside him burst out in a series of teeth-clenched, moaning sobs. It scared me to death. And I was never so relieved in my life.

I did what cats do. I jumped on his chubby lap and meowed, right in his face.

I felt his hand come down softly on my back. It was hot and sweaty and shaking. He kept on crying but it wasn't so scary now. The tension was gone out of it, and he just let go. It was a long time subsiding. When he finally stopped, he picked me up in both hands and looked me straight in the eyes.

"*She* sent you, didn't she, Fido?" he said. "Jessie wanted you here to keep her old man company when he died. God bless her, she's watching over me, even now."

I don't know that I've ever seen more pain in a human's eyes. But Charlie was smiling. Imagine that.

CHAPTER 32

"Yoo hoo! Mr. Worthman!"

"Uh oh," Charlie muttered under his breath. "I'm right here. Is that you, Gladys?"

"Yes, Charles. Pretty day, isn't it?"

Charlie crawled out from under his car. He'd backed it into his driveway, where he was working on it this morning. I was nodding on the dry grass of his postage-stamp-sized lawn, enjoying the sun.

"I made you a little something," the overlarge, white-haired woman said. She was dressed up like she was going on a date, and made up too, little circles painted on her pale cheeks. "I thought you might be hungry."

"Well, isn't that nice of you," Charlie said, taking a covered dish from her hands. "What is it?"

"Tuna casserole. You said you liked it when I dropped some off Christmas morning?"

Charlie lifted the lid and took a sniff. "Appreciate it, Gladys. You shouldn't have gone to the trouble...."

"Nonsense," she said, waving a hand full of sparkly rings and jangling bracelets. "No trouble at all. I enjoy having someone to cook for," and she batted her eyes like a teenager.

Charlie's body language seemed to betray a certain lack of enthusiasm about all this. But I had no problems with it at all. The scent of that baking fish wafted over the lawn and woke me up like smelling salts.

"Let me take this inside," Charlie said. "Would you like a cup of coffee? I have some ready."

"Oh, I don't want to be any bother…. Charles! There's a kitty cat following you!"

"That's Fido," Charlie said, laughing. "He follows me everywhere."

And I *was* following him, too, right through the garage and into the house. I was going to get me some of that food if I had to carry it in myself.

"He's *adorable!*" Gladys bubbled. "I didn't know you liked cats, Charles. Is he yours?"

"Seems to be," Charlie said, taking the dish into the kitchen. "Much as he's anyone's. Make yourself to home, Gladys. I'll bring out that coffee in a sec." The kitchen door swung closed before I could get through. It almost slammed on my nose.

Kitchen doors couldn't stop Gladys's mouth.

"Fido," she shouted. "That's a funny name for a cat."

"Clmpff nmm," came Charlie's muffled voice.

"Pardon?"

Charlie kneed open the door; he was carrying a cup and saucer in each hand.

"Clarence named him," he repeated. "Friend of mine, I think you met him once. Anyway, we found this fella up ice fishing in Colorado, and Clarence thought he acted more dog than cat. So, Fido."

I was sitting on the rug, heartbroken. I was figuring tuna and all he brought was coffee and lame conversation. Gladys took the drink and sat her bulk down on the plastic covered couch, which squeaked and hissed like it wasn't enjoying it.

"I've always been fond of kittens," Gladys gushed. She patted her thighs, "Come here, sweetums. Come, come … uh … Fido? I still think that's a silly name, Charles. Is he friendly?"

"I guess," he said. "Is to me, anyway. He should be kind of wild, though. We found him all by his lonesome up there. And hungry as a lion."

Gladys patted her legs and called me again. I slunk over to Charlie's recliner and hid under his feet.

"The poor thing," she said. "I suppose he's just shy."

Yeah, that's it lady. Now go home.

They made small talk for a while. Charlie was getting restless to judge from the way he was squirming in his seat. Finally Gladys took the hint.

"I should let you get back to your car," she said.

"Yeah," Charlie grunted as he got up. "Time to get to work. I sure thank you for the casserole, though. I'll have some for lunch."

"You're quite welcome, Charles." Gladys walked over to me and knelt down. She was light on her feet for such a big woman.

"Aren't you just the most precious…." she cooed, tickling my head with her manicured nails. "He does look a little skinny," she said, standing up. "Would you like me to look after him when you're at the airport, Charles? It would be my pleasure."

Charlie picked me up, hands under my front paws, the rest of me dangling in midair. "Would you like that, Fido? Spend some time with Mrs. Apple here?"

No! But Charlie didn't speak cat yet.

* * *

I must be a gentle soul, deep down. I know I can be a hard ass, just ask anyone who ever messed with me, or anyone who fell in love with me right before I took a powder. But as averse as I was to this woman, who was obviously using me to get next to a man who didn't know how to say no, I cut her some slack, instead of cutting her face.

And I'm telling you, it was all I could do to keep my claws sheathed. When, early the next morning, Charlie dropped me off at Gladys's townhouse—as much a museum as his place, but brighter and loaded with dolls, stuffed animals and ceramic figurines—she started in on me and didn't leave me alone until he picked me up that evening. Wherever I went, there she was. When I thought I'd found a private place her piping voice would follow me, giving me no peace. When she let up long enough for me to fall asleep I'd wake up five minutes later with her big paws all over me. It was almost enough to make me wish I was back at the lake.

Except for the food. The old woman could cook, I'll give her that. And she thought that canned cat food was tantamount to animal abuse. If only she'd shut up once in a while.

This semi-happy state of affairs went on for about a month. I gained weight and Gladys got to see Charlie twice a day, when he dropped me off and picked me up. She was glowing and I was getting silky and sleek again, but Charlie wasn't looking well at all. Part of it might have been awkwardness at fending off Gladys's affections, but most of it was sickness. I could smell it on him.

I might have stayed in joint custody forever, or at least until spring came and I was ready to take the road west again, and it would have been okay. But it wasn't to be. Gladys overplayed her hand.

I think the cold weather gave her the idea. And it was plenty chilly, though it never got as frigid as the lake.

For a woman who rarely left the house, Gladys stayed busy. When she wasn't talking to me she was talking on the phone, and when she wasn't cooking she was fiddling with two metal sticks and a ball of yarn.

Don't ask me why, but next to catnip nothing drives us crazy like a nice fuzzy yarn ball. One boring day Gladys tossed me a softball sized globe of the stuff and I went ape, to her great amusement. Maybe she figured it was better for me to shred wool than to crash all her porcelain dollies, which I had been known to do. But when I kick-pawed the ball until yarn was wrapped around my body so bad she had to extricate me, I saw a light go on in her eyes.

"Look at my little precious," she said, fussing with the knots and tangles. "What a silly boy!" When I was unraveled she went into a big wicker hamper and pulled out another ball.

No thanks, I was thinking, had enough for now. But she didn't give it to me. She just held the yarn against my fur and nodded.

"This will be perfect!" she yawped. And she sat back in her rocker and got those sticks to clicking. In a week it was done.

They say that cats don't have facial expressions, but that's not quite true. If you're a cat person, a sensitive, observant cat person, you can read our feelings in the cast of our eyes, the rake of our whiskers, the set of our ears. Charlie didn't know cats from quacks, but he read me when it counted, bless his ailing heart.

"Hello, Gladys. How was my boy today?"

"Good evening, Charles. You wait right here, I have a surprise for you!"

I had squidged myself into the far corner of the living room, trying to hide. Gladys came over and scooped me up.

Have you ever seen a cat in a sweater? Neither had I, neither had Charlie. A poodle maybe, but they deserve it.

Gladys handed me to a wide-eyed and speechless Charlie.

"Don't you just love it?" she bubbled.

"It" was a big, itchy, hand-knitted sweater that covered my trunk like a tube top. It was snug as a sleeve and hot as a stove; I never felt so humiliated in my life.

"My, my, my," Charlie said, stuck.

"I thought with it being the weekend tomorrow, and you two maybe outside...."

"It, uh, must have been a lot of work."

"And so cold and all lately...."

"Well.... Thank you." But there was a question mark on Charlie's last word.

"Would you ... would you like to stay for dinner?"

Charlie is holding me and I'm looking up soulfully into his eyes. My ears are flat against my head, my jaw slack, tip of my tongue hanging out, almost panting. My proud tail hanging straight down like a flag in the rain.

"Charles?"

For a moment it was like Charlie didn't hear her. But he heard me.

"...Ah, no thank you Gladys. I'm kind of pooped, I think we better be getting home."

"Oh, of course, you need your rest. I'll see you later. And I'm so glad you liked it!"

No sooner had her door clicked shut than Charlie whispered in my ear.

"Damned crazy woman...."

And no sooner had Charlie's door slammed shut than he pulled the monstrosity off me—forward, over my head, which not only almost suffocated me but cost me a claw. I think it was the kindest thing a human not called Doc or Fern ever did for me.

"Think you might want to spend some time over at the airport with me, Fido?"

I didn't know how to nod my head and I didn't know how to say yes. But I knew how to purr.

Our new regimen started that Monday. I never saw the sweater again and I never saw Gladys, either. Nor, as far as I know, did Charlie. I think he was the more relieved of the two of us. But, then again, I liked her cooking more than he did.

Charlie had an office at the airport, that trailer I told you about before. It was a big metal thing up on blocks, the kind you'd see at a construction site. Outside, a few rangy shrubs made a bad attempt at homey landscaping, inside was a confusion of old aircraft parts, broken instruments, piles of charts and books, a desk littered with a couple of clunky computers, a toy airplane and a phone, and an asthmatic space heater on the floor that singed my fur if I got too close. He set me up with food and a litter box, but after being cooped up for so long I was happier to be outside when the weather was decent. Charlie let me come and go as I pleased; there were birds to chase and mice to hunt, sand to pee in and airplanes with big, high wings to sun myself on. It was a pretty good setup and I was happy.

That airport wasn't the busiest place in the world, but it seemed like everyone who came through there knew Charlie and dropped by the trailer for a chat. Once in a while a student would appear, all eager and nervous, and Charlie would go flying for a couple of hours. But that didn't happen very often. Mostly he just sat on a squeaky office chair and held court. I was the new kid in town, and I got plenty of attention. When it got to be too much I'd go outside and scare the rodents.

After a few days of going back and forth to the townhouse, Charlie started leaving me at the airport. That was fine by me, I hated the car rides and it always seemed I was in the middle of a sweet dream when it was time to go. I quickly found my spots and made the place my home; I liked the airport.

Besides, his house was dark and depressing. And Charlie didn't seem so sick when he was among people; going to work seemed to revive him.

Until one day, when he didn't show up.

CHAPTER 33

I have to admit I didn't even notice that he was gone until most of the morning was too. It was a pretty crappy day, gray with an on and off icy drizzle; I spent most of it under the trailer staying dry. After a few people trooped up to the office, knocked on the door, waited a while, then walked, drove or taxied away again, it hit me. Where was Charlie?

Charlie's car had a distinct sound, a big old American car sound I could hear coming a quarter mile away. I'd gotten into the habit of listening for it and meeting him on the trailer doorsteps. When I finally realized he was missing that morning, I kept an ear on the traffic noise, straining to catch the note of Charlie's Caddy in the drone. It never came. But Clarence did.

"Hey Fido? Where you at? I got your food. You here, cat?"

I pretended I didn't hear him—for about three seconds. Then I came trotting out from under the trailer, tippy-toe, making little mewling sounds as I rubbed against Clarence's pants leg.

"There you are. Don't you look fat and sassy? C'mon inside. Cold as death out here." Clarence turned the key and went into the office; I followed him. It was even colder inside, but I barely noticed. I was too busy eating.

Clarence didn't pay a whole lot of attention to me. After he fed me and plugged in the heater, he sat at Charlie's desk and picked up the phone.

"Charlie Worthman room? Yeah, thanks...."

"That you numbnuts? What you tryin to do, scare a Negro? Yeah, I'm there now.... Him too, he's right here."

Clarence looked up from the phone. "Charlie says hi, Fido."

"He's eating. What the hell else he do?" Clarence spoke into the phone again. "So what are they telling you?

"Uh huh ... okay ... all right," Clarence nodded as he spoke, doodling on a pad on Charlie's desk. "So when you come home?"

Clarence stopped doodling. "You funning me, right? You just got there!"

He covered the mouthpiece and spoke to me.

"Man's a fool," he said softly. "Tonight my ass."

Clarence took his hand off the phone, "What's the doc say about that? Yeah, I bet. You ought to at least let 'em check you out a few days, you mule....

"All right! Damn, whatever you say. It's your funeral. So, you want I should take Fido?... No, he seems fine. Damn sight better than you."

I had a hunch I was being discussed. I sat at Clarence's feet, cleaning my muzzle with long tongue flicks, then wetting a paw and doing my ears. I missed a few words.

"….now you're making some sense, for once. Rest up tonight in the hospital, just don't go having no more episodes. I'll drop by your crib tomorrow night…. Thanks, you too."

Clarence had the phone halfway to the hook, then put it back to his ear.

"What? What you say?"

Pause.

"All right, all right, all right! I'll fill the damn bowl until it don't hold no more! But I just brought the one can, where you say you keep it? Bottom drawer? Done. Now rest yourself, *and* me. I'll see your lame ass tomorrow. Bye."

Clarence frowned as he hung up the phone. He heaved himself off the chair, walked over to the filing cabinet, opened a drawer and shuffled around inside. When he stood up again he had an armful of cans.

"What you in the mood for, Fido," he said, peering though the bottom of his glasses to read. "Chicken with rice, Catfish filets, or Liver pate and beef?" Clarence did a take, staring at me and then reading the can again like he didn't believe his eyes.

"Liver pate and beef? Damn, cat, you eat better than me! Mind if I join you?" And he laughed a deep Santa Claus laugh.

The good news is that Clarence left the heater on, and I had food and water for a herd. The bad news is that he left me locked up in that office overnight. That doesn't sound so terrible now, but at the time I didn't know how long I'd be stuck there. By morning

I was feeling thoroughly claustrophobic, sniffing the corners for air leaks in case I had to start digging.

The only window in the trailer faced front, towards the runway. It was as gorgeous today as yesterday was bleak; I really wanted to be outside. The next best thing was to sit at the window, watching the planes take off and land. There was more of that going on than usual, because of the weather, I guess, and all that action made a lot of noise. So I missed hearing Charlie coming until I felt his footsteps on stairs.

I saw him before he saw me. It was the strangest thing, he looked like he'd lost ten pounds and he was more stooped than ever, but he didn't have that veil of sick gloom on him. When he blinked the noontime dazzle out of his eyes and saw me, he reached down and picked me up, a smile on his face like he'd never been sick a day in his life.

"That idiot leave you cooped up in here?" Charlie said, scratching my belly. "Well, he's gonna have to do a whole lot better than that."

I was purring as loud as those airplanes; I *felt* the change in Charlie. No pain—this guy isn't in pain anymore. He seems downright ... serene.

Charlie sat in his chair and put me back down on the floor. There was a mini-fridge under his desk; he reached inside and took out a plastic bottle, unscrewed the top, dug into his jacket for a vial, shook out a couple of pills and guzzled them down.

"Shouldn't oughta do that before I go flying, but what the hell. It don't make no never mind now."

He stood up and swung the door open for me.

"You want out, Fido?"

I did. I hate to use a dirty litter box when there's a whole world to spray. After taking care of business in the sand behind the trailer, feeling glad to be alive, I went looking for the sunniest spot I could find. Charlie had a couple of different airplanes, but the best one for sunning was the one I'd flown in on. It had its wings way up high, about six feet off the ground. And getting up there was easy—just hop on the tail and scoot around the rudder, up to the left wing and out towards the edge, away from the stinky gas cap. It was a trick I'd pulled many times before, and the only times Charlie had caught me at it was when he was getting the plane ready to fly. He'd come peeking over the wing, standing on a stepladder, checking out whatever it is that you're supposed to check before you go up, see me, and shoo me off. I could always tell when he was coming because I'd hear him unlock the airplane door before he got up on the wing, but I'd make him chase me off anyway. I'm bad like that.

I was only up there for about half an hour before Charlie came out to the airplane that sunny afternoon. I woke up hearing the door swing open and waited for his head to appear over the wing. But it never did. Instead, he started calling my name.

"Fido! Fiiidooo! Where you at, boy?"

Some instinct told me not to move a muscle, so I didn't.

"Fido! Where *is* that damned cat?"

I kept quiet, don't ask me why. He stomped around calling me for a full minute, but never thought to look up on the wing. Then he stopped, right under me, and began beeping numbers into his cell phone. I could hear every word he said.

"Hey Clarence, you there? Pick up…. No? Well, look, pal, I need you to do me a favor. I got me a charter to Tahoe. Couple of guys showed up and wanted to go right away. I'll be gone a few days. I need you to come over and pick up the cat, take him to your place. He's around here somewhere, if I can find him I'll put him in the trailer, if not, just come by and give him a holler. He'll show up, eventually. Soon as you can, okay? Thanks buddy," and he snapped the phone shut.

"Fido? Phweet! Phweet!" Charlie tried whistling and that almost did it. Usually whistling pulls me like a magnet, but not this time. I knew I was waiting for something, I just didn't know what it was.

Then Charlie, a study in calm today, got frustrated. He cursed, sighed, and went pounding off to the trailer, still barking my name. When he disappeared around back, I dove off the wing. The airplane door was wide open. I knew now what I'd been waiting for. In I jumped—to the floor by the rudder pedals, scooting between the front seats, up and over the back seat's bench, down through the baggage compartment and all the way back to the deep, narrow space behind the light glaring through the rear window.

If you make yourself a tight enough ball and the air isn't too bouncy, you can almost fool yourself into thinking you're still on the ground, and maybe all the noise is just the Missus going crazy trying to vacuum your hair out of the couch. There was a time, back in my Doc and Fern days, when even that was enough to send me careening into the basement. But look at me now.

Or rather, don't look, because I was hiding. I couldn't have told you why, back then, if my life depended on it, which it did. To this day I'm not sure. All I know is that if I had shown my face before we got off the ground, Charlie would have put me off the airplane and I'd probably still be wondering what happened to him. And I might never have made the final third of my journey, that difficult last leg that brought me back to the land of my birth and the loves of my life.

Then again, if I hadn't been on that plane I wouldn't have used up two of my nine lives in a single afternoon.

Little airplanes don't have rear view mirrors, or at least this airplane didn't. That allowed me to climb out of the baggage nook and onto the back seat, right behind Charlie, without being seen. I was going to make my presence known eventually, but not quite yet. Not until I had figured out what had me so hinky all day. The longer I waited, the longer the little oddities kept adding up. But adding up to what?

Like, what did it mean that Charlie wasn't talking to anybody on his radio? He had his headset on, but unless I missed it in the noise, he never spoke a word into the microphone.

Not that he was silent, he just wasn't talking. The old, sick dude who had rescued me from freezing, who only yesterday defined grumpy and had the stink of pain on his every labored breath ... was singing! You'd almost have to be there to understand how strange he was acting that day; it weirds me out even to remember it.

"Off we go, into the wild blue yonder, flying hiiigh, into the sun!" On and on like that.

Another thing—when had he changed clothes? I could only see the sleeves and collar, but he wasn't wearing that jacket when he got to the airport this morning. In fact, I'd never seen it before and I would have noticed if he'd ever worn it—even from behind I could see that it was way too tight and had braids and stripes and metal ornaments pinned all over it.

When I wasn't watching Charlie's jacket or listening to him groove, other stuff caught my attention. Like how low we were flying, how screamingly fast the scenery was ripping by the side window. How high, monstrous and *close* the white tipped peaks were, scraping by beneath us. Like the way the sun worked its way forward no matter how fast we flew, creeping lower and lower in front of our left wing. And how we seemed to be flying in a straight line. Even after the occasional bounce or bump we'd always come back to west, towards that imaginary spot in my mind's eye that marked home. It was like Charlie knew where I wanted to go, and was taking me there.

That idea couldn't have been more wrong.

I saw the ridge a long way off. The air was as clear as it ever gets, it could have been a hundred miles away—I wasn't built to judge distances that far, so it could have been more, or less. But for sure that ridge was bigger and taller than the random hills we were crossing now. Even this far away I could see the jagged peaks cutting the sky like a sawtooth, from the tip of our left wing to the tip of the right. And, little by little, as we got close, those mountains began to bulk up huge, seeming to grow up into the afternoon sky, looming and shadowed in front, spiky and gleaming on top.

It was all very beautiful and awesome, I was captivated, but it didn't seem connected to me. I felt like a spectator, like a human must feel watching a movie. I wanted to see it better, so I took a chance of being discovered and hopped on the top of the back seat for a straight ahead view.

Again, you have to realize I was out of my element, it took me a while to understand what I was seeing. But when I "got it" my fur stood up on end and my heart tripled its beat. A great, big, clawing mountain was right off the nose, filling the windscreen. And it was *higher than we were.*

I don't know how to fly. I don't know anything about the up and down and left and right of it. All I knew was Charlie, Charlie, Charlie.

"Charlie!" I howled. It came out as "screech!" but it was no good. He couldn't hear me through his earphones. *I* could barely hear me over the motor noise.

That mountain looked close enough to touch now. I could see single trees on its flanks. Enough being coy. I flung myself straight off the back seat—right at Charlie's head.

That scream I heard. The nose of the airplane pitched up violently, then swung hard right as Charlie slapped me off his scalp and into the passenger door. I hit the side window face first, and for a moment there, I was looking straight down. All I could see was mountain. I bounced off the door and clawed the seat fabric in a death grip, bracing myself, ready for anything.

Except the two things I saw next. First was the ground falling away sharply as Charlie quickly got control of the plane, lifted the nose and arced into a shallow banking climb.

Second was Charlie's face, streaked with tears. He looked at me with so much sadness I thought my heart would break. Did I do that? All I wanted to do was crawl on his lap and meow until he felt better, but his look told me to keep away.

"Now why'd you want to go and do that for?" Charlie whined like a hurt child. "How'd you get in here? Now I can't..." he sobbed. Some pilot's reflex made him look away, and out the windscreen. He flew the plane for a moment, straight and level, until he had time to compose himself.

"Come here, Fido," he said, reaching for me. I hopped onto his legs and put my paws on his belly.

"I was so close, boy. And now I can't," he said again. But this time it didn't sound like an accusation.

Charlie rubbed his face, wiping away the tears and a thin trickle of blood that ran from the punctures I'd made in his head. He looked at his hand and chuckled.

"You got me pretty good, didn't you Fido," he said, patting me between the ears just a little too hard. "So what the hell am I supposed to do now?" he continued. "Take the lousy chemo?"

"Meow?"

"No way. No goddamn way." The anger was returning to Charlie's voice. That didn't scare me. But when I felt the plane turning towards the sun again, towards that sky-scraping mountain, that did.

"Shrivel up until they gotta blow food up a tube to keep me alive? Uh uh. Ain't gonna happen. Not to the kid."

Turn back! I mewled. Turn around! Let's go home…. I suddenly realized that this was the first time I *wanted* to turn back—away from that spot under the setting sun I'd been following for so long—that this was the first time I'd called anyplace else "home."

But none of that mattered to Charlie. When I meowed in his face he only grinned, showing about a hundred teeth. I jumped on his shoulder and wailed in his ear, I licked his cheek, I scratched at the headset that hung around his neck, where my mad leap had knocked it. Charlie just reached up and held me by the scruff, my face against his, both of us watching that mountain coming closer.

"Shhh," he said. "Shhh. It's okay."

My whole body was vibrating like a tuning fork, my eyes were bugging out like they were trying to escape my head. The piney scent of woods invaded the cabin, just before we crashed. But we didn't crash; we climbed. The peak of that ridge slowed its terrifying climb up the windscreen … froze … and began to creep downward, and then down some more.

Then it was gone. We were over.

Charlie sighed and pointed the nose of the plane to the right of the sun, where it had been most of the day. Below us, peaks and valleys ranged as far as I could see, the near parts in deep shadow. But each ridge we passed was lower than the one before. I began to calm down as we droned on into the sunset, the same noise that was driving me crazy now reassuring, comforting.

And then it stopped.

All I could hear above my ringing ears was the wind, pulling us back, slowing us down. That, and Charlie's voice.

"Oh shit," he said. There was no more passion in his voice than if he'd dropped a wrench on the floor. No fear, either.

CHAPTER 34

Charlie picked me up and placed me on the right seat, soft as snow. Then he got busy. Flipping levers and switching switches, muttering their names to himself as he checked them off, one by one. He was totally calm as he did it, which is more than I can say for me. I wasn't sure what was happening, but I knew it wasn't good. But Charlie moved with unhurried precision, like he was doing a dance he learned years before and never forgot.

"Eighty glide, carb heat, mags, left tank, right tank," he called out softly as his hands danced, "primer, throttle, mixture. Again...."

"Mawk," I croaked, sounding like Rass. I wonder how *he's* doing, I thought. Probably better than me at the moment. "Mawk!"

"Easy big boy," Charlie said, reaching over to pet me. "No biggie. I just ran us out of gas. Can you believe it? Fifty-five years of flying and two wars and this is the first time I ever ran the tanks dry! On my last flight. Don't that just beat all?"

I rubbed my cheek against his right hand. Get me out of this, Charlie. I'm too young to die.

"Well, I guess I better get on the horn," he said. "Sure wish I could belt you up, Fido, this could get rough."

Charlie clamped his headset back over his ears, pushed some buttons on his panel.

"Mayday, mayday. Sacramento radio, this is Skylane six eight zero tango alpha, about twenty-five southwest of Lake Tahoe, descending through niner thousand, out of fuel."

I could only hear one side of the conversation, but I could tell Charlie had raised someone on the first try.

"Squawking seven seven zero zero and identing," he said. "Roger. No flight plan. Blue and white Cessna 182.

"Uh, on board? Two...." and he cracked up laughing.

"Sorry. Make that one. One and a cat.

"No, I'm fine....Don't you worry about me, sonny, I been doing this a while. Now, you got vectors for me or what?"

Charlie took his thumb off the microphone button and turned to me.

"They think I'm losing it up here, Fido. But never you mind. I'll get you down in one piece and that's a promise."

"Say again, Sacramento? You want me to go where? That's how far north? Uh, unable. Give me something west. If I can't make an airport, I want to put it down on the flat. All I see up north is big bumps."

"Roger. Two five zero on the heading. Amador County? What's the altitude? No, I don't have that chart. Long story. One thousand six hundred ninety? That means I have about six thousand to play with. What's the wind supposed to be up here? Got it. This is gonna be close."

Charlie banked the plane slightly to the left. I started to crawl back onto his legs, he brushed me away.

"Not now, Fido. I've got to do this just perfect if we're gonna land on pavement."

"Yeah, Sacramento. I'll keep you posted. Nothing yet, it's getting kind of dark down there. It's a non-towered field, right? Well, you want to see if there's someone there can fire up the beacon? I know it's early, but it might help."

"Goddamn eyes," Charlie said, rubbing them with the heel of his hand. "Can't see, can't breathe, can't barely walk, haven't had a woman since Jessie died. But I can still fly this son of a bitch, you just watch."

"Hey, Sacramento, what's the freq for Amador's pilot controlled lighting? One two two eight. Changing frequencies now, I'll be right back with you."

Charlie clicked a button on the yoke several times, squinting into the distance.

"Uh ... hmm ... maybe," he said under his breath. "Yeah! That's it! There it is, Fido, right off the nose. What did I tell you?"

"Sacramento? Zero tango alpha has the airport in sight. But you might want to get some equipment out there. I'm gonna have to stretch the hell out of this glide to make it."

The lower we went the darker it got. It was like a sunset speeded up, like we were going from the land of the living to the land of the dead in about ten minutes. I could tell we were getting close from the look on Charlie's face. There was tension there, lips sucked in tight, eyes darting, nose flaring like he was sucking wind. But mostly it was intense concentration, he was so focused on what he was doing that I felt almost alone. That part didn't feel good.

Neither did the bumps. As the ground reached up for us, the air got angry. I could hear every creak and groan of that old airplane now that the engine was silent, and every bounce became our last in my terrified mind's eye.

"Sacramento, zero tango alpha. Getting kind of low here. I'm going to shoot for the south-facing runway. What's the heading?

"Roger, one niner. I'm going to traffic frequency now. Wish us luck, and I'll talk to you from the ground."

Charlie took a deep breath, reached across the seat, unlatched the passenger door, scooped me up and held me in his lap. He seemed calm and in control, but his big belly was pouring out heat, and I could feel the pain in it. I could smell it too, mixed with the piney scent of the trees we were probably going to land in.

"Don't claw me, Fido," he said, his tone soft but his voice thick and strangled. "You're gonna be just fine." He popped his door open a crack, too. "Once we get on the ground you get the hell out of here fast. Nothing blows like empty tanks."

My mouth was so dry I couldn't even croak. Charlie thumbed his mike switch:

"Amador traffic, Cessna six eight zero tango alpha, about five northeast at three thousand five hundred. Out of fuel, coming in left base for runway one niner. Anyone in the pattern, get the hell out of the way."

My head was pressed against Charlie's stomach, his grip tight and sweaty. I could hear his wheezing breath, feel the gurgling thuds rumbling through his body. I was scared out of my mind, but the feel of Charlie deftly massaging the controls as he held me close gave me hope. Inside his body and outside the plane, everything was going to hell. How could he be so calm?

"We ain't got the altitude, Fido," Charlie said to me like I was his copilot or something. "Unless maybe I can pick up some lift off that ridge …. Wind is right … what the hell. Let's try it."

I felt the plane bank slightly to the right. The bumps got worse, Charlie rode the bucking plane, muttering curses under his breath.

"C'mon you SOB … come on … Yeah!"

It wasn't much. Just a soft push from beneath and a moment of smooth air. But through the sweat beaded on Charlie's face, through the pain that tore at his insides, through the wracking breaths he struggled to take, I saw a smile.

He held the plane steady for another moment, his eyes flicking left and right, waiting for something that only he could see.

"That ought to do it," he said, kicking the plane back to the left. "*Hell* yes, I'm good! Lookie there, Fido," he said, pointing out the windscreen. "I might even have to use flaps!" And he laughed out loud.

"Amador traffic, Cessna zero tango alpha, short final runway one niner. Thanks for staying out of my way."

Charlie hauled back on the wheel and the nose came up. I felt us slow and sink, felt all the tension go out of Charlie's body. For a moment we seemed to hover … then "chirp!" Just like that, we were on the ground, rolling.

I don't know much about flying, but I knew that we were safe now. We were back on earth, where all good cats belong. My heartbeat slowed down from its jackhammer pace, I even managed a small meow of relief.

Runway lights trundled past the plane as we rolled along. And rolled along. Why weren't we stopping?

"Uh, dude, any time now," I thought.

Thinking didn't do it. I tried a howl.

"Charlie?"

We ran out of momentum before we ran out of runway. The plane creaked to a stop and just sat there. The doors that Charlie had unlatched swung open halfway, letting in a soft, herbal breeze.

And the sound of sirens. I got scared again.

"Mrrorrw! Come on, Charlie, let's get out of here."

No response. I looked up at him, his head was rolled over on his left shoulder. I crawled up his chest, licked his sweaty face, tasting of salt and ashes. He didn't even twitch. His hands were frozen on the wheel, his feet flat on the rudders, still as a statue, like a museum exhibit labeled "Pilot."

And there was no pain coming off him anymore, no suffering, no breath, nothing.

The sirens got closer.

"Son of a bitch," I thought. "You went and died on me. You got what you wanted, after all."

Flashing red lights painted the interior of the airplane. I didn't want to leave him like this, not after all we'd been through. He'd done this for *me*, to keep *me* from getting killed. I was his last passenger and somebody ought to know it.

Home never felt closer; I could feel it pulling on my whiskers, even in this terrible moment. But I couldn't leave Charlie. After crossing most of a continent and leaving a trail of live humans behind me like roadkill, it was the dead one that finally had a hold on me.

Tires crunched to a stop on the pilot's side of the plane. Doors slammed and voices called out, boots pounded the runway, men so near I could smell them.

I waited for the last second, then a couple of seconds more. I waited long enough that I could hear their startled voices trailing behind me as I darted out the passenger door.

"Hey, you see that?"

But they were too busy to follow. I sped across the runway, past the bordering lights, over gravel and grass, cool mountain air, rich and scented, filled my lungs.

Good-bye, Charlie. Rest in peace. Now how do I get home from here?

CHAPTER 35

In a way, I was home already. State lines don't mean much to a cat, but this place felt *right*. You'll have to trust me on this, it's called a homing instinct for a reason, and I don't understand it anymore than you do. I just knew that I was getting close, all the little hints only a cat's senses are sharp enough to pick up were telling me the same thing: You're almost there, Doo Doo.

Almost, but not quite. I still had a ways to go. And while I didn't know exactly how far or how long, I knew one thing for sure. I needed to avoid people. I'd had about all I could take.

Spring comes early to California, and it was clearly spring here. I passed that first night alongside a small stream, in a stand of woods between the airport and the small town it was attached to. Food was everywhere, the night air no worse than chilly. Survival wasn't going to be a problem, there was no reason to go anywhere near the little city or anyplace else where people lived. There were only two people I wanted to see now, only one place I wanted to go.

The way home was down. I could tell from the thickness of air that I wasn't too high up, but this was still rough, broken country. I figured the best way to avoid roads and get off these foothills was to follow the stream. I hunted early, slept late, and got off well before dawn.

That first day put the town far behind me, by the third the woods were thinning out and the pitch of the land began to ease up. Occasionally I could see glimpses far ahead, down into what looked like an endless, hazy valley. Maybe I should have been discouraged, that valley was big, and no matter how hard I stared, I couldn't see the ocean, but my spirits soared with each step I took.

I'd give anything to be that young again. My body took to the exercise like it was hungry for it. Unlike my last mountain trek, this one didn't use me up, it *built* me up. The weather was fine, food abundant, water never more than a lick away. I didn't even get sore; I'd spent the winter romping around my airport, not trapped in a cage, my fur was thick and my muscles strong.

But the best part was what I was leaving behind. Where I was going was still out of sight, but where I'd been and what I'd seen filled my head and made me crazy. I needed to be free of those visions. The farther I got from those places, the better.

Cats have vivid memories, did you know that? They can come on so strong they're almost hallucinations. Did you ever see your kitty chasing ghosts around the house? They were real enough to him. And I couldn't get the memory of Charlie's head, lolling dead on his shoulder, out of my mind. But distance helped, and I was making good time. I was almost sane when I came upon the greenhouses.

I first saw them by moonlight. The foothills had given way to just plain hills and rolling meadows, the ground cover mostly grasses and shrubs. What trees there were bordered the creek, now wider and slower as the land flattened. I climbed one when I saw the lights.

A road, maybe three miles off, with a few stationary glows that could have been signs or streetlights, and cars that came so infrequently I had to watch a while to be sure it *was* a road. But even out here roads weren't so uncommon that I was surprised to see one. I'd passed under a few where they'd bridged my creek. No, what caught my attention was what was between me and that road. Row after row of long, thin, low buildings, their white roofs catching the moonlight and sending it back to my dark-adapted eyes in a ghostly gleam.

If I'd have stuck to my plan, I would have given them a wide berth. Where there were buildings there were people. But, you know, I'm curious. And there was more than light coming off those buildings. There were also smells.

So many scents I couldn't pry them apart. Every flower and every herb I'd ever encountered—and then some—seemed to be growing down there. And maybe a little hint of ... something extra? I had to go check it out.

What I couldn't see until I got close was the fence. Six feet high of cyclone fencing, with three rows of razor wire at the top. A gravel road ran along the property, following the fence like a moat, the grass on the shoulders cut so low there wasn't enough cover for a cockroach. They obviously didn't want anyone—or any critters—messing around their precious buildings. But they didn't count on me.

This wasn't the kind of jump you could walk away from if you missed. A cat could leave a leg up there, easy. I went looking for a little help, starting at the right hand corner, walking left. After a few hundred yards I found it—some kind of utility box, maybe two feet tall and about a foot away from the base of the fence. Perfect.

I hopped on and practiced the leap, the way you've seen cats do—crouching and bobbing, gauging the effort, getting the muscle memory in place, half-springing, settling back and doing it again. The fourth time I went for it and sailed right over. The way down was farther than the way up, but I landed on soft grass, almost silently. It was like a lawn inside, manicured and even. They know how to keep a nice place, I thought, but not how to keep me out. I was pleased with myself no end.

Up close the scents started to differentiate, some buildings flowery, some herby, some didn't have much smell at all. I sniffed around about a dozen of them before I came upon the aroma that had drawn me here. Catnip.

Oh yeah. There it was, unmistakable. Sweet, fresh catnip, and only a slab of glass between me and *it*. I couldn't see it, the glass-sided walls of the greenhouse were frosted, but I knew it was in there. And I knew I wouldn't have to throw my body through a windowpane to break in. The smell was too strong, there had to be an opening around here somewhere.

In fact, there were several. A row of windows belted the greenhouse about four feet off the ground, the kind that were hinged at the top and swung out at the bottom. The good news was that every third window was open, the bad news was that they were only open a little, the bottoms angled out a few, tight inches.

What to do? Well, first, check 'em all. I traipsed around the greenhouse, head up like I was waiting for honey to drip from the sky. But, after circling the building, I couldn't find much to chose from. All the windows were open the same three or four inches. It was scary precise, like a robot had done it.

In the end, I chose the window where the catnip smell was strongest. I figured if I was going to lose some fur in this operation, I might as well land in medicine.

Those of you who think I brag too much about my physical prowess should have seen that first attempt. I came up short, clunked my head hard on the metal frame of the window and went spinning back to earth. Ouch. Frustration made my second attempt even worse, I jumped so high I landed on the open pane, my claws screeching down the glass as I slid backwards, and I wound up right where I started. But I learned something that time. The window bounced when I hit it—it didn't close, it stayed open at the same angle—but it had moved under my weight. That meant it was *loose.*

Now I had a plan. My next jump should be softer, lower. I'd aim for the edge of the sill and slip my front paws just under the opening, keeping my head below the frame, out of harm's way. If it worked I could pull myself up by my claws. But I'd need a bull's-eye to pull it off.

Now it's time to brag. I hit that spot like a marksman, dug my claws around the aluminum frame, ducked my nose under the opening and hauled myself up. It was tight, just like I figured from the ground. But I'd gotten my forehead under the frame, and once I was wedged in snug I reared back with all my strength, like I was doing a pushup. And just like I figured from the ground, that sucker *moved*—enough to let my head through. And like I've said before, where my head can go, my body can follow.

Every junkie can tell you about the Big Score. Even a reformed one, years sober, will get a sparkle in his eyes remembering the time he hit a jackpot so huge it seemed to go on forever. It never does, of course, and the bigger the high the harder the fall, but that's not the part that sticks with you. Looking back now, through a whole lifetime, I can still feel the thrill that young cat who used to be me felt when he fell into The Great Catnip Factory that spring evening.

And the consequences that followed? Well, I remember them too, when I think about it. How could I not? But they seem disconnected, as if my self-indulgence had nothing to do with the price I had to pay. Nostalgia colors my hindsight now, to the point where I remember them as separate events. The dream of a young tomcat driven half-feral by crazy life and countless miles who beat the system for one splendid night of joy. And the nightmares that came barking on its heels like a pack of wolves.

Tables of nip. Aisles of nip. Tender, just sprouted nip. Taller, getting ready to flower nip. Catnip in all its delicious manifestations. And I did it all.

I never thought you could OD on the nip and I guess that's true, if by OD you mean, like, die. But I came closer that night than ever before, or since.

I went wild, romping from table to table sampling the wares; some of the stuff made me feel giddy, some woozy, some horny, some just itchy. I can't lie to you, I had a hell of a time—as long as I was awake. I remember feeling the hard luck and sad memories melting away in the drug haze, peeling back layer after layer until I was a kitten again, still in my momma's paws. Bad choices I'd made and remade got undone, bliss took their place and everything was all right and was going to *be* all right forever—which is pretty funny when you consider the bad choice I was making right then. But as long as I was awake, I was high and happy.

Then I fell asleep.

It started like a normal catnip nod, warm and comforting. Momma was on my mind, of course, she always is when I'm in the throes of nip. My earliest memories of her came back—her sweet breath like a halo on my face as she licked me. I was so tiny I rolled over like a dustball with each loving flick of her tongue. And nothing to do all day but romp with my brothers and sister and nuzzle on momma's belly when I got hungry or tired.

Those are the moments that drove me to catnip in the first place, and I got my share that wild night. But I took it too far, because it didn't stop there, and no matter where it went I couldn't wake up.

It started going wrong when Rass appeared. My little buddy was still stuck in his cage, just where I left him, and screaming like he was being murdered. This time I just *had* to free him. In my dream I was big as a human, but with cat paws. Clawing and fumbling with the lock, I finally managed to open the door, but Rass wouldn't come out and he wouldn't stop screeching. He was howling like the damned, and the damned was *me*. I went in there to try to drag him out, but when I got inside, it wasn't the cage anymore, and Rass wasn't alone.

I was in a small, dark place, crowded with souls. They were all there—Kathy, the homeless woman who snatched me up like I was a kid in a custody battle and took me so far from home, Silver Fox, my first love, who got me into the fight that almost cost me an ear, the truck driver with no name, Doug and Kimberley, Clarence and Charlie, Gladys the lovestruck widow. They were keening my names, Rusty, Lucky, Fido, Tuffy, ghostly voices that gave me the chills, scary but irresistible. I didn't know which way to turn.

The walls of the room receded in a rush; either that or I was shrinking. I felt ice cold inside, like I was about to disappear. The wraiths around me grew enormous, even as they began to fade away. Running in a mad panic, I tried desperately to reach someone, anyone, everyone I knew or used to know. And I reached them all, one by one, but they were all dead. Not a spark of warmth anywhere, just corpses, falling away from me, eyeholes blank, mouths open, making breathless noises that sounded like my name.

It got so bad I tried to wake myself up, like I was dreaming that I knew this was a dream. But I couldn't do it, and the pain just kept coming. I cringed as I shrank, no bigger than a housefly now, and let it all wash over me. The broken hearts and busted lives, grasping hands that knew my fur, hands that fed me, held me, missed me, gone forever, a drowning wave of dead regret. And then I got so small I fell through the floor.

I was me again. The voices stopped. I heard a patty pat and looked up. Doc was standing in front of me, slapping his thighs the way he did when he wanted me to come to him. The smile on his face was blinding, the smile of a person who hadn't seen his cat for a year and never expected to see him again, a smile of shocked surprise and delight. It was exactly what I'd been hoping for, what I wanted to see, what I hoped he'd feel when I got home. Fern stood right next to him, looking just as happy as her husband, but a little mad too, as if to say, "Where were you, you naughty boy? You had us worried sick."

I'm so sorry, I'm so sorry. I'll never, ever do it again.

Pat, pat, pat.

Yes, I'm coming!

I leapt off the rug, past the tattered furniture that I knew so well, the living room furniture that *I'd* tattered. I threw myself onto their mercy, into their arms, back in their hearts.

And I flew straight through them. They were just ghosts.

I told you it was a nightmare. The dread went on and on, too. I won't trouble you with the details, as long as you promise me you'll lay off the nip. Suffice it to say that I wanted it to end as much as I've ever wanted anything in my life. And it did, eventually. The dreams went away and I fell into a blank coma for hours and hours, until I slept it off.

But wouldn't you know, when I finally woke up, I was in worse trouble.

CHAPTER 36

"**G**otchya!"

That was the first word I heard that morning, and it wasn't a good one. Worse yet, it was true. I had a pair of gloved mitts around me so tight I could barely breathe, much less fight back. The guy they belonged to must have been six-five, two-fifty. Hands as big as a rake and strong as steel.

"*Look* at this place!" he snarled. "What the hell were you doing? How'd you even get *in* here?"

Loosen that grip a bit, Moose, and I'll tell you. But he wasn't in the mood to listen.

"Son of a *bitch!* What a mess. You must've knocked over fifty plants, you piece of crap. Guess who's going to have to clean it up! And Mario is gonna be pissed. *Damn* it all."

This was all spat—juicily—in my face as the giant goose-stepped me down the aisle of the greenhouse. From the look in his eyes you'd think he'd just caught me eating his children. My head was swimming and I was hung over as hell. Fear started cranking up its engine and regret came along for the ride.

But I didn't panic, not yet. Bad as the situation was, I figured okay, we're on our way out of here. At worst he'll heave me over the fence and I'll be down the road with a couple of thumbprints on my abdomen. But I figured wrong.

As soon as we got outside he shoved me into a big burlap sack, knotted the top, hoisted bag and cat high in the air, and started walking. The mesh of the dirty burlap was coarse enough that I could see shadows through it. Sometimes the shadow was his tree-trunk of a leg as it slammed into me full stride, setting the bag spinning.

Trapped, hung over, insulted, and now dizzy; I was getting fed up. Time for some payback. Next time his leg came in range I fired my back claws through the cloth as hard as I could, which wasn't very hard since I had nothing to brace against. But it was hard enough.

"Ow! You asshole!"

Moose punched me in the guts, right through the bag.

That's when I really started to worry.

"Edgar, I got invoices up the wazoo here. Why you giving me a headache?"

"You think you got one now, you oughta see what he did to fourteen."

"Oh hell. How much damage we talking about?"

"Fifty, sixty plants. Catnip mostly, fescue, some sage."

I'd been howling myself hoarse since I'd caught my breath. The sack must have been used for fertilizer or chemicals, because the dust burned my throat something awful.

"Christ, he sure has a mouth on him. He's making my ears hurt. Well … what's done is done. Just make sure it doesn't happen again."

"What am I supposed to do about it, boss?"

"Hell, I don't care. Does he have a collar?"

"I don't know. Let me check."

Between screams I'd been fanging the bag, but it was too stretchy and tough; it wouldn't tear. When I saw Edgar's bulk coming for me again, I shrank back and hissed, awaiting the blow that never came. Instead, he untied the bag, reached in, and dragged me out by the scruff. His other hand grabbed all four of my paws at once, so I was pretty much immobilized. He turned me over and gave me a shake, like he expected me to rattle.

"Don't see one," he said to his boss, who was sitting behind a cluttered desk in his fluorescent-lit dump of an office.

The boss glanced up at me for all of about a second, then back to his papers.

"Get rid of it."

"What do you mean, get rid of it, Mario?"

"What, I got to draw you a picture? What do I pay you for?"

"Oh…. I dunno, boss. I mean, damn…."

"Just get him the hell out of here, Edgar and make sure he never comes back. I don't want to know. And tell Donna to come in here on your way out. Ditzy broad has me double-paying these vendors, sure as shit."

Back in the bag for me. I didn't know how much trouble I was in. If I had, I doubt I'd have made like a finch when they throw a rag over its cage. But that's just what I did when Edgar dumped the sack in the corner of the greenhouse and left me there all morning. I slept.

* * *

"Can I take a look, Eddie?"

"Sure, doll. Let me," Edgar said as I woke up again, or maybe I should say woke up for the first time, because now my hangover was gone, my head clear, and my sense of danger sharp. This time I had every muscle primed, ready to pounce the instant I saw daylight. And pounce I did. Right into the giant gardener's humongous paws.

"Awww," the bubble-haired woman said, bending forward to look at me but keeping her distance. "He's *cute*! What did the bastard tell you to do?"

"Kill it."

"No!"

"You surprised?"

"Not really."

"I was pissed off at *him*," Edgar said, thrusting me towards the woman, "until I saw Mario. I wouldn't even have told the SOB if I didn't know he'd try to take the damage out of my paycheck."

"He's a piece of work," the woman said, shaking her poofy hair. "Are you gonna?"

I had more than a casual interest in hearing his answer. But Edgar just shrugged.

"We ought to find better jobs, Donna."

"Wish I'd been born rich instead of beautiful," she cackled.

Edgar laughed with her, then said: "They've got a pound over in Jackson, I might take him there after work. Or either drown him in the crick. That could be more merciful."

"What a shame. If I didn't have dogs…. But David would whine about it."

"The more I think about it the angrier I get. It's not just the cat, it's Mario. I'm a *gardener*, dammit, not an executioner. What he pays us, let him do his *own* dirty work." Edgar's grip on me tightened, and it was pretty snug to begin with. That squeezed a pitiful squeal out of me. It probably saved my life.

"Awww," Donna said again, drawing closer as Edgar reached down for the bag. "Uh … wait a sec, Eddie."

She kept her hands to herself but gave me a good long look this time.

"Huh. You know what he reminds me of?"

"I give up."

"You remember the ballgame last August?"

"Sure. The company 'picnic.' Three hours each way and the crappiest seats money could buy. Giants lost, too. Why…. Oh!... You think?"

"It was on the Jumbo Tron. He looks just like him."

"Sports Center was all over it for about a week, too. But it can't be. Can it?"

Donna reached out and touched the top of my head with a single finger, like she was afraid of burning herself.

"He doesn't *seem* dangerous," she said.

"That guy pitched for Denver, how could this be the same cat?"

"It probably isn't," Donna said. "Still, it's a shame, poor thing."

"Gotta be a million orange cats like this, right?"

"Right."

"Sure looks like the one, though."

"Are you trying to talk yourself into something, Edgar?"

"No," he said. "Out of something."

* * *

At least I was out of the bag. Edgar sealed me in a packing crate with a dish of water. No food though, and I was ravenous. What's worse was that no one could hear me—I was in a shed outside the greenhouse, lonely, hungry and scared.

I didn't take it lying down, the crate was wood and cardboard, and I got to work on it right away. If I had enough time, I could probably bust out, and if I could get out of the box, I'd figure a way out of the shed. But I didn't have that much time, and I knew it.

What I didn't know was what Edgar had in mind when he came for me. I took some comfort in the thought that if he was going to off me, he probably would have done it already. Or tried to do it. No matter how big and strong he was, he was going to have a fight on his hands. But I also knew the odds, and they weren't good.

At the same time, I never felt so *close*. I felt that one more shove, one good leap, would put me in Fern's arms, safe and home. Maybe I was too young to imagine my own death, too strong to believe in failure, but hope never left me, even in that black box in a shed, trapped in the middle of nowhere.

Hope came wafting my way on a trail of cigarette fumes, late that afternoon. The shed doors squeaked open, a moment later the top of the crate was lifted.

Donna was staring down at me, veiled in smoke. Edgar tossed a handful of dry food onto the floor of the crate, then slid the top back on, offset a few inches. He was puffing away, too.

"I called the Giants at lunchtime," I heard Donna's voice say.

"What they tell you?"

"If it's him, there's a reward."

"No shit? How much?"

"Ten. Ten thousand."

"Damn! So how we supposed to find out?"

"They said bring him by."

"Wow. To the ballpark?"

"Yes."

"That could be fun, even if he's not the right cat," Edgar enthused.

"I hope he is, and not just for the money, you know what I mean?"

Edgar gave a grunt that I chose to interpret as sympathetic. "Yeah, I guess so. Better be him, though. So, you wanna go?"

"When?"

"Tomorrow, skip work?"

"Uh … sure, why not."

"David won't mind?"

"Oh, he might. But he does what I tell him."

"Wrapped around your little finger, huh? Why am I not surprised? Fifty-fifty okay with you?"

"That's generous of you, Edgar." Donna sounded flirty.

"Nah, I wouldn't even have thought about it, not for you."

"Well, let's not count our chickens...."

"Before we shove them down Mario's throat," Edgar finished.

They left me alone after that. I scarfed up the kibbles he left me like it was lobster, I was that hungry. When I was done, I started hacking at the walls of the box. I picked a spot between the floor and the first wood rib and got to work. It was slow going, but I was making progress. Pitch black though it was, I could feel my claws tearing into the wall, going through the tough cardboard skin, sending a shower of confetti onto the floor of the box around my back feet.

But I was getting tired. Big as the box was, and if I had to guess I'd say it was six feet long by four feet wide and tall, the air was starting to get pretty foul in there. At the point of exhaustion, I felt my claws break through. My front left paw punched a tight hole in the wall, it almost got stuck and I had to twist it to pull if free. For about two seconds I was elated. And then I got confused.

Why no light? It was dark inside the shed, but not that dark. I should be able to see the hole I'd made, but I couldn't see a thing. I didn't smell any fresh air pouring through, either. I reached back up and started chipping away at the sides of the hole until it was large enough to shove a leg through. Probing deeper and deeper, at an awkward angle, until I was a couple of inches in, I hit it. The outer wall. Damn, damn, damn.

There was no way. I'd have to make a hole in that first wall almost as big as me, just to get at that second one. I backed away through the shredded paper littering the floor to the opposite corner to rest and think.

And I did come up with one useful idea. My bladder was about to burst, and that confetti was almost like litter. I gave it a good soak and felt better. But I was still trapped and the foul air was funky now, too. I *had* to get out of there, but how?

The same way I got in, that's how. Edgar pulled me out with one of his steam shovel paws.

He looked me straight in the eyes. I got ready to fight for my life.

"Whoa, there, Lucky," Edgar said holding me so tight all I could do was writhe and not much of that. "Is that your name, Lucky? I hope so, for both our sakes."

But I didn't see malice in his face, which was a good thing, because there wasn't a damned thing I could do about it. And then the bastard threw me back in the bag.

* * *

"You bring the carrier?" Edgar asked.

"Yes," Donna answered. "But I have a better idea."

"What's that?"

I was hearing this from the back of a pickup truck where Edgar had thrown me, still in the sack, about half an hour ago. We hadn't gone anywhere, Edgar just leaned up against the side of the truck smoking. Occasionally, when I got too loud, he'd pet the bag, which beat a punch in the guts anytime.

"You feeling tired?" Donna voice asked.

"Uh, kinda, why?"

"Because," Donna said in a voice rising with excitement, "I want to go tonight!"

"They'll be closed…"

"I know, but this way we're there first thing in the morning. And anyway, San Francisco! It'll be fun. We can stay with my sister, for free."

"What's David say about this?"

"He told me to be a good girl."

Edgar let out a grunt that I think was supposed to pass for a laugh.

"So, will you?" he asked.

"We'll see," Donna giggled.

CHAPTER 37

Dog stink. Old dog stink. *Scared* dog stink. We cats aren't as celebrated as some mammals for our sense of smell, because we won't go chase convicts for a living, but don't let that fool you. Our noses are as acute as our eyes, and as delicate as our ears—which accounts for some of our so-called fussiness when it comes to meals. We're not carrion eaters in the wild, we prefer our food fresh and sweet. The least little "off" scent puts us off our feed, and if you could smell what we do, you'd be more careful with what you put into our dishes, *and* yours.

So, being trapped in a box of funk isn't our idea of a good time. The beat-up plastic dog carrier I was stuck in *reeked* of sick, scared dog. And the one, overpowering stench among wet-fur dog, skunked dog, infected dog, and old, rotting-from-the-inside-out dog, was last-ride dog, on-the-way-to-be-put-to-sleep dog, might-as-well-be-dead-already dog. It was horrible, the smell triggered my fight or flight instinct, and I could do neither. It made my skin crawl.

But at least I wasn't in that bag anymore. And there was the mercy of some fresh air, wafting through the half-open windows of Donna's rattletrap SUV, diluting if not dispersing the smell of dying mutt.

And, amid the ripe odors and my own, low-key terror, there was the diversion of watching the queer, edgy interaction between Edgar and Donna, who was driving. I tried to concentrate on that. It was hard, what with the death funk and fright, but I tried.

"I love this time of night, don't you, Edgar?"

"Yeah...." he drawled in a deep voice that managed to sound confused and manly at the same time. "What do you mean, exactly?" he finally added.

"It's just that I'm not usually out and about at this hour. I find it ... well ... thrilling." Her last word was an invitation.

"I, uh, I know what you mean, Donna," he stammered. I was pretty sure that Edgar had just RSVPD her invite.

The ways of humans never fail to captivate me, even when I'm in a fight for my life drowned in dog B.O.

And besides, there was maybe an opening here. The more attention they paid to each other, the less they'd be thinking about me. And I do believe what they were doing together came under the category of attention—especially when Donna pulled the car onto the shoulder of a dark country road and they *parked* for half an hour.

I began to figure it all out later, when we hit the freeway, Donna and Edgar nuzzled up close, both of them smoking something *close* to catnip, but not quite. I was *incidental* to this little adventure. I was an *excuse*.

But what I didn't understand, being a cat and all, was that I was also ten thousand dollars. That kind of money doesn't mean a thing to us, but it concentrates the minds of humans remarkably.

They tried to be nice. I remember that about them, they weren't cruel, not even big brute Edgar. But they sucked at it, they knew cats like I knew cash: *i.e.*, not at all. I'd had fast food before—homeless Kathy gave it to me all the time—but nobody ever thought of feeding me taco meat until this duo that night.

We'd just driven through a big city, Sacramento as it turns out (not that I saw any of it then or ever) when the munchies hit them. They left the freeway, found a drive-through, got a big, steaming bag of food and ate in the parking lot, right off their laps. Class all the way.

Edgar turned to me on the backseat, his mouth was full and there was a piece of cheese stuck to his chin.

"Here you go, Lucky," he said. And he reached through the door of my cage, tore the paper off a burrito and unrolled it, flat on the bottom of the box.

It actually smelled pretty good compared to the dog stink, but I would never have touched that pile of grease if I hadn't been starving. But it wasn't the grease that got to me. It was the spices.

"I don't think he likes it," Edgar said.

Oh? What gives you that idea, genius, my retching or my gagging?

"We'll get him some proper food when we get to Fiona's," Donna said. At least she waited to swallow before she spoke.

"Fiona's your sister?"

"Yeah."

"Is she gonna be cool … you know … with us?"

Donna laughed through her nose, "Cool," she said, "that's Fiona all right. I don't think she'll be any problem at all."

"Something you're not telling me?"

"She's a kid. Twelve years younger than me, and she's not too crazy about David. Not too crazy about men...."

Edgar tapped his chest with a taco-laden hand.

"Well, you know..." he said, "I *am* one."

"So I noticed," Donna said dryly. "Don't worry, she'll be fine with you. Just don't hit on her."

"Hey! What kind of a dawg you think I am?"

"A cute one," Donna touched Edgar's face. "But Fiona's not into *men*."

"Oh!" Edgar finally got it. "You mean your kid sister bats from the other side of the plate!"

"Good lord," Donna sighed. "That's *one* way to put it. But don't let Fiona hear you say that. She's very ... uh ... militant."

"Jesus! Where you taking me, woman?"

"Anywhere you want to go, big guy," Donna said, starting up the car.

* * *

I remember Charlie talking to a young flight student, in the trailer after a lesson late one afternoon. Charlie was very animated, using his hands like little airplanes, swooping them this way and that while I tried to stay balanced in his lap. He was trying to make a point.

"See, if you hold your altitude, just right, and you come around on the steep turn back to the heading you started from, you'll feel a *bump*."

Charlie waved his hand up and down to illustrate.

"Bump!" he said. "That's you hitting your own wake. That's how you know you did the turn right and you've made a complete circle."

The next time my illicit lovebirds/capturers stopped the car it was to pay a toll. We climbed up a long ramp and crossed a bridge. Then we came down the other side.

Bump!

Circle complete.

I was home.

* * *

Sorta.

"There's one!"

"Yesss…" Donna hissed, swerving the car hard to the right. "Great! A spot in San Francisco. Fiona's only a block from here."

"I guess maybe he is lucky, after all," Edgar laughed, pleased with himself.

"Leave us hope," Donna said, shutting down the motor. She turned and leered at me with a mouth that looked like a wallet.

I didn't care. I was so excited I damn near peed myself. Edgar grabbed the cage off the backseat and hauled me into the sweet, ocean air of the big city. That hot spot I'd been pursuing all this time now burned mere inches from my face. You can't be as territorial as a cat and not have a strong sense of place. And somewhere, very close, was home, *my* place.

Come on, guys! Let me out. Just let me sniff the air and I swear, I'll find it straight away. Hell, I think it's just over that hill! Please!

"It's us!" Donna shouted into the speaker.

Bzzzz. The door swung open and we were inside.

Stale apartment air doused the flame.

* * *

"So, is this the one you told me about?"

"Which one, Edgar or the cat?"

"I prefer cats, sis. No offense, Edgar."

"Uh, none taken. You mind if I smoke?"

"Not at all, but you can't do it in here."

"Uh … okay. Where should I put the box?" Edgar asked.

"I'll take it," Fiona said.

"It's heavy…"

If you could hear a scowl, and cats almost can, that would be the time. Fiona reached for the dog cage and snatched it away from Edgar.

"Not too," she said. She marched me over to a couch in the small living room, sat the cage down and knelt in front of it.

I couldn't take my eyes off her. She had more ink on her arms than a newspaper, and you know how cats love newspapers. Never were two sisters less alike. Fiona was tiny where Donna was tall, she was skinny while Donna was pudgy, and she was as dark as Donna was blonde.

But the biggest difference was in the eyes. Donna's dull eyes showed a simple soul that was about as kindly as one could be that never gave a thought to anybody else in its life. Fiona's showed a burning, angry intelligence and were as deep as my mountain lake before it froze over.

And I'll be damned if they didn't grow as she stared at me, right into my hungry core.

Her tight little mouth softened, she drew so near she almost kissed the wire door.

"Wow," she whispered.

"What?" Donna honked. She'd plopped down, uninvited, on the end of the sofa. Edgar stood rooted where he'd been since we got there, just inside the door. He shifted his weight from leg to leg like a kid who needed to use the bathroom, or maybe he just needed that smoke.

"This cat is.... Special," Fiona chanted. Her tone was reverent, almost sacred.

Donna laughed. "We sure hope so. He could be worth serious cash if he is."

The scowl was back. "I love you, sis, but you are *so* crass."

Donna was unfazed, "I just know where my bread is buttered, you hippie," she sassed with wise-ass sweetness.

Fiona let it pass. But then, as if in a trance, *my* trance, she unlatched the cage door!

Mute Edgar found his voice.

"Don't!" he blurted.

"Pardon me?" Fiona demanded. And she reached in the box and pulled me out.

Yes!

I heard the argument that followed snuggled on Fiona's bony legs. But it wasn't much of a contest, she basically just laid down the law to her country cousins.

"I don't approve of this at all," Fiona pronounced.

"Don't approve of what?" Donna asked.

"Any of it. Selling this creature for money, even bringing him here from his home in the woods. It's just plain wrong."

"All's we're trying to do is get him back to his rightful owner," Donna protested.

"Oh, please."

"So what's wrong with making a few dollars? Not all of us have big jobs, you know."

"I work for motor vehicles, sis. And I'm not going to stop you, or your … *friend* … from doing what you want when you leave here. But I will not have this animal being abused in *my* house."

"Abused?..." Edgar spat.

"Is someone speaking to you?" Fiona shot back.

Edgar caved. "I think I'll go outside for a smoke."

"You do that. Here…" Fiona tossed him a set of keys.

"Be nice to him, sis," Donna said when the door closed. "He's kind of sensitive."

"He looks it," Fiona sneered. She was working her fingers through my coat back to front, as she spoke. That was fine by me, contrary to popular opinion, there *is* no wrong way to rub a cat, only wrong people.

"So, where'd you meet *this* gem?" Fiona continued.

"Work. He's one of the gardeners."

"Well, he's better than that lame husband of yours. At least he looks like a man, even if he is an oaf."

Donna laughed like she'd just been paid a compliment. "So, you don't mind if we stay, really?"

"Not at all. You two take the bedroom, I'll sleep here on the couch. But the cat stays with me, I will *not* let him fester in that cage all night."

"Aw, that's great of you, honey."

"Well, it's not like anyone else in the family ever comes to visit. I think I scare them."

Donna let her horse laugh loose again. "You scare *me*, Fi."

"I should," Fiona answered. "Now why don't you see if your man can scare up some food for this fellow? There's a twenty-four hour over on Folsom. Do you have money?"

Donna nodded. "You're the best, sis," she said getting up. "I'll go with; Eddie doesn't know the city at all. We'll be right back, you take care of Lucky."

"Somebody needs to," Fiona said cryptically. Her skinny fingers reached between my back legs and scratched my stomach.

CHAPTER 38

M ake your plan and be patient. Wasn't that what Matilda told me, back at Foothill Ranch? It was advice I didn't follow then, and it almost cost me. I got lucky that time, but I couldn't count on being "lucky" again, even if that was supposed to be my name.

The real name is Doo Doo, and I know where I want to go. Every time I turn around it seems like somebody new is making plans for me. No more. I'm going to find a way out of this apartment and the next time a human hand touches me it's going to belong to Doc or Fern or nobody.

Patience. I scoped out the place so casually I don't think Fiona even noticed, and she watched me like I was a star and she was a groupie. Inside, I was a nervous, lost kitten, outside I acted like I owned the place. I'm just stretching my legs, Fiona, just walking the carpet. Pay no attention to the curious pattern of my pauses, my stops and starts, my upward glances as I fake biting an imaginary flea on my back. Pay no attention to the mental map I'm searing into my muscle memory.

Three windows: two on the far wall of the living room, one in the kitchen, all closed. A little L-shaped hall leading to the locked front door, another closed door that probably led to the bedroom. Situation not promising. But I'd figure out something.

I missed my first chance. With my scouting mission complete, I was back in Fiona's lap when the lovebirds came home. If I'd have been closer to the front door, I might have made a break for it, right then. Which would have been a mistake, because all that would have done is put me in the hallway on the sixth floor, and I'm too short to reach the elevator button.

"We brought beers!" Donna proclaimed as she breezed in.

"Got there just in time," Edgar added. "Five minutes of two. Want one?"

"Pass," Fiona said.

"Oh, come on sis. Don't be a party pooper."

"Some of us have to work in the morning."

"We got the *good* stuff," Donna tempted, holding up a bottle of something or other.

"Did you remember the cat food?"

"Of *course*," Edgar blurted. He shook the bags he was holding. "Food. Litter. Tray."

"Give me," Fiona said. She put me on the rug and stood up. "I'll feed him," she said, heading into the kitchen. "You guys want glasses?"

"Nah, but we still want you to join us. Just one?" Donna asked.

"Okay. Whatever. But only one. I need to get to sleep. Come with me, kitty, you must be hungry."

Actually I had to pee so bad I was about to blow a kidney. But Fiona was a "sensitive" and she got it. She set up the litter tray on the kitchen floor and even had the manners to leave me alone to use it in peace. That did more than ease my bladder, it gave me the clue I was looking for. I could work this woman's mind. All I had to do was get her alone, and stay out of the cage.

Fiona was as good as her word, she only drank the one beer. But in the time it took her to finish one, Edgar and Donna drank several. And with each bottle they downed, their voices upped. Fiona's contribution to the party consisted mostly of "Shhh!"

I was curled up on a footstool, watching the action through slitted eyes, trying not to draw any attention to myself. I needed to be a ten-thousand dollar afterthought, safely asleep in the living room when my captors slept it off a thin, crucial door away. Go to bed, you crazy kids. You've been waiting for this all day. Go have your fun, I'll be fine right where I am.

"Well…" Fiona yawned theatrically, "it's about that time."

Edgar turned out to be a courtly drunk, drat the luck.

"We don't want to put you out of your bedroom," he said. "Donna and I can stay on the couch."

"Poor couch!" Fiona laughed. "No, that won't be necessary. I fall asleep out here half the time anyway."

"But, uh, what about Lucky?" Edgar asked.

"What *about* him?" Fiona said with an edge to her voice.

"Maybe he should come with us?" Edgar tried. "You know, so he won't bother you and all?"

Moment of truth. I was counting on Fiona. But it was the beered-up sister that saved me.

"Leave him be, Eddie," Donna said.

"I was just asking…." Edgar complained.

"Don't make a federal case. Come with me, honey. I think they *both* need some sleep. But bring the rest of that six," she leered.

Edgar did a slow, blurry take.

"You're the boss," he said, as he wobbled to his feet.

"For about five more minutes," Donna mooned.

"Yuck," Fiona said under her breath, but *I* heard.

Edgar retrieved the carton from the fridge.

"Nitey nite, sis," Donna said, one hand on her man to steady herself.

"Yeah, thanks for everything," Edgar added. "See you in the morning."

Depends on what you mean by "you" big boy, I thought. You just underestimated the magic cat.

Patience. Don't rush it, don't scratch yourself, don't pad around, don't make any noise, wait until she's fast asleep. Wait for the gross sounds emanating from behind that bedroom door to fade away. Just lie here on this footstool and listen to the hum of the city drum against your own soft purr of anticipation, knowing it will be soon, if only you wait, if only you don't blow it. Patience.

For once I couldn't sleep, not even catnap. That made the minutes creep by like hours and got me so antsy my pelt twitched. Fiona was on her back, covered by a fancy knitted thing that looked hand-made, like something Fern would buy in a craft store and Doc would hate. But *everything* reminded me of them lately. Now that I was so, so close, the pull of their love was overpowering. Those original two humans I'd bonded to, the chosen ones who had come into my life when I *needed* it, when I missed my momma so bad I ached—perhaps rationally not so different from the long list of people who had loved me since—were my driving obsession. Maybe that makes no sense to you, but to me they were special, uniquely *mine*, and anyway, cats aren't rational creatures.

But not rational doesn't mean not smart. And I've always considered myself the smartest of cats—when I can control my impulsive side, which was hard as hell tonight. For my plan to work, I had to wait until Fiona was so deeply asleep she'd still be half in dreamland when I woke her up. And I had to be sure that those redneck drunks were dead to the world, because if they heard what was going down when I made my move, it would be disaster.

Of course it figured Fiona was a light sleeper. I may be magic, but who ever said magic was easy? She tossed and writhed and murmured slurry words I couldn't make out, words that sounded quizzical, even angry. I didn't know if she was battling demons or having a gas attack, but it wouldn't do. I had to wait until she was far, far away, deep in the ether, hooked up to that intuitive place where she wasn't fighting herself, at peace, in touch with the hidden power that was the source of her "difference," the part I could *reach*.

Finally her breathing smoothed out, her nose made soft, popping noises, almost a light snore. I waited to make sure she stayed there. She did. It was time.

Your cat has done it to you, when he was hungry or lonely and you didn't want to wake up. Maybe he was just messing with you, or had some agenda you never could figure out, but if you live with one of us, something like this has happened.

It's very late at night, you stir in your bed, maybe you feel the weight on your chest, the breath on your skin, maybe you whine and wriggle, trying to get us to go away, trying to stay asleep. Then comes the claw—the one, delicate, insistent, sharp, won't-leave-you-alone claw, poking your face until you can't take it anymore and you give up and open your eyes.

Now, depending on who you are, you either swat little Snowball off the bed with the back of your hand, pull her under the blanket with you for a settle-down snuggle, or get up and see what she wants.

What *I* wanted was the worst thing possible Fiona could do to her sister. She'd have to get the message from a mute cat, a stranger she'd just met, and act on it like it was *her* idea, before she had the chance for second thoughts. The magic cat gathered all his powers and hopped on the couch.

I crawled up very close, almost on her neck, and waited. She mumbled a few times and then got to snoring softly again. In slow motion, I lifted my left paw, extended my claws, and oh-so gently hooked the longest one on her lower lip.

Gentle tug, no response.

I pulled my paw back, then brought it down again, tapping her eyelid, once, twice…

Her eyes slid open. Mine were six inches away, staring into hers, unblinking, beseeching, commanding.

"Get up, Fiona. Get up and open the window. Do it silently and do it now. Set me free."

"Kitty," she whispered. "What…."

She almost understood, but she was confused and groggy. I couldn't risk a meow. I'd have to show her. I slithered out from under the hand she'd placed on my back, climbed off the couch and leapt onto the windowsill.

"Here," I said silently, "come here." Fiona looked at me, unmoving. I sent beams of pictures from my mind to hers. An open window, a flash of tail, a cat home where he belonged. Moments passed, heartbeat to heartbeat.

She pivoted on the couch and sat up, paused there a while, then placed her hands on her knees and pushed herself to her feet like a sleepwalker. Three steps later she was standing above me, her head tilted like a bird that hears something.

"I have to go now, Fiona. It would be good to get to know you. Maybe sometime. But now I have to go. Open the window."

Confusion covered her face like a veil. She reached for me, touched my ears, blinked. Suddenly I was terrified she was "waking up."

"Are you.... I couldn't," she whispered.

I was concentrating on the magic *so* hard. My whiskers flexed forward like antennae, screaming out my silent message. "Do it do it do it."

Fiona pulled her hand away, leaned back on her heels like she was trying to get some perspective, trying to regard this situation from a distance but couldn't because her feet were stuck in the mud. She folded her arms across her chest and closed her eyes.

I waited until I just couldn't wait any more. Looking back on it now, it was probably no more than five seconds, but at the time it felt like forever. I was afraid she was going to fall asleep where she stood. I had to take a chance. Turning to face the window, I reared up on my hind legs, stretched to my full length, and skittered my claws down the glass. When I turned back around Fiona's eyes were open and she was nodding. She was nodding yes.

Soft air ruffled my fur through the open window. The never-quite-dark city sky glowed above me. Below me, six stories down, the dim forms of an urban backyard, shrubs, fences, other shapes too indistinct to make out. I heard the sounds of distant motors, a wheezy bus, leaves rustling in trees that were too far away to jump for, the light rush of the wind that never dies in San Francisco. *Home* was out that window, I could feel it, stronger than ever, but this jump was intimidatingly high. After all my preparation, I was scared: I hesitated. Then Fiona inhaled a cough like a tiny gasp, mere inches behind me. She was waking up to what she'd done.

That was my cue. It was now or never. Crawling down the bricks with my front paws, my back claws clinging precariously to the wooden windowsill— not *nearly* ready—I threw myself off the edge of the building.

CHAPTER 39

Cats have no collarbones. Did you know that? That's why we can make idiot jumps of sixty feet straight down, land on all fours, and walk away—sometimes. Picture a suspension bridge, where our legs are the piers and our bodies the road. That's how it looks when we land, our tubes suspended from our shock-absorbing legs, our bellies sometimes even hitting the ground before springing back up again. If we had a collarbone connecting our front paws like people, it would explode into sawdust. We don't, so we can fall a long way and live.

But there is a limit, and sixty feet is well past the no-injury distance. To fall six stories and not hurt something bad takes two things: Technique, and luck.

Luck I always had, and it didn't desert me now. As soon as I looked down, at the very instant that gravity began to take hold, I saw a row of big, square, plastic trash cans, lined up about six feet from the wall. Plastic *gives*, plastic is softer than concrete, and concrete was what those cans sat on. I had my aiming point.

Technique was making sure I got there. And getting there was going to be a challenge, because I hadn't pushed off the side of the building very hard. If I didn't do something, I was going to fall short.

I splayed out my back legs as wide as I could and aimed with my front. Have you ever seen pictures of a flying squirrel? It was kind of like that. Cats are a whole lot heavier than squirrels, there isn't much glide *in* us. But I didn't need much, just about three extra feet.

I got two and a half. My front paws caught the lid of the can, my back legs slammed into its side. And that's where my luck came into play again. The can was *empty*. I knocked it clean over on its side at impact, and I rode it down.

And back up. The can flexed like a diving board and bounced, throwing me forward, upside down in a tumbling rebound. My back legs were propelled over my head as I traced a backwards arc, six feet high. Just enough time to get myself righted, feet down, head up. I landed facing the building, opposite the way I'd jumped, against my momentum. Cats don't land pretty going backwards, but the can had taken most of the shock, so all I did was stagger hindwards, fall on my ass, and stop—crazed, because all this had happened in a flash, much faster than I can describe it here, but unhurt.

I *must* have been crazed because the next thing I did made no sense. What I should have done is gotten a move on. Being in the middle of all that commotion, I didn't realize how much noise I'd made—though I might have taken a hint when the windows of that big, blank wall started lighting up like a pinball machine. Prudence dictated a quick exit, but I couldn't hear her for the rage in my soul. Pride and freedom and shock had me all worked up.

I jumped on top of an untoppled garbage can, arched my back like a warrior, stretched my neck through a ruff blown up and bristly as a bottle brush, faced the sky ... and *howled.*

"Harroooo!"

Take that, you sonsabitches. "Horrrowwwl."

My heart hammered in my chest as I waited for that building to hit back. I was ready to fight the world, all my frustration and anger at being hijacked, hoodwinked, bagged, hauled, hugged, slugged and thwarted refused to be held in for a second longer and came pouring out my mouth.

"Yih-raahhrrr! Rawwwwk!" That's for Rass, you bastards. That's for every cat trapped behind those dirty curtains, living with some dweeb who thinks the world's best predator is "cute." "Yowwwl!"

I saw Fiona's face silhouetted in the open window, six floors up, trying and failing to see with human eyes what I could see with mine.

"Hisssss!" Here I am, you silly girl. That's right, right here. Take a last look, I'm on my way home. I hope you don't catch too much hell from your sister and her "friend" for letting me loose. But you didn't have much choice, did you?

Time to haul ass. If I keep this up, somebody's going to wing a shoe at me, sure. I'm purged clean, light as a feather. It feels so damned good to be alive.

* * *

That rush of energy burned itself out almost as fast as it hit. Dawn came, gray and sulky, within minutes of my escape. I don't know if it was fatigue or not having the sun to guide me or what, but I was also kind of lost. I wasn't used to this flat, streets-and-sidewalks part of San Francisco—my radar was failing me. The last decent sleep I'd gotten was days ago, back before the greenhouse, and I hadn't had to deal with city traffic for months. That traffic was picking up alarmingly and my sense of direction was shot. By the time I'd covered five paranoid blocks the danger bells in my head got too loud to ignore. Stop! Sleep! Find a place to hide before you get yourself run over.

Good idea, but there were a couple of problems. One, it was real urban here, no grass, no bushes, just stores and buildings and sidewalks and, increasingly, people. And two, whenever I came to an alley or even a stoop that offered a bit of cover, it *reeked* of cat. Every foot was enemy territory, marked and claimed, and I was in no shape for a fight. And each time I came to the end of a block, the challenge of crossing the street got harder, the traffic heavier. The temptation to crawl under some parked car and hope it *stayed* parked was growing on me, but I knew better. So I kept going, staying close to the buildings, avoiding people, watching for hostile toms, and praying for a break.

I didn't get one. What I got was a boulevard. I should have just hung a right and tried the next corner, but what little homing instinct I had working told me I needed to cross right here. But "right here" was lanes and lanes of traffic with a concrete median and yet more lanes on the other side. From my vantage point, a foot off the ground, the street looked like a canyon, the far side a blinking blur I could barely make out through the speeding cars and lumbering trucks. And one more thing—legs. Suddenly, I was surrounded by a pack of people.

Of course I don't know what a stoplight is, I'm a cat. But I can tell the difference between standing and walking and when that phalanx of high-heeled and booted titans started moving I moved right along with it.

These were no-nonsense, morning commuters, I had to trot to keep up. That was fine by me, but after I almost got kicked in the head a couple of times I figured I better move to the front of the pack.

I've made plenty of bad moves in my life, and most of them were pretty obvious, in hindsight. If I had a do-over, I'd do them differently or not at all. But not this one. This one was insignificant, a matter of a mere foot or two—yet the consequences cascaded until they were damn near fatal.

You see, what I hadn't realized was that nobody had noticed me down there, snaking around that forest of legs. But the moment I sauntered ahead they *all* did.

"Hey lookit!"

"Cat!"

"Watch out, kitty!"

"Somebody grab it!"

"Car!"

Those voices hit me like spotlights on a bare stage. I turned on the jets.

Right over that median in a two-hop, ten-foot leap, down across the other four lanes of the boulevard to the far sidewalk. Almost.

"Nooo!"

"Watch out!"

I caught the movement out of the corner of my right eye while I was in midflight. Low slung and sleek, in the curb lane, coming fast.

My brain did a quick calculation and decided it was going to splat right into that chrome bumper. I tried swimming, legs flailing, willing the ground to come to me so I could claw the pavement, dart away, stop. Everything slowed down; I felt like a helpless spectator as gravity did its deadly job, arcing me to my doom. Behind me I heard screams, The yahoo in the sports car saw and heard nothing. I braced myself.

They call it right turn on red. That's what almost killed me and that's what saved me. The jerk in the I'm-late-for-work car was shooting for an open lane, looking to make a fast right through a busy intersection. Actually it's called right turn on red *after stop*, but this moron had no intention of stopping.

But he had to slow, just a little, to take a look. To make sure his precious Turbo Chickwagon didn't get sideswiped by a truck. I don't think he ever touched the brakes, but he eased off just enough that I hit the asphalt a few feet and a half second before he hit me.

There was no time to think, it was pure reflex—I pronged straight up, as fast and as hard as I could, like I was a spring loaded, four-legged pogo stick.

Look, I already fessed up that I was an idiot in full thoughtless panic. That ought to buy me one simple immodest brag, especially when it's the truth. And the truth is this—for all their fame and fortune, there isn't a human athlete in the whole wide world who could come close to doing what I did. Compared to me a gold medal gymnast is a slug. If a human could do what I did, spring straight up four times his height, he could dunk a basketball from a standing start into a 24-foot-high hoop. To an ordinary cat even your sports gods are plodding, heavy, stiff-necked statues. And I'm no ordinary cat.

The speeding car's sloping hood wedged under my outstretched claws while I was still on the way up, moving so fast I smoked the wax. I still remember that smell. The windshield dealt a hard, angling blow to my right flank, launching me skyward too quick for the pain to keep up. That would have to wait for the breath to come back into my shock-imploded lungs.

Then the idiot hit his brakes. All he ever saw was a flash of gold blasting into his windshield, and gone so fast it could have been his imagination. He never even got out of his car. But I believe I ruined his paint job. That thought helps keeps me warm in my old age.

But back to the poor, body-slammed kitty staggering half-speed down the sidewalk, gasping for air, right side both numb to his brain's instructions and on fire in a burning crescendo of pain. He could sure use a break. The Good Samaritans were gaining on him. It was beginning to look like he'd pulled the most dramatic escape of his life, only to fall into the hands of yet another set of strangers with who knows what consequences. Maybe they'd think the place for a hurt, stray cat was the pound.

My left side was still working, the other side not so good. I kept veering to the right, bouncing off buildings like a wind-up toy, scalloping down the block. I'd be about to fall over and I'd bang into the bricks again and rebound out to the sidewalk. I made it halfway down the block like that, then swerved right one more time. Or one last time, I should say. Because that time I didn't bounce off the wall. I went straight through.

And I was back in the woods again. My old friend, come to save me, a sweet, resinous oasis of soft scents, here in the hard city. Or at least that's how it smelled. What it looked like was lumber.

Piles of lumber neat stacked, heaps of lumber scattered like jackstraws, shards of lumber littering the fresh-gouged earth. I had stumbled into a construction site—not as much of a coincidence as it first seems, if you know San Francisco. Where I got lucky was in finding the only gap in the board fence that kept the gawkers out and the workers working. There was exactly one missing tooth in that quarter-block whitewashed smile, and fate blew me through it without so much as a splinter.

What's more, the place was deserted. Maybe it was their day off, maybe they hadn't started building yet and they were just piling up supplies; I wasn't asking. I was just happy to be alone.

But for how much longer? There were people hot on my tail, I had to hide in a hurry. I saw one likely spot—a tarry pile of torn roof shingles, broken beams, twisted wire and rusty nails at the very back of the lot—the bulldozed mess of a torn-down house.

Quick as I could I worked my way into that maze, leaving a bit of fur behind on every splinter and shard in my haste, which, considering my condition, wasn't all that hasty. But I was desperate to get invisible, and I succeeded. Scrabbling frantically through the wreckage got me to a small hole where I could curl up and ache in peace. It also got me a face full of plaster dust. Just when I'd managed to fall off the end of the earth and disappear, I sneezed.

CHAPTER 40

Nobody cared. Can you believe that? I waited in dust-covered, white-faced suspense and not a damned thing happened. Nobody came, nobody at all. I suppose I should have felt relief. I mean, I'd almost killed myself getting away from those people, but I was kind of … disappointed. I expected to see a mass of humanity come pouring through that fence, little cat-sized stretchers in hand, ready to whisk me away to the animal hospital.

I mean, I'm Doo Doo, for chrissakes, the Magic Cat! And they're content to go on their way and forget about me, after what we'd been through? The nerve!

I sneezed again, louder. No takers.

That's the way it's gonna be? The hell with them. I actually started to sulk—until I remembered why I was here in the first place. Oh yeah, *that.* Home.

Sooner or later I'd have to get moving again, but right now I needed to take inventory. I'd lost a couple ounces of fur, had a bone bruise or two and my ribs ached when I breathed, but I decided it was still worth the trouble. Everything hurt, nothing broken, lots to make my trip painful, nothing bad enough to stop me. I could tough it out.

But where the hell was I? When I was three thousand miles away, I knew *just* where to go, but now that I was so close to my goal, I'd lost the "spot." My compass was spinning, pointing this way and that and nowhere in particular. Just like those fickle people, running after me a moment ago but gone now, it felt like home itself had deserted me.

I gave it up and let the sadness wash over me like an old friend, feeling alone in the world, abandoned. But then my *real* old friend came along and rescued me. It was as much swoon as sleep, and mercifully, for once, it was dreamless.

I woke up in the dark; I'd slept the whole day away. But that rest had done me a world of good—mentally. My body I couldn't vouch for until I tried using it.

Sore, achy, stiff. It hurt all over, and when I tried to stand I shook so hard it was pure luck I didn't collapse the pile around my ears. But my parts all moved when I asked them to, which was important, because I needed to get out of there in a big way. I'd picked the dustiest spot in town to hide, and I'd breathed in most of it during my twelve-hour "nap." I was parched and wheezing.

Carefully retracing my way through the maze of rubble, trying not to bang into anything sharp and leave what was left of my pelt behind, I emerged into the vacant, lumber-strewn lot and breathed some cool, clean air. It felt so good to cough that chalk out of my lungs I decided to shake it off my body. Big mistake. My bruises bit so hard I had to stifle a scream. I decided dirty wasn't so bad; I'd try again in a year or two. In the meantime I'd go looking for a way out other than the street.

That turned out to be easy. Once I stepped around the pile I could see the back of the lot. There was a gap in the fence there big enough to drive a truck though, which is no doubt what it was for. Across that gap ran a single chain, about a yard off the ground. Apparently cats weren't their main concern. Better yet, it bordered on an alley, not a street. I walked under, looked both ways for cars or people, saw neither, and traipsed.

I still didn't know where I was, but I knew I wanted to avoid big, commercial avenues. This was a good start, in the middle of the block, no corners to deal with, no busy intersections. Across the alley were small, detached houses with driveways and backyards, places where I could *maneuver*.

Let's try this for a while; I'll figure out where I'm going later. For that I'll need an open space where I can get my bearings—preferably one that isn't paved, because it's hard to get your bearings with headlights bearing down on you.

With a little judicious zigging and zagging, I managed to make some decent progress, crossing small, residential streets mid-block, through one set of alleys and yards to the next. And I noticed something important on the way. While it was still flat here, the land was beginning to slope, ever so slightly, upwards. That felt right.

But then I hit another avenue, a big, wide, nasty one. There were stores and lights on the far side of the street and people galore. I was on a roll and I didn't want to stop, plus I was still thirsty as all get out; I had to cross right here. Happily, traffic was light at this hour, and it's actually easier at night because you can see them coming. I only had to wait a minute for a nice, clean shot, and then I blew across that asphalt, post-haste. It hurt like hell, but my speed was still there.

With no gaps on this side of the street I had a decision to make. Left or right corner? Something told me left, so I went left. And something was right.

As soon as I was pointed in that direction, I could smell it. Coffee. More precisely, coffee *shop*—with tables on the sidewalk at the corner. Light poured from big windows, music leaked out into the street. And right by the entrance sat a big metal bowl, throwing glints off its curved sides, practically whistling to me.

"Water."

I'd seen this before. I knew who that water was for—dogs. Lots of coffeehouses have taken to this custom, I'd seen it in San Francisco and I'd seen it in New York, and usually there was some big, slobbery mutt in that bowl, snout deep.

But I didn't see any dogs now. I paused in the shadows, sniffed the air, then darted under the first, unoccupied table, three short of the door. All the rest were lousy with customers. If I was going to check out that bowl, I'd have to run a gauntlet of people.

What the hell. You're thirsty. This is your town, and this coffee shop on this corner is *in* your town. Make like you own the joint.

And that's just what I did.

Tail up, strutting the sidewalk top cat style, right past people dunking Danishes and lapping lattes. Right past the Table Toads who were croaking nonstop, leaning forward, giggling, paying too much attention to each other to pay any to me. I was invisible again; I approached the bowl unmolested.

Anticipation had my whiskers twitching, I was *so* thirsty. And, hurray, it *was* water, four inches deep and as big around as one of those Frisbees the pooches seem to love more than life itself. But lordy, was it foul! Oily dog spit slimed the surface, repulsive floaties—bits of dog biscuit no doubt, bloated and mushy—added to the pollution. But this was no time to be finicky. I hate to snitch on my own species, but the truth is our fussiness is just an act. We know if we turn up our noses when your offerings displease us, you saps will go for the upgrade, every time. But this was an exception under the emergency clause. There were miles ahead of me and I needed water like a mosquito needs blood. I swallowed both pride and scum and sucked down that soup ... with relish.

Relish, a few clots of Doggie Treat, one drowned moth, some hair that looked like it came off a Pomeranian and a couple of not-quite dead ticks to provide that much-needed crunch. No problem—I was going to need protein too—fuel is fuel. And it's better to eat ticks than vice versa.

I had the tank pretty much topped off when I was swallowed by the Cone of Silence. It came along with the Pool of Darkness—both being manifestations of the Mountain of Blubber which had oozed itself between me and the coffeehouse door. The bulk of the man sucked the vibrations right out of the air on the side of the world where he stood.

That's what got me to look up from the revolting bowl of dog backwash I was gargling down with such noisy determination—all of a sudden I couldn't hear myself. I was being loomed like I've never been loomed before.

So unready was I for the amazing sight my eyes were pumping into my unbelieving brain that I forgot to close my mouth. A single strand of viscous water trailed from my tongue to the bowl.

Man-mountain began to widen at the base, yards of fabric folded and billowed, a head shaped like a beer-keg left orbit and began to descend, looming even larger now. From the apex of all that flesh came a rumbling grunt, half human, half volcano; he was kneeling down!

I knew I'd probably encounter people when I went for the bowl, and I'd promised myself that this time I wouldn't panic. And I kept that promise, but I deserve no credit. The strangeness of his pinhole eyes—staring out at me like an animal trapped inside a cave—made it impossible to move or even to look away. I felt a shiver start at my whiskers, pulse past my ears, pass through my pelt and exit my trembling tail.

Those buried eyes crinkled into what I think was supposed to be a smile.

"Awww," the Mountain cooed.

That wasn't what I expected at all. I unfroze long enough to blink.

"Here's a nice kitty," he rumbled. He'd gotten himself squatted down so low his face was just above mine. I couldn't imagine how he'd get up again.

This was just a man. An *enormous* man—getting really, really close, but just a man. The spell was broken and I'd drunk all the water I could hold. There was nothing keeping me here.

So why didn't I run away? Why was I drawn to this mound of flesh that had to speak before I was sure it was human? Gravity?

"You sure are purty," he said, and bracing himself with one hand on the ground, swung the other towards my head!

I saw that tree trunk coming and shrank away.

"Shhh," the Mountain said. And he dragged his massive palm across my back.

It was like being petted with a roast beef. But I could tell he was trying to keep the weight off me, this was probably as close as he could come to delicate.

And I'll be damned if it didn't work. My twitchiness vanished and I let the heat and random love of the moment take me. As it took him—he was getting even more out of this chance encounter than I was, and I found that strangely reassuring. My motor started going and the big fella was eating it up, stroking my body and grinning like a fool.

"It's a nice pussy. Is it thirsty? Oh, the water is yucky!"

I hate baby talk. This time it didn't bother me.

"Let me get you fresh," he said.

The hand that had been petting me now grabbed the bowl. Man Mountain grunted, swayed alarmingly—for a moment I thought I was going to get squashed—and stood up in stages, like moving so much mass required rest stops.

"Be right back," he said when he was vertical.

He turned around and blubbed away, bowl in hand, squeezing sideways through the coffeehouse door.

I watched him go. I knew I wasn't going to be here when he came back.

That's another one, Doo Doo, I thought. How many does that make? How many times do you need

to prove it to yourself? Don't you think maybe you're pushing your luck?

I turned around and curled up the right side of the corner, heading up the block in the direction that felt most like west.

I got my second wind after that, and picked up the pace. The next several crossings were easy, no more crowds or heavy traffic, just small streets and a couple of nearly deserted boulevards. That upward tilt of the land I'd noticed before continued and got a bit steeper—though not nearly enough to deserve the word hill, nor anything like the peak-and-gulch part of town where I was born. I was just winging it, trying to go in more or less one direction so at least I wouldn't make useless circles. Impatience made that difficult—the faster I went the loster I got.

It was still too built up here to do what I needed to do, which was find a place to stop and get oriented. I needed a good, clear acre of land—something bigger than a vacant lot, a small park would do nicely. And if it was a little bit higher than its surroundings, I'd like my chances. But none appeared. Spooks did—I could feel cats' eyes peering at me from the alleys, hear dogs barking behind each fenced yard and dark hedge I crossed. This was no good. The *last* thing I needed was a fight—or flight. I was lost enough already.

And angry. Where the *hell* was that park? This is San Francisco, the city is rotten with them!

Try getting your head out of your butt, idiot. Look, over there, to your left, where those streetcar tracks disappear underground. Isn't that a hill? Aren't those trees?

CHAPTER 41

So how does a cat find his way from somewhere he's never been to wherever it is he wants to go? You've all heard the stories; I'm not the first of my kind to make an "impossible" trip home. We can't all do it, but some of you can't play the piano. It's a skill, partly talent, partly learned. And it's very hard to describe in terms a human can understand, but I'll try.

There are two distinct elements to it, homing and tracking. Homing is what I've been doing until now. Homing is following that bright spot on the horizon, that sense of direction that shows you where something you can't see *is*. It's not like a map—that's a human thing. It's more like some internal gyro that always points to the same place, no matter what twists and turns our bodies make. It's a pull, more or less strong and steady, but not very specific. Imagine a person navigating by compass. He can see where the needle points, but how does he know when he's reached North?

Tracking is a fine art of tiny things. It's all about senses, but our senses are so much sharper than yours that the comparison is misleading. We pick up on things you'd never even notice. The closest human example I can think of is when one of you goes blind, or, better yet, is blind from birth. In some uncanny way you've heard about, but can't understand, those poor folks can develop their remaining senses to such a pitch of sharpness that they can *know* things, things the sighted could never sense. Well, take that skill and multiply it by ten and that's what the average cat has all the time, and I'm no average cat.

So here's what I was trying to sense when I trotted up that pocket-sized park on the industrial fringes of the city. How salty is the air? Is that distant rumble the ocean? What is the stronger scent from this direction, asphalt or grass? How about that direction? How does the ground tilt under my feet? And a dozen other things you have no words for at all.

Then I tried to put it all together. Buried in all that information was the one, specific combination of everything I could sense that meant *home*. Tracking is trying to move so that all the needles line up, and you need a clear place from which to start, a place close enough for the evidence to *show*.

That's what I was doing on this grassy knoll, and that's the best I can describe it. You'll just have to take my word for the rest.

The little park was wooded, but it had a bald spot in the middle and that's where I parked myself. I sniffed and tasted the air, felt the breeze, arced my ears this way and that, and got myself oriented. I thought I had a pretty good idea where to head next. But trees blocked the view; I'd have to step out and see the lay of the land before I could gauge the task that awaited me. And I was too tired for that at the moment. My battered, used-up muscles needed a two-hour catnap, minimum. So I ate a few blades of grass, put my head between my front paws and drifted off right there, out in the open. I figured I could hear anyone or anything that came my way in time to scamper off, if I had to. And luckily, I didn't have to.

The night was darker when I woke up. It was thick overcast. The San Francisco high fog that so often covers the city on summer nights had come early this year, and now that it was late there were fewer lights reflecting off the bottom. It was quieter, too. Every now and then I heard a whispery boom that had to be the ocean. That got my pulse going. Ocean meant *home.* All I needed now was a fix, a target, and for that only my eyes could serve. Time to take a look. I stretched out my stiffness and paid the price in pain, licked off the dew and leaf litter I'd picked up while I slept, and weaved my way through the copse of trees to the other side of the park.

I had my general direction; I was looking for a hint, a glimpse, something to orient on to narrow it down. When I came clear of the trees and reached the curb on the west side of the park, I got more than a hint. I got the jackpot.

The Candelabra. Ask anyone who has ever been to S.F., they've seen it. A tall, ugly, three-pronged antenna perched on top of the highest hill in the city. There it was, lights winking on its spires, on my right at about one o'clock, maybe three miles away as the crow flies. The sight that would have driven me streaking heedless through the streets, had I seen it a couple hours ago, before I composed myself, before I slept.

Because the last time I'd seen that tower, more that a year ago, I was sunning myself, *in my own backyard.*

* * *

So this was it. The homestretch. I was *so* ready for this to be over. Hunger went away, fatigue went away, aching muscles and bruised ribs didn't, but they faded into the background, I was going *home.*

Cats are built for speed, not for distance. Pounce, eat, sleep: That's what our genes tell us to do, that's what our play is all about—streak across the room like crazy for ten minutes, bouncing off the furniture, chasing ghosts, amusing our "owners" no end—then slow, stop and drop. Four totally inert hours later we're ready to do it again.

But I hadn't come across the continent in a sprint. I'd learned a thing or two about pacing myself. If I wanted to get this last little jaunt done before morning I'd need to take it slow and make constant corrections as I got closer. It wouldn't do to go flying off like a bottle rocket, overshoot the target, backtrack, blast past again, get lost, get tired, get discouraged, get stupid, get caught. No more adventures; I'd had about all I could take.

So I walked. I walked and sniffed, walked and looked, walked and stopped, turned a few degrees right or left, then walked some more. From street light to porch light, over hedges and under fences, from dark place to dark place whenever I smelled dog or heard person. I walked for a couple of hours, and it was like one scene on an endless loop, little fragments of grass and sidewalk and tarmac, repeating, a treadmill city falling beneath my feet, flickering images, always changing but all the same. And nothing could touch me, I was invisible, invincible, in a fugue state of perpetual motion. Soon that beacon on the horizon grew a sound, just a whisper at first, but then louder and louder. It was calling my name.

"Doo Doooooo…. Doo Dooooooo," a foghorn bellowed silently, "come here, come home."

Soon that sound wasn't on the horizon anymore, it was much closer, much louder. The land tilted steeply upwards and the blocks got bigger and the streets got crooked. This was familiar, this felt right, home was getting near and the sound screamed in the foreground. I could *feel* it, just over the next rise, pulling at my insides so hard that uphill felt like downhill. I had to set my feet against my heart and the effort dragged a purr past my throat. Here I was, in the wee, small hours of the morning, all alone on the back streets of San Francisco, purring like an idiot. It was about as close as a cat can come to crying.

* * *

One more hurdle awaited me. Home was on the shoulder of a very steep hill, not far from a flat spot to the east. That flat spot marked the edge of my territory, back when I lived there. I'd explored up to it but not beyond it, and for a very good reason. That reason rose up now and slapped me in the face.

I was congratulating myself on my good luck and better navigation when the street I'd been following stopped. That wasn't so surprising, streets in San

Francisco have a habit of doing that, and I'd already done considerable zigzagging to stay on course. But now there was no place to zig; this stump of a street dead-ended into a steep, overgrown embankment.

Climbing through that thorn-filled thicket was tough enough, and I got reminded of all my dings and aches on the way up. But what was worse was having to come right back down.

How could I forget the freeway? I'd heard it all my young life, I could even see it from the roof of my house, but somehow it had totally skipped my mind. I didn't know I was in trouble until I ran into the fence at the top of the hill.

The fence wasn't the problem, I could find a hole or burrow through the bottom, or climb right over, come to that. The problem was twelve lanes of concrete spread out over a quarter-mile wide roadbed sunk thirty feet below me. There wasn't much traffic on that superhighway, but what there was flew by scary fast, mostly big trucks, headlights jittering ahead of them like death rays.

There was no way. I was stymied as sure as if I'd hit a steel wall. Maybe I could make it over safely, nine times out of ten, but I'm not that much of a fool. Just rash sometimes. I had to backtrack.

Okay, a minor disappointment. Once I got back down the embankment and over my pique, I realized the happier truth. That freeway was within sight of my house, therefore *I* must have been within sight of my house. All I had to do was find a way across, then I should be on home turf, at long last. One last barrier and I'd be in high catnip, eating Fern's food, lolling on Doc's lap. Home!

So, which way? I walked back to the corner and sat on a lawn for a few minutes, trying to reconstruct what I'd seen through that fence. The land had been flatter to the left, or south, hillier to the north. So right would probably bring me closer to home. I struck off in that direction, along the sidewalk of a street that more or less paralleled the embankment, looking for a way through.

What I found was a way over. A road on stilts, far overhead, that angled down towards my right, away from the freeway. If I wanted to get up on that bridge I'd have to go several blocks east. I didn't like that idea, and I couldn't tell where that overpass really went, either. It could have crossed over the freeway, or it could have ramped right onto it.

Tempting, but no. I did four or five more unhelpful blocks and then decided to change my strategy. The street I was on kept curving away from the embankment. If I didn't want to miss my crossing, I'd need to be right up against that hill, road or no road. The going might be tougher, but there was no other way to be sure. I took the next corner to the left, back towards the freeway, back towards the place these little streets went to die.

It was pure luck, one last time. This new cross street curled gently to the left, I couldn't see where it ended. But it was well-lit, and what I could see, right away, were its street lights angling *down*. I rounded the bend and there it was, an *underpass*, with that big slab of road passing right over the top. It even had sidewalks on both sides so I wouldn't have to risk the street. Haven't I told you, time and again, that I'm a lucky cat?

I trotted through that tunnel on tiptoes, so high on anticipation that my claws peeked out of my feet and clattered on the cement, making little skritchy sounds echo off the slab-sided walls.

The underpass ended at a climbing cross street in a little commercial area, deserted at this hour. Oh yeah ... this was my neighborhood for sure. I was seeing it from a different angle, from below rather than above, but I knew this was it. That long, low building, all lit up, that was the subway station. I could see its glow from the living room window when I perched on the sill at night. Over there, at the intersection, a stoplight blinking on and off. I'd seen that from the front stoop too, way up the hill where my home was, where my home *is*.

But where, exactly, *am* I? As close as I was, I still needed to find the right alley, the particular strip of wild urban jungle that led to my house. My usual hangout was behind the houses on my block, above their redwood fences, in the steep mini-forest where I'd been born. But there were *lots* of places like that tucked away in the folds and gullies spiraling above me. Somewhere, around half a mile up, there should be a *special* gap in the line of row houses that terraced the hill. One that I would instantly recognize, even in my agitated, forgetful state. Or so I chose to hope.

It figured this last bit would be tougher than it looked. Such a prize needs to be worthy of the effort, I told myself. I guess even cats can rationalize. But all I knew was that it was hard to keep my sense of direction straight, because *nothing* was straight here— not the streets, not the contours of the mountain I was climbing, not the impenetrable arcs of two- and three-story homes, not even the vital but infrequent gaps I needed to keep going up, up to the next tier of curlicue streets, where the maze offered its next challenges and detours.

Sure, all the cues were trending right, the smells, sounds, and angles were telling the same tale: You're getting warm, very warm. But despite all that, I didn't know where the hell I was or where "it" was. I needed to find something unmistakable, someplace I knew so well that it would give me a flashback—oh yes, I've been here before! But that checkpoint was elusive, I kept climbing, kept hoping, kept straining every sense to find the "fix," and all I got was dizzy.

When I found it, it caught me totally by surprise. It was the last thing I was looking for, because looking had nothing to do with it. But it was a memory of my past life nonetheless, one I hadn't given a thought, but one no cat could ever forget.

The Bark. "Barkbarkbark!" Crazy, loud, constant, pathetic. "*Bark!*"

Of course! Only one dog sounded like that, wailed like that, barked like that. A poor, neglected, balcony-exiled pooch, treated like a disease. If he'd been a cat he'd have taken a powder long ago and I couldn't have used him as the neighborhood sonar. But his balcony was thirty feet high, and dogs are so loyal they'll take abuse even if escape is possible. They're built that way—the more you beat them the more they love you. I'd always felt pity and contempt for Crazy Balcony Dog—hollered at, banished to a four-by-eight slab, but still begging for forgiveness. "What have I *done*? Why do you do this to me? Why won't you let me *in*!" You could hear unrequited love in every bark and wail.

But now his neurosis was my godsend. Because that miserable, tiny apartment balcony was *directly behind my house!* That whimper, those trilling whines, that anguished bark, were pure joy to me. Follow those sounds, find that balcony, and I'd be right there, just a flimsy fence away from paradise, from owners who *never* abused me, were *never* unkind. On the contrary, they loved me, made a fuss over me, gourmet-fed me, gave me the keys to the kingdom and a pillow to sleep on. They even kept a supply of catnip on hand at all times—growing in the yard, stuffed inside toys, leaves they'd spread around the house like candy—sweet, sweet catnip junkie enablers.

I got a buzz just thinking about it. I homed in on that pitiful, screaming dog like a magnet.

It was close, just a few blocks away. "BarkbarkBARK!" Any minute now, and my long-lost idyllic life, so full of comfort and love, would be mine again. I'd made a terrible mistake, been led astray, and paid for it with a million miles and a hundred years. But now my exile was minutes away from being over.

Then mere seconds. I found my jungle strip, my birthing place, and there was that fence with the hole at the bottom, the one I'd used countless times to leave my yard, and more to the point, return again. Home was on the other side of that hole, a ragged gap two feet wide, four inches high and one inch thick between me and the promised land. All my fear and fatigue and bad choices were on this side, all my hopes and love and redemption were waiting for me on that side. I slithered under the weathered fence, pink nose, golden paws, white chin, and emerged into the backyard I knew, and missed, so well. And there was the house! *My* house, with *my* people, no doubt still mourning my loss. I bet they miss me even more than I miss them!

I walked down the steep yard with an overflowing heart. Here I am, people! Let the love fest begin.

CHAPTER 42

So why isn't the light on? I know it's very late, but Doc and I had always, and I mean *always*, seen the dawn together before he went to bed. He'd be reading on his couch with the patio door cracked open to let the cigar smoke out and me in, the lamp on the bookcase glaring into the backyard, letting me know he was still up and open for business. But now all was dark as I walked down the hill.

And speaking of cigar smoke, how come I couldn't smell it? Even when he wasn't smoking that scent would linger in the air, coat the concrete deck, settle with the dew on the grass. A human couldn't smell it then, but I could. Where was it now?

Something wasn't right. The house looked the same, but it didn't *feel* the same. Now that I looked more closely, I noticed things were missing—like the ratty patio furniture I used to sun myself on, the big, greasy barbecue grill that always smelled tantalizingly of meat and charred fat, and the flower pots Fern planted with fresh catnip for me, and replanted whenever I ate it down to the roots. Where the hell was my catnip? Where the hell was Doc? Where the hell was I?

Okay, settle down, big boy, you've been gone a long time. The catnip died, they threw out the grill, Doc quit smoking. Maybe he's taking a nap, he did that sometimes. Stop skulking around and *do* something. Open a mouth, make some noise, wake them up, they'll be thrilled to see you.

Wait, better yet, surprise them! See over there? You're so freaked you forgot about the cat door! There it is, right under the kitchen window, just like always. You *are* home, now go tell them about it.

It was a short, two-foot hop from the deck to the cat door in the back wall of the house. I charged in the way I always did, leaping fast and flat to push through the rubber flap ... and crashed back to the concrete with a knot on my head. The cat door was closed.

That hurt, but it wasn't pain that screeched through my throat now. It was fear.

"Hooowll!" (Where *are* you?)

"Screeech!" (You're gone?)

"Ruhh, uh, raaawr!" (No, no, *no!*)

I got all worked up. I was beside myself, crazy with fright and loss, howling at a moon I couldn't see beneath the fog. That got the dog working overtime. The more I cried the more he barked. And I cried plenty. The backyard became a symphony of pain.

How long I kept up that shameful hysteria I don't know. All I remember now is the red rage and helplessness that surged through my body and rasped out my mouth. That, and a tiny voice telling me to get ahold of myself. However long it took, finally, I started to listen. Beat on the door, Doo Doo. You need to find out, you need to *know*.

I stilled my cries and walked slowly to the patio door. Rearing up on my back legs, front claws out, I got ready to scratch that glass to dust if I had to.

But I didn't have to. The light came *on*. And then I heard the familiar "click" of the lock, and the door rolled open. Oh yes!

"What the hell is going *on* out there?"

Oh, no! You're not Doc. Where is he, where is Fern?

The backlit form was too short by a half a foot to be Doc, the shrill voice too high by an octave. I couldn't see this stranger's face and I didn't want to. I knew.

"Scat! Go on.... Git!"

"Hissss." I didn't intend to do that, it just came out.

The silhouette let out a yip and rattled the screen door like he wanted to scare me away but was afraid to come out and do it in person.

He should have been. If I could have gotten at him I'd have clawed him to ribbons, just out of frustration. But my heart wasn't in it. I left the patio and trudged back up the hill, the dog's barks mocking me the whole way.

* * *

Day came and confirmed the awful truth— strangers were living in my house, *my* house. There were three of them, a man, a woman and a kid. They might as well be nobody. I crawled through the fence and watched them once or twice, hiding in the dense undergrowth of the unkempt yard. At least that hadn't changed. But everything else had. Most of all, me.

For the first time in forever, I didn't know what to do with myself. I was fresh out of purpose, I had nowhere to go. There was nothing for me here and nothing pulling me anywhere else. I was stuck; I fell into a deep, listless depression.

Sleep helped, it was an escape from thinking, from disappointment, and I did plenty of it. My body was beat up almost as badly as my spirits, but I'd live. That was the easy part. If there was anyplace in the world where I could live feral and alone, this was it. There were mice aplenty on that strip between the yards. Water still flowed at the storm drain on the corner, the same houses kept out dishes of food, some dog, some cat, that I could steal if times got lean. All my hiding places, all my lookouts, everything I needed was here, just like I left them half a lifetime ago. Only one thing was missing…. Make that two.

The survival instinct is strong in a cat. With nine lives to protect, we get a lot of practice. So that's what I did—survive. I became a drone, eating, drinking and sleeping aimlessly. I watched my old house, hoping for a change that never came. My only interactions were with animals, some I hunted, some I fought, some I ran away from. Springtime is heat time for kitties, and I took advantage of that diversion when the opportunity presented itself. But those moments of pleasure were fleeting.

I denied myself all human contact. There was nobody I wanted to be cute for, nobody I cared to talk to, nobody I wanted to respond to my antics, my voice, my purr. I just wanted to be left alone, and, if you can call that a goal, I achieved it. Stay away from people. Avoid trouble. Don't speak. Keep out of sight. Little by little I began to forget.

Time passed, even my dreams eased up on me. Once in a while I'd see Momma or Fern while I slept, but mostly my dreams were as dull as my days. Safe, simple and boring. It had been so long since I'd heard my name—*any* of my names—that I almost forgot it. I was getting stupid and I didn't even care. I didn't think about it much, I didn't think much at all. Even the lonely began to wear off in this numbing, pointless existence. I was all hollowed out, even as my body got strong and sleek. I became an idiot. If cats have souls, I still had mine, but it was getting weaker every day.

It was almost too late. Little bits of my past were dropping off me all the time and I never noticed. Maybe the day would come when I could pass Doc on the sidewalk and not know who he was. I doubt it, but maybe. For sure some things stopped being triggers. There was a house near the end of the block that puffed out cigar smoke now and then. The first couple of times I smelled it, I got a heart rush, galloped over, got disappointed, and slunk back to whatever I was doing, usually nothing. But now even the connection between my Doc and the smell of a cigar was gone, erased, extinguished. It was just another stink.

It was just another sound. Maybe in a week or a month that's what it would have stayed. But here on the edge of oblivion, one more lost cat in a world that has millions of them, after almost too long alone in my urban jungle, that sound began to bother me.

Motor noise. Nothing unusual about that, the street out front wasn't a busy one, but cars droned past all the time. I spent my time in back, away from the street; what happened out there didn't matter to me. I couldn't even *see* out front unless I climbed a roof, and the only way there was between a break in the row houses halfway down the block.

So I wasn't paying attention to the slightly louder than normal engine noise that throbbed its way from west to east before slowing to a halt nearby. It was a glorious late afternoon in autumn, a time when, if no fog rolled in, the sun would angle its steep rays straight down the gap between the backyards above and fences below, where I lived. Basking in that sunlight, strong enough to warm the fur but low enough that all the sting was out of it, was one of my few pleasures these days. I was in my favorite spot, nestled against the sunny side of an enormous tree, its lower branches so high that the light blasted beneath them, heating me and the trunk and the ground delightfully. This was *my* place, I'd marked it, used the rough bark as a scratching post, defended it once or twice from impudent interlopers, nothing bothered me here.

So why are my ears twitching? What dares to disturb the idiot cat's slumber as he fails to notice the passing of another day? What the hell *is* it about that sound?

I had to know. Once an idea takes hold in a cat's mind it sticks there and pulls until we do something about it. That's how we got the rep; once our curiosity is aroused we're like people with OCD—we can't help ourselves.

But we're also lazy, in case you hadn't noticed, and never more so than when grogging vacantly in the luxuriant sun. I was at the absolute pinnacle of the prime of life that day, and it still took me ten seconds to struggle to my feet, stretch the sloth out of my body, and get moving—slowly. There were three backyards between me and the shortcut to the street, an unfenced yard surrounding the block's one detached house.

The motor idled haltingly, somewhere near that gap. "Lobe, kalunk, lobe, kalunk." The closer I got the more it drew me, every clink and thrum became more distinct, more compelling. I rounded the last fence and started down the hill towards the street, moving faster now. Everything in my body was waking up, the haze in my head began to clear, memories were firing in my mind in tune to the engine's spark. Could it *be*? Could it possibly be?

Fifty feet from the sidewalk, trotting through the tall weeds, and that damned motor stops cold. What's worse, so do I. The sudden silence shocked me still for several seconds.

Those seconds cost me hours of nervous worry. But they were nearly catastrophic, I *almost* turned around and walked back up the hill. It was my newly awakened curiosity that saved me. Curiosity saved the cat.

I started downhill again, nosing slowly through the grass, front paw, back paw, down to the flat. One last hop through the weeds and I'm on the sidewalk, parked cars gleaming in the sun, crowding the curb, blocking my view. What am I looking for?

"Tink, clink, tink," the sound of a cooling motor across the street. Oh yeah, that's it. Passing underneath a pickup truck, standing right in the middle of the road, I turned to face that sound.

"Tink, clink, tink."

Doc's Jeep.

* * *

Big and battered and black, it sure *looked* like Doc's Jeep, but where was Doc? The street was deserted.

I tried sniffing the air, trying to pick up his scent, but I couldn't do it. There was too much wind, everything was all mixed up. I wasn't even sure I remembered his scent, I wasn't sure of anything. Would I even know him if I smelled him, heard him, saw him? Was I imagining the whole thing?

What to do? When all else fails, try screaming.

"Howl, howl, howl."

Funny how a cat's voice doesn't carry during the day like it does at night. The sea breeze took my cries and shredded them, I could barely hear myself.

Suddenly a car rears up close, and I'm in the middle of the street, wailing like an imbecile. Get a *grip* on yourself, Doo Doo.

That was too much to ask, but my reflexes put me safely on the far sidewalk when my mind failed me. I *am* seeing things now, my head full of images of home, Fern, the ghosts of Rass and all the people I'd seen and spurned that put me here, breathless and crazed, at just this moment.

What to do? I look around dizzily, through the clouds in my eyes, and find that Jeep again. Go *there*. It *is* Doc's car, I tell you. Go there.

Still breathing hard, making little chirps with each step, I close on that big hunk of metal and glass. I'm facing its front, its two big eyes and vertical mouth, stalking slowly, like it's alive and I don't want to spook it. Every time I blink it looks a little more real, every nick and dent speaks to me. When I finally get there, it looks so much like home I want to move right in.

And that's exactly what I do. The plastic side windows are zipped down this warm day. Doc always did that. I measure the height and spring from the curb, sailing into that dark hole, landing on the passenger seat. The car I hated so much, the noisy wreck I escaped forever ago, sending me on a lost voyage to god knows where and back—yes, and back!—it had won after all. Take me home, Jeep. Take me home.

But the Jeep just sat there, and the sun went down.

Darkness was usually my friend. Not tonight. I started worrying about the reception I'd get when Doc showed up—I was sure it was his car now, his scent was all over it—and that gave me a case of the frights. He had every right to be mortally pissed off at me. I mean, the last time I was in this very Jeep I skedaddled without a backwards glance, out of his arms and into oblivion for more than a year. Now all of a sudden I show up and I'm expecting catnip and cuddles like it never even happened? What am I, a fool? If the fur was on the other paw I'd have tossed me right back on the sidewalk and good riddance to bad rubbish.

So I'm thinking sweet thoughts in that vein, getting more and more agitated and wishing like hell I could pass the time the way I usually do—asleep—but that release is denied me. I get to experience every minute of the next three hours in a tizzy of restlessness and anxiety, wide awake and hating it. I couldn't sit still but I didn't dare go anywhere for fear of missing Doc when he came back.

All I could do was pace the two foot square seat cushion. And every screen door's creak, every footfall, every muffled voice brought me up short, straining to hear, poking my head out the window to see. I was so wired it felt like I had ants on my skin.

The wait was killing me. After a while it was all I could think about; even the fears that were torturing my imagination took a back seat to my screaming impatience.

How long will this go on? How does it all come out in the end? Am I home or am I lost forever? I *have* to *know!*

CHAPTER 43

The Happy Ending

I *don't have as many teeth now as I did back then. My back legs are stiff on cold mornings and I'm not the athlete I once was. But my mind is as sharp as ever, maybe sharper than it was on that last, lost day all those years ago. If my memories are a little fuzzy it's because I was a little fuzzy* back then, *not now. I still had a lot of youth to go when this story ends and, I'm happy to say, I lived it very well. So much has happened since, I could be forgiven if the odd detail dropped into the discard pile of the past in the intervening years.*

But I'm telling the story the best I can, and what I've dredged out of my memory rings true to me now. This has been a process, one that grew and deepened as I undertook it. The more I remembered the more I remembered, it was almost like living it all over again. I've tried to make it real for you.

The words you are reading weren't typed by me, of course. Cats don't have fingers. But Doc does, and he's using them on the keys of his laptop right this second, his fingers clicking and twitching, the muscles on the bottoms of his forearms tensing and relaxing as they rest across my back. He fancies himself a writer—did I tell you that? He thinks he's *writing this story.*

Well, it was his idea, I'll give him that much. He never got over wondering what the hell I'd been through and where in the world I'd been in the fifteen months I was gone. He'd ask me and ask me, like if he kept asking I'd acquire the power of speech, rear up on my hind legs and go, "See Doc, it was like this...." And there were times I wished I could talk, because I thought I owed him an explanation.

Finally he decided that if he couldn't know, he'd quiet his curiosity in the way he knew best—by making it up. And that's what he thinks he's been doing for the past year, as we come to the end of our tale.

But I'm here to tell you that each and every scene, every smell, every taste, every idea, every hurt and loss and love he's put on these pages came straight out of my mind, beamed into his, while he worked the keys and selected the words. This is my story, this is the truth, and I think he knows it. Otherwise he would have erased these last few lines before you ever read them.

So, come on Doc. It's almost daybreak and I'm running out of days. I promised these nice folks a happy ending. Let's give it to them.

* * *

One moment I'm alone in the Jeep with my craziness—three hours of moments actually. The whole time I'm waiting for Doc, waiting for Doc, fretting about it and waiting for Doc. And when he comes, I'm surprised.

The driver's door opens and Doc—who is a tall, skinny thing—swings his butt onto the seat, unfolds his legs, grabs the wheel and shoves the key into the ignition in one, articulated, praying mantis motion.

The motor coughs to life before I find my voice.

"Mrrorw?"

Doc jerks his head my way, narrows his eyes and stares.

"Mrrorww!"

He shuts the motor down.

"Doo Doo?"

I stand up.

"Oh. My. God. Doo Doo!"

"Ru-rarararr…" my purr vibratos my meow. One paw reaches over the console of the Jeep's unlit interior and finds that leg, the same jeans-covered leg I'd touched a million times, my claws snagging the cotton, feeling his warmth, my whole body humming with anticipation.

"I don't believe … where the hell … dammit, boy!"

Oh no. Don't be angry, you *can't*.…

Big spidery hands reach around my tube and pull me up in the air. He turns me so we're face to face.

"It's *you*," Doc marvels. "It's really you!"

He's not angry. He's shocked. He's *amazed*.

A funny sound glugs in Doc's throat. He blinks. I'm spun sideways in his hands. He buries his face in my body. Hot tears wet my fur.

The surprise overwhelmed him, I guess. But not me. What *I* felt as Doc used my flanks for a crying towel was *relief*. I was as relieved as it's possible for a kitty to be. I let my body go limp in his hands and let it all soak in. Go ahead, Doc, I know what you mean.

* * *

Home at last? Almost. First there was the matter of a little drive to a place I'd never seen. Home might be the same, but house had moved.

"You aren't going to jump again, are you?" Doc said as he pulled away from the curb.

How can I? If I was any closer to your belly I'd be your belt.

Doc had me clamped tight, but he needn't have worried. I wasn't going to make the same mistake twice.

Okay, so maybe it wasn't a total mistake—the things I'd seen, the people I'd known, the purpose I'd discovered, and most of all, Rass…. But one cross-country odyssey per cat is enough.

"Where *were* you all this time?" Doc asked for the first of a thousand times. "Were you here in the old neighborhood all along? Did somebody kidnap you or something? We looked everywhere!"

Not quite everywhere, Doc. Now when do I get to see Fern? Are we there yet?

Yes we were.

The new house was pretty much the old house, five minutes away. Maybe a little bigger on a lot that was flatter, with a nice front porch where I could already picture myself eating potted catnip while I watched the traffic.

Doc stopped the car, opened the door and got out without ever relaxing his death grip on my scruff. He wasn't crying anymore—which was also a relief because that kind of scared me—he was as giddy as a child.

"Man, Doo Doo. Fern is going to *freak out!* A day doesn't pass that she doesn't say your name at least once. If you only *knew...*"

Doc tossed me over his left shoulder, my back legs in his right hand while the left worked the latch. We walked into a darkened house that smelled a lot like the old one, but with a little something extra that I couldn't identify at first.

"Quiet now," Doc whispered to me pointlessly because I wasn't making a peep. "Fern's asleep. Let's go surprise her."

Doc clicked on a hall light and opened the bedroom door. He held me against his chest and sat down on the bed, next to a lump.

That would be Fern. She liked to sleep in a cocoon of blankets, only the tip of her head exposed, her hair puddled on the pillow, and, often as not, me sleeping right on top, like a hat.

Doc leaned down and kissed the lump, then whispered:

"I brought you something, baby."

"Uhhuuuuh..." Fern whined. She hated being awakened in the middle of the night. But then again, who likes it?

"I got something for you, sweetie," Doc said in a voice that couldn't quite contain itself to a whisper.

"Nnnn! Gotta work n'morning!" A sweet, angry voice mumbled. Fern flinched away, pressing herself deeper into the bed, desperately trying to hold onto the threads of sleep.

Doc snuggled up to her from behind, peeled the covers away from her chin, and gently placed me there, curled up under her neck.

"Yaah!" she yelped. Fern always startled easy, but only for a moment. I heard her hands rustle under the sheets, seeking the source of this fuzzy, tickly heat.

She knew me before she saw me.

"Doo Doo," she claimed, her words pitching up at the end like she was asking a question. But there was no question in it. She knew

And so did I. People say the soul is in the eyes, but cats know better; it's in the touch. She held me for the longest time, rocking her body gently, making a nest between her hands and the curves of her neck.

"Sushhh…" she whispered, addressing herself not to the silent voices of her husband or her kitty, but to a din of emotions so loud the room could barely hold them.

"Shhh," she crooned. "Momma knows … momma knows."

CODA

Now I'm supposed to wrap up all the loose ends and tie my life story with a nice, neat bow, right? Well, I can't do that. I'm sixteen now, I was only three when I fell asleep in Fern's arms that morning. So unless Doc wants to write—and you want to read—another thousand pages, we'd better stop here.

Not that I made any more 6,000-mile trips, mind you. One of those per catlife is enough—though I never did lose my wanderlust. From time to time I would go walkabout, right through my long, robust middle age. I don't do that any more. Now a big trip is to the porch and back. But my life has had adventures galore, too many to tell, and I'm growing tired of reminiscing. I'm growing tired in general.

However, I don't think the Feline Authors' Union would mind if I added a detail or two here at the end. We're a small group, and being cats, we don't take the rules too seriously anyway. So consider the following a little gift, a thank you for your patience and attention.

* * *

The new neighborhood was cat city. There must have been fifteen of them on the block when I showed up, including a couple of toms that outweighed me a good five pounds. Well, there are a lot more now, and most of them are *my* great, great grandkittens. It didn't take me long to let the neighborhood cats know—there's a new boss in town.

It was no contest. I'd been places and done things all these rubes put together wouldn't be or do in a lifetime. I'd faced death in ways and multiples a regular nine-lives cat would never know. I was trouble in a day, top cat in a month. Even now, in my dotage, I lord it over them on sheer reputation. I never even have to fight anymore, which is a good thing because my fighting days are long gone.

Doc and Fern are getting older too, just like me, but much more slowly. They continue happy and well. If you're looking for drama in that department, read a human author, they specialize in that kind of fantasy. Doc and Fern are plain old happily married, childless, cat-crazy folks. Doc doesn't even get into the people nip nearly as much as he used to, and, truth to tell, I'm losing my taste for the cat variety. But every once in a while …well … let's just say we ain't dead yet.

So, do I think of the long, lost past very often? No, mostly I'm just here, thinking no farther ahead than my next nap and no further back than my last meal. But sometimes, when the wind is right, it all comes back to me. Sometimes, when the meager changes of San Francisco's seasons prompt my memory, I'm on the road again.

Flying high with a dying pilot, romping the carpet-short grass of a minor league diamond, dodging subways in those manmade caves under New York City, freezing cold, clawing through ice to get a drink at Halfway Lake, burning hot under the TV lights in the arms of a pitcher falling in lust with a newscaster, buried in the belly of a jet, sprinting free over the high, dry foothills of a Colorado summer.

And the people? Sometimes I miss them all—Doug, Charlie, Fiona, Kimberley, even the homeless drunks that started it all not five miles from here. But it's not the people I miss most. I think you know that.

Which brings us to our last detail. Remember that odd, unfamiliar smell I noticed that first night in my new home? Well, it turned out to belong to a tiny dandelion of a three-month-old kitten that Fern and Doc had gotten to heal their cat jones once they were sure I was gone forever.

She was black and white and already chubby, with hair so thick it stuck out of her round body like a porcupine. And she was scared of everything and everybody but Fern—and me.

She lived in a shoe box. That's where I saw her for the first time later that morning. Her pink-nosed, clown-patterned face peeked above the cardboard and watched me with skittish little eyes.

"Hello ... who are you?" she said.

"I'm Doo Doo and I run things around here, who are you?"

She hopped out of her box and started sniffing me all over.

"Momma?" she meowed.

"Uh, no, I'm not your momma," I laughed.

"Momma!" she mewled and nuzzled up against my body like she was going to feed.

Something made me indulge her. I flopped on my side and she snuggled up tight and licked my belly, an indignity I endured by nipping at her neck.

"You know I'm not your momma, right?" I said when she stopped licking and started kneading.

"Yah," she purred. "You're nice."

Stupid cat, I thought. But I was purring too.

"Watch the claws, Rass," I said when she got a little too enthusiastic.

"Wha?" she skittered to her feet and looked at me with her wild, marble eyes, so much like *his*. "What you call me?"

"Rass."

"My name not Rass!" She rolled on her back and started swinging her little feet wildly like she wanted to fight for joy.

I grabbed her by the scruff and gently pulled the thrashing pill of fluff back to my belly, where she immediately settled down.

"There you go, Rass."

"Why you say that? My name not Rass!"

I tapped a paw on her head like a benediction.

"It is now."

About the Author

Allan Goldstein lives in San Francisco with his wife, Jordan, and a minimum of two cats. His op-ed newspaper column, "Caught off Base," has appeared in San Francisco 's *West Portal Monthly* for the past decade. Satire, invective and humor are specialties.

He also blogs regularly on opednews.com, and on hypocrisy.com under the pseudonym Snark Twain. Other work has appeared in *Spitball, The Baseball Literary Review, The Potomac Review,* and several magazines including *Rock and Gem* and *Pilots Preflight.* He is currently at work on his third novel. You can read most of his published writing on his website, allangoldstein. com, and contact him at allan@allangoldstein.com.

Doo Doo cat lived in San Francisco with the above family. He wants you to know he was as beautiful, loving and wild as described in these pages, and continues to be so in the eternity beyond. He considers Mr. Goldstein to be his faithful literary executor and will expect his cut of the royalties when they meet again.

Made in the USA
Lexington, KY
19 December 2016